The Wedding Pearls

ALSO BY CAROLYN BROWN

CONTEMPORARY ROMANCE

Love Is

A Falling Star

All the Way from Texas

The Yard Rose

The Ivy Tree

Lily's White Lace

That Way Again

The Wager

Trouble in Paradise

The PMS Club

The Ladies' Room

Long, Hot Texas Summer

Daisies in the Canyon

The Yellow Rose Beauty Shop

HISTORICAL ROMANCE

THE OKLAHOMA LAND RUSH SERIES

Emma's Folly

Violet's Wish

Maggie's Mistake

Just Grace

DRIFTERS AND DREAMERS SERIES

Morning Glory

Sweet Tilly

THE LOVE'S VALLEY SERIES

Choices

Absolution

Chances

Redemption

Promises

BROKEN ROADS SERIES

To Trust

To Commit

To Believe

To Dream

To Hope

THE PROMISED LAND SERIES

Willow

Velvet

Gypsy

Garnet

Augusta

The Wedding Pearls

CAROLYN
BROWN

Montlake Romance

This is a work of fiction. Names, characters, organizations, places, events, and incidents are either products of the author's imagination or are used fictitiously.

Published by Montlake Romance, Seattle

www.apub.com

ISBN-13: 9781503954441 (hardcover)
ISBN-10: 1503954447 (hardcover)
ISBN-13: 9781503949539 (paperback)
ISBN-10: 1503949532 (paperback)

Cover design by Laura Klynstra

Printed in the United States of America

To my awesome agent,

Erin Niumata:

Thank you for taking a chance on me all those years ago, for sticking with me through these many years, and for everything you do to make me successful. It's been said that some people cross your path and change your whole direction.

I'm sure glad that our paths crossed!

Chapter One

Being adopted never bothered Tessa as much as being clumsy. Her biological parents, whoever they were, could have given her an ounce or two of grace. But oh, no! She had inherited the gene to fall over nothing more than air, and she gave a whole new meaning to the term *butterfingers*.

Her adoptive mother, Sophie, was a different story. Tall, thin, and graceful as a runway model, she taught dance to students from age four through high school. When Tessa was four years old, Sophie put her in ballet classes, but after the first year, when both of them cried at every lesson, she admitted defeat.

By the time Tessa was twenty-five she'd stopped praying for a miracle called grace to fall into her lap. At nearly thirty, she'd accepted the fact that the clumsiness, like her blonde hair and blue eyes, could not be given back to the DNA gods.

If it could go wrong that last Friday in August, it did; if it couldn't possibly go wrong, it found a way to do it anyway.

Tessa'd spilled two cups of coffee and had to change her shirt both times. Thank goodness she'd learned long ago to keep extra clothes at work. She'd dropped two fat files and mixed them up, which resulted in an hour of hard work getting them separated.

Thirty minutes before closing time, she sat down behind her desk and picked up a thick romance book. Just another half an hour, and surely to God if she sat right there until it was time to leave she could avoid another disaster.

On Monday her partner and cousin, Clint, would be back at work. Sorry sucker had taken all four weeks of his vacation time in the same block so he and his wife could tour Europe for their fifth wedding anniversary. As mad as she had been at him for leaving her in the middle of the summer to run the travel agency alone, she sure looked forward to him being back in the office.

She'd read only a few words when the door pushed open, bringing in a blast of hot, muggy air and a tall, good-looking cowboy. Tessa was glad she was sitting down or she would have tripped over her own thoughts and fallen right into his arms. He looked like one of those old Marlboro ads and a CD cover of Blake Shelton all tossed in together. Her pulse kicked in a little extra giddyup, and her heart did one of those thumps that came along these days only on special occasions.

"Hello, is Tessa Wilson here?" he drawled.

She closed her book without using the bookmark. "I'm Tessa. What can I do for you?"

He nodded toward a chair and asked, "Mind if I sit?"

"Honeymoon?" she asked.

"No, ma'am." He removed his hat, laid it on her desk, and raked his fingers through thick, dark hair that feathered back perfectly. She could read people, and this man was damn sure nervous. Maybe he was married and planning a trip with his mistress. It didn't matter—her job was to put him at ease and work a little magic to get him a good deal. Where he went—or with whom—wasn't a bit of her business.

He inhaled and let his breath out slowly. "I guess I am planning a trip, but not one that you can help me with. I'm here on official business." He slid a business card across the meticulously clean desk toward her.

She picked it up, glanced at the name, and looked up into the sexiest green eyes she'd ever seen. He looked far more like a rancher than a lawyer. The hair, the eyes, a square face with the perfect amount of chiseling and a perfect-size cleft in his chin. She held her hands in her lap with her fingers laced tightly together so she wouldn't reach out and touch that little chin dent.

Holy crap! She didn't let clients affect her like this. It had to be that the steamy sex scene in the romance book she'd been reading had set her mind and hormones into overdrive. She glanced down at the cover image of a cowboy with a bare chest, hip-slung jeans, and a cowboy hat in his hands. It was exactly like the black felt hat sitting there between herself and the new client. She undressed him with her eyes and decided that he wouldn't look so very different from the model on the novel. She quickly closed her eyes and willed the wicked thoughts away, then opened them again and glanced down at the card one more time.

"Branch Thomas, what can I do for you?" Her throat was dry, but she was afraid to uncap the water bottle on her desk for fear she'd drop the thing and make another mess.

His eyebrows knit together into a frown. "I'm not sure how to put this in words, and it might come as a shock. I guess the only way to say it is to blurt it out. You'd think this would be easier, since I'm a lawyer."

"Spit it out," she said.

"Okay, then." He nodded seriously. "I'm here on behalf of your biological mother and grandmother. They would like to meet you. And that trip I was talking about, they're leaving on Tuesday for a monthlong road trip around the perimeter of Texas, and they would like for you to go with them so y'all can get to know each other."

Tessa was so intrigued with his eyes that his words, which tumbled out so fast, didn't sink in for several seconds. "I'm sorry, we don't usually plan trips like that, but if you'd tell me how far they want to travel each day I could maybe work up some tourist sites and hotels." And that's when she clamped a hand over her mouth. "What did you say?"

He picked up his hat and laid it in his lap. "You did know you were adopted?"

She nodded.

Any minute he was going to bolt and run. She could see it in his eyes. "And you did know that you had a biological mother somewhere?"

Another slight tip of the head without losing eye contact with him. "I've always known I was adopted. It didn't matter, and I'm comfortable with it."

"The rest is pretty self-explanatory. Your birth mother and grandmother would like to meet you this weekend. They live in Boomtown, Texas, a few miles east of Beaumont." He looked at a travel poster on the wall behind her left shoulder as he talked. "It's about a three-hour drive from here. They are willing to come over here, or if you wouldn't mind the drive, they would like for you to come to Sunday dinner to discuss this trip."

"Is this a joke?" she asked bluntly.

His eyes shifted to her forehead. "I realize it's a lot to take in, Miss Wilson, but please don't shoot the messenger. Your mother is Lola Laveau. Her number is on the back of the card, along with Frankie Laveau's. That would be your grandmother."

He pushed up out of the chair and settled his hat back on his head. "I've written my cell phone number on the front there so you can contact me over the weekend if you want to decline any or all of this. I'll be glad to deliver the message for you. Or if you have any more questions, you can call them or me. Sorry to drop this in your lap, but like I said, I'm just the messenger."

Then he was gone, leaving her in stunned silence with his card in her hand. She was still sitting in the same spot, her mind going over every word, every name, and looping back to repeat them a dozen times, when the door opened again and her mother pointed at the clock.

"It's five thirty. Did you fall asleep and forget that you close at five?" Sophie asked.

Dressed in a pair of khaki shorts and a bright-orange shirt, she was as cool as a snow cone from that stand down near the park. Her blonde ponytail didn't have a speck of gray in it, and even after a day of dancing with her students, her makeup was still perfect.

Tessa handed the card to her mother and held her breath. Sophie looked at the front first and frowned, then flipped it over. "Well, well, well." She smiled. "I haven't seen Lola Laveau in almost thirty years, but I have thought of her often."

Tessa pinched her leg, and it hurt like hell so she knew she wasn't dreaming. But she still felt as if she were in a vacuum and all the air had disappeared. Her chest hurt even worse than her leg. Maybe if she shut her eyes and then opened them again, she would wake up to find it was a dream. She blinked slowly and sucked in a lungful of air. When she opened her eyes, she saw nothing had changed, so it was definitely not a dream.

Emotions flooded over her—mostly shock because this was not a surprise to her mother. And then fear, denial, excitement, anger—each emotion lasting only a few seconds before another pushed it out of the way to take center stage.

"You knew my birth mother?" Her voice was raspy, and the words came out one at a time with seconds between them.

Sophie sat down in the same chair that Branch had been sitting in and nodded. "I did. We were good friends back then."

Was she hearing her mother right? Had her clumsiness affected her hearing? "You never told me."

Sophie shrugged. "You never asked. I was prepared to tell you all about this years and years ago, but you never seemed interested in knowing about your birth parents. I'm starving, my child. Let's go down to that Cajun place you like and get some shrimp gumbo and I'll answer any questions you have."

Tessa turned out the lights, locked up the business, set the security alarm, followed her mother out of the store, and settled into the passenger's seat of Sophie's van. Questions were a jumbled mess in her brain, one leading to another and none of them making a bit of sense. Thank God it was Friday and she had the whole weekend to process this mess before she called that sexier-than-hell cowboy Branch and told him no, thank you, to Sunday dinner, visits, or a cockamamie trip. She needed a drink—hell, she needed a whole bottle of Jack.

Wanette, a familiar hostess at the restaurant on Main Street, took them to a table in a back corner and asked, "How's that granddaughter of mine doing in ballet? I was afraid she'd have two left feet."

"Don't you worry about Yvette. She's a natural," Sophie said. "I think we'd both like a good, strong, top-shelf margarita, and I do mean strong."

Wanette winked. "Yes, ma'am. I'll make it myself so it'll be exactly right. Need a few minutes to look at the menu?"

Sophie shook her head. "We'll both have the shrimp gumbo, but the drinks first and maybe a basket of bread with some butter and honey."

"Got it." Wanette smiled.

Sophie reached across the table and covered Tessa's hand with hers. "Okay, for the next hour, I'm all yours. What do you want to know?"

"I don't know where to start or what to ask. It never mattered to me, Mama, and I'm not sure it does now. *Adopted* was just a word. Remember when you gave me my first journal and you wrote on the first page?" Tessa asked.

Sophie smiled and squeezed Tessa's hand gently. "I told you that you didn't grow in my tummy but in my heart. I remember well. You wrote in your journals until last Christmas, when Matt broke your heart. I think it would do you a world of good to start writing again, *chère*."

"I haven't got anything to write about." She paused. "I was comfortable with being adopted, Mama. You and Daddy are the best parents a kid could ever have, and even now that I'm an adult, I don't want to think about life without either of you. God, I'd like to go back to this morning and start all over again. I don't like this can of worms that cowboy opened."

"Cowboy?" Sophie asked.

"Sexy cowboy, but that's not important," Tessa said. "Just tell me what I need to know, because my brain isn't working well enough to ask questions."

"We were in the same commune together up in central Kentucky. Way back in one of those hollers that nobody can find unless they have a map, and even then it's iffy," Sophie started.

"Commune as in . . ." Tessa stammered over the words.

Wanette brought their drinks, a basket filled with bread, and a bowl with packets of butter and honey. "Y'all enjoy. Your food will be out soon."

Sophie broke a hot roll in half and buttered it. "As in free love, all for one and one for all? Yes, that kind of commune. We were all hippies born about twenty years too late, but we hated the establishment and decided we could live off the grid. It wasn't bad, and most of us stayed with the partner we brought to the party in the beginning."

"But you're from Louisiana and so is Daddy, and Lola"—the name sounded strange on Tessa's tongue—"is from Texas. Does Daddy know that you lived in a commune?"

Sophie slathered butter on the other half of the roll and handed it to Tessa. "He went with me. Our best friends had gone up there and we followed them. We'd been there three years when Lola and her boyfriend showed up. He survived only a couple of weeks before he packed his bags and left, but Lola stayed. We had a two-bedroom trailer, so she stayed with us when she wasn't out with the sheep."

Tessa bit off a piece of the bread and chewed slowly. "Sheep? As in furry animals?"

Sophie sipped her drink. "Of course. Her job was to take them out to the pasture to feed each morning and bring them back in the evening. There were about twenty ewes and a couple of rams, and she named every one."

Tessa picked up the oversize margarita and gulped three times before she set it back down. "Was her boyfriend my biological father?"

"No, he was not. She got pretty wild after he left, so she never knew who your father was. Told me it could have been one of four of the fellows who weren't attached to a particular woman at that time. Don't be quick to judge her. She was right out of high school and thought the boyfriend loved her. And then he left her more than a thousand miles from home and she didn't want to go back and face the music. Matter of fact, *chère*, she didn't know if she could go home."

Tessa took a deep breath and spit out the words before she lost her courage. "Did you and Daddy . . . I can't even say the words, but did you?"

Sophie shook her head. "We were committed to each other, and we didn't cheat on each other. That part was totally optional. We were a couple and everyone knew it. We grew our own food and ate a lot of mutton, barbecued goat, chickens, and vegetables. We canned and froze food for the winter and lived very simply. We moved back to Louisiana right after you were born."

"Drugs?" Tessa held her breath and waited.

Sophie shook her head. "Our bodies were our temples. We didn't do drugs, but one of the guys, Skip Morton, did make a mean batch of moonshine up in the hills, and I can't say we didn't partake of it. Eat some more bread. The way you are downing that drink, you're going to need it."

Tessa popped another bite into her mouth. "This is a lot to take in all at once."

Wanette set two piping-hot bowls of gumbo in front of them. "Tessa, I swear you're pale as if you saw a ghost walkin' across the Bayou Teche. What you need after that gumbo is a plate of beignets and some good black coffee. That'll cure you up fast, *chère*."

Tessa pasted on her best fake smile. "I'm fine, Wanette, thank you. Just had a long day."

"That Clint better get his sorry ass home like he said he would this week. I miss him comin' in for lunch, but you need him at the agency. What was he thinkin', runnin' off for a whole month like that?" Wanette fussed as she hurried off to take care of another customer.

"Any more questions?" Sophie asked.

Tessa needed another sip before she could make the words leave her mouth, so she picked up the glass and took two long gulps. "Why did you adopt me?"

Sophie hesitated so long that Tessa wondered if she'd even said the words. "Lola had a real hard pregnancy, and when it came time to deliver you, our midwife couldn't do the job. We called an ambulance and I went with her, mainly because she wouldn't let go of my hand and I thought for sure she'd die. No one deserves to die alone. You couldn't get through the birth canal so they had to do an emergency cesarean, which meant she had to stay in the hospital a few days."

Tessa ate more of the hot roll, not tasting a single bit of it. "You didn't really answer my question."

Sophie grimaced. "This is tough. I don't want you to judge her before you meet her. She was a sweet girl, Tessa, but the pain was horrible and she must have equated that with you, and then there was the fact that her boyfriend had left her and she'd turned away from all her upbringing and gone wild for a while. It all caused a great deal of guilt." She stopped and drained her margarita. "I was the one that bonded with you as if I'd given birth to you myself. Your dad and I knew from the time we got together that I couldn't have children, but there you needed a mother and there I needed a baby. Then Lola got an infection and they had to do a hysterectomy, and that was the only thing that made Lola happy. She never wanted another child if it meant going through nine months of hell. I asked if I could have you and she said yes. I was real glad you turned out to have blonde hair like mine and blue eyes like your daddy's. It made things easier when we came back home, and unless someone asked, we let everyone think we had you while we were gone."

The alcohol had begun to ease Tessa's nerves somewhat. The gumbo actually tasted good when she dipped into it. "What about the adoption papers?"

"She took care of that. Said she had some money that would pay the lawyer, and six months after we came back to Louisiana he called to say that the papers were in order." Sophie followed Tessa's lead and dipped into the gumbo. "We drove over from New Iberia to Beaumont, Texas, and signed them. Didn't see her and she didn't see you. I was glad because I was terrified that she'd take you from me. And then you know how it is with our nosy family. Someone found out that we'd been to Louisiana and the word got out that we'd adopted you."

"I don't want to see her," Tessa said bluntly. "She didn't want me then and it's too late."

"I think you should," Sophie said softly.

"But, Mama, she didn't want me then. In all these years, she's never made a move to get in touch with me or you . . ." Anger replaced all the other emotions. Tessa's ears burned as if steam were really flying out of them. Her hand shot up to cover her mouth and her eyes widened. "Has she talked to you about this?"

Sophie leaned across the table and put her fingers on Tessa's lips. "No, *chère*, we haven't talked since the day she left the hospital after you were born. And Tessa, I will always be your mother, but you should at least get to know Lola and her mother. They are family by blood. And, honey, she was every bit as clumsy as you are."

The anger disappeared at her mother's touch, and Tessa smiled. "Really?" she asked incredulously.

"Really." Sophie nodded.

Chapter Two

Tessa argued with herself as she crossed half the state of Louisiana. Several times she considered turning around and going right back to New Iberia and never looking in the rearview mirror. But her parents thought it would be a good thing if she met her biological family, and she was curious. Besides, she'd given her word, and her father said in a Cajun family that was as good as a binding contract.

The call to Branch the night before had been very businesslike. She'd told him she would drive to Boomtown on Sunday and be there at noon but that she probably would not go on the trip. He'd thanked her for the call and said he would let Frankie and Lola know what she'd decided, and they'd said good-bye and that was that.

She drove into the little town of Boomtown and nosed into the school parking lot where Branch told her he would meet her before leading her out to the Laveau place. Being early to appointments was as much a part of her as that obsessive thing she had about keeping everything in order. Even a hairpin on the vanity worried the devil out of her until it was put away.

She checked her reflection in the mirror. Lipstick was all chewed off, so she reapplied that. The rest of her makeup still looked good, but the curls she'd worked so hard to put in her shoulder-length hair that morning had drooped. Her mama could fix her hair in the morning and work out with kids all day long and it would still look good that night. Tessa's curls fell out within a couple of hours, and perms did nothing but turn her hair to straw. Maybe, like her clumsiness, it was a genetic thing and she could blame that on Lola, too.

A horn blasted right beside her dark-gray Chevrolet and she jumped, dropped the still-open lipstick in her hand, and groaned when it smeared down across the light-gray fabric on the passenger's seat. She grabbed it up, twisted it shut, and put the lid back on it, then reached in the backseat for a baby wipe. She never, ever left the house without them and bought them in bulk when she went to the discount store.

When she finished getting the mocha-colored lipstick wiped from the seat, she turned around to find nothing but the window separating her face from Branch Thomas's. She quickly hit the button and rolled down the window. Hot, sultry air rushed in as the cool air escaped.

"You scared me."

"Sorry about that. I figured you could fall in behind me. I didn't want to get out of my truck in this heat," he said.

Today his jeans were faded and he wore a dark-green knit shirt the same color as his eyes. And Lord have mercy, but he smelled good enough that she wanted to lean out the window and kiss him right smack on the lips.

"So I'm to follow you, then," she said.

"If you want to go out to Frankie's, you do. There's more twists and turns to get to her place than you can imagine. As we go through town, look over to your left when we pass the Dairy Queen. The sign isn't huge, but that's Lola's shop. She buys and sells antiques." Without waiting for a comment, he turned around and headed back to his truck. The tight little strut he had in scuffed-up cowboy boots made her wonder how in the hell he'd ever gotten to be a lawyer. He was a cowboy through and through and looked like he'd be more at home on a tractor than in a courtroom.

"Well, who pissed in your oatmeal this morning?" she mumbled as she turned her car around and followed the big black truck.

Lola's Antique Shop was in a metal building that looked like an old warehouse. The windows were clean, and what she could see of the displays going down the road at thirty-five miles an hour looked really nice.

Branch made a couple of turns, and her hands slipped on the steering wheel as she followed. She quickly pulled a tissue from a box on the console and dried them, but it didn't last long, not as nervous as she was. With the next turn they left the paved road and hit gravel. Dust boiled up behind his big black pickup truck thicker than a foggy Louisiana morning.

She shouldn't be here, and besides, who in the devil lived out here in the sticks like this? Any minute now, she expected to see a single-wide trailer with a bunch of coonhounds under the porch. Trip, her ass! They probably drove an old Volkswagen bus and the trip would involve camping out along the side of the road with a bush for a bathroom and a creek for a bath.

They crossed a cattle guard, and less than a quarter of a mile down a pecan tree–lined lane, Branch stopped in the middle of a circular drive in front of a lovely two-story, white-frame house.

"Wrong about that psychedelic VW, but I'm not getting my hopes up about these people," Tessa muttered as she stared at half a dozen white rockers on the wraparound porch. They rocked gently in the morning breeze as if someone had just left them moments before. The flower beds were every bit as meticulously cared for as her mother's were. Roses flourished with lantana, daisies, and petunias all trimmed and blooming abundantly. A few morning glories still hung on despite the afternoon heat bearing down on them, and the impatiens were absolutely gorgeous.

She swung the door open and called for a big dose of bravado as she stepped out of the car. She was every bit as nervous as a hooker at a church social, but she damn sure didn't intend to let anyone know, especially that cowboy who was walking toward her.

Legs out gracefully. Feet on the ground. Branch holding the door open for her and a hand extended to help.

Like a lady, she put her hand in it and stood up, grateful that she didn't get off-balance and fall against him. "Thank you." Dammit! His touch wasn't supposed to make her go all soft inside. A man that handsome had a woman somewhere in his life. She'd bet her agency on that much.

"You look lovely today, Miss Tessa. Your hair is the same color as your mother's." He smiled.

"So you do know how to be nice," she said.

"What's that mean?" The smile faded.

Confidence built with that first step she took without her clumsiness surfacing. "You looked like you could eat nails back there at the school."

"I don't really want to be here today. I'd rather be out at my ranch, but the job comes first. Sorry if I came off rude. It's not your fault, but it is part of the job. Our law firm handles all of Frankie's affairs, and when she says 'Jump,' all my dad says is 'How high.'" He dropped her hand.

"We all do things we don't want to do, I guess." Dammit! She liked that feeling his touch gave her. She hadn't had anything like that in almost a year. If she was honest, more than a year, and it felt good. "When you said that about my hair, did you mean my birth mother?"

He walked beside her but kept a foot of space between them. Still, the scent of that woodsy shaving lotion had no trouble reaching her nose or sending her hormones into overdrive.

"So your adoptive mother is a blonde also?" he asked.

"Yes, she is." Tessa took one step, tripped over nothing more than hot summer air, and was on her way to the gravel, facedown, when big, strong arms encircled her waist and held her tightly.

"I'm so sorry." She gasped as her arms flew up to circle his arms for support.

Crimson filled her cheeks. Of all the days for her clumsiness to come out, it had to be this day when she wanted to make a good impression. His chest was hard against her breasts, his biceps like steel in her hands.

"It's okay. Just glad you didn't fall on the gravel and rip that pretty blue dress. If you decide to go on this trip, you'd best bring a big hat and lots of sunblock, as fair as your skin is." He smiled down at her.

She pushed away from him, righted herself, and took a deep breath. "I guess there's no putting off going inside, is there?"

Branch's mouth turned up at the corners. "They're good people. A little earthy. A lot eccentric. I don't want to say too much so you can form your own opinion, but don't let this place or the fact that they have money scare you."

The door flew open, and a short, round woman wearing jeans and a flowing overshirt with more sparkling bling on it than anything Tessa had ever seen outside of Mardi Gras ran out the door. The oxygen tank she pulled rattled along behind her on the gravel like a puppy on a leash. She grabbed Tessa in a bear hug that sank Tessa's face right into a set of big, smooshy breasts that were the size of cantaloupes.

"Hot damn, Branch! I got the first hug. I won't ever let Frankie hear the end of this. She's out back havin' one last cigarette to calm her nerves. Lola is in big trouble for keeping this big secret, I'm here to tell you. And she deserves it for not tellin' me and Frankie about this gorgeous child all these years. Well, don't stand out here in the heat. Come on inside before Blister blows plumb up in this heat."

"This is Ivy, your grandmother's best friend." Branch made introductions. "Ivy, this is—"

"Hell, Branch, I know her name! It's all we've talked about around here for days. We're going to have such fun on our trip, Tessa. Me and Frankie, we been plannin' this for years, and now that she's retirin', we decided to do it as a celebration. The fact that you're going has made her day. Come on, come on. I can feel these damn tubes in my nose meltin' as we stand here." Ivy led the way into the house.

"Blister?" Tessa looked up at Branch.

"That's the name of her oxygen tank," he explained.

Yep, eccentric was right, and she hadn't met the real family yet.

"She's here! She's here!" Ivy yelled like a drunken fishwife as she entered the house.

Another blush lit up Tessa's face. Would it be all right to hide behind Branch or to turn tail and run back to Louisiana without a backward glance? Lord, to be announced in a booming voice that could be heard all the way back to Louisiana was so embarrassing.

A woman about Ivy's age, only with short, gray hair cut in a chin-length pageboy that fell from a center part, came through the sliding doors at the end of a wide hallway. "You old bitch. Why'd you go out there and meet her first? I ought to jerk that tube out of your nose and watch you die right here in my foyer." She stopped three feet away from Tessa, and her blue eyes got bigger and bigger. "Well, I'll be damned. I can see you are sure enough her daughter. You've got Lola's hair and you look a lot like she did when she left home. You sure you are almost thirty? I swear you don't look a day over twenty."

She quickly crossed the short distance and wrapped Tessa up in her arms. Frankie didn't smother her with the hug, but she did almost asphyxiate her with the lingering cigarette smoke. "You can call me Frankie, and you've met Ivy, the hussy. She knew I wanted to see you first."

"Hello, I'm Lola." A short, blonde-haired lady stepped out from a doorway. She wore a pair of jean shorts and a halter top that showed off tats on both arms and one ankle. "Welcome to Boomtown, Tessa. I'm glad that Sophie named you that. It was my first choice of a girl's name."

"Well, come on in the kitchen," Frankie said. "Alice has the dinner ready to put on the table, and we'll visit while we eat. I hope you like fried chicken, Tessa. I can't tell you how happy I am to finally have a grandchild, and I got to admit, it's kind of nice that you come already potty trained." Frankie threw an arm around her shoulders and giggled as they followed Lola into the dining room. "You can sit right here beside me and across from Lola. Branch, you take the other end of the table. And Ivy, you can sit beside Lola. And that kid already seated is Melody. She's Ivy's great-niece who got into trouble for smoking pot at school and got thirty days of community service for her stupidity."

Tessa stiffened at the doorway and couldn't force her feet to take another step. So many new faces, some even relatives by blood. A strange house that drew her eyes to pictures, furniture, and things that defined the owners. Smells of food wafting toward her. Too nervous to eat, yet hungry. Crazy vibes from Branch shooting across the room like a whole bevy of falling stars. Panic mode was setting in. Fight or flight, they called it. She didn't want to fight with these people. But flight—now that sounded pretty damn good.

Branch seated Frankie first and then Tessa before circling the table to do the same for Lola and Ivy. Melody sighed and rolled her eyes.

Ivy laid a hand on Tessa's arm before she rounded the end of the table, and just the touch of the old gal's hand was calming. "Don't mind her. She's pissed because she has to go on this trip, do all her schoolwork online, and send it in to her teachers. It's a special thing because I know the judge, or else she'd be sitting her pot-smokin' ass in detention and still doing all her homework online. It's not a tough enough punishment, but the judge was lenient because we're old friends."

A middle-aged woman started bringing out food and setting it down the length of the table. "That's all, except for dessert. Lola, you can take care of that, right, so I can get home to my family?"

Lola nodded. "Yes, and thanks, Alice, for working on your weekend off. We'll make it up to you."

The short, round lady with salt-and-pepper hair smiled. "You already did. A month off work with pay. That's a good job in anyone's book. See y'all at the end of September, and if you want to come home early, call and I will get the house ready and some food cooked up. And Tessa, I'm glad you came to visit. Frankie has been so excited I was afraid she'd have a heart attack."

"Thank you, darlin'. Don't know what we'd do without you, Alice," Frankie said.

Alice disappeared into the kitchen, and Tessa heard a door somewhere back there open and shut. It said something that they were so good to their hired help, didn't it? And Alice said they were excited about her coming to see them, so maybe her mama had been right.

Frankie picked up the platter of chicken, slid a breast and a wing onto her plate, and handed it to Tessa. "Now let's talk about you, Tessa. Branch wouldn't tell us a damn thing. Are you married? Engaged?"

Tessa put a leg on her plate and started to pass the platter on. "Neither one. Not even dating."

"Better get two legs if you got any notion that you'll want another one. This chicken had eight and Lola can eat at least six." Frankie laughed.

She put another one on her plate and handed the platter off to Melody, who immediately passed it on to Branch. "I'm, like, a vegetarian. That means I, like, do not eat meat," she said.

"Too bad marijuana ain't meat. Then you wouldn't be in trouble," Ivy said.

"Let it, like, rest," Melody smarted off.

"I will not. You did a stupid-ass thing and you can put up with what I want to say until you learn your lesson," Ivy said.

Melody was a cute little red-haired teenager. Probably about fifteen or sixteen, dressed completely in black with a ton of black makeup on her face. Not that it did much good, because freckles were still shining across her nose. She was small built and looked like a little kid in a Halloween costume.

"I've got a question," Tessa said.

"Shoot," Frankie said. "We'll answer anything you want to know."

"What if I'm a fake? What if I'm not your daughter and I'm here to rob you blind?" Tessa asked.

"Then we'll shoot you," Lola said bluntly.

It started off as a giggle that Tessa smothered with her hand, but it wouldn't be denied and turned into laughter that bounced off the walls, with Lola joining in.

"What's so damn funny?" Melody asked.

"You'd have to have their sense of humor to understand them," Ivy explained. "No one understands Lola's humor, but evidently her daughter does."

Lola wiped her eyes on her dinner napkin. "I knew Sophie and Derek. I trusted them with you, and I'm sure they brought you up right. Sophie fell in love with you the day you were born. You sure don't look like you could be twenty-nine years old. I bet they ID you when you order a beer."

Tessa's laughter stopped as suddenly as it had started, and she steeled herself for the question on her mind. The room went so silent that the flapping of butterfly wings would have sounded like an approaching tornado. She had to ask, had to know before she exploded. It was the question that hung over her like smoke in an old honky-tonk.

"Why did you give me to Sophie?" Tessa looked Lola right in the eyes and asked softly.

Lola hesitated several seconds before she answered. "I was young and stupid and scared. And at the time I didn't know if Mama would let me come back home after the stunt I pulled. I was afraid if I told her I had a baby, too, that she'd definitely say no, and that commune wasn't any place to raise a child."

"Regrets?" Tessa took a big scoop of mashed potatoes and sent the serving bowl to Melody, who filled a fourth of her plate with them.

Lola shook her head. "They were better parents than I could have ever been."

Ivy raised her hand like a little girl in the schoolroom. "I've got a question. What is it that you do?"

"As in a job?" Tessa tasted the potatoes as she waited on the green bean casserole. "My cousin Clint and I own a travel agency."

"If you can get away for any or all of my retirement trip, I would be mighty happy," Frankie said. "We could fly you back to Louisiana whenever you say the word if you can't make the whole trip."

Tessa had agreed to meet these people only to please her mama, and yet there was something about them pulling at her heartstrings. Something about this moment that felt right. No, it was more than just right; it was deeper than that. Something she couldn't put her finger on, something she'd have to analyze and sort out over a glass of good old Jack Daniel's. Not a double shot or three fingers, but a glass half-full that she'd sip on all evening as she tried to figure out why these people could find their way into her heart over the course of one lunch. Did blood and shared DNA really mean something after all?

"Well, crap!" Lola pushed back her chair and dabbed at her legs with her napkin after she'd knocked a glass of water into her lap.

Frankie waved it off with a flick of the hand. "It's an everyday occurrence. Funny thing is that she can handle a thousand-dollar tea set in the store and never break a thing but she can't walk across a room without stumbling or falling over her own feet. And meal-times are always a disaster."

Ivy picked up a bowl of candied sweet potatoes and started them around the table. "Her daddy was like that, too. Frankie here, why, she could tiptoe across hot coals and never lose her balance, but her daddy, Lester, that man was so clumsy it was downright pitiful."

"Was?" Tessa asked.

"Been dead now about thirty years," Frankie answered. "Did it bother you that you were adopted? Did you ever wonder about your other family?"

"Being adopted never bothered me as much as being clumsy. My mama and I both cried every day of dance lessons for a whole year before we figured out I had two left feet," Tessa confessed. "It broke Mama's heart and mine because I felt like I'd let her down. I was only four, but I remember trying so hard to be graceful."

Lola picked up the corn that had spilled on the floor and carried it to the trash, returning with a fresh napkin for her lap and one to spare.

Well, dammit! Why did I have to say "mama" twice in one explanation? Tessa thought.

Frankie smiled. "I can read your mind, child. Sophie is your mama, darlin'. She deserves that, and don't you ever feel bad about it. I'm happy to be Frankie, and Lola, here, well, she's happy to just be Lola. We'd like to be your other family if you'll let us, and we'd sure like to get to know you. Right now, we've probably come on too strong but we don't know any other way to do things, so bear with us."

"Thank you." Tessa felt heartstrings pulling at her. Could she really leave her home on Tuesday morning and go on a trip with complete strangers? Even though they were blood relatives, she didn't know these people. Did she want to?

"Good chicken. Reckon you could send that platter back this way, Tessa?" Branch changed the subject. "I'm glad Ivy left a breast for me."

"Oh, honey, I've always got a breast for a good-looking cowboy."

"Dear Lord!" Melody rolled her eyes at the ceiling.

"He is at that," Ivy chuckled.

"This is like cruel and unusual punishment. I'm never, like, getting in trouble at school again," Melody whined.

Ivy's old eyes twinkled as she looked across the table at her great-niece. "Well, that's a step in the right direction. Now, if you'll give up smoking that dope, maybe your brain cells won't be fried. You are lucky the judge let you keep that tablet thing for your lessons and your phone, but remember, he said the phone could go if I thought you were spending too much time on it."

༺༻

The sun was a big orange ball setting in her rearview mirror and casting a glow over her entire car as Tessa drove back into New Iberia that evening. She'd tried for more than two hours to sort out her feelings about this new wrinkle in her life and the trip that the whole bunch of them were so happy about. She'd barely gotten into her apartment and kicked off her shoes when the jingle of keys and her doorknob turning announced that her mother couldn't wait to talk.

"I know you probably need some time to get things sorted out, but I couldn't wait to talk to you. I drove by and saw your car. How did it go?" Sophie looked worried.

Tessa patted the sofa beside her. "Just got here. Sit with me?"

Sophie handed her a small gift bag. "I'll open up a couple of cokes and then we'll talk."

"What's this?" Tessa asked.

"Open it and see."

"A journal?" Tessa frowned. "Mama, it's not Christmas."

"I know that. This is a special journal for a special trip."

Tessa ran her hand down the outside of the soft brown leather with the word *Memories* engraved in gold on the spine. It was by far the fanciest journal that she'd ever had, and there were twenty lined up on the bookcase in her bedroom.

"I told you that I'd open a file on my laptop and record the whole trip, and that's only if I decide to go," Tessa said. "I tried to make up my mind all the way home. I did the pro and con thing and tried to talk myself into it, then tried to talk myself out of it. I can't decide."

"Then let me decide for you. Your father and I want you to do this, Tessa. You need to do this, especially after the Matt situation." Sophie set two bottles of coke on the coffee table and plopped down on the sofa beside her daughter. "That journal is to record your private feelings. You can use your laptop to keep track of the places you've been, the things you've seen and maybe even use all that on your travel agency's website. This is for personal and private ideas and thoughts about your trip and new family. Someday you'll want to go back and remember more than the long ride all around the state of Texas. You will want to know how you felt at the beginning of a day or at the end of it. What emotions that day evoked. You are an excellent writer, and I know you will be happy that you recorded more than events."

Tessa laid the journal on the coffee table. "Thank you, Mama. But this is all more than a little surreal. I don't know if I can really do this. I've never thought about finding my birth parents or really cared about all that. You and Daddy and all my Cajun cousins were enough for me." Tessa smiled. "This can't be easy for you."

Sophie laid a hand on Tessa's knee. "Your dad and I are secure in our place and we never want you to look back and wish you'd taken a different path. After the way Matt's mother treated you when she found out you were adopted, well, I don't want that hanging over your head. I want you to know that you came from good people biologically. Lola made bad choices, but that does not make her a bad person. You need to know that deep down."

Tessa wiped away a tear. "I love you and Daddy."

"And we love you, *chère*. Promise me you'll write in the journal."

"Like my first diary." Tessa laughed.

"You were five," Sophie remembered.

"And it started me on journals. You gave it to me because I was too clumsy to dance and said that someday I'd be a famous writer. That pretty often authors were eccentric and couldn't dance." Tessa nodded. "I'm just a travel agent. I'm still waiting on a life-changing experience that will make me a famous author."

"Patience, my child," Sophie said. "That life-changing event will happen and when it does you'll be glad that you recorded every minute. Now, tell me about Lola and her mother. Three of you on a trip for a whole month. I think it will be fun."

"Three?" Tessa sighed. "Try five!"

Sophie sank into the sofa beside her daughter. "Lola had more children? Did she adopt them?"

"No, but Frankie has a friend and that friend has a niece who rolls her eyes and acts like a spoiled brat," Tessa answered.

"How old is she?" Sophie smiled.

"Melody? She's sixteen."

"I remember a little girl who rolled her eyes and was a spoiled brat when she was sixteen. The proof is in your journals from that time." Sophie laughed softly.

"You can't read emotions like that in words," Tessa protested.

"Oh, yes, you can," Sophie disagreed. "Tell me about the dinner. I want to know everything. Your first emotion when you walked into the house, when you saw Lola for the first time, what you ate, all of it."

"Well, Ivy met me in the yard, toting an oxygen tank behind her that she calls Blister because it's like a blister on her ass. She hugged me first and then Branch and I went inside. Around the table was Ivy, Frankie, Branch, Melody, Lola, and me." She went on to tell her mother every single thing that she could remember, except the way that sparks danced around the room every time she looked at Branch. That much she kept deep in her heart. Lord, help! The cowboy might be engaged or in a relationship. He wasn't married, because she'd checked his hand for a ring, but that didn't give her any rights, not even to the electric vibes she felt when he was close.

Tessa threw an arm around Sophie and hugged her. "Mama, I'm not sure I want to go. It was a crazy day and I'm not sure if I'm up to this trip. Besides, Lola might have given birth to me, but now that the can of worms is opened, I don't know if I want to know the woman who didn't want me," she said longingly.

"It will always, always bother you if you don't go, and I do not want you to look back on your life with regrets," Sophie said.

Tessa barely nodded as a picture flashed in her mind of that table with all the ladies and Branch around it. She nodded again, this time more emphatically. Her mind was made up in that instant.

She would go on the trip, not because it would make her mother happy but because she didn't want regrets later in her life. Fate had dropped this into her lap, so she'd play it out, one day at a time.

Chapter Three

Tessa got lost four times on the way from the school parking lot to Frankie and Lola's house. Each time she called Branch and he told her what to do to get back on course. When she finally parked her car in the circular driveway, crossed the driveway without falling over a single chunk of gravel, and made it up the steps without stumbling one time, she was feeling right proud of herself. She hit the doorbell with her fingernail and waited.

"Just go on in. They've got their things loaded up already and are waiting on you," Branch said right behind her.

She whipped around so fast that one toe hung on the welcome mat, and she pitched forward right into his arms again. It was one of those déjà vu moments that embarrassed her more than the last one.

"We've got to stop meeting like this," Branch said.

"I'm so sorry. Clumsy is my middle name, but you know that from the dinner conversation we had on Sunday." She put her hands on his chest and righted herself and wasn't amazed one bit at the way her heart tossed in a couple of beats.

"Sounds like you might share a name with Lola," he said. "I was out in the garage getting things arranged. If you'll give me your keys, I will put your car in the garage and get your suitcase arranged in the trunk. Is it in the backseat? And hopefully you followed Frankie's orders and brought only one. With six folks going, we had to limit the amount of baggage."

"Yes, it's in the backseat and yes, there is only one, but it's packed pretty heavy," she answered.

"She's here! She's here!" Ivy squealed behind her as cold air rushed out the door and hit Tessa in the back.

She turned slowly and kept her eyes on that pesky doormat. "Good morning."

"Come on in. Are you hungry? Need a cup of coffee to go?" Ivy asked.

"I'm good except for maybe a trip to the bathroom," Tessa said.

"Frankie and Lola have been on pins since Saturday. They were scared to death you'd back out." She held the door open for Tessa.

Melody met her in the foyer and did one of those insolent eye rolls. "Thank God you're here. They would have been, like, horrible if you hadn't shown up. You are, like, the chosen one who can do no wrong. Did you pack your wings and halo?"

"I'm not that important. I'm like the new puppy. Wait until I spill a chocolate milkshake all over the car seats. They'll be ready to put me on an airplane and send my clumsy butt back home." Tessa smiled.

"They'd probably have it, like, cleaned up and put in a shrine," Melody smarted off.

The girl was dressed in designer jean shorts and a black tank top, and her red hair had been pulled through the hole in the back of a black cap. Hot pink lettering in glittery script on the bill said *I'm Retired*. "And we have to wear these shitty caps because Frankie and Aunt Ivy said so."

Tessa escaped into the bathroom, glad for the excuse to be alone one more time.

When she came out Lola was waiting beside the door, holding a cap and a ponytail holder. "We aren't wearing these for style even if Mama did have them special made for us." She touched the bill of her cap. "Turn around and I'll get you all fixed up and ready to go. They are to keep our hair out of our eyes and mouth and to provide shade for our faces so we don't burn. This is a big thing for her and Ivy, and she is so excited that you agreed to go."

"And you?" Tessa asked.

"I've thought about you every day, Tessa, for the past twenty-nine years and hoped I made the right decision that day when Sophie asked if she could adopt you. I don't expect to be your mother, but I would like to be your friend. And yes, I'm tickled that you are going with us," Lola whispered softly. "Now let's get that hair up or else Mama will come back in here and fuss at both of us for holding up the big send-off."

Tessa pulled a hairbrush from her purse and handed it to Lola, who quickly whipped her blonde hair up into a ponytail and put the cap on her head.

"You will have to adjust it. Did you bring sunglasses?" Lola asked.

Tessa took a pair of huge white-framed sunglasses from her purse and put them on and adjusted the hat. "There's an extra pair in case I drop these. I buy cheap ones because I break at least one pair a week."

"Me, too." Lola smiled.

"Nine o'clock on the button. Time to get this wagon train rolling," Frankie yelled from the driveway and gave a shrill whistle.

Tessa half expected to see a covered wagon coming from around the back of the house where she figured the garage was located. She breathed a sigh of relief when the nose of a red car made its appearance, but when the whole Cadillac was parked in the front yard with Branch sitting in the driver's seat, she was almighty glad she had on sunglasses.

"It's my first brand-new car. My husband bought it for me in 1959 when his first oil well came in like a gusher," Frankie explained. "He promised me a trip in it all around the state of Texas someday, but he didn't live long enough to retire."

"Branch is going?" Tessa's heart threw in an extra beat.

"He's our driver," Lola said.

As if on cue, Branch unfolded his long legs from the car and opened the back door like a chauffeur. "Ladies," he said with a big smile and a wave of his hand toward the broad backseat.

He wore khaki shorts, a snowy white T-shirt, and sandals. His eyes were covered with mirrored sunglasses and a snap-bill cap set on top of his head. He looked better in tight jeans and a cowboy hat, but either way made Tessa's mouth go dry.

She started to crawl into the backseat, but Frankie laid a hand on her shoulder. "Darlin', this is my retirement trip so I call the shots. Ivy and Blister get to sit behind Branch, then Melody in the middle and me on this side. You are sitting in the middle of the front seat with Lola on the passenger's side. That's our seat assignments for the whole trip. And Tessa, I can't tell you how glad I am that you are along for this trip. It means the world to me. It'll give us time to really get to know one another."

"Why can't I, like, sit in the front seat? I hate riding in the backseat," Melody said.

"Do you upchuck when you ride in the back?" Ivy asked.

"No, I just don't like it," Melody answered.

"Then suck it up, buttercup!" Ivy popped her on the fanny as she passed on her way to the other side of the car. "Your job is to take care of me and Blister. It's not a vacation for you."

Tessa scooted across the wide leather bench seat to sit between Lola and Branch. "So the oxygen tank is Blister," she said. "Does the car have a name, too?"

"Oh, yes," Lola answered as she buckled her seat belt.

Frankie reached up and touched Lola on the shoulder. "I can hear you. Haven't you learned anything in your forty-eight years, girl? I have the hearing of a bat and the memory of an elephant and I've got eyes in the back of my head. Don't never try to put anything over on me. This baby girl is named Mollybedamned."

Tessa dug between the seats and found the end of the belt. "As in first name Molly, second name Bee, and last name Damned?"

"No, as in all one name," Frankie said.

"It comes from an old western movie we watched years ago. You probably never heard of it," Ivy said. "Hey, Frankie, we need to watch that on this trip."

Melody mumbled something.

Ivy nudged her on the shoulder. "Girl, you'd better enjoy the sunshine and wind blowing in your face and remember that you could be spending eight hours a day in detention hall lookin' at the back of a cubicle. It will do you good to watch *The Brothers O'Toole* with us one evening, so don't you be bitchin' about it."

Melody threw her head back against the seat and pretended to snore.

Frankie winked at Ivy. "She won't have time for movies. She'll be doing schoolwork every single night, won't she?"

"Okay, ladies, Mollybedamned is raring at the bit to get this trip started. Let's leave with a bang!" Branch settled into the driver's seat and put the car in gear.

Both old ladies in the back threw up their hands and screamed, "Hell, yeah!" at the top of their lungs.

"I don't hear you," Branch singsonged.

They got louder.

He shot a grin toward Lola. "Mollybedamned says she hears the backseat crowd, but she isn't leaving until the front seat shows some enthusiasm."

Lola nudged Tessa and threw up both arms. Tessa did the same and started yelling at the top of her lungs. Sweet Jesus! It felt good to scream and yell out the tension from her body. The fact that it was in fun made it even better. Finally the Caddy pulled forward with three generations of women yelling at the top of their lungs, their arms waving in the air.

Things had finally settled down when they crossed the cattle guard, but when they reached Boomtown, a police escort took them down Main Street with the high school band following behind, playing "Waltz Across Texas." Folks came out of the businesses to wave and throw confetti at the Caddy as Branch drove all of five miles an hour down the short street.

"Holy smoke," Tessa said.

"It wasn't hard to arrange. The band practices every morning anyway and the policeman is a friend," Lola said just loud enough for Tessa's ears.

"Pretty impressive," Branch said out the side of his sexy mouth.

"Why are you driving? I thought you were a lawyer." Tessa's shoulder and hip pressed tightly against Branch's and the temperature in the convertible was a hell of a lot hotter than what the sign on the bank declared that morning at nine fifteen when they left town.

"Branch is a damn fine lawyer and as long as he's behind that wheel, he's billing me for his hours," Frankie said from the backseat. "And he'd damn sure better not cheat me a single minute or I'll move my business."

"Yes, ma'am." Branch looked in the rearview and winked.

Tessa had ridden first class in airplanes that didn't offer the comfort that the old Caddy did. If only there weren't that stormy upheaval in her hormones because of Branch, she might look forward to this trip a lot more.

"Music. It's not a party without music," Frankie said. "Tessa, turn on the radio. It's set to the country music station I like. When we get out of Beaumont range, you'll have to find another one."

Tessa turned the dial to hear Willie Nelson's rough voice singing "On the Road Again."

"Hope you like country music, because that's what we'll be listening to for the next month," Lola said as she nudged Tessa on the shoulder.

"Love it," Tessa said.

Branch kept time to the music by tapping his thumbs on the steering wheel. Ivy and Frankie sang along at the top of their lungs with every song for the next half hour. Tessa couldn't see Melody, but she'd bet the girl was either texting her little friends or else about to succumb to a case of acute boreditis, a disease that affected lots of teenagers and got them in trouble. Lola leaned her head back on the leather seat and snored.

Tessa folded her hands in her lap and pinched the inside of her wrist. It hurt like hell, so this was not a dream. She was really riding between her biological mother whom she'd met only three days ago and the sexiest man in the universe, who could be engaged or in a committed relationship.

If someone had told her last week at this time she would be riding in a vintage Caddy, listening to songs that were popular when the car rolled out of the factory, she would have had them committed, and yet the red spot on her wrist said that it was true.

"You asleep?" Branch asked.

She shook her head.

"What do you think of Mollybedamned?"

"I want to own her. Never rode in anything like this," she said.

"Want to take on her upkeep, too? She gets about eight miles to the gallon." Branch flashed her one of those brilliant smiles and her pulse quickened.

"Anything this beautiful deserves to be high maintenance," she told him.

Branch lowered his voice to a sexy drawl. "Are you high maintenance, Miz Tess?"

"High maintenance and awkwardness do not make good bed partners," she answered and then wished she could shove the words back in her mouth when she got a sudden visual of Branch tangled up in pure white sheets on a nice big king-size bed.

"You telling me that you didn't fall into my arms on purpose?" he teased.

"That's right." She nodded.

"Well, hell! I thought I was finally getting to be as irresistible as my older brother." He chuckled.

"You mean there are two of you?" she stammered.

"There's only one of me, but I have two brothers, making three of us. It's my oldest brother who's always been the pretty boy. I'm the ugly duckling," he answered.

She crossed her arms over her chest. It didn't help much, especially when his leg brushed against hers. It was definitely going to be a long, long month, and she didn't see a bit of boreditis in it for her.

"I bet you use that line a lot. Does it work?" she asked.

One side of his mouth turned up in a crooked smile. "Sometimes."

Ivy poked him on the shoulder. "I'm dying for a cigarette and so is Frankie. Pull over at the next wide spot in the road. And Miss Priss back here is beginning to wiggle, so I reckon she could find a bush and cop a squat."

"I'm not peeing on the ground. God, Aunt Ivy! What if something, like, bit me?"

"Might be easier to scratch a bug bite on your ass than put up with an exploded bladder or wet underwear if you pee your pants.

I saw those things you call underbritches. Lord, girl, there's not enough material in them thong things to flag down a train," Ivy said.

"There's a roadside rest up ahead. That will do fine." Ivy pointed to a sign advertising the place a quarter of a mile ahead.

Branch tapped the brakes and came to a stop at a place barely big enough to pull the big red car off the highway. "It's not much of a place."

"Hey, it's got a picnic table and one of them portable pot things. It will do fine. I'm dying for a cigarette and a Dr Pepper. And would you look at that, Melody." Frankie pointed at a faded green portable toilet. "You don't have to worry about bugs. No self-respecting bug would live in a place that smells that bad."

"It beats a bush," Melody said.

"Are we there?" Lola yawned.

"Not by a long shot. We're stopping for smokes and cokes. Might as well get out and stretch your legs," Frankie said.

"Not this time. Maybe in an hour. I'm going back to sleep," Lola said.

Ivy took the oxygen tubes from around her ears, turned off the tank, and hustled from the car to the concrete table. She'd left a perfectly comfortable seat in the car and yet she sighed in relief as she sat down on the concrete bench and propped her back against the table. She pulled two cigarettes from her purse and handed Frankie one before she lit hers. "Ahhh, this is the life. Good company. Nice warm day. No hurries. No worries. A good nicotine and Dr Pepper fix. Yes, ma'am, I'm loving this retirement party."

Melody made a beeline for the toilet and closed the door behind her. No way was Tessa going in that thing. If there was a spider, even a tiny one hiding in the corner, she'd panic and in her awkwardness most likely tilt the thing over trying to get out.

Branch held the door for Tessa to slide out the driver's side, then he opened the trunk and took out a Dr Pepper from a red cooler and another from a blue one. "Ivy does not share these things with anyone, no matter who they are, and she gets cranky if she doesn't have one at ten, two, and four."

"Just like the bottle says." Tessa nodded. "But she shares her cigarettes."

"Yes, she does. Watch her pull that flask from her purse and add a little kick to her Dr Pepper. At least that's what she calls it." He grinned. "She shares other things as well, but not her stash of Dr Pepper."

Tessa leaned against the fin on the back fender and kept an eye on the old girls and the green outdoor bathroom at the same time. Ivy stuck the cigarette between her lips, twisted the coke cap off, removed the cigarette, and took a swig. Then she pulled a bright-silver flask from her purse and poured a healthy shot into the bottle and offered it to Frankie, who'd already taken enough out of her bottle to give room for a little kick.

The idea of whiskey or vodka or moonshine in Dr Pepper was enough to gag a maggot. Add that to the horrible scent that wafted across the warm morning breeze when Melody opened the toilet door and it was enough to make Tessa want to curl up in the trunk and close the lid tightly.

"You survived. It's a miracle," Ivy told Melody.

"They must've, like, cleaned it this morning. It smelled like roses and I only had to kill one spider and have a stare-down with, like, one old rattlesnake. Piece of cake. Can I have a bottle of peach tea, please, Branch?" Melody said.

He took one from the cooler and handed it to her. "Your lies are almost convincing."

"I've decided they aren't going to get the best of me, at least not anymore today," she said. "Truth is, I held my breath and never peed so fast in my life. Got a whiff of it after I shut the door and it's still in my nose. I'm hoping the tea will help."

"You're learning," Branch drawled.

Half an hour later, they were back in the car and Blister was furnishing oxygen for Ivy. Mollybedamned hummed along smoothly and Lola continued to snore.

"I swear to God this is a wonderful trip," Ivy said with a long sweet sigh.

"Wait until we're out in West Texas where there's nothing but scorpions, dirt, and sky," Branch said.

"It's the moonshine talking right now. Your old ass is going to be draggin' by the time we get to Jefferson," Frankie told Ivy.

"I bet yours is draggin' worse than mine," Ivy popped right back. "And besides, we get to stay two nights in that hotel so I'll be all ready for the next leg of the journey. Melody will probably be real disappointed that we're not staying in the one downtown that's haunted."

Melody shivered. "For real? Like with ghosts and chains and howling? No, I don't want to stay in that place."

Frankie giggled like a little girl. "Yes, ma'am. Me and Lester stayed there one time and I heard footsteps in the hall, someone beating on the walls and moaning. I could have sworn I heard chains rattling against the old wooden floors. Scared a whole year off my life. I hear that the ghosts have figured out a way to get out of that hotel, especially at this time of year, and sometimes they go visiting different ones in town. You might get to hear them in the place where we are going to stay."

"Mama, stop trying to scare that child," Lola said without opening her eyes.

"Go back to sleep, Lola. I swear, ever since my daughter was a little girl she never could stay awake in a car, but she hears in her sleep and smarts off without waking up. We tried letting her help us drive down to Corpus Christi one time when she was sixteen. Damn near ran off the road and barely missed sideswiping a police car while she was at it. He made her do a Breathalyzer test and almost took us all into jail."

"You shouldn't have let me get behind the wheel," Lola mumbled but she smiled.

"I'm not a child," Melody protested. "And I'm, like, not afraid of ghosts. Like, I know how to protect myself."

"How's that?" Ivy asked.

Melody crossed her arms over her chest. She probably didn't weigh a hundred and ten pounds soaking wet with rocks in her pockets, but something about her expression said that Ivy and Frankie might have met their match if they cooked up something to scare her.

"Well?" Ivy pressed.

Melody raised her chin a notch. "I carry pepper spray."

Ivy pulled the flask from her purse and had a swig and then passed it across Melody to Frankie, who did the same.

"Well, that's good to know. But don't you know that pepper spray turns ghosts into zombies?" Frankie said.

"What's in that bottle thing? Are y'all, like, high on something?" Melody changed the subject.

"It's medicine and you ain't sick."

"I don't like whiskey or vodka. I like daiquiris," Melody said.

"Well, you won't be getting anything with liquor in it on this trip, and besides, this isn't whiskey or vodka." Ivy put the flask back in her purse. "It'll be time to refill it when we get to the hotel, Frankie. Did you bring enough to last out the trip?"

"Probably not, but what I got will make it halfway and by then maybe we can find someone who knows someone." Frankie laughed.

"Moonshine." Branch leaned slightly and whispered in Tessa's ear.

Tessa nodded. Thank goodness Branch was driving or they'd wind up in a ditch for sure, with Lola falling asleep when she rode in a car, two old ladies sipping on moonshine and putting it in their Dr Peppers, and a petulant teenager who'd probably run the wheels right off Mollybedamned.

At noon Frankie told Branch to take the next ramp because she had seen a burger shop advertised back down the road at that exit.

"I'm starving for a big old double bacon cheeseburger, fries, and a chocolate shake," Frankie said. "And we'll get this straight right now. Branch is holding a credit card that I gave him this morning since it's only right and proper for the man in the family to pay for the meals. This trip is my retirement party, and none of y'all are buying food or paying for rooms. If you want to shell out money for extra clothing or for souvenirs, that's on your dime, but the trip itself is on me."

"That ain't necessary. I got a chunk of plastic to pay for me and Melody," Ivy protested loudly.

"This is the trip of a lifetime and I'm payin', especially since I get to call the shots on where we stay and where we eat. Conversation over," Frankie said, her expression leaving no room for argument.

"Thank you," Tessa said.

"Ditto," Ivy chimed in and nudged Melody.

"Thank you," the girl said petulantly and went back to texting.

"My pleasure, folks." Frankie sighed with pure pleasure. "I can't believe that Tessa is on the trip with me."

"Well, I can't believe my great-niece is on the trip with me." Ivy laughed.

"Lucky, ain't y'all," Melody said.

"Someday when you have kids or find one that you didn't know you had, you'll know how lucky you are," Frankie said.

"Speakin' of kids, you remember the day Lola was born?" Ivy giggled.

Tessa turned down the radio so she could hear. This was her biological history and she didn't want to miss a single story, but Branch took the next exit and pulled into the burger place parking lot before Frankie could answer.

Branch opened the door for Ivy and helped her get Blister out and rolling. Melody slid across the seat and stretched as far as her slender arms would reach, peeled off her sunglasses, and headed toward the entrance without waiting.

"I got first dibs on the bathroom," she threw over her shoulder. "Too bad y'all can't keep up with me."

Branch shut the door and rounded the back side of the Caddy, opened both the back door and the front one, and held out a hand to Frankie.

She took it and smiled up at him. "You don't forget to use that logbook and write down the times. I'll pay you them high-dollar billable hours while you drive and pay for your food and bed, but I ain't payin' you for nothing but driving."

"Yes, ma'am," he said.

"I need a cigarette so bad it's terrible, but I need a bathroom worse. We'll have to wait for our smokes until after we eat," Ivy said when the rest of them caught up to her and Blister.

That the old girl could walk that fast with bad lungs amazed Tessa almost as much as the fact that she still smoked.

"Remember when we got caught in the school bathroom smoking cigarettes?" Ivy giggled again.

"Shhh! Don't you let Melody hear that or she'll never let us forget it," Frankie said.

"She's already inside with them damn things stuck in her ears. I'm probably lucky that I can't hear the shit she listens to." Ivy looked over at Tessa. "Back then cigarettes didn't cause lung cancer or emphysema or any of those other diseases. Hell, they didn't have a notice on the packages until we'd done smoked for forty years. They had a bull pen out back of the school for kids who wanted to smoke."

"Really? Are you pulling my leg like you did Melody's with the ghost stories?" Tessa asked.

Ivy used her free hand to cross her chest. "It's the god-honest truth, ain't it, Frankie?"

"It is. Only good girls didn't go to the bull pen. No, sir! Our mamas might be sittin' home smokin' up a storm, but their daughters best not be seen out there in that bull pen with them wild boys," Frankie said.

Tessa cocked her head to one side. "What happened?"

"Tilting your head to one side like that is something else that you got from Lola. She always does that when she's worried or when she asks a question," Frankie said as she kept walking. "But to get back to the story, Ivy can cry on demand, and she brought on the tears. Our principal let us off with a warning, and believe me, we never got caught again."

Ivy pursed her lips together. "That's right. From then on we opened the window and brought along Delores to stand watch for us. Look at those two old geezers over there in that window looking at Mollybedamned."

"Old farts wouldn't know what to do with that much power if they did get to drive her," Frankie said.

Tessa bit back the giggles. If the whole trip was like this, she wouldn't have wasted a single minute of it. Those two should take Blister and Mollybedamned to New York City and do comedy shows.

Ivy nudged Frankie with her elbow as they got in line to order. "Bet neither one of them would know what to do with two good-lookin' broads like us, either."

"Ivy!" Tessa gasped.

"Hey, I can take the oxygen off for ten minutes at a time. Fifteen with a little jacked-up Dr Pepper. That's twice as long as it would take an old fart like that to get the job done," Ivy said.

"What job?" Melody asked as she stepped into line with them. "I thought y'all had to, like, go to the bathroom."

Frankie winked at Ivy. "We do, but we're going to order and then go. Takes us longer to get up and down than it does you youngun's."

"Don't mind them." Lola poked Tessa on the upper arm. "They go on like that all the time. Been best friends since before they went to school, and there's never a dull moment around them."

"I want to be like them when I grow up," Tessa said.

"Be careful what you wish for, you might get it," Branch said so close to her neck that she could feel the warmth of his breath.

Tingles danced up and down her spine. She could blame it on not having had a boyfriend in nine months, but that wouldn't be true. But that did not mean anything would ever happen between them. A month might be long enough to form a friendship, but a relationship took much longer. Still, it was nice to know that she still had a hormone left in her body. She'd begun to think they'd all dried up and died after the stunt her last boyfriend pulled.

Chapter Four

A blast of cool air greeted Tessa as the hotel's automatic doors opened for them when they stopped for the day. Lord, it felt good to stand a few feet away from the desk under a vent while Branch did all the paperwork to check them into the hotel. A few feet in front of Tessa was a lovely staircase leading up to the second-floor rooms. The dining room where breakfast would be served the next morning was to her right and to the left was a nice comfortable sitting room with couches, wingback chairs, and tables. On past that the hallway where the first-floor rooms were located ran west to east. She didn't care if her room was on the top floor or in the basement as long as it had air-conditioning and a shower.

She hadn't had time to cool off when Branch brought three room keys tucked away in little envelopes to Frankie. From the numbers, Tessa figured they'd be lined up side by side and wondered if she'd be sharing with Frankie and Lola. That would give Branch his own room and put Ivy and Melody together. But she was wrong.

Frankie looked at the keys and tucked one inside the pocket of her shirt. "This one is for me and Ivy and Melody."

"But I wanted to, like, stay in the room with Tessa and Lola," Melody fussed.

Ivy's eyebrows show up. "Too bad, darlin'. You are here to wait on me, not have a party."

Frankie handed the second envelope to Lola. "You and Tessa will be right next to us, and Branch, this one is for you. And so we don't have this argument every night, this will be our sleeping arrangement for the rest of the trip. Now, Branch, would you see to it our bags are put in the right rooms, and then you can log out for the day." Frankie looked like she could fall on her face and take a nap right there at the foot of the staircase.

"Yes, ma'am. Your chauffeur will do that for you," he said tersely.

Frankie shook her finger at him. "Don't you get pissy with me, young man. You get to stop work in the middle of the afternoon, which is more than you'd do if you were at home."

"And besides, since you can't resist being a gentleman, you'd do it anyway," Lola told him.

He folded his hands across his chest and flashed a brilliant smile. "Y'all are ganging up on me."

"Yes, we are," Ivy said. "But you're a big, strappin' cowboy. You can take it. Now, rather than stand here and argue, I'm going to my room and taking a shower. I swear to God, I've been sweatin' like a barnyard turkey the week before Thanksgiving, but it was worth every drop to get to do this today."

Branch grabbed a luggage cart from the hotel foyer and pushed it out to the parking lot where he'd already put the Cadillac's top up, locked the doors, and put Mollybedamned to bed for a nap until supper time.

Frankie led the way down the hall, checking room numbers until she found the right one. "Okay, y'all. We will meet up in the lobby at six fifteen this evening. Tonight we're going to a little Italian restaurant that Lola found online. They have tiramisu and cheesecake on the dessert menu, and I love cheesecake. Reservations have been made for six thirty." She opened the door and pushed it open, letting Ivy and Melody go on ahead of her. "That'll give us time to get cleaned up and rested, maybe even take a little nap."

"Next one is ours." Lola took a few steps and slipped the key card into the door. "You can listen for Branch." She peeled off her shirt and threw it on the floor next to the closet door. "I'm hot, sweaty, and already tired of riding in a convertible, but don't tell Mama. She and Ivy are twenty again when they get in that car with the top down. I hope it at least rains a few days so we can ride in air-conditioned comfort." Her khaki shorts landed somewhere by the desk in the corner.

Tessa sank down on the sofa. "Mollybedamned has air-conditioning?"

"Not in the beginning, but when I was about sixteen Daddy had it put in over at the Cadillac place in Beaumont. Mama liked the top down but he hated to be hot and miserable, so they compromised." Lola kicked off her flip-flops. One went toward the window, the other scooted up under the bed. "Top stayed down until noon and then it went up for the afternoon."

Next was the bra and then the cute little hot-pink bikini panties as Lola made her way to the bathroom. The door shut, and Tessa heard the sound of shower.

One thing was for absolutely sure, Tessa had not inherited Lola's lack of modesty. That she had to have gotten from Sophie, along with her penchant to have things in order at all times. She fought the urge to pick up all the clothes, fold them neatly, and stack them on the end of the desk, but she sure didn't want to get off on the wrong foot this first night with Lola.

Branch rapped on the door and yelled, "Bellboy with your luggage."

Tessa bounded off the sofa and slung the door open. He unloaded two suitcases, a fancy pink leather laptop case, and a cooler right inside the door and was on the way out when he stopped and looked Tessa right in the eye.

"Don't ask questions and don't move. Not an inch. Just keep your eyes on the floor," he said.

"What?" she asked. "Is this a joke or a prank?"

"There is a spider above your head, and if you start flailing around it's going to land in your hair," he answered.

She froze and became a statue with her eyes closed tightly. "Get it and flush it down the toilet."

"I don't think Lola would appreciate me going into the bathroom right now. I've got his remains wrapped up in a tissue. I'll take him to my trash can," Branch said.

Tessa waited until the door was closed behind him, and then she crawled up in the middle of the bed and sat cross-legged as she checked the entire ceiling and the corners for any more of the vicious varmints.

Lola came out of the shower with a towel around her slender body and one wrapped turban style around her head. "What is the matter with you? You look like you saw one of those ghosts that Mama and Ivy teased Melody about."

"Spider," Tessa gasped.

In one leap, Lola stood in the middle of the bed. The towel that had been around her head hit the pillows and the one around her body slipped down below her breasts. She pulled it back up and tucked the corner firmly under her arm. "Where? Kill the sumbitch. I hate spiders. That's why I wouldn't go to the bathroom in that god-awful place we stopped this morning."

"Me, too!" Tessa told her about the fuzzy creature only slightly smaller than an Angus bull hanging above her head on a tiny thread. "I don't see another one, though, so I guess he was traveling alone."

Lola checked the floor cautiously and stepped off the bed. "Well, thank God for Branch. If I was ten years younger, I'd go over to his room and thank him properly."

Tessa eased off the bed. "Lola!"

"Well, I would. Your turn in the bathroom. I'm going to fire up my laptop and check on Inez, the lady who helps me run the store. After supper tonight I plan on a quick swim in the hotel pool. My body feels like it's been riding all day, and it needs a good loosening up. Too bad that's the only way I can get the job done." She smiled.

Tessa opened her suitcase and removed her laptop and set it on the sofa. "What's that supposed to mean, and how did you get away with bringing a cooler and a laptop case? I was told one piece of luggage."

"I had to have the cooler. I'm a bear if I don't have a Diet Coke first thing in the morning, and Mama knows it. The laptop case I snuck into the car after Mama and Ivy had their baggage in there. My suitcase was too full to fit it inside." She smiled.

Tessa nodded and headed toward the bathroom, but she did not leave her clothing lying all over the hotel room floor. Letting the hot, pulsating water massage her back, she propped her arms on the tile and buried her face. What in the hell was she doing in a hotel room with a tattooed stranger and a big, hairy black spider? This was not Tessa Wilson at all. She was not impulsive. She didn't do anything without planning it to the last detail. That was her job—planning trips for folks with every possible point covered and taken care of before they ever boarded the airplane, bus, or train. She damn sure didn't run off for a month with strangers without an itinerary and a plan. What in the devil had come over her?

No answers shot out of the shower, so she lathered up her hair and then used conditioner. When she finished, she wrapped a towel around her body and one around her head, exactly like Lola had done.

When she stepped out of the bathroom, Branch and Lola were deep in conversation, and she pulled the towel tighter around her body. Why did a towel that covered up a hell of a lot more than a bikini make a woman feel so naked?

"Branch, did you see how tired Mama was?" Lola said. "I'm glad we're staying two nights here, and we may have to do more of that if she starts to wear out more and more. She thinks she's twenty, but we all know the truth about that."

Sparks danced around the room between her and Branch so that Tessa was surprised Lola didn't see or hear the crackling noise they made.

"We'll watch her closely," Branch said. "I should be going now. I've got some business of my own to take care of. Thank God this place has free Wi-Fi. See y'all in a little while."

"Why didn't you tell me he was here? And why did he come back?" Tessa fumed when he left.

"You're covered up. It's not a big deal. He called to see if I'd brought an extra memory stick for the computer and then came to get it," Lola explained.

Both of Tessa's eyebrows shot up. "Easy for you to say. You're dressed."

Lola's laughter filled the room. "Our first fight, and it didn't take a week to get here."

Tessa dug in her suitcase for fresh underwear and a nightshirt that would do until it was time to dress for dinner. "I'm not fighting. I'm stating facts. You are dressed."

"Sure I am. I'm wearing a ratty old nightshirt and boxer shorts and no bra. My hair is hanging limp and my toenail polish is chipped, while you stand there looking like a fresh little flower with dew hanging on the petals."

"I'm mad at you right now, and it doesn't have anything to do with Branch," Tessa said bluntly.

Lola settled into the desk chair and stared right into Tessa's eyes. "For giving you away at birth?"

"Hell, no!" The words spewed from Tessa's mouth.

"Then what did I do?"

"Being adopted has never bothered me at all. It's this damned clumsiness that I could strangle you for." Each word got louder.

"Well, darlin', that is a Laveau thing, and I could have strangled my daddy for the same thing. I couldn't even be a cheerleader in high school."

"I'm still mad," Tessa said honestly.

"You can get glad in the same britches, or lack of britches, as the case is right now. I see you got the smart-ass attitude that we get in exchange for the awkwardness."

"Yes, I did, and I'm sure it will surface plenty during the next few weeks. Sometimes it embarrasses the hell out of me."

"Welcome to my world," Lola said and went back to work on her computer.

Lola was working on her computer when Tessa finished dressing for the evening. She'd chosen a bright floral sundress with lots of cornflower blue in it and sandals to match and hoped she hadn't overdressed.

Lola pushed her reading glasses down on her nose. "You look real pretty, Tessa."

"Thank you and so do you." Tessa nodded.

Lola looked like a gypsy child in a flowing multicolored gauze skirt, an orange tank top that hugged her slim body, and bright-blue flip-flops. She'd curled her blonde hair, but the curls were already falling.

"Thanks. Mama likes me to get dressed up occasionally." Lola's smile was almost shy.

Tessa tucked her room key into a tiny purse that held her cell phone, credit cards, and cash. "I'm going to go hang out in the lobby and wait for everyone."

"Mama will probably be there. She's always early and I'm usually late to everything. Guess you got that early thing from her, not me," Lola said. "I've got half an hour, so I'm going to Skype with a friend of mine in Boomtown."

Tessa waved as she shut the door. "See you later then."

She spotted Frankie when she turned the corner. She still looked tired, but her eyes brightened when she looked up and saw Tessa. She motioned her over to the empty chair beside her.

"You sure do look like Lola this evening," Frankie said. "Have a seat and let's talk. We haven't had much time for you and me by ourselves."

"Thank you, and you look all spiffy yourself." Tessa had never seen so much glitter and glam on a knit shirt or had any idea that a grandmother would wear big diamonds on every finger and in her ears. "Maybe we'd better get Branch a pistol to protect all that jewelry."

Frankie patted her big black purse setting on the table beside her. "Branch don't need a gun, honey. I carry a .38 Saturday night special right here in the pocket of my purse and I'm not afraid to use it."

"Good grief, Frankie. What scares you enough that you need to carry a gun?" Tessa stammered.

Frankie giggled. It wasn't a chuckle or laughter, but a little girl giggle that didn't go with the idea of a six-gun right there in her purse. "Not a damn thing, but if it tries, it's going to be wigglin' on the ground tryin' to breathe. Now have a seat, darlin', and I'll tell you a story."

Tessa chose the empty chair right beside Frankie and turned in the seat so she was facing her. "I love stories."

"Good, because today I'm going to tell you about your grandfather, and each day on this trip, I will tell you a story of some kind about this part of your family."

"I'd like that," Tessa said.

Frankie sat up straighter and smiled. "Lester Laveau was a romantic soul, and I fell in love with him when we were freshmen in high school. My mama wouldn't let me date until I was sixteen, but Lester was allowed to call on me on Sunday afternoons."

Tessa made a mental note to remember all that she could of the stories and type them into her laptop each evening. She'd have the stories to tell her own children someday when they asked about her ancestors.

"Then I had a birthday, and we were allowed to sit in church together and go to church socials, but always with a chaperone." Frankie's eyes twinkled and her mouth turned up in a smile so big that it totally erased all the wrinkles around it. "Sometimes Ivy and I would go for a walk and Ivy would wait under this big old scrub oak tree while me and Lester had some time alone up in the hay loft. It was there that I got my first kiss, and I liked it so much I went back for lots more."

"What did he look like?" Tessa asked.

"Oh, he was a handsome one, with blond hair and blue eyes. Not much taller than me, but tall enough I could wear high heels. In those days a woman never wore shoes that made her taller than her feller. Lester had a little old forty-acre place with a two-bedroom house on it down between Boomtown and Beaumont. His granddaddy left it to him, so that's where we moved when we got married right out of high school in 1949. He worked in Beaumont for an oil company and seemed to have a knack for learning the business."

"And you?" Tessa asked.

"In those days, I kept house, raised a garden and chickens and milked a cow twice a day and waited on the babies to come along, like any good wife." A sweet smile appeared as Frankie thought of those days. "Only there were no babies, and the damn Korean War started and Lester got drafted and sent. He was gone for fifteen months and

I had to hold down the place and live on what piddling little the government allotted me, but I made it. Ivy was working as a secretary over in Beaumont at a different oil company, so she moved in with me and paid me whatever it would've cost her for an apartment and used our old Chevrolet to get back and forth to work. And I waited every day for a telegram telling me my Lester was gone."

It was the passion in Frankie's voice that drew Tessa into the story as she sat spellbound, waiting for the next part.

"He came home in one piece, but it took a long time for the light to come back into his eyes. It's the eyes that tell the stories, not the words or the smiles or frowns. It's all in the eyes. They don't lie. You watch a person's eyes when they tell you something and you can tell if they're sincere." Frankie's voice cracked and she dabbed a tear with her finger. "We'd lie in bed at night and he'd weep for his friends who either didn't come home or came back with parts missing, and I wept with him."

Tessa laid her arm on Frankie's. "I'm so sorry."

"Don't be. That drew us even closer together, and finally I got pregnant. We were twenty-three that year and had been married five years. I lost the baby and four more after that in the next seven years." Frankie's tone had gone softer.

Tessa could feel the pain right along with her for the loss of those five little babies. How in the world did a woman keep her sanity after burying one baby after another in such a short length of time?

Frankie's eyes went dark and cold. "Doc said I was fertile enough, but my body wouldn't hold on to a baby. So there I was, thirty years old, and we gave up on having a family."

Tessa tried to steer the conversation away from all those memories. "What happened to Ivy?"

The light came back into Frankie's blue eyes. "Oh, she moved out the week Lester came home. Said we needed our own space, and she had a new job in Boomtown working as the school secretary. She stayed at that job until she was sixty-five and retired. She never married and she never stopped being my best friend."

Tessa pulled her hand free, kicked off her sandals, and tucked her legs up under her. "When did you move to Boomtown?"

"I'm gettin' there," Frankie said. "It was 1958 and Lester used the last dollar we had saved to drill for oil on our forty acres. Turned out to be one hell of a wise thing, because he hit a gusher and used all that beautiful money to buy some more land he had a gut feeling about, and pretty soon he had whole pastures full of oil wells."

"And he bought that Caddy out there with the first oil money?" Tessa asked.

Frankie clapped her hands. "You remembered what I told you. That's wonderful."

"I'm enjoying the story," Tessa said. "We've still got time. Tell me more."

"By 1960 he was ready to put in a real company and it seemed like Beaumont was a better place to do it than Boomtown, so we put in an office and I went to work with him, answering phones, filing papers, and making appointments. It took a few more years to get established, but we finally decided to hire full-time help and he surprised me with the place in Boomtown. I remember the day that he took me out there to see it and gave me the keys. Lord, I thought he'd bought me a mansion."

"And it was closer to Ivy, right?" Tessa whispered, wanting more and more of the story.

"Oh, yes," Frankie said. "We'd settled in real good, and then boom, I was pregnant again. We didn't figure I'd have any luck, but I carried the baby to term and before the two of us turned thirty-six we had Lola. And here comes the rest of our dinner party, so that's enough for one night. Besides, I'm starving to death and I need a beer."

Chapter Five

The dimly lit restaurant was cool and the aroma floating from the kitchen set Tessa's stomach to growling. She could eat a whole cake pan full of lasagna, two baskets of bread, and six bowls of salad, and then two desserts.

"Maybe not quite that much," she mumbled.

"Planning your supper by the kitchen smells?" Branch asked.

She nodded. "I'm hungry, and everyone knows that whatever you eat on vacation has no fat grams or calories."

"I wish that were true." Lola laughed.

The waitress led them to a table in the corner and Branch seated each of the ladies before he took his place beside Tessa. His leg brushed hers when he sat down and for a split second food was running a distant second to pure old desire. One day she'd been in this cowboy's company and she had never, ever let her hormones have the upper hand. She didn't date anyone she didn't know, and even then there was a definite protocol to the way things progressed.

Melody picked up the menu the moment the waitress laid them on the table. "Thank God, they've got eggplant parmigiana. I was, like, afraid I'd only be able to eat a salad."

"There's bread and marinara sauce," Ivy said.

"Teenager cannot live by bread alone." Branch chuckled.

"She must have peanut butter," Tessa said.

Frankie cackled out loud. "Aha! She did get a bit of the Laveau smart-ass. I told you that she wasn't all peaches and cream, Ivy."

"What are y'all havin' to drink?" the waitress asked.

"A pitcher of beer for me and Ivy," Frankie said.

"If y'all will share with me"—Lola looked over at Tessa and Branch—"I'll order a bottle of red wine."

"Gladly," Tessa said. Lord only knew how badly she needed a glass of wine, a good stiff margarita, or even a shot of Jack after the story Frankie had told her.

"I'd rather share the pitcher of beer," Branch said.

"Me, too," Melody piped up.

"Over my dead body," Ivy protested loudly.

"Peach tea, then." Melody sighed.

One waitress brought out the drinks and another brought a tray filled with bread sticks and two family-size bowls of salad.

Frankie started the process of ordering after she'd taken a long draw of beer from a frosted mug poured from the big glass pitcher the waitress set in the middle of the table.

"So what did you two find to talk about in the lobby?" Ivy picked up her mug of beer and held it up. "A toast before you answer that. To the trip that we've planned since we were twenty years old. To our retirement, Frankie. And to nothing but happy times from here through eternity."

Lola raised her glass of wine. "Hear, hear!"

Frankie's eyes misted as she held up her beer, her diamond rings glittering in the candlelight. "To family, both old and new, and friends and whiny-assed teenagers. I'm glad you are here to join me on the trip of a lifetime."

Glasses and mugs clinked together.

"Retirement?" Tessa asked.

"We're calling it that because it's our last hurrah. Folks these days make a bucket list. This is the first thing on our list and then we'll really retire." Frankie grinned.

Tessa smiled back at her.

"Well?" Ivy said.

"Well, what?" Frankie asked.

"Your talk in the lobby? What was that all about?"

"Oh, that." Frankie sipped her beer before she answered. "I was telling Tessa about Lester."

"With or without your rose-colored glasses?" Lola asked.

Frankie shook a long bony finger at her daughter. "When it comes to Lester Laveau, I don't have anything other than rose-colored glasses."

"Salad?" Melody filled the bowl in front of her and passed it to Ivy. "I do love Italian dressing. I'm glad it's, like, not made with meat."

Lola took it from her hands when she sent it that way. "How long have you been a vegetarian?"

"Two weeks. My boyfriend and I made a pact," she said.

Tessa put the red onion rings to the side and dipped deeply into the salad when the second bowl was passed to her. "It's a good thing you like vegetables."

"I know." Melody smiled.

If the child would wash all that black tar from her face and dress in brighter colors, she'd be a knockout, but who was Tessa to say a word. She'd gone through her rebellious years at that age, too, and had refused to wear anything but bibbed overalls and T-shirts for a whole year. And yes, there was a boyfriend involved in that decision, too.

"What happens if he breaks up with you?" Tessa laid a bread stick on the saucer.

"Not my Creek. He and I are like soul mates," Melody said.

Ivy's jaw dropped. "Creek?"

"His real name is Albert, but he chose a new name when we decided to be vegetarians."

"And you didn't?" Frankie asked.

"Oh, yes, but I wouldn't expect you old people to understand or to call me River Dance."

"Good God, the world is going to hell in a handbasket," Ivy said. "And hell, no, child, I will not call you River Dance."

Tessa ate her supper and listened to the easy banter between Ivy and Frankie. She had tiramisu for dessert and managed to get through the evening without the heat that engulfed her every time Branch's hand or leg brushed against hers burning down the restaurant. But by the time they got back to the hotel, she was ready for a quick swim, more to work the kinks out of her mind than from her body.

ᔓ

Lola did manage to toss her skirt and clothing somewhere near her suitcase when she peeled out of them and donned a bright-green bikini and left the room. Tessa planned to follow her, but first she had to call her mother and report on the first day of the trip, and then she answered a long e-mail from Clint concerning a client who wanted to book a round-the-world trip for himself and his wife on their golden anniversary.

Lola was back by the time she closed her laptop. "The water is nice, but now I need another shower to get the chlorine out of my hair. It'll turn green in a hurry if I don't. You probably already know that, but if you don't, then take a page from my lessons-learned booklet."

"Will do." Tessa mumbled, slightly irritated at Lola for telling her something that she already knew. She was almost thirty, not sixteen, and her real mother had warned her about the effects of chlorine on blonde hair when she was just a kid.

She carefully hung her dress in the closet with her strapless bra draped over another hanger and set her sandals on the floor neatly. She put on a tankini in the same shade of blue as her eyes and a cover-up of white lace and headed toward the pool, her rubber flip-flops making little noise as they slapped against the carpet.

The outside pool was small, but there was a decent breeze that evening and she had it all to herself. She dived in, swam to the shallow end, flipped, pushed off with her feet, and made it to the other end before she stopped. She propped her arms on the side and suddenly felt as naked as she did with only a towel around her when she realized Branch was staring at her from no more than three feet away.

His broad chest was covered with exactly the right amount of soft dark hair that narrowed as it traveled downward across a ripped abdomen into the waistband of his bright-blue swimming trunks. "Did you need some time away from it all to think?"

"Are you married?" she asked bluntly.

He shrugged. "No. What has that got to do with anything?"

"Engaged?"

He shook his head. "Was, but that ended last Christmas when she wanted me to sell my ranch," he said.

"Me, too," she said.

"You, too, what? You want me to sell my ranch?"

Tessa shook her head. "I was in a relationship that ended at Christmas also. And to answer your question about getting away from everything, it does get more than a little bit overwhelming," she said. "I probably should have stayed at home and gotten to know them in little doses, but I'm committed now and I'll see it through."

Branch extended a hand and she put hers in it. She jumped and then she was sitting beside him with only six inches of air separating them. "Frankie said you could go home anytime you wanted. I don't have that option."

"Why did she choose you to drive?" Tessa asked.

Branch's grin lit up the night more than the lights and the stars. "She says Mollybedamned likes me and that the Caddy hates Lola."

Tessa laughed out loud. "That's the lamest excuse I've ever heard."

"Exactly what I told my father, who is senior partner of the law firm where I work. But he said he's not losing our biggest client, and my job is to make her real happy."

"Mollybedamned or Frankie?" Tessa enjoyed talking to Branch. His quick wit and funny sense of humor reminded her of her cousin Clint.

"Both." He grinned. "So I guess we're in it for the long haul. At least we've got each other to talk to if the journey gets rough."

"What do you think Lola was talking about tonight when she said that about rose-colored glasses?" Tessa asked.

"I never knew Lester Laveau, but my dad did, and he says that he was a tyrant when it came to runnin' his company. Evidently, he was a different man when he went home, but still I'd bet that Lola saw him in the real light more than Frankie did."

"Guess everyone has a story and sees things in their own way. Race you to the other end and back, and then I'd best get on back to my room. I've got some things to take care of before I turn in for the night."

"And the winner gets?" he asked as he wiggled his dark eyebrows.

"To be the winner." She dived in without waiting for him, but he beat her and was sitting on the side by the time the race was done.

"I'm the winner." He grinned.

"Yes, you are, but don't enjoy your pedestal too much. The trip isn't over and winning one battle doesn't mean you get the trophy for winning the war. We both should be getting back inside," she said.

"Thanks for the conversation and the race." He stood up and disappeared into the night air.

ɞ

Tessa picked up her brand-new journal and opened to the first blank page. Emotions rambled around in her heart and mind like marbles in a tin can. Right beside her on the end table with the lamp was the hotel's complimentary pen and note pad. She picked up the pen and decided that she'd write in the journal each evening but only with whatever ballpoint pen the hotel provided. That way, she'd take home the ink from each stopping place along the way.

You are superstitious. The voice in her head was Clint's.

"Am not," she mumbled.

"Am not what?" Lola looked up from her laptop.

"Are you superstitious?" Tessa asked.

"Yes, ma'am. I never walk under a ladder. I would drive six miles in a circle to keep from going across the road that a black cat crossed, and if all the numbers on the clock are the same, then I have to wait until it changes before I go to sleep," Lola answered. "Why do you ask?"

"Some folks think I'm superstitious, too," she answered.

"I think everyone is to some degree." Lola started typing again.

Tessa scribbled on the notepad to get the ink flowing and wrote *September 1* at the top of the first page. That was as far as she got for several moments. She stared at the wall and wondered how in the hell she was supposed to put what she felt on paper. It was so raw and so emotional, even worse than last Christmas when her relationship had ended so abruptly. Finally, she started to write.

> *Day one has ended and thirty more stretch out before me. I'm still not sure that I will last through the whole trip, but I made it through the first day. I wish I could say that I've made up my mind to stay one more day and then tell them that I'm going back home on the next bus, plane, or rental car that I can find. Or that I've made up my mind to go the whole journey. But I haven't done either, and I don't like indecision.*
>
> *It's like every nerve in me has been scraped raw and I can feel what these people feel. It can't be because we are blood kin, because I don't share genetics with Melody, Ivy, or Branch.*

She held the pen in the air and smiled. Today had been like an episode of *The Twilight Zone* or maybe *The X-Files*. She picked up the pen and started writing again, this time faster and with less attention to what she was putting on paper, ignoring the eerie music from those scary shows until it finally stopped altogether.

> *Compassion is what I feel for Melody. She's struggling to find her place in the world. I don't think I had all those pent-up feelings when I was sixteen, but then I had Clint, and he was my rock in a topsy-turvy world. Maybe she needs a friend like that and fate has sent me on this trip to help her through this dark time in her life. Lord, I appreciate my mama more tonight than I ever did. A teenager can find friends hiding under any rock, but they get only one mama.*

She looked up at Lola and damn sure didn't feel like she had a second mama.

Indifference is what I feel for Lola, with her tattoos and aloofness. She says that she's glad I came on the trip, but I'm sure I remind her of a painful time in her life.

Clint's voice popped into her head again. *Don't judge too quickly.*

"Stop it," she said loudly.

"Talkin' to me or to yourself?" Lola looked up from her work.

"The voice in my head," Tessa answered honestly.

"I have those, too. They're a bitch, aren't they?"

Tessa nodded and went back to work.

I really like both Frankie and Ivy. It would be difficult not to like them, as open and entertaining as they are. Traveling with them is like watching reruns of The Golden Girls. *Ivy is a mixture of Blanche and Dorothy. Frankie has a touch of Rose when she talks about her husband and a lot of Sophia in her. But right now I wonder if I can ever cultivate real people feelings for them.*

And that brings me to Branch. I'm not a teenager with raging hormones, but . . . what can I say? He's sexy as a model for the cover of a romance book, plus he is kind to the old gals, patient with Melody, and tolerates Lola. I bet kids and dogs would flock to him like bees on clover in the springtime. And everyone knows you can't fool a child or a dog when it comes to people. Too many times today his elbow or his knee touched me when one of us shifted positions and the heat that shot through my body was not brought on by the wind blowing through the Caddy. I'll have to be careful with Branch Thomas. Oh, yes, Madam Journal, I surely will.

I wonder what they'd be writing about one another and me if they had a journal. Not that it matters, but I do wonder what their thoughts might be.

Chapter Six

Mollybedamned created quite a stir when Branch drove into town the next morning. Like celebrities or visiting dignitaries, Ivy and Frankie waved to the people on the streets. Melody kept her head down and tried to slide up under the front seat, but Tessa could almost feel the heat from her cute little red cheeks pushing past the backseat. Poor thing would probably never smoke pot again.

Branch kept the speed at least five miles below the speed limit and his smile and that cute little dimple in his chin let every woman in Jefferson, Texas, know that a very sexy cowboy had come to town, even if he was driving a vintage Caddy instead of a pickup truck. He parked in the first available spot in front of a store specializing in antiques and quilts and like a good chauffeur held the door for the ladies to crawl out of the backseat first and then took care of Lola and Tessa.

"I am going to sit on that bench right over there." He pointed to a wrought-iron bench between two stores. "That way I can keep an eye on Mollybedamned. She might get lonely, and she wouldn't like anyone touching her seats or her steering wheel."

"That car is not a person," Melody said flatly.

"Shhh, you'll hurt her feelings and then she'll make life miserable for you," Branch declared. "You might apologize to her to be on the safe side."

Melody tossed her head back defiantly. "You are all crazy. I'm not apologizing to a stupid car."

Tessa patted the hood gently. "Remember, Mollybedamned, she's a teenager. She doesn't understand that you are like a fine wine to be appreciated and adored. Don't make the rest of us suffer because you are angry at her."

Branch chuckled.

Lola smiled.

Melody rolled her green eyes. "I had high hopes that you might be the sane one."

Tessa let her face go blank. "I guess I lost my place as the chosen one."

Branch picked up the oxygen tank and set it on the sidewalk, then extended a hand to Ivy. "Next thing we know, she'll be insulting Blister."

"That's when I'm sending her to the detention home," Ivy said. "And enough rolling the eyes, young lady. One of these days they are going to freeze like that and you are going to be forever looking up at the sky."

Melody must have believed her great-aunt, at least a smidgen, because she started another eye roll and immediately stopped, looked at a sign down the street a ways, and pointed. "Look, there's an ice cream store. Can we go there?"

"Maybe in a little while," Frankie said. "Right now we're going into every antique store in town. Lola wants to check out their stock and maybe send some stuff back to Boomtown."

Melody sighed dramatically. "I don't want to look at dusty old antiques. Can I get my laptop out of the trunk and walk up there to that library and sit in the cool and do my homework?"

"Only until lunchtime," Ivy said. "And when you come out you'd best have every scrap of it done for this day. After lunch we've got some more stuff we want to do in this place and your job is to help take care of me, not run off to text with your boyfriend and pretend to be doing homework."

"I'm mad at him so I'm, like, not going to answer his texts or call him until tonight," Melody declared with a toss of her red hair.

"What he do? Change his mind about his new pot-smoking name?" Ivy asked.

"No, he and my best friend, like, sat out in his car at noon and, like . . . never mind," Melody said.

"Made out?" Ivy pressed.

"No! If they'd done that, I would have never talked to either of them again. They did a little smoking and she, like, had a vision, and now she has a new name and it's not fair. That was supposed to be, like, our thing and I didn't share it with her and now he has. And her new name is Dove Feather, which is prettier than River Dance and it's going to take me all day to, like, get over it." She pouted.

Branch opened the trunk, handed her the computer, and she flounced off in the direction of the library.

"Oh, to be young again." He laughed.

"I can't believe she volunteered that much information," Frankie said.

"She had to get it off her chest and tell someone, even if it was four old ladies. Don't look at me like that." Ivy pointed at Lola and Tessa. "In her eyes you two are only slightly younger than we are."

"Would you want to be sixteen again?" Lola asked.

"Living through that one time was enough for me. Branch, there's a place across the street to get a cup of coffee or something cold to drink if you get thirsty," Frankie said. "Mollybedamned won't get mad if you forsake her long enough to get something to drink. Now, the rest of you, let's start with this store. I like that quilt in the window, Lola. It would look real good on that old iron bedstead that's been in your store for more than a year. Might even sell the thing for you."

Tessa followed them into her first ever visit to an antique store and fell in love the moment she walked inside. She roamed from one place to the other, drinking in the beauty of the antiques. If those old hand-stitched quilts could talk, they could fill books with stories of cold winter nights, picnics under shade trees with children chasing fireflies at dusk, or maybe brand-new lovers wrapped up in the afterglow like they were in a cocoon. She ran her fingers over a marble-topped oak buffet, the cold surface reminding her of another buffet, not so different from this one. It was in her grandmother's house, and many times all the pretty geegaws had been put away so that it could be covered with shrimp gumbo, étouffée, and every other Cajun dish the family brought in for a gathering.

There was comfort in old things, like the warmth of real love filling the heart. She stopped at the hall tree and leaned forward to catch a whiff of the scent coming from it. Someone in the past had sat right there and smoked, and the smell had found its way into the wood. Someday, when she had a house instead of a one-bedroom apartment, she wanted a hall tree in the foyer.

Branch settled in on the bench and watched the people. There was something about Tessa that got under his skin—in a good way. It damn sure wasn't love at first sight, because he didn't believe in that shit anymore.

"Hey, there, young man, you mind if I sat down here with you?" someone asked.

When Branch looked up, he saw skinny legs sticking out from the bottom of baggy khaki shorts and a T-shirt that bragged about a trip to Las Vegas.

"Not at all, sir," Branch said.

"You waitin' on a woman?"

Branch nodded and smiled. "Five of them."

The old guy combed back his wispy gray hair with his fingers and whistled through his teeth. "God must be testin' you for somethin' to lay a burden like that on you. That beauty right there." He sat down and tilted his head toward the Caddy. "Does she belong to you?"

"No, sir, but I'm the driver for the next few weeks. Takin' those five women all over the state of Texas for a retirement party," Branch answered.

The man stuck out his bony hand. "To get to drive a beauty like that, I'd drive the devil and his favorite disciples around as long as they wanted. I'm Herman."

Branch shook it, surprised at how firm his handshake was. "I'm Branch. Pleased to make your acquaintance. Her name is Mollybedamned."

"Fittin' name for a gorgeous redhead."

"You want to take a drive around the town in her while we wait?" Branch asked.

"It'd be an old man's dream." Herman sighed.

The four women came out of the store at the same time Branch stood up, and Frankie smiled. "Sit on back down. We're just gettin' started. Would you put this in the trunk? We'll need to go to the post office and pack it into a box to mail, but we can wait until we get all our purchases down before we do that."

"Frankie, this is Herman. We're going to take Mollybedamned for a little spin around town while we wait on y'all," Branch said.

Herman jumped to his feet and stuck out his hand. "So that beautiful lady belongs to you, ma'am?"

"Yes, she does," Frankie answered. "And since Mr. Herman here thinks she's beautiful, she won't mind him riding in her seats. Y'all have a good time."

"Thank you, ma'am. Do you think she'd mind if I got Branch here to use my phone and take a picture of me with her? Nobody back home in Pennsylvania will believe it if I don't have the proof." Herman's old green eyes twinkled.

"She might smile for you after those sweet words," Frankie said.

"Did you find anything that took your eye?" Branch asked Tessa.

She shook her head. "A gorgeous hall tree, but it won't fit in the trunk. Maybe I'll find something in the next store that won't require a moving van to get home."

"Well, let's go see what we can find," Lola said. "I bet we can get all the way to the library by noon, and I want to eat lunch at the barbecue place that lady in the quilt place was talking about."

After a flutter of the hand waving good-bye to Branch, Tessa joined the other ladies and pulled Blister for Ivy, keeping pace with the older lady while Lola and Frankie went on ahead.

"That cute little blonde your woman?" Herman asked on his way to the car.

"No, sir. It's a long story but Frankie is the one with the gray hair that you shook hands with. The one with the tattoos is her daughter, Lola, and the pretty blonde is Lola's daughter. The one with the oxygen tank is Ivy, Frankie's best friend."

"That's only four. Where's the fifth one? Oh, I get it. Mollybe-damned is the fifth lady, right?"

Branch opened the car door for Herman and waited for him to get settled before he shut it. "No, she's the queen. The fifth one is a sixteen-year-old great-niece of Ivy's, and she's at the library doing her schoolwork for the day."

Herman settled into the passenger's seat. "Why ain't she in school?"

"Got caught smokin' pot in the bathroom," Branch said and wondered why he was telling an old man he'd just met personal things. Maybe, like Melody, he needed to tell someone and a stranger was the best option he had.

The old fellow belted himself in. "This is downright wonderful. But you really ain't with Lola's daughter?"

Branch started the engine and shifted into reverse. "Her name is Tessa, and I'm really not with her. This is only our second day on the trip and I barely know her."

"You go on and get to know her, son. Your soul already does. Your body and mind have to catch up, and sometimes they run a mite slow," Herman said. "Last time I sat in a car like this was back in 1960. My brother got married and rented a Caddy convertible to take him and his wife from the wedding chapel in Las Vegas to the hotel. Me and my girlfriend, who's now my wife, got to ride in the backseat."

"And you've been married how many years?"

"Fifty-three this summer." Herman grinned. "Takes work and a lot of waitin'. Sometimes a woman don't know what she wants and we have to wait for her to figure it all out, but she's been worth it. That pretty blonde will figure it all out if you've got the patience to wait."

"And if I don't?" Branch asked as he drove slowly down the street.

"Then it'll be your loss." Herman waved at all the gawkers who stopped on the sidewalk to point and stare at Mollybedamned. "Look at all them jealous people. Guess I ought to call Marybelle and tell her what I'm doin' or she might get worried. I told her I'd be right there on that bench when she got finished lookin' around."

Branch bit back the laughter when Herman explained five times that he was not in the car with a serial killer and that the man wasn't going to rob him and throw him in the bayou for the alligators.

When he ended the call, he looked over at Branch sheepishly. "Damn technology. Too many of these magic things like a phone you can use anywhere and it ain't even got a cord. Gets a woman to thinkin' foolish things. Now, where was I? Oh, yes, we were talkin' about all the people bein' jealous. Ever had a woman on your arm that people were jealous over?"

"I was engaged to a woman named Avery, and she was beautiful. Trouble was, she knew it," Branch answered and then wondered again why in the hell he was telling a stranger something so personal.

"Was?" Herman asked.

"I'm a lawyer. So is she. She wanted me to sell my ranch, and I love ranchin' more than lawyer work so I said no. End of story."

"That kind of woman ain't even worth waitin' on. What about that cute little blonde you got ridin' with you? She hate ranchin', too?"

"Don't know. Haven't asked her."

"Well, don't let her get too far down the road before you do." Herman chuckled.

Tessa wandered around the second store full of all kinds of craft items with a few antiques in the rental booths. She was looking at a cream pitcher in blue and white when Lola walked up beside her.

"You've got a good eye. That's the Walker Blue Willow, and it's been discontinued for years. That's an excellent price at ten dollars. I could get forty for it at the store."

"Are you going to buy it?" Tessa asked.

Lola picked it up and looked it over. "You saw it first. I wouldn't steal it out from under you."

"I think I'll start a cream pitcher collection on this trip. If I choose one thing to collect as we travel, maybe I won't send too much home for a one-bedroom apartment," she said. "So yes, this is going to be my first purchase."

Lola handed it to her. "If it had chips or nicks it would lower the value, but this one looks great."

Tessa carried it to the counter. "I don't care if my collection isn't in top shape. I want it to remember the days we're all spending together."

Lola picked up a carnival glass bowl and checked it out. "This is fun, isn't it? Thank you for coming along. It means a lot to Mama, but Tessa, it means as much to me."

"Thank you," Tessa said past the lump in her throat. Now, why in the hell should she be getting all emotional over a mother who gave her away almost thirty years ago? It didn't make any more sense than that flutter in her heart when Branch was nearby.

"I'm too tired to tell stories tonight, Tessa," Frankie said when they were back at the hotel. "Me and Ivy are going to watch television and drink a bottle of wine that we bought in that little specialty shop."

"And eat every bit of that marzipan chocolate with it," Ivy said.

"I've got my homework assignments done for two days. I don't know why I, like, have to go to school. I bet I could, like, do a whole week's worth of work if I kept after it all day, so I'm going to swim and text my friends all evening," Melody said.

"Creek?" Tessa asked.

"No, I'm, like, punishing him for another day. One of my other friends—not my bestie, Natalie, only now she is, like, Dove Feather—told me that he's still hanging around Natalie and they're, like, all chummy, so I'm not talking to him. I've only been gone two days and this is the way he treats me?" she whined.

"I'll call pizza in to be delivered at six thirty. What kind do you and Ivy want, Mama?" Lola asked.

"Meat lovers' with extra cheese, and make it a large," Ivy answered quickly.

Frankie tossed her purse on the bed and stretched out beside it. "Her eyes are always bigger than her stomach. I'll share with her. Tell the delivery boy to bring us a six-pack of Coors. I like bottles better, but we'll take cans."

"Mama, you've got wine." Lola rolled her eyes.

Frankie held up a palm. "Don't fuss at me. It's my retirement party and I'll damn well eat and drink and do whatever I want this month. When we get home, I promise to be good the rest of my days."

"Okay." Lola shook her head slowly. "But I can't believe you've promised to be good for at least seventeen years. You've always said you'd live to be a hundred."

Frankie chuckled and shut her eyes. "If I live to be that old, I will be good and eat right and live on the memories of the night I ate cholesterol-filled pizza and chocolate and drank too much and me and Ivy giggled until midnight. Jesus, you'd think I was the child and you were the mother."

"Role reversal," Lola said. "So meat lovers' for that room. What do you want, Melody—or should we call you River Dance?"

"Hell, no! And don't look at me like that, Aunt Ivy. I'm renouncing my vision name. I'm, like, just Melody," she said. "And since I'm no longer River Dance I'm not a vegetarian so I, like, want a sausage pizza with extra meat and cheese, and I'll have one of those beers."

"You might not be River Dance, but you'll have a soft drink or juice from the vending machine," Ivy said.

Her chin shot up in the air and she looked down her nose at Ivy. "You aren't a bit of fun. I bet you drank beer when you was sixteen."

Ivy lowered her head and squinted until her eyes were nothing more than slits. "What I did or didn't do when I was your age doesn't have a thing to do with what you are going to drink tonight or any night while we're on this trip. Go on in the room and crawl your scrawny little ass up on your bed and talk to your friends with your thumbs. I swear to God on a holy Bible that if someone were to break a teenager's thumbs, they might as well shoot the kid in the head."

Tessa kept the giggle at bay until she and Lola were safely in their room. Then she threw herself back on the sofa and the laughter bounced off the walls. Tears streamed down her eyes, ruining every bit of the makeup that was left. Lola went to the bathroom, brought out a box of tissues and tossed them at her. She caught them midair and pulled half a dozen from the slot on the top.

"What is so funny?" Lola sat down beside her on the sofa.

"All of them. I should be writing a script of this whole trip. Lord, it would make a movie that would rival *Fried Green Tomatoes.* 'Towanda!'" She raised one arm and giggled at the line in the movie.

"You are way too young to remember that movie," Lola said.

"No, I'm not. My mama loves it and we've watched it together a dozen times," she said.

Lola's smile faded and she grew serious. "Strange. I don't ever remember watching a movie with my mama."

"Really? What did you do when you were a teenager?"

Lola did one of her famous shrugs, both shoulders spiking up until they almost reached her ears. "Stayed out of their way, mostly."

Tessa straightened up. "Their?"

The shoulders dropped but the expression on her face said that it was not a happy memory. "Mama and Daddy."

"Tell me about them," Tessa said.

"First I have to call in pizza. I need to holler at Branch and see what he wants, so you've got a minute to decide." She picked up the hotel phone and hit the number for the room next door. "Hey, we're ordering pizza and I'm about to call it in. What do you want?" She wrote on the hotel pad as she listened and then said, "It will be here in about twenty-five minutes. I'll have it brought to your room since you've got the credit card, so holler when it gets there and I'll pick up ours and the ones that go to Mama's room." Lola put the receiver back on the base and looked over at Tessa.

"Taco," Tessa answered the unasked question.

Lola frowned. "Taco pizza?"

"My new favorite," Tessa answered. "Our pizza place started making them about a year ago and I fell in love with it."

"What's it taste like?" Lola's nose curled slightly.

Tessa shrugged. "Tacos and pizza kinda mixed together, I guess. Don't go judging it until you try it."

"If I order chicken and pineapple, can we share both?" Lola asked.

"That's my second favorite," Tessa said. "So yes, ma'am, we can share. And maybe bread sticks and marinara?"

"You got it, kiddo," Lola said.

Tessa liked that title. Not *daughter* or *my child* but *kiddo*! It fit both of them fine. She didn't mind being Lola's kiddo at all.

Lola called in the order and then motioned for Tessa to move over on the sofa. Back against the padded arm, she sat with her feet crossed Indian style and took a deep breath.

"So do you have a vision name?" Tessa turned and faced her, drawing her knees up and wrapping her arms around them.

Lola's full mouth turned up in a crooked, mischievous smile. "What brought that on? Are you saying we should do a little pot smoking tonight?"

"It's the way you are sitting," Tessa said.

Looking down at her legs, she chuckled. "No, I don't have a vision name, but my first love had a nickname for me so I guess it could be my vision name. I hadn't thought of it in years."

One of Tessa's eyebrows rose slightly. "Are you going to share?"

"It started out as Lola Bunny and then he shortened it to Bunny and he bought me little rabbit things. All the other girls got teddy bears at Valentine's. I got a rabbit of some kind or sort. I still have them all in the attic in a box with all my cards, letters, candy bar wrappers, and everything he gave me."

"Is that why you've got that bunny on your shoulder?" Tessa asked.

Lola nodded. "Yes, it is. We got them together when we ran away from Boomtown and headed for the commune. And this one"—she pointed to the rose on the other shoulder—"is because I was going to name you Tessa Rose."

"I like that, but my name is Tessa Ruth." Tessa let that name slide off her tongue silently a few times. She did like it, but not as well as her given name. Sophie had told her that it was a modern name with old-world charm, and that always made her feel important.

Lola's eyes misted. "My middle name is Ruth."

The empathy that Tessa didn't realize she had made her eyes water a little, too. "I didn't know where it came from until right now. I actually wondered if she'd gotten it from the Bible. She and Daddy are faithful churchgoers."

A pregnant pause filled the room, as if they were both waiting on the other to say something.

Finally, Tessa swallowed the lump in her throat and said, "You were going to tell me about Frankie and my grandpa? But tell me about that other tat on your ankle first."

Lola pulled up her skirt tail. "This little symbol means happiness. I got it to remind me that happiness is not a destination but a day-by-day journey. We get up in the morning and we decide to be either bitter about the past or happy that we have an untainted future. I try to choose the latter every day," she said.

A hard rap on Branch's door right next to theirs brought Lola into a standing position. "That will be our pizza, and he's early. I'll go on and get Mama's and deliver it, then bring ours so we can have girl talk."

"I'd like that." Tessa wasn't sure if the warm flush sweeping through her was family love, curiosity, or acute hunger, but she wanted to know more. This was why she was on the trip, after all—to get to know her biological family.

Deep in her own thoughts about Lola, she didn't hear Branch push open the cracked door and enter the room. It wasn't until he set three pizza boxes on the coffee table that she realized he was there. And then she squeaked like a mouse caught in a trap.

"Hey, it's only me. I didn't mean to startle you," Branch said.

"I invited Branch to eat with us since he would be all alone," Lola said on her way back into the room, letting the door shut behind her. "Besides, he's got pepperoni and he offered to share."

Tessa's eyes widened at the sight of so many big pizza boxes. "You bought large pizzas for all of us? And bread sticks and marinara?"

"They were on special. Any size for only ten bucks, and the bread sticks were half-price if you ordered more than three pizzas. It was a great deal and we might as well get all the bang we can for Mama's money. Besides, we can eat leftovers until we go to bed and I'm always hungry after a swim." She opened the boxes and plopped down on the floor on the other side of the coffee table. "Y'all can have the sofa. Maybe if my mouth is closer to the pizza I won't drop half of a slice in my lap."

Branch sat down and opened three bottles of beer before he grabbed the first slice of pepperoni pizza. Tessa took a long draw from her beer and then set it down on the coffee table. The taco pizza looked scrumptious, but she was so damned clumsy and worried not only that she might drop half or all of it in her own lap, but that maybe she'd do one of those reaching maneuvers that would cause it to end up upside-down all over Branch. Her stomach growled, and still she didn't want to pick it up.

Branch pointed at her pizza. "What is that?"

"Taco pizza," Lola answered. "It sounded horrible when she ordered it, but I'm thinking I might like it."

"Are you going to eat it or stare at it?" Branch asked.

"First I'm going to cover my lap in napkins, and if you'd like to take yours to the desk chair or sit over by the door, it's okay." She set about picking up napkins from the stack that came with the pizza and arranging them on the skirt of her sundress.

"I'm fine right here," Branch said. "There's not one part of me or these clothes that can't be washed."

He bit into a slice of his pizza and chewed slowly.

"Now, tell me, did y'all think Frankie looked really weary tonight? Do you think she's really going to make it for a whole month?"

"She will or she'll die on the trip. She's stubborn as an old Missouri mule," Lola said. "Oops, there went the first chunk of pineapple right down into my bra. Hopefully, that's all the mishaps for this evening."

Tessa picked up a slice and transported it from box to her mouth as carefully as if it had been a cup of tea in the finest china cup in the world. "Mmmm." She made appreciative noises. "This is absolutely wonderful. Y'all have to try it."

Nodding his head, Branch finished the slice he was eating. "Okay, I will try both of those sissy pizzas."

"Sissy?" Lola and Tessa said at the same time and in the same tone.

"Well, it damn sure isn't a man's pizza. We eat meat lovers' and pepperoni and sausage or maybe sometimes we might have hamburger, but not chicken and pineapple or taco, for God's sake," he said gruffly.

"Don't pass judgment until you taste it, smart-ass. What's the matter with you?" Tessa asked with a frown.

"Smart, whatever!" he shot back.

"Ass, whatever!" she smarted off. "What's got your tighty-whities in a wad right now?"

He held up a palm in defense. "I'm sorry, ladies. I got a phone call before I came in here that aggravated me. It had nothing to do with y'all and it wasn't very nice of me to take it out on your sissy pizza. I'd be glad to have a slice of each, and y'all help yourselves to my man's pizza."

Lola reached for a slice of his pizza. "Thank you. As unladylike as I am, I'll be glad to partake of your peace offering. I can probably make as big a mess with it as I can mine."

"Me, too," Tessa said.

He reached toward the taco pizza and his arm brushed against Tessa's. "Like mother, like daughter."

She gripped what was left of that pizza like it was a long-lost sister, digging her nails into it. If the heat generated from his touch had been able to escape through her fingertips, the poor crust would have broken into blazes.

After eight months and nine days of celibacy, hell's bells, any sexy cowboy's touch would turn me into a melted pot of hot hormones. It's not the man; it's me needing a boyfriend. As soon as we get back home, I will find one and prove it, she thought.

"We did it, kiddo!" Lola shouted.

"We did what?" Tessa asked.

"We didn't get anything on us other than the tiny piece of pineapple that I fished out of my bra. We must be good for each other. If we are together, we aren't as clumsy. Did you realize that we didn't make a mess at supper last night or when we had barbecue for lunch today? That's a miracle."

Tessa popped the last bite into her mouth and nodded. It was beyond miraculous. It was sheer magic.

Branch took another bite. "Pretty damn good. I might change my mind about this. I bet my guys would love it on poker night," he said. "I should be going, though. I've got about an hour's worth of business to take care of on the computer before I can go to the pool. You reckon I could take a box back to my room with some of all three?"

"Sounds like a plan to me." Tessa grabbed a pepperoni slice before Lola and Branch started divvying up the leftovers into two boxes.

Yes, sir, she definitely had to start seriously looking for someone to date when she got home. She'd call her mama or text her later tonight and tell her that she might be ready to go out with that new youth director at her church. He wasn't nearly as sexy as Branch, but her daddy said he was a good guy. Maybe a good guy was exactly what she needed.

ᔕ

Tessa opened her journal that evening, picked up the pen from the nightstand, and started to write without hesitation.

Day two—GUILT.

She wrote the word in print and in all capital letters, then went over it three times to make it bold.

That is my emotion for the day. I had so much fun with the whole bunch of them, but I shouldn't, not this quickly. I owe it to Mama and Daddy, who took me when my own mother didn't want me, to not get close to these people this fast. And yet I've let my guard down with all of them today and felt like I was with friends on a girls' day out. Then tonight I was flirting with Branch as if something could ever come of this outrageous infatuation I have with him. Crap, Tessa Ruth! You've got to get control of yourself. Branch is only here because he has to be. Melody doesn't want to be here. Lola could care less, and Frankie and Ivy have each other. You don't really fit in.

And yet, today I did. I was part of the whole thing. Lola helped me pick out the cream pitcher for my new collection and there was a thin bond there between us. I felt it, and now I feel guilty for it. Mama deserves my love and attention. She was the one who held my hand when I was sick, who cried with me when I could not dance, and who has been there for me.

Add CONFUSION to the GUILT. Mama would be the first one in line to tell me that I shouldn't feel guilty because I share genetics with two of these women and it's all right to make new friends, no matter what their age is.

Chapter Seven

Dark clouds drifted over the sky that morning when Mollybedamned left the hotel parking lot at ten o'clock. Day three of the trip had begun, and the next stop was around Gainesville, according to what Ivy and Frankie were already discussing in the backseat. The top was down to start the day, but the sky looked like it might dump cats and dogs and baby elephants down on them at any time. Branch pulled out onto the highway heading north, with plans to stop in Paris, Texas, for lunch in a couple of hours.

"Clouds will make it cooler," Ivy said. "But y'all better get out your sunblock if you didn't already put it on this morning. Remember that sunburn you got back in '59, Frankie."

Branch glanced in the rearview mirror to see Frankie nod. "I'll never forget that damned thing. Me and Lester went on a drive the summer we got Mollybedamned. It was a day like this, and I spent a week flat on my stomach in bed with a bad burn on my shoulders and back. I was wearing one of those strapless dresses, but at least I did have on a great big old floppy hat and it saved my face from the same kind of blisters."

"You ever had a burn?" Branch asked Tessa.

"Not one time. Mama bought sunblock lotion for me and her by the case. My Cajun cousins got brown as toast in the summer, but not me. I've always looked like I was soaked in buttermilk," she answered. "How about you?"

"I turn a little red and the next morning it's brown. Could have some Cajun in me, too. Listen to them." Branch tilted his head toward the backseat.

"I love their stories." Tessa smiled.

The old girls were well into the *remember when*, *remember what*, and *remember how* stories when Branch tuned them out. Instead of listening, his thoughts went back to the old guy and his stories from yesterday.

He glanced down at Tessa, who was intently listening to the stories coming from the backseat. Her shoulder and hip pressed against his, creating some kind of wild, hot electricity. She wasn't his type, but something drew him to her. Maybe Herman had been right, but most likely what the old guy saw was nothing more than Branch going too damn long without a woman. Now his body was reacting to a woman's touch, no matter who she was, and Tessa deserved a hell of a lot more than a quick romp in the sheets. And that's all Branch had to offer after the mess Avery made of his heart.

Lola reached into a tote bag at her feet and brought out a piece of knitting attached to round needles. She wound the thin pink yarn around her fingers and went to work, humming some kind of lullaby that was barely audible from the other end of the wide bench seat.

Tessa watched the process a few minutes before she finally asked, "What are you working on?"

"Baby caps. I make them for the hospital down in Beaumont and the one in Houston to put on newborn baby girls," she answered.

"No baby boys?" Branch asked.

"I like pink, and"—she glanced over her shoulder—"my therapist says it's good for me. It takes me to my happy place, thinking about those baby girls wearing my little knitted hats. I am humming to keep the noises from the backseat out of my head. I left my music and earbuds in my suitcase. I've heard the stories they're telling a million times."

"Will you teach me to do that? I've always wanted to crochet and knit both, but with my two left feet, I figured I might be all thumbs, too," Tessa said.

Branch kept both hands on the wheel, but he really wanted to throw an arm around Tessa and assure her that because she couldn't do ballet dancing did not mean she couldn't learn to two-step. Maybe someday he'd show her rather than tell her.

"Sure, I'll teach you." Lola kept throwing the yarn over the needle and doing something with the other one and suddenly a stitch appeared. "If I can learn to do this, anyone can. I like making baby caps because they're small, soft, and I can make two or three a week. It's simple, basic knitting so I don't have to learn anything like cable stitching. It's mindless work where I can think about anything but what is going on around me. We can have our first lesson tonight. I've got extra needles and yarn."

Ivy touched Branch on the shoulder. "We got so wound up in remembering the past that we forgot our music. We can't take a Caddy trip without listenin' to Waylon, Willie, and the boys."

"Crap!" Melody's earbuds and MP3 player came out of her purse.

"You go on and listen to that shit that you young people call music," Ivy told her. "Someday when you grow up, you might recognize the good stuff, but first you got to grow up."

Branch turned the dial and found a country station. He kept time with the music with his thumbs on the steering wheel as Rascal Flatts sang "Bless the Broken Road."

"You're pretty serious this morning," Tessa said.

"Just listening to this song. You ever traveled down broken roads like they're talking about?" he asked.

"None as broken as the one I'm traveling right now," she said. "How about you?"

"Ditto," he answered. "I've known Frankie, Lola, and Ivy most of my life. I can't begin to imagine how overwhelmed you must be or why you agreed to this."

"My mama and daddy thought it would be good for me," she said softly. "If I know the people that I share a bloodline with, well, then I wouldn't feel like . . . never mind."

Branch frowned. "I could never understand what you are feeling, Tessa. It's way too deep for me, but if you ever need to talk, I'm here. Do you live with your parents?"

Tessa's pretty full lips almost turned up in a smile, but it didn't materialize. "Thank you, but this is all so raw and new I wouldn't know how to put it in words. And, no, I haven't lived with my parents since I graduated high school and went to college. I have my own apartment. Do you live with your folks?"

Branch shook his head. "I have my own ranch out east of Beaumont. Just one section of land, but it's got a couple of oil wells and a hundred head of the best Angus cattle in the state on it."

The sun peeked out from behind the clouds and caught her bright smile. "And who is running all that while you are gone? I love animals and always wanted to live outside of town. Do you have cats and dogs as well as cows?"

Branch's heart threw in an extra beat. Could Herman have really known something, after all? "I do have cats and dogs, and my foreman, Corky, is taking care of things for me. He stayed on when I bought the place and I'm lucky to have him. Who's running the travel agency?"

"My partner and cousin, Clint. He got home from a four-week holiday in Europe and thinks I've lost my mind to waste my whole year's worth of vacation time on this trip. Offered to send me to a therapist," she said.

"I wish my father would have given me that option." Branch chuckled.

"Whoa, hosses," Lola yelled and pointed. "Mama, did you see that?"

Tessa had been so deep in her own thoughts about how she would describe her feelings to Branch that when Lola shouted, it startled her. She jumped and Branch laid a hand on her knee.

"Whoa there, Miz Tess! You were about to bust that seat belt and fly," he said with a twinkle in his eye.

Her heart settled somewhat, but her pulse still thumped like a drum against her wrist. "I was a million miles away," she said softly.

"You scared the shit out of me, girl. For a minute I thought Jesus was coming down through the opening in those clouds to get me," Frankie said.

Lola put her knitting away. "Oh, hush that talk. I told you that you're going to live to be a hundred and we're going to have a big festival in Boomtown to celebrate and you're going to ride down Main Street in Mollybedamned that day."

"Well, then what were you talkin' about?" Frankie asked. "We ate a big dinner in Paris an hour ago. Are you already thinkin' about ice cream?"

"I saw a little sign back there stuck on a barbed-wire fence. Turn right where those balloons are waving in the air, Branch," Lola said. "It's a big church bazaar festival and yard sale, about five miles up this road."

"Hot damn!" Frankie said. "Me and Ivy love bazaars, and you might find something for the shop. And I thought you disappeared into a foggy place where you don't see jack shit when you pick up that pink yarn."

"I hate yard sales. I'm not getting out of the car." Melody leaned her head back on the seat. "When do we get to the hotel? Does it, like, have a pool?"

"This is our trip and we love junk, so get used to it. You've been so quiet all day that I thought maybe you'd gone into a stupor," Ivy said.

She put up a palm and closed her eyes. "I'm, like, in mourning, and my music is the only thing that can console me."

Branch made the turn onto a two-lane road and drove north, and Tessa read the signs tied to the fences along the way.

"I hope it's not all gone," Frankie said. "The folks who go to these things are there at the crack of dawn, so we might be gettin' the leftovers."

"You're all, like, in a basket load of trouble if you think you can use a credit card at this place," Melody said. "My mama helps with the one at our church and, like, it is cash only."

Ivy pulled an earbud from one of Melody's ears, leaned over, and yelled, "Honey, these two old gals don't leave home without a full flask, a cooler of Dr Pepper, a couple of cartons of cigarettes, and enough money to buy any damn thing we want."

"Well, I'm staying in the car and mourning," Melody said.

That was twice she'd mentioned the word in less than five minutes. Tessa made a mental note to talk to her that evening and offer a listening ear, a shoulder to cry on, or a sounding board to cuss at. Being sixteen was tough in any world, but the poor little lamb was enduring a lot on this trip—even if she shouldn't have been smoking pot.

"Look at all that stuff—and I smell chili." Frankie opened the door before the car had fully stopped. "I am going to buy a jar to take to the hotel room for our supper. We'll stop and get paper plates and bowls and have a feast in the room."

"I only have about two quarts of chili left. Want me to get it ready for you?" the lady behind the table spread with baked goods and food asked.

Frankie nodded. "Yes, I do. Set it back along with whatever that is I smell that has cinnamon in it."

Tessa left Ivy and Frankie with the lady in charge of the food and followed Lola to a table on the other side of the church parking lot. She picked up a cream pitcher from the end of a table holding several lamps. "This is pretty. Is it an antique?"

"Not really but it's not modern, either," Lola answered. "It's in good shape. Two bucks is cheap for it. Back in the early part of the last century, that stuff was what they gave away at carnivals. Most of it is an orange and yellow swirly mix or else purple and blue."

Tessa kept it in her hand and picked up a small dish. "Like this?"

"No, that one is a rarer piece. It's called black amethyst. See those swirls of black and purple with a hint of a weird shade of green? It's a steal, kiddo. In the store, I'd mark it at twenty dollars. I thought you were going to limit your purchases to cream pitchers." Lola ran a hand over a white hobnail glass cake dish.

"I was, but it's only fifty cents and . . ." Tessa let the sentence drop.

"And that's why I own a store." Lola laughed. "I started with a carnival glass compote that I found at a garage sale and in a year I had to rent a storage unit and then Mama said my addiction had to have an outlet so we put up the building and I really went to work."

"So is this the beginning of a second job, Miz Tess?" Branch asked.

She liked that nickname every bit as much as she liked that Lola called her *kiddo*. "I don't think so, but I'm still buying this cute little bowl. I'll put it on my dresser to catch bobby pins and ponytail holders."

"Want me to find a place in the trunk for those?" Branch asked.

"No, I'll pay for them and they're small enough to fit in my purse until we find the place to mail them," she answered.

A pretty yellow-and-black butterfly caught her attention as it flew past and straight toward the food table. "Looks like they are selling sweet tea by the glass. Y'all interested? I'll get them when I go pay for these two things."

"I'm shopping some more," Lola said. "Y'all go on and sit under the shade tree if you are finished, though. Right now I want both hands free to pick things up."

Branch pointed at an empty picnic table under a big pecan tree. "I'll wait right there, and I'd love a glass of sweet tea."

The lady took her money and poured up two big disposable cups of tea. "I've also got lemonade, but it's that instant stuff, not the real thing," she said.

Tessa put the change from the ten-dollar bill in her purse. "This is fine. We were afraid we might get here too late to get anything."

"Oh, honey, you got here at exactly the right time. We opened up at noon and most of our crowd was here to eat then. They'll come back after work to browse. We planned on having this on Saturday, but it's supposed to rain that day so we moved it up two days. We were gettin' bored so we're real glad y'all stopped by. You got one mighty handsome boyfriend sittin' down there waitin' on you."

"He's not my boyfriend," Tessa said quickly.

"Oh, your husband? I didn't see a wedding ring so I assumed you were dating." The middle-aged lady blushed.

Tessa matched the crimson dots on the woman's face with her own high color. "Not that, either. I haven't known him a week."

The lady smiled and lowered her voice. "Well, honey, the way those dreamy eyes of his have followed your every move since y'all got out of that big old Caddy tells me he might be your boyfriend before long." She patted her on the forearm. "Take my advice. Don't close the door until you are sure you don't like what's behind it."

"Yes, ma'am." Tessa carried the red plastic cups to the table and set one in front of Branch.

"Thank you. I owe you," he said.

She pulled the cream pitcher and the little bowl from her purse and set them on the table between them. "Does it hurt your little manly pride for a woman to buy you a sweet tea?"

"A little bit," he answered. "But not enough to push it aside and not drink it."

She sipped the tea. "Mmm, the perfect amount of sugar, and it hasn't been boiled. See how light it is? That means it was steeped, like tea should be. And about that pride thing, you can buy me a vending-machine coke tonight at the hotel and we will be even."

"Deal." He stuck his hand out.

She shook it and blamed the heat on the day and the bright sun that had broken through the clouds. It couldn't be anything else, could it?

"So why did you buy those two pieces in particular?" He dropped her hand and nodded toward the cream pitcher and bowl.

She picked up the bowl and imagined it full of hairpins and ponytail holders. Maybe when she bought a real house, she'd furnish it around the items she bought on this trip. "I liked them. I wanted something to remember each event on the trip and decided I'd buy cream pitchers. I'm writing a journal about what we do each day and the things I learn about my birth family."

"And the bowl?" he asked.

"Just because I liked it," she said. "No reason other than that. Why?"

She wasn't about to tell him or anyone else that the strange shade of green reminded her of his eyes and that's what she intended to write in her journal that evening.

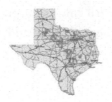

Chapter Eight

Tessa was deep in thought for the second time that day when Frankie let out a squeal from the backseat and Branch had to hold her down again. Lord have mercy, it took more than a few seconds for her soul to settle back inside her body.

"What?" Lola's head whipped around.

"Look at that sign," Frankie said.

"WinStar Casino a mile over the line in Oklahoma." Ivy pointed. "Y'all can have a feast in the room. We're going to the casino, aren't we, Frankie?"

"Mama!" Lola scolded.

Using her finger, Frankie made the sign of a cross over her heart. "I promise I won't get caught again counting cards. I swear to God, it looks to me like I should be able to use all that bookkeeping shit I learned to play a little poker," she said.

"Ivy?" Lola kept staring.

"Okay, okay, I won't get caught, either," Ivy said.

"That doesn't mean they won't do it," Branch said softly out of the side of his mouth. "It means they won't get caught."

Ivy and Frankie could hardly wait to get out of the car when Branch parked Mollybedamned under the awning in front of the hotel. They marched right up to the desk to talk to the clerk about a limo for the evening. And as luck would have it, the hotel had a service on speed dial—for a fee, of course—but Frankie didn't bat an eye at how much it would cost. When Lola said she would go with them, they declared that they didn't need or want anyone's company. According to Ivy, it would mess up their juju at the blackjack tables.

By four thirty, they were both dressed in white dress slacks and flowing tops with enough dazzling sparkle to light up a moonless night. They wore too much perfume, too much jewelry, and their cute little purses probably held more money than Tessa made in a year at the travel agency. But it was Frankie's bucket list trip and she was making memories, so Tessa hugged them both and wished them lots of luck.

"Be home before twelve. That limo out there turns into a pumpkin at the stroke of midnight," she warned. "And if you do get caught doin' something you aren't supposed to do, then call me and I'll come get you. You do have your cell phones and they are charged, right?"

"Yes." Ivy giggled. "But we won't be takin' calls from none of y'all. Not unless you call three times within three minutes, and then we'll know it's an emergency."

"And"—Frankie held up a hand with enough big diamonds to put Tiffany to shame—"you'd better damn well have broken bones or blood if you call us."

"Why aren't you takin' the fancy car instead of a limo?" Melody asked.

"Because someone might key her or hurt her in a parking lot that big," Frankie said. "If I win a lot of money, we'll stop tomorrow at the mall in Wichita Falls and you can spend a hundred dollars on anything you want to get you out of your mourning."

Melody threw her hand over her forehead in a true Scarlett O'Hara gesture. "Retail therapy won't even, like, work. I may never wear anything but, like, black again."

Ivy patted her on the shoulder. "Maybe you'll change your mind by the time we get to the shopping mall."

Tessa looped her arm through Melody's as they watched the limo pull away from the hotel. "Want to go for a swim or maybe even a jog?"

"Yes to a jog. I feel like my body is molded into the shape of the backseat of that car over there." Melody nodded toward the Caddy. "Mourning doesn't, like, mean I'm going to get fat and ugly. Having red hair and freckles is enough. I have to, like, protect my body."

"Hey, now, you are putting down one of my newest friends, and I don't let people talk about my friends," Tessa said quickly. "Your hair is lovely and your freckles make you irresistible. Want to join us, Lola?"

Both her palms went up defensively. "No, ma'am. Jogging is not for me. I'll take a swim later to get the kinks out of my spine. Y'all go on and have a sweatin' good time. I'm going to Skype with Inez about the lamps."

Melody glanced at Branch, who shook his head. "Not today, ladies. I've got some lawyer work to do. Maybe we'll meet up later at the pool."

"Then I guess it's me and you, kid," Tessa said.

"Meet you in the lobby in five minutes."

Tessa dressed in hot pink running shorts, a matching tank top, and her favorite shoes. She waited on the bench in front of the hotel for Melody, who showed up less than a minute later, wearing a hangdog expression that matched her black shorts, tank top, and shoes.

"You ready or do you need to stretch?" she asked Melody.

"Let's go," she said and took off. "We can go slower if you get winded."

Tessa's lips curled in a smile. "I'm not thirty yet, girl."

"That's ancient."

"How about eighty? What's that?" Tessa asked.

"That's petrified, and I know who you are talking about. Don't tell them, but I like those two old girls. I want to grow up to be like them. Dolling up in ridiculous outfits, hiring a limo, and, like, going to casinos. I want to live every day like it was my last and, like, never look back," Melody said softly.

"Then why are you in mourning? You're wasting precious time letting some stupid boy ruin your days to live."

Melody stopped and fell back on the grass, hands to her sides and eyes straight up at the big white puffy clouds. "That stupid boy can kiss my freakin' ass. He got what he wanted. Talked me into, like, smoking pot with him and then right into my pants. Then I smoked it in the bathroom so I wouldn't be afraid to, like, have sex with him again and got caught."

"Well, now, that puts a new light on everything," Tessa said.

Melody shut her eyes tightly. "You're not going to yell at me for having sex with him?"

Tessa's heart went out to the girl. She'd given away a precious gift and some smart-ass kid hadn't been mature enough to appreciate it. "No, it's done and can't be undone."

"Are you going to tell Aunt Ivy?"

Tessa sat down beside her, drew her knees up to her chest, and wrapped her arms around them. "No, I am not. Did you make him use protection?"

"Duh!" Melody slapped her head. "I'm, like, young. I'm not dumb."

"Okay, then, the way I see it was that it was your decision, although I think we should castrate him for getting you high so you'd say yes," Tessa said.

Melody giggled. "Now, he's already dating another girl, Tessa. He's the quarterback of the football team and she says that the head cheerleader is, like, supposed to date the quarterback, that it's, like, tradition."

Tessa lay back in the grass still wet from when the sprinklers did their job earlier. "How many girls are in your little clique of friends? Tell me about them. Who's the most popular? Are you cheerleaders?"

"I was a cheerleader until I got caught, so now I'm, like, off the team. The other four were smoking pot with me, but they got out before the teacher caught me. They promised that they'd still be my friends." She pointed up at the clouds. "That one looks like an angel."

"And that one looks like a teddy bear." Tessa pointed in the opposite direction. "So how are the other girls reacting?" Tessa pushed on.

"Natalie is the head cheerleader and is, like, just the most popular girl in the whole school. If the others don't do what she says, then she will figure out a way to, like, get them kicked off the squad, so we all basically do what she says. Oh. My. God! Do you think she got me kicked off the squad so that she could have Albert? She's the one who is dating him now!" Melody clamped a hand over her mouth as if she'd only that moment seen the big picture.

Tessa laced her hands behind her head. "What do you think?"

Melody sat straight up. "I wondered why they all had to, like, leave in a hurry, and right after they were gone, a teacher came right in the bathroom. Surely she wouldn't do that. I mean, we've been best friends since, like, summer started. She's the one that told me all the girls were having sex and I'd better get with the program or she'd see to it I wasn't a cheerleader."

"And who was your best friend before Natalie?"

Melody slapped herself on the forehead. "I'm, like, so stupid, Tessa. My best friend was Jill and has been since kindergarten. We planned to finish high school and go to college together and then, like, open up our own computer tech business. We're both good at that. What have I done?"

"Were you happy when Jill was your friend and these mean girls weren't controlling you?" Tessa asked.

Melody nodded and wiped a single tear from her cheek.

"You made a big mistake, but I bet it can be fixed. What you ought to do is go up to your room and call Jill. Talk to her and tell her that you've missed her being in your life. Share everything with her like you used to do and go back to being the girl you used to be when you were happy," Tessa said.

"I was happy before all this cheerleading shit." Melody nodded seriously. "But, Tessa, what if she won't talk to me? If she'd deserted me for a bunch of cheerleaders, I wouldn't talk to her."

Tessa laid her hand on Melody's. "Never know unless you try."

"How'd you get to be so smart?"

"I lived through being sixteen." Tessa bit back a giggle. This was far too serious to Melody to laugh about it. "Want to continue this jog, or have you got other things to do?"

"I'm going to take a shower and then call Jill," Melody said.

"Good luck." Tessa sat up. "See you at six thirty for supper."

"Thanks." Melody popped up on her knees and wrapped her arms around Tessa, hugging her tightly before she stood up and ran back toward the hotel entrance.

Tessa hoped that Jill and Melody could get over their differences. Everyone needed a friend in their corner. Clint had been her Jill, and she couldn't imagine being sixteen and not having him around to support her.

A squeak took her attention to a side door into the hotel. Branch came through it, crossed the yard in a few long strides, and sat down right where Melody had been not two minutes before. "I started out to the Caddy to get my laptop. Forgot and left it in the trunk when I saw you talking to Melody. It looked serious, so I didn't want to disturb y'all."

"Girl problems. Being sixteen isn't easy," Tessa said.

"That's the gospel truth whether you are a girl or a boy at that age. We're probably putting grass stains on our shorts."

"They sell khaki shorts in your size every day at Walmart." She smiled.

"Want to tell me what girl problems our young friend is having?" Branch asked.

Tessa shook her head. "Can't break the laws of confidentiality."

"Lawyer-client privilege, huh?" He grinned.

"Something like that. More like friend-slash-friend privilege," she answered.

"So does that mean if we talk about things that you won't tell anyone?" His hand closed over hers and he squeezed gently.

"If we are friends?" She nodded. Why, oh why couldn't Frankie have hired an old gray-haired married man to drive them around the state?

"Maybe we can make that happen." He moved his hand.

She wrapped her arms back around her knees and laced her fingers together. They felt hot and tingly, but at least they didn't have the ability to blush.

He popped up on his feet and extended a hand. "I've got one more phone call to make and I'll meet you in Melody's room in half an hour for supper."

"Thank you, but I think I'll sit here a few more minutes before I go inside. I think Lola needs some privacy."

"Oh?" He raised a dark eyebrow.

"A couple of times I've walked in and she's been chatting—or maybe I should say Skyping—with a man on her laptop, and she looked happy. I caught his face a split second before she pushed a button and he disappeared. All I could tell was that he wears glasses and has a thin face."

"Really? I wonder if Frankie knows," Branch said.

"Have no idea. I thought I'd give her some privacy if she needs it. See you in half an hour," Tessa said, and she watched him from the corner of her eye until he disappeared into the hotel.

Chapter Nine

Folks must've thought that Frankie and Ivy were true celebrities, with the huge bodyguard escorting them into the casino that evening. He walked a respectful foot behind them, but his eyes kept sweeping the whole place as if he were looking for the paparazzi.

"I feel young again," Ivy said.

Frankie chuckled. "Smart move in giving Horace extra money to pretend to be our bodyguard, wasn't it? I bet he was a marine or maybe a pro football player."

"No, ma'am." Horace chuckled. "I was in the navy and I was a cook. I come from real big people. Miz Ivy, you sure you don't want me to take care of Blister for you?"

Ivy glanced over her shoulder. "No, you keep acting like you are our bodyguard."

"Y'all really do need one, you know. What with all that jewelry, someone might knock you in the head to get at it," he said.

"Horace, I carry a pistol in this big purse, and there ain't nobody takin' a thing from any of us," Frankie said.

"Then I'll keep the paparazzi away like I been doin', ma'am." Horace chuckled.

"So what do you think of those looks that's been goin' on between Tessa and Branch?" Frankie changed the subject.

"I reckon they like what they see, but I'm tellin' you right now, us old farts are stayin' out of that deal. We got involved in Lola's love life and look what it got us. She ran off, came back broken, and never has been the same since. I never understood why she knitted all them pink baby caps until now," Ivy said.

Frankie sighed. "I wouldn't mind if Tessa and Branch fell in love. Lola would have family closer that way. You are right, Ivy, we shouldn't have interfered with her and that boy she was in love with, but Lester, he wasn't having a hippie kid like that for a son-in-law. If he'd been clean-cut and tucked his shirttail in and maybe shaved that scraggly stuff off his face before he came to the house that first time, things might've gone different."

Ivy drew her painted-on eyebrows down and shook her finger at her friend. "We're here to have fun, not worry about the kids. Lord, I'm glad I never had any."

Another gravelly chuckle came from Frankie and she pushed her way up off the bench. "Honey, it took both of us to get Lola raised and we didn't do such a good job even then."

Horace stopped at the entrance into the gaming room. "Where would you like to begin? Blackjack tables? Slots? Name your poison."

"Blackjack," Frankie said.

"If we win more than ten thousand, we're going to give you a thousand-dollar bonus," Ivy said.

"Well, then." Horace kissed them each on the forehead. "That's for good luck. Now, let the winning begin."

Lola was sitting cross-legged in the middle of the bed, her blonde hair up in a towel, makeup all washed off and a green mask applied to her face. A picture was on the computer screen and the speakers picked up deep-throated laughter.

She smiled. "Stop laughing. I've been riding in a convertible with the wind blowing on my face, so I need this moisturizing mask or else I'm going to come home wrinkled up like an old prune. You wouldn't love me if I looked like I was a hundred and ten."

"You would look beautiful in a tow sack, darlin'," he said.

Lola was glad the green goo covered up the blush. Even after more than a year of secretly dating Inez's younger brother, Hank, she still had trouble with compliments. "I know exactly what I look like. I've only got a few minutes until I have to wash this off and go to Mama's room for supper. She and Ivy have hired a limo to take them up to that casino over the line into Oklahoma, but Melody is here and we're having supper in that room."

"Pizza again?" he asked.

"No, we stopped by a church festival on the way here. Did Inez show you the pictures?"

"Oh, honey, she squealed when she saw what all you've found. I miss you, Lola. I can't believe we have to go a whole month without seeing each other. Think if I showed up in the same town you could sneak out for a night?" he asked.

"That ain't damn likely," Lola said. "I'm rooming with Tessa and I wouldn't have any idea how to explain that to her."

"So how is it going with you two? That picture of her and Branch sitting at the picnic table reminds me of you. But not her eyes. Do those belong to her father?" he asked.

"I didn't know which of those guys fathered her until she showed up that Sunday for dinner. I do now, and it would have to be the worst in the lot but the prettiest one. She reminds me of him in the way she smiles. She's got my awkwardness and Mama's big heart, but there's something else, probably from Sophie. It's a softness that neither Mama nor I have."

Hank wasn't handsome or rich, but he made her feel special and he always put a smile on Lola's face. "Sounds like you are kind of proud of her, but honey, I disagree about that softness. You've got it, but you keep it tucked away pretty deep so folks can't hurt you."

"I am proud of her. I realize she won't ever think of me as her mother, but I think we might be good friends. She's a better person than if I'd stayed in that commune and raised her."

Hank leaned forward until all she could see was his eyes. "Who are you trying to convince? Me or you?"

"Oh, hush. I'm going to wash my face, get dressed, and go eat chili and soup and fresh-baked bread and chocolate chip cookies. And I think Mama bought a tray of lemon bars." She winked.

Hank sat back and folded his arms across his chest. "You are horrible, mentioning lemon bars to me when I'm too far away to get any of them. They're my favorite. Now, that's what I want and the bakery in Beaumont is closed. I may show up on your doorstep to pay you back for that."

"I know. I'll take a picture of them and send it to you in tomorrow's e-mail."

Hank chuckled. "You do and I'll put the one I snapped off my screen on Facebook and declare that I am in a relationship with Lola Laveau."

"They will never find your body if you do that." Lola groaned.

"Then don't mention lemon bars to me unless you are standing in front of me with them in your hands. Good night, and Inez told me before I left the shop that she sold four thousand dollars' worth of stuff today. I'll talk to you tomorrow night!"

Sophie started talking when she answered Tessa's call. "Where are you? Are you okay? I've been waiting by the phone all evening. Please tell me your father and I didn't give you bad advice. If we did, say the word and we'll be there to bring you home as soon as we can get there."

Tessa had dreaded making the phone call, but now that she heard her mother's voice everything was fine. "Mama, you and Daddy didn't give me bad advice. We are in Gainesville tonight. And everything is okay."

"Are you keeping a journal like I suggested? What does Lola look like these days?" The anxiety in Sophie's voice settled and now she was being a nosy mother.

"I don't know what she looked like in those days. Did she have tattoos?" Tessa sat down in an uncomfortable chair in the lobby.

"One on her shoulder of a bunny. It wasn't healed up all the way when they got to the commune. Does she have more now?"

A family checked in with two little children who eyed her from behind their mother's skirt. "Now she has a rose on the other shoulder—said she thought she might name me Tessa Rose, so that's why she chose that one—and a symbol on her ankle that means happiness."

Sophie sighed.

"Are you all right, Mama? You're not sick, are you?"

"No, I miss you."

Tessa laughed softly. "I miss you, too. I was sitting here thinking about you and your dance class today. Then this cute little blonde-haired girl came in wearing a tutu. I wish I could have danced for you."

Sophie laughed. "Oh, hush. You'll have me in tears. I'm glad you are who you are. So you have a tutu mama and a tattoo mama."

"I have one mama. Lola and I are probably going to be friends, but you are my mother," she said.

"Thank you," Sophie said with a catch in her voice. "I hope you are friends."

Tessa winked at the little girl and she smiled shyly, then turned her head away. "Lola is like a bird with a broken wing and she needs me to be her friend, but she's satisfied with our relationship; I can feel it. She knits pink caps for newborns and hums lullabies."

The silence was so long that Tessa held out the phone to be sure she hadn't lost service. "Mama?" she said.

"I'm sorry. Poor Lola. You said it right, Tessa. She really was like a little bird that had fallen out of the nest too early. Wasn't sure how to fly or how to stay away from the predators. Bless her heart," Sophie said softly.

The little girl waved as she and her family pulled their suitcases to the elevators. Tessa wiggled her fingers at the child.

"Lola is going to teach me how to knit," she told her mother.

"Good luck with that." Sophie laughed.

"I know. It's probably an impossible situation." Tessa laughed.

"Oh, not that it has anything to do with your condition," Sophie said quickly. She never used the words *clumsy* or *awkward*, not once in Tessa's lifetime. It was always *her condition*. "I tried to knit when you was a baby. I wanted to make you a special blanket. That thread crawled up my arms and tried to strangle me to death."

It was Tessa's turn to sit in stunned silence.

"Tessa Ruth, are you still there?" Sophie asked.

Tessa gasped. "I thought you had a Super Woman cape in your closet. I didn't think there was anything you couldn't do."

"Sorry, darlin'. But there are no capes hiding anywhere in this house. I can dance, but I cannot knit, crochet, or do any of those things that require finger dexterity. I got all my talent in my feet, along with a healthy supply of rhythm and balance. If you learn to knit, I want a scarf for Christmas. Purple will be fine."

"I've got fifteen minutes to get a quick shower and go to Frankie's room. That's where we're having supper, but she and Ivy won't be there. They hired a limo to take them to a casino, so there will only be the four of us. I'll send you a long e-mail later telling you about Melody. I think I made friends with her today."

"Tessa, honey, you make friends wherever you go. You've always drawn people to you, especially those with problems that need fixing. That's you. Good night, and I'll look to hear from you in a couple of days, right?"

"Right. Love you, Mama."

"Love you more."

Chapter Ten

The first thing Tessa noticed when she reached Frankie's room that evening was the complete difference in Melody. With a freshly washed face, no makeup, and her red hair swinging from a still damp ponytail, she looked more like a happy teenager.

"So how did it go with Jill?" Tessa asked.

"Well"—Melody drew out the word into six full syllables—"we had a long talk and she said that Natalie is dating Albert and that they make out in the halls, like, right in front of everyone and that they are dealing pot, like, right out of her purse. And"—she paused to catch her breath—"when I get home and back in school she is going to, like, come over to my house for a sleepover that first day."

"That means she forgave you, right?" Tessa asked.

"She's a good friend." Melody nodded very seriously. "I've learned, like, a big lesson."

"Good!" Tessa hugged her just as a gentle knock on the door preceded Lola and Branch arriving.

When they'd finished heating bowls of chili in the microwave and eating, Melody helped clean off the coffee table and put the food back into the refrigerator. That she was deliberately moving slowly was plain to Tessa. She didn't want to be alone all evening.

"Hey," Tessa said, "I saw a commercial a while ago while I was drying my hair. Y'all want to curl up on one of the beds and watch an old rerun of *Steel Magnolias*? It's coming on channel thirty-four in about five minutes."

Melody hurried with the rest of the cleanup and nodded the whole time. "I'd love it if y'all would stay. I was dreading a long evening in here all by myself. What kind of movie is this that you're talking about?"

"A chick flick," Branch answered. "But I don't want to spend an evening alone, either, so I'm in, but only if y'all don't make me stay on a bed all by myself. I'd feel like a leper."

"This is my favorite Julia Roberts movie, so I'm staying. Here, it's your room, Melody, so you get to control the remote." Lola pitched it to her and took up residence on the far side of the bed closest to the television.

During a commercial break Melody declared, "If my two little brothers act like that the day I get married, I am going to strangle both of them. Shelby is a better person than I am. They're going to be real sorry for the way they've acted, because when they get married, I hope she really acts up. Or better yet, I hope she has a bunch of mean little boys that ruin their wedding."

Tessa had seen the movie half a dozen times and knew how it would end, but she didn't say a word to spoil it for Melody.

Lola slipped back into her spot and patted Melody on the knee. "So you like Julia's character, Shelby?"

"I want to grow up and be like her. I might start wearing my hair all big and use lots of hair spray. And pink might be my new signature color," Melody said.

Branch moved closer to Tessa. "You mean that you are going to give up black?"

When his bare leg touched hers she thought the duvet might catch plumb on fire. Four grown people on one queen bed did not allow for much space between them.

Melody raised her chin a notch. "Yes, I'm going to wear pink, even if red-haired women aren't supposed to wear it. Tomorrow we get to go to the mall, and if Aunt Ivy and Frankie win tonight, I get to buy something new and it's going to be pink. Maybe bashful or blush. Not hot pink."

"You're really getting into this, aren't you?" Tessa asked.

"Yes, and shhh." She put a finger over her lips. "Now it's time for the next part. I wish we'd find a festival like Shelby is at and I could eat fried catfish fresh out of the grease."

"Good thing you aren't a vegetarian anymore."

"Shhh!" Melody hissed.

The movie ended after Shelby's funeral, and Melody threw herself into Tessa's arms and sobbed until she got the hiccups. "Oh. My. God. This cannot happen. It's not fair. She wasn't supposed to die. Those two old women, Ouiser and Clairee, could die, but not Shelby. She was too good to die."

Branch reached across Tessa and laid a hand on Melody's shoulder. "It's a movie, Melody. It's not real life."

Her head shot up and she pointed a finger. "No, it's an epic film. I'm going put it at the top of my Christmas list so I can watch it without commercials. I may go back into mourning for a whole week because Shelby died."

Lola rolled off the side of the bed and picked up the pan of lemon bars from the desk. "We need sugar. Here, Melody, indulge, and remember, you can't wear pink if you are in mourning."

Melody took two lemon bars from the pan, holding one in each hand. "I may need to eat the whole thing before I get over this. Shelby wouldn't want me to wear black. They can have those stupid bracelets that have WWJD on them. I want one that has WWSD, for *What would Shelby do?* and I may never take it off." That set off a whole new batch of tears.

"Eat, sweetie, and don't cry anymore. It'll make your eyes swell shut, and you're making me all weepy," Lola said softly.

"What the hell?" Ivy and Frankie both said at the same time when they pushed their way into the room.

"What is going on in here? Did her mama die?" Ivy asked.

"We watched *Steel Magnolias* with her. She'd never seen it and it ended about five minutes ago." Branch slid off the bed. "Tessa is trying to console her and Lola is trying to help her get through the tears with sugar."

"Poor baby," Ivy said. "I cried the first time I watched that movie, too."

Tessa glanced at the clock. "It's not midnight."

Frankie set about removing her rings and putting them in a pouch to lock up in the hotel safe. "They threw us out."

"Mama, for God's sake, were you counting cards?" Lola gasped.

"I don't use anything other than my fingers and toes, so what's wrong with that?" Frankie asked. "Horace didn't mind a bit when I handed him a thousand-dollar tip."

Melody's hands came away from her eyes. "Horace? Who is that?"

"Our limo driver and bodyguard," Ivy said.

"A thousand-dollar tip?" Tessa's head reeled at that. "How much did you win?"

"I won ten but Frankie won forty before they told us we had to leave. But when they caught us we'd only won about five each that round so that's all we had to give back," Ivy said.

"Thousand?" Tessa gasped.

"Well, honey, we wouldn't have given Horace a thousand-dollar tip if it had been ten and forty dollars." Ivy laughed.

"Holy shit, Aunt Ivy! Does that mean I can really go shopping tomorrow then?" Melody squealed.

"It does, darlin'. My purse is full, and I'm not stingy with my winnings. Now, tell me what has happened since I left, other than you're all sad about that movie. You look different without all that makeup."

"My new signature colors are bashful and blush pink. I'm never wearing black again," Melody declared. "And I'm only wearing as much makeup as Shelby would have worn."

Ivy's rings clanked together when she clapped her hands. "Well, hot damn! I should've made you watch it a long time ago when you got this silly crap in your head about wearing black and all that damned makeup. Your mama is going to be very happy."

"I can't believe you really won that much, Mama. You usually cash out long before they catch you these days." Lola laughed.

"I know, but we was having so much fun. I'll take you shopping and you can buy anything you want tomorrow," Frankie said. "Did y'all leave us something to eat? We only nibbled and now I'm hungry."

"There's plenty of soup and chili in the little fridge, but the chocolate chip cookies are gone," Lola said. "And you know I hate to shop for anything other than stuff for my store, but thank you for the offer."

Branch picked up his flip-flops. "I do believe we've had enough excitement for one night, so I'm going to my room. And I'm not surprised that you won that much money. I am surprised that they caught you! Good night, ladies."

Tessa watched him as he crossed the room and shut the door. Her heart tossed in an extra beat and her palms were slightly clammy. Lord, she had to get a grip and start thinking about dating again. She'd called explicitly to tell Mama that she was ready to go out with that new youth director at the church, but the conversation had gotten sidetracked. What was his name? She touched her chin trying to remember.

"Tessa?" Lola said.

She looked up to see Lola with the strangest expression on her face when the youth director's name—Matthew—came to her mind. It didn't matter that they called him Matthew and not Matt. She couldn't date that man, not when he had the same name as her ex-boyfriend, the very culprit who had broken up with her at Christmas.

"What?" Tessa asked. "Do I have food on me?"

"No, it was . . . nothing. I'm going to my room, too," Lola answered.

Tessa bounced off the bed. "Thanks for being such a good hostess this evening, Melody."

"Anytime." Melody smiled.

ഗ

Lola grabbed a book and crawled between the covers in her bed. "Something sure turned that child around. You know anything about that? It was like the difference in night and day from when Mama and Ivy left until we walked into her room."

Tessa shrugged. "Maybe she woke up and smelled the bacon."

Lola laid the book to the side. "I think maybe you were the one frying that bacon. She's a kid, so she'll spill it all eventually, and I'd be willing to bet dollars to doughnuts that you gave her some real good advice out there on that jogging trip."

"Doughnuts! Why did you have to say doughnuts? Now I want one or a dozen," Tessa whined.

"Right out of the bakery with maple icing," Lola said.

Tessa fell backward onto her bed and groaned. "Yes! That's my favorite kind."

"Mine, too. We'll make it a point to stop tomorrow and buy some if we see a doughnut shop. Maybe they'll have one in that mall we're supposed to go to so Melody can buy something pink."

Tessa rolled over on her elbow. "That's the second time you've looked at me like that, Lola. What is it?"

"It's a story for another night."

"We never did get around to the one about Lester and Frankie."

"We will later. It's a long time until the end of this trip, and I'll tell you lots of stories before then. See you in the morning. I thought I'd read but I'm sleepy." Lola yawned.

"Good night. I'm not sleepy, so I'm going to e-mail my cousin and see how things are going at the travel agency. Will the light by the sofa bother you?" Tessa asked.

"Not a bit. Good night, kiddo," Lola said.

She curled up in the corner of the sofa with the laptop on her knees and pulled up Facebook to find Clint's name on the side.

"Hey, what's going on in our area of the swamp?" she typed as a private message and hit "Send."

"I talked to your mama and she said you are alive. Shit, girl! I thought they'd hauled you off and sold you into the sex trade," he answered.

"You've been watching too much television. They might have sold me off to be a maid, but I'm not sex trade material." She giggled as she wrote. "Besides, what are you doing up this late? You've got a travel agency to run tomorrow and you are an old bear if you don't have eight hours of sleep."

"Call me so I can hear your voice or we can Skype," he wrote back.

"Can't. Lola is sleeping and I don't want to wake her."

Little dots appeared showing that he'd seen the message, and then she saw: "Tell me about Branch. Your mama said he's the only man on the trip. Poor guy with all you yappy women. Is he single?"

She smiled. "Out of five people I described and told Mama about, you picked up on Branch?"

"He's the only male in the bunch. Is he fat and bald?"

"He's a tall, sexy cowboy."

"You *have* to call me tomorrow and tell me more. I want to hear your voice. I can tell more by that than words on a message."

She slapped a hand over her mouth to keep the giggles from echoing off the walls. "You are an old woman. I don't know how you ever found a woman to marry you, much less stay with you five years," she typed.

"It's because I'm sensitive," he sent back.

"Good night, Clint. I will call you tomorrow evening or the next day. Sometimes it's difficult to get away by myself, and there's no talking in the car with Branch on one side and my birth mother knitting on the other."

"You are a witch from hell" flashed on the screen.

"Hey, I watched *Steel Magnolias*."

"Was Branch there?" Clint asked.

"In the bed beside me."

"Tessa Ruth Wilson!"

"With a teenager and my birth mother. Come on, Clint, I've only known him a little while. What did you expect?"

"I like him if he watches chick flicks with you. My gorgeous wife is home from one of those baby showers. I hope it didn't give her ideas," Clint wrote.

She made soft clicking noises with her tongue even though he couldn't hear her. "Tick-tock . . . that's the biological clock."

"You're the same age I am."

She smiled and sent a smiley face before she shut her computer and picked up her journal.

Day three. I've decided that like Melody said, I want to be like Frankie and Ivy when I grow up. They live every day like it's their last one on earth and have so much fun. I could feel the energy in the room when they got all dolled up for their night at the casino. Don't think I've ever seen two old gals so blinged out in my life. Not even Mrs. Adams, who flies to Switzerland every winter. I swear it's only so she can show off her full-length sable coat. But this journal is supposed to be a journey into what I feel. And yet the lightness in my heart when Frankie and Ivy crawled into that limo was a feeling. And it had nothing to do with guilt.

I felt like I'd peeled a layer of onion from the outside today when it came to Lola. She knits those pink caps for babies because she feels guilty about giving me away as a baby, but like Mama said, she's a little broken bird. I wonder how many layers there are and what I'll find when I reach the inside of the onion. Somehow I don't think it will be the hardhearted woman with tats that I thought it would be three days ago. It's not pity that I feel for her, but maybe closeness because of the guilt.

My heart came close to jumping out of my chest today when that lady thought Branch and I was a married couple. And in that split second I let myself entertain notions about what it would be like to be his wife, to go to bed with him each night and wake up to that brilliant smile each morning, to share a life and sex with him—it was a damn heady couple of moments before I got control of it. But it did solidify the thought that I need to begin to date again. I'm ready now.

Talking to Melody made me feel like I had a little sister. I'm glad that she couldn't read my thoughts when she told me that that rotten boy had coerced her into sex. And it's a good thing that thoughts can't kill people, or they'd be toting him off to the morgue about now. I've never known such protectiveness to surface in me, not for anyone, except maybe Mama, and that's so very different.

So today, I've run the gamut of emotions. I've been a wife, a big sister, a daughter of sorts to a woman I'm beginning to understand, and a friend. Oh, and a granddaughter, too. It's more than a little bit tiring to realize that I have no control over my feelings, that they come and go at will with no forewarning. And it's scary as hell because I don't like being out of control in any aspect of my life.

Maybe that's what Matt was saying when he told me that I wasn't passionate enough for him. I wonder if it is because I'm adopted and there are underlying feelings of abandonment even though I've had the best life a woman could hope for. Is that why it's so easy to let my guard down with this eclectic bunch of people—because the time has come for me to admit that I need to throw caution to the old proverbial wind, and let my heart out of the protected cage?

She laid the pen to one side, closed her journal, and headed toward the other bed.

She laced her hands behind her head and shut her eyes. *And now I feel all better.*

Bullshit, a strange voice in her head said. *Now you are more confused than ever, but you are beginning to understand yourself. Get some sleep. Tomorrow is a brand-new day of wonderful adventures.*

Chapter Eleven

Branch folded his arms over his chest and leaned against the hood of Mollybedamned. "If I'm going to stay out here in the heat and protect this gorgeous lady, then I should be on the clock."

"You ain't drivin', so clock out." Frankie glared at him.

"I'm following orders, so I'm not clocking out." He shook his head from side to side.

"We agreed that when you were behind the wheel, you were on the clock. Other than that, I'm not paying lawyer hours for a driver. Hell, Horace would drive for me cheaper than you do," she said.

"Then get Horace and I'll go home," Branch said. "But if I'm not getting paid to sit out here, then I'm going inside. I can sit in the mall where it's cool and read a book or work on my laptop in one of those free Wi-Fi cafés," he said.

Tessa wasn't sure how much was bluff and how much was real. Frankie's eyes were twinkling and Branch had trouble controlling the grin that begged to be turned loose.

Ivy finally got between them, her back to Branch and facing her friend. "Hell, Frankie. We'll only be in there two hours. One of Mollybedamned's rearview mirrors costs more than what he'll charge you. Or think about that time you had to replace the taillight."

"Or the paint job if someone keys her," Melody piped up.

"Okay, then, but if I come out here and there's a fingerprint on her, I'm holding you responsible," Frankie fussed.

"Yes, ma'am." Branch opened the door, got comfortable in the seat, and tilted his hat down over his eyes. "I will protect her with my life, Miz Frankie."

"I hate to lose a fight," Frankie fumed.

"Was that a fight? I thought you two were teasing," Tessa asked.

"They were," Lola said. "Mama is bitchy because she hates to shop."

"I love to shop," Melody singsonged. "And I'm starting in Victoria's Secret."

"Sweet Jesus!" Ivy rolled her eyes upward.

"He can't save you from this. It's your punishment for counting cards last night," Lola said. "And for promising to take Melody shopping. You didn't tell her where she could go, so now you have to go into the panty store. You could buy some bikini britches for yourselves."

Tessa glanced over her shoulder as they walked away from the car. Her eyes locked with Branch's. He held up one thumb and capped it off with a wink. Those two gestures put a spring in her step.

"So what are you, like, going to buy in the mall?" Melody swung a slim hip over and bumped Tessa.

"Who knows? Something might catch my eye," Tessa answered. Except that what she'd like to buy wasn't in the store but out there protecting Mollybedamned. However, some things in life were not for sale, and she was sure Branch fell right in that category.

"Cool air," Lola said when they were inside the mall. "Wonderful cool air."

"Don't even think about putting the top up," Frankie scolded.

"Who, me?" Lola acted surprised. "You know how I love the heat and sweat."

"Don't be sarcastic with me," Frankie said.

"And here's the store. Y'all have fun. I don't need a thing. I'm going to wait for you on that bench right there." Lola pointed.

Tessa picked up a red thong on the first table in the store. "I'll buy you each one of these. What size do you wear?"

"Holy shit, girl!" Frankie grabbed at her heart. "That's not underbritches. That's a sin waitin' to happen."

"Do decent women wear those things?" Ivy asked loudly.

"Yes, Aunt Ivy," Melody said. "I've got three right here in the stack of things I want and they're all pink."

"Does your mama know?" Ivy frowned.

"Of course. She wears them, too," Melody answered. "I don't need to try on any of this, but here's what I like and y'all can help me pick out how much I can have. Three pink shirts and shorts to match, the panties, and a new pink bra."

"I can see that the shirts and shorts are pink, so why do they have to write the word across your boobs and butt in glitter and diamonds?" Ivy asked.

"It's their signature, Aunt Ivy. And pink is my new signature color like Shelby's was on *Steel Magnolias*. I was going to ask Santa for that movie for Christmas but I'm going to buy it with my own money before we get home so me and my friend Jill can watch it the first night I'm there." Melody shoved the pile of clothing toward Frankie. "And besides, when you and Frankie went to the casino last night, you had glitter and glam all over your boobs."

"You can have all of it." Frankie took a step back. "I don't care how much it costs. Let's pay for it and get me out of this store. I swear I've heard all the boob talk I want to hear for a month."

"I'll pay for it," Ivy said.

Frankie nudged her on the shoulder. "You can pay for the next store."

Melody squealed and did a two-second happy dance right there in front of the counter. "You mean I get to shop some more! Can we go to Rue 21?"

"If it's not a panty store, that's fine," Ivy said, "and whatever this bill comes to, you can have that much at the next store, but remember, it all has to go in one suitcase, so you might have to pack up some stuff this evening to send home."

Melody shook her head back and forth. "Send home, nothing. All that black shit is going in the next hotel trash can. Don't give me the old stink eye, Aunt Ivy. You say that word all the time."

Frankie pulled a couple of bills from her stash of winnings from the night before and paid the clerk, who told Melody that she could pick out one pair of panties free from a table beside the checkout since she'd spent over a hundred dollars.

"What size do you wear, Aunt Ivy? I'm going to get my freebie for you since I don't wear granny panties. You want silk or cotton?"

"Silk and size eight." Ivy waved Melody away with the flick of a wrist and then turned to Tessa. "Anything to get this kid out of this store. I'm getting hives."

"We're going down the mall to some place called 21," Frankie said when they reached the bench where Lola waited.

Lola pointed down the center of the mall. "They're setting up kiosks down the center of this place and a feller passed me with a big, wide dolly full of antique glassware. I'm going there while y'all visit the next place. Want to go with me, Tessa, or with them or hike out on your own and meet us back here in an hour?"

"Only an hour? I can spend half a day in Rue 21," Melody whined.

"Well, darlin', you've got one hour and the same amount of money that you spent in that pink store back there, so you'd best shop real fast," Ivy said.

Tessa had absolutely no interest in going to a teenagers' clothing store, so she sat down on the bench beside Lola. "I'm going to stay with Lola."

"I'll pay you to take Melody to that store and I'll sit on the bench." Frankie groaned.

"Oh, no, you will not!" Ivy said. "If I have to go, so do you." She looped her free arm in Frankie's and pulled her along.

Lola pushed up off the bench. "We might as well be the first ones there when he unloads his goods. I think I saw a cream pitcher or two. I'm looking for white milk glass. It seems to be the rage right now with collectors."

The vendor had only one piece of milk glass, but it was a lovely one, a compote with the grape pattern that wasn't easy to find. Lola negotiated with him and bought it for five dollars less than the asking price. Tessa found a lovely little green cream pitcher and sugar bowl to match, but he wouldn't budge on the price and he wouldn't split the pieces.

Lola led the way back to the bench, sat down, turned sideways, and pulled her legs up to sit cross-legged. "Those were made in the forties so they're not really antiques yet but not many of them have survived so you really got a pretty good deal on them."

"Will you tell me the story of Frankie and Lester while we wait?" Tessa asked.

Lola's expression changed from happy to sad in an instant. "No, but I'll tell you how they affected me."

Tessa wished she hadn't asked. "I'm sorry. If it's painful, you don't have to go there."

"You deserve to hear because you agreed to come with us." Lola hesitated a long time before she went on. "I'll condense it as much as possible. Mama lost so many babies and she'd given up all hope and resigned herself to never having children. It was either that or she inherited a flaw, because she had no mother instincts. She was more like my friend than my mother."

It might be rude, but Tessa couldn't keep her eyes off Lola's face. She could feel Lola's pain but had no idea what to say to make it go away.

Lola went on, "I'm not complaining, because I understand her now. But growing up was different. She and Daddy had each other and they'd learned to accept it, and then I came along and upset their apple cart. She was good to me. She took care of me, provided for me. I never wanted for anything and always had the best money could buy. But there was something missing . . . something she couldn't give me because she didn't have it to give. It's hard to explain, Tessa. But I didn't ever feel that tender loving care that kids want and need from their mother. I loved her and she loved me, but the closeness . . . what you and Sophie have . . . wasn't there. Don't look at me like that. I can see it in your eyes when you mention her and hear it in your voice when you talk to her. It's what I wanted for you, so I'm damn sure not complainin'. I was terrified that I couldn't ever give it to you because I didn't know how—" She paused.

Several seconds passed and Tessa wondered if she was waiting for her to say something, but she was trying to process what Lola had said.

"I saw right away," Lola went on, her face showing the pain of the words, "that Sophie had whatever it was that was missing from my gene pool. I wanted you to have that. I don't expect you to understand."

Immediately, Tessa wondered if she would have the same flaw. Had Matt seen that she wouldn't make a good mother, or had he worried about it because no one knew her biological family?

"So I rebelled and went looking for what I didn't have at home. In my young mind, I thought sex and love was the same thing." Lola hesitated as if she was getting her thoughts together. "Then I learned that there are different kinds of love and they can't be interchanged. I'm probably confusing you. Like I said, it's taken almost thirty years for me to get a handle on all this."

"I'm listening, but you don't have to explain anything to me." Tessa heard what she said, but her heart didn't want Lola to stop.

"Daddy was a hard man and demanded a lot, with respect and obeying at the top of the list, but I never sat on his lap or he didn't read books to me or have tea parties with my little china sets at Christmas." Lola's tone had changed to a monotone. "I guess it was pure rebellion when I ran away with Tommy, my boyfriend, to live in the commune. Then he left me there and I knew better than to go home. Daddy wouldn't have let me in the door, not when I was unmarried and pregnant."

Tessa's sharp intake of air startled Lola out of the trance.

"What? Aren't all fathers like that? When they speak, aren't we supposed to jump?" she asked.

Tessa shook her head. "I can't imagine my daddy not letting me come home. He would lay down the law and I'd have to toe the line, but he'd be so glad to see me that he'd open up his arms to me."

Lola unwound her legs and sat up straight on the bench. "And that is why I let Sophie and Derek have you. That's what I wanted for you, Tessa. I went through four different men right after Tommy left me stranded. One a week, and none of them brought me a bit of happiness. And then I was pregnant and didn't know which one was the father. I was so ashamed of myself and guilt ridden that it almost destroyed me." There was another long silent stretch. Then Lola wiped a tear from her cheek with the back of her hand. "If it hadn't been for Sophie, I would have probably overdosed and finished my life right there. But she saw me through it, listened to me cry at night, held my hair back when I threw up every day for the first three months I carried you, and then never left my bedside when you were born. Did she tell you that she slept in a chair so she'd be there to take care of you for me?"

Tessa wanted to ask if she'd figured out which man got her pregnant, but she didn't want to sidetrack her, so she kept quiet. Tessa tried to remember her feelings when she'd last held a baby. One of the women at her church had a baby girl around Christmastime last year. Holding that baby had made Tessa want one of her own, but if she did have a child, would she feel the same after it was born?

"I lived with Sophie and Derek until I went into labor." Sophie grimaced as she remembered. "And that's the day I understood my mother for the first time. They put you in my arms and I only felt pain. I handed you off to Sophie and she sat down in a rocking chair and started humming a lullaby. I had no idea how to love you, and you looked at me as if you didn't know who I was. But when Sophie held you, you snuggled into her arms, and I realized my mother and I shared the lack of mothering instincts. You deserved better than I had, so I gave you to Sophie."

Tessa scooted over and slung an arm around Lola's bent shoulders. "I've had a good life, Lola. My mama and daddy both love me very much."

"I know they do. I can see that and I have no regrets."

Tessa bit her lip and drew her eyes down.

Lola smiled. "Your birth father did that same thing when he was worried. I'll tell you what little I know about him later on. But now, back to this story. When I was twenty years old I started knitting, and I thought if I only made pink hats for new baby girls and if I hummed while I worked, maybe it would ease the guilt."

Tessa squeezed her shoulder gently. "And then it got to be a habit, right?"

Lola's smile was shy. "Yes, but babies don't interest me, no matter how many hats I knit. Folks come in the store with these newborn babies and Inez goes all gaga over them. I try, but I must've been standing behind the door when God gave out mother instincts, because I failed to pick up any at all."

"And Lester? Was he glad when you came back home? Did you show up on the doorstep or call first?" Tessa asked.

Lola leaned against Tessa. "Sophie called the number for me and talked to my mama, who wired her the money to put me on an airplane and send me home. When she came back into the hospital room, I was staring at you in that bassinet and trying to feel something. She told me that my dad had been dead for six months and that my mama wanted me to come home."

Tessa shivered from head to toe. "Oh, Lola, I'm so sorry. That was too much for anyone to have to take in. You probably had something like PTSD."

Lola nodded. "That's what they said at the center where Mama took me. She met me at the airport, took one look at me, and drove me straight to something between a hospital and a rehab center. Because of the privacy thing, they couldn't tell Mama anything that we discussed, and I didn't tell her about the hysterectomy for ten years. I didn't tell her about you until last month."

"After all these years, why?"

Lola shrugged. "She was whining about how much she wanted a grandchild and I spit it out before I even thought about what I was saying."

Before she could say anything else, Melody, Ivy, and Frankie showed up and Lola looked up, and just like that the sadness was replaced with a smile. But it did not reach her eyes.

Tessa stood up and pointed at the bag Melody carried. "I'd say from the size of that bag that you'd best do some suitcase arranging when we stop at the next postal place. Lola found something I need to send home, so I'll get the GPS up on my phone and we'll stop by one on our way out of town."

"What did you find?" Frankie asked Tessa.

She removed the cream pitcher and sugar bowl from a sack, unwrapped them from the newspaper, and held them up. "Aren't they cute?"

"We used to get those in oatmeal, or was it laundry detergent?" Ivy said.

"I had a whole bunch of them in my hope chest when me and Lester married. His mama about had a fit when she saw them on my table because they weren't good stuff. I had a notion to tell her that I didn't put out the good stuff for old biddies like her," Frankie said. "Now, let's get out of this place and back on the road. I've had all the shopping I want to do for the rest of my life."

"Thank you, thank you, thank you, for everything," Melody gushed as they left the cool mall and a hot Texas wind hit them square in the face. "I can't wait to take selfies and send to Jill."

"I thought your best friend was Natalie," Ivy said.

"Ex–best friend. Jill has been my friend since I was in kindergarten and I was stupid to forsake her for those hateful girls. I hope Natalie gets caught selling pot on the school grounds. Soon as we get to the hotel tonight, I'm having a fashion show in all my new stuff and I'm going to take tons of pictures." She rattled all the way to the car.

Chapter Twelve

Lola was stretched out on the bed and talking quietly on the phone when Tessa gathered up all her dirty laundry, stuffed it into a plastic sack, and eased the door shut behind her. She should have packed more underwear, but she'd really thought she'd give the trip until the end of the week and then catch a bus or a taxi to the nearest airport.

She was such a meticulous planner and packer that she had used a public laundry only a few times in her life. In college, she and Clint had shared an apartment that came with a washer and dryer. When she graduated and got her own apartment, she'd made sure that one did, too. Hoping that she had enough quarters to wash and dry two small loads, she pushed into the tiny laundry room, stumbled over nothing but air, and fell right into Branch's arms.

"I'm so sorry," she mumbled.

He held her tightly against his broad chest. "We've got to stop meeting like this. People are going to think you are falling for me."

She pushed back and sighed. "I imagine they'll think I'm naturally clumsy."

His smile lit up the closet-size room that held two washers on one side and two dryers stacked on top of each other and a folding table the size of a card table on the other side. He'd already sorted his things on the folding table into two piles, which meant it would be at least half an hour before she could get her things going.

"From the size of that bag"—he pointed to her hand—"I'd say that you've probably got two small loads, too. Why don't we combine them? We can each pay for a washer and a dryer to make it fair. I plan on doing laundry on Fridays while we're on the road to keep from having to buy new things. How about you? Shall we make this our Friday night thing?"

Where were the excuse gods when she needed them? Probably having wine with the gods of grace and laughing about who they'd abandon the next day.

"Sure." She'd been in a long-term relationship that involved laundry, but putting her underpants and nightshirts in the same washer with his things seemed so personal. There were his white Jockey shorts all mixed up with her Victoria's Secret hip huggers. The blush started at her neck and crawled up to her cheeks in record time.

"Hot in here, isn't it?" she said.

He picked up the whole bunch and tossed them in a washer, put the money into the slots, and added detergent. "Little bit. Want to go sit beside the pool while they wash? I checked before I came in here and it looks like there's a few of those chaise lounges in there. I still owe you a soft drink."

She kept her eyes away from her underpants going in the machine with his. "Sounds fine to me. I'll have a Dr Pepper, not diet."

He chuckled. "High-octane, huh?"

She wondered how in the devil he wasn't married with a smile that showed off enough dimples to be masculine and that oh-so-sexy five o'clock shadow. "That's right. I only allow myself to have a real one every few days. They're full of sugar and empty calories."

Branch finished getting the next washer going and tucked her arm into his. "You don't have to justify anything to me, Tessa."

"But I do to me." She simply had to find a boyfriend when she got home. This business of electricity between her and Branch was about to undo her hormones.

He led her out of the laundry and pointed toward a door leading outside. "There's a Coke machine out there by the pool. Cans only. No bottles, since it is a pool area and there's a big sign that says that anyone who throws a can into the pool will be banned. So I hope you aren't feeling rebellious."

"Not today." She was glad there was no one at the pool and doubly glad that she wasn't wearing a bikini because there had to be a red handprint on her arm where his hand had rested. The heat was too fierce for it not to be crimson. She stretched out on a lounge and took a couple of long, deep breaths while he went to the vending machine under an awning in the corner.

Branch brought back two cans and handed one to her. "One high-octane Dr Pepper right here. Tab pulled and ready to drink. Feels good and cold, too."

She tipped it up and took a long drink. "It is really good. It's a treat to get something that's not diet."

He claimed the chaise right next to her and leaned back in it, shut his eyes, and for a few seconds she thought he'd gone right to sleep. But then, without opening his eyes, he said, "You mentioned that you hadn't had a boyfriend since Christmas."

"That's right." She could have given him the exact number of months, days, hours, and minutes since Matt broke up with her.

"And that was the end of it, no calls, no texts, nothing?" he asked.

"Why are you so interested?" A cold coke did not give him the right to open up old wounds.

"I need someone to talk to, and everyone in my life is either severely pro or con in this issue. I need some advice from someone who is totally neutral," he said.

Lord, help! When had she become the therapist on this trip? She was a travel planner, not a problem solver. Hell's bells! She couldn't even get her life straightened out, what with all this new family. Throw in the sparks between her and Branch and it thickened the troubles by ten.

"Okay." She nodded. "Tell me all about it. But remember, I can fix it if you want to go to England on a shoestring budget but I'm not good at relationships. My past is testimony to that."

Branch removed his cap and laid it to one side. "That's the problem. I don't want it fixed. I've moved on and I don't want Avery in my life. She left me for a bigger firm and for one of the older partners in that firm who did not own a small ranch."

"And?" Tessa asked.

It was Branch's turn to talk in a monotone. "She started calling and when I refused to answer or return her calls, she started sending long, lengthy e-mails. After the first two I wrote her a note and said I was deleting them all from that point on. Now it's texts. Ten a day at least, mainly to let me know that she's not giving up."

"And?" Tessa raised an eyebrow.

"And I quit opening them today. Did you have the same problem and is this normal?" he asked.

"No, his name was Matt, and he broke up with me. He's been married since March and his wife is pregnant, which means he was cheating on me long before we broke up. I hope he doesn't start stalking me like that," she said.

Branch sat up so fast that his movements were a blur in her peripheral vision. "It is stalking, isn't it?"

Her head bobbed a couple of times. "That's what I'd call it. Maybe after a month, she'll get the message, but then she might get desperate and decide if she can't have you, no one can."

Branch shivered. "She's pretty vicious in the courtroom. I wouldn't put it past her, the way she likes to win."

Tessa laughed. "She's too smart to try to kill you, Branch. So she's a lawyer?"

He nodded. "And your Matt? Is he in the travel business?"

"He's not my Matt. And no, he is a computer consultant for a large firm out of New Orleans. He's from New Iberia originally and his parents live there. We went to high school and college together and we kind of fell into a relationship," she answered.

Branch turned around and slung his legs out over the side of the chaise lounge. "What happened?"

"He said that we grew apart and the fizz went out of our relationship. And his mama wasn't real sure that she wanted her son to marry a woman that had no idea what kind of people she came from." Tessa had never wished for a roll of duct tape so badly in her life. Even a little six- or seven-inch length of it would be enough to tape her mouth shut. Had she inherited the need to talk too much from Lola along with her clumsiness?

A frown drew Branch's eye brows into a solid line. "Because you are adopted?"

"It's a big thing when someone can trace their ancestors back to the sixth day of creation and wants to know what kind of blood is coming into their family. And"—she lowered her voice—"there was that scandal when Sophie and Derek ran off to the commune for those years. Who knows what kind of weird stuff they might have put into their adopted child's head?"

"That is a foolish way of thinking," Branch said. "Did you see that woman after the breakup?"

"Of course. We go to the same church. I see her sweet little gloating face every Sunday," Tessa said sarcastically.

"Does Matt go to that church, too?"

"When he's in town visiting his folks, which is about once a month. But he and his wife, who is also a computer geek, stay in New Orleans most of the time. I hear that she has an uncle who practices voodoo, but no one is telling Matt's mama. She'd probably have a heart attack. Now your turn," she said.

"For a heart attack or to stick pins in a doll that looks like Avery?" His eyes twinkled.

"You know what I'm talking about. If I'm telling stuff, then you have to do the same. Tell me more about Avery," she said.

He tipped up his coke, finished the last of it, and tossed the can toward the big black trash bin across the room. It landed smack in the middle and he pumped his fist. "That was a three-pointer."

"You play basketball? I would have guessed you were a football player."

"No, basketball is my participation game. Football is my armchair game. Who's your favorite team?" he asked.

"You're not getting off that easy, buster. I'm not interested in football tonight. I want the Avery story," she said.

"It's time to put the clothes in the dryers. You sit tight and I'll be right back. Won't take five seconds."

She watched him walk away with that easy swagger that marked him as more rancher than lawyer, and tried to imagine him in a tailored three-piece suit in a courtroom. It wouldn't materialize no matter how tightly she shut her eyes. He would always be the six-foot cowboy with dark hair and sexy green eyes who'd walked into her travel agency that day with the most earth-shattering news of her entire life. In the picture in her mind, his face, with the perfect amount of chiseling and a perfect-size cleft in his chin, always had a smile for her and sometimes when he looked her way, she even got a sly wink.

He whistled an old Ernest Tubb tune as he returned. It took her a minute but finally she remembered it jazzed up, high school band style. "Waltz Across Texas" had never been her favorite country song because she didn't like Ernest Tubb's voice. But it did have a catchy melody when Branch whistled it. He flopped down on the chaise lounge. "Now, where were we? Talking about your favorite football team?"

She narrowed her eyes into nothing but slits. "We are going to talk about Avery. You made me spill my guts. Now it's your turn."

Branch shrugged and stretched out on the chaise again. "She's tall, dark haired, and brown eyed, and she's a crackerjack lawyer. She'd joined our firm and was a go-getter. I had no idea she set her head for me, not for the person I am but because I was my father's son and she wants to be partner in a firm."

"Were you blind?" she asked.

"Yes, ma'am, but believe me, I've got my eyes wide open now."

"And she broke it off with you, because you wouldn't give up your ranch and be only a lawyer, right?"

He gave her a thumbs-up sign.

"I bet she's not clumsy, either." Tessa smiled.

"Not a bit. Graceful as a ballerina. But I'd take clumsy over a calculating and manipulative serial killer."

Tessa hummed a few bars of the hair-raising music from a horror film. "She'll kill you, Branch, like a black widow spider kills her lovers after she's finished with them. If not your body, your soul."

"That's exactly what I'm afraid of, so I'm steering clear of her. And thank you, Tessa, for sharing and for listening."

"Phone is vibrating, which means I've got a text." She checked the message coming in. "Lola says that the food will be here in thirty minutes. It's being delivered to Frankie's room."

"That should give us time to fold clothes and put them away." Branch led the way to the laundry room. He pulled the still-hot clothing from the dryers and tossed them on the folding table. Their hands got tangled up when she grabbed for a pair of underpants and he went for his white briefs at the same time. Static electricity sent sparks flying when they pulled them apart.

"Wow!" he said. "Looks like they formed a tight relationship in that dryer."

"Looks like it." She blushed.

Dammit! She'd rather have the clumsiness than the fiery-hot cheeks.

"You ever felt sparks like that in a relationship?" he asked.

"Let's get this folded and go have supper. If I felt sparks right now it would be from hunger," she answered.

"I have," he said.

"Oh?"

"Yes, one time I have felt sparks like that, and it scared the hell out of me," he said.

"Avery?"

"No, ma'am. Didn't feel anything like that with her. It happened after she left."

Tessa wanted to know who had created sparks for him, but she couldn't make herself ask the question. Not when they were folding underwear.

He stacked all of his things in a pile and picked them up. "I've got mine all done. I'll see you in Frankie's room in"—he checked the clock above the washing machine—"ten minutes."

"Me, too, Branch Thomas, and it scares me every time it happens," she mumbled after he was gone.

Chapter Thirteen

Hey, y'all." Lola passed out paper plates and plastic forks. "I called down to the front desk and asked the clerk if there was a movie place in town. And he told me that they'd restored the old Palace Theater here in Childress. There is a play going on there tonight, kind of like an Off-Broadway thing. Anyone want to go with me?"

Melody stopped opening all the square boxes on the desk and raised her hand. "Me. Count me in. I don't care what it is about. I want to go."

"Not me," Ivy said. "This old broad is tired."

Frankie yawned. "I'm already in my caftan. I'm not getting dressed again. Go on, Branch, and get started. You don't have to wait for us womenfolks to load our plates."

Branch followed orders. "Plays are not my thing. I'd rather watch a movie. Is there another theater around these parts?"

"Only if you want to drive fifty miles down south of here. They've got an old drive-in that stays open until the first week of October," Lola answered.

"You mean one like in the old movies where you watch it from your car?" Tessa asked.

"You've never been to a drive-in?" Frankie asked. "Oh, Branch, you've got to take Tessa. It doesn't matter what's playing."

Tessa filled her plate with sweet-and-sour pork and fried rice, and then carefully carried it across the room. She set it on the table and eased down as gently as possible to the floor. Lola and Melody each claimed an end, which left Branch and Tessa across from each other on the cramped table.

Branch picked up his fork. "Never was any good with chopsticks. Looks like we're dining in a fine Oriental restaurant tonight. Seems only right that we take in a movie afterward. Besides, I haven't been to a drive-in since I was a teenager."

"Then Lola, you call a taxi to take you and Melody to the Palace, and y'all"—Frankie pointed at Branch and Tessa—"can take Mollybedamned to the drive-in. She hasn't been to a theater in forty years. She'll enjoy the outing."

"Fifty miles is a long way to drive for a movie," Tessa protested. Besides, it would mean a few hours in the front seat of the Caddy with no one but Branch, and she wasn't sure that was a good idea.

"Since I'm driving, do I get to log the hours?" Branch asked.

"Hell, no! I'm not paying you to go have a good time, and believe me, I will check the logbook to see if it matches the one I'm keeping," Frankie answered.

"I haven't been logging in nearly the hours that I would be if I was back at the office. Dad may see my numbers at the end of the week and tell me to rent a car and come home," Branch argued.

"You tell your daddy to talk to me before he makes a fool decision like that. I can always take my accounts to another firm," she said.

"I'll remind him." Branch winked at Tessa.

Ivy poked Tessa on the shoulder when they'd finished supper. "Come on outside with me to smoke. I swear, I miss those old motels we used to stay at back when Mollybedamned was brand-new. Folks could smoke right in the room. Next thing you know, they'll be making us go outside to fart."

"Why?" Tessa asked.

"Hell if I know, but the way things are going, they will," Ivy answered. "I'm glad that I won't be around to see the day."

"Not to fart. I can understand that as small as most of these rooms are. Why do you want me to go with you?" Tessa asked.

"Because Frankie says that she's too tired and these two have to get their asses in gear because that play starts in an hour. And your movie isn't going to begin until it gets dark so you don't have to leave for an hour and someone has to babysit Blister so I don't blow him and me both up." Ivy headed toward the door, oxygen tank rattling along behind her.

"I'll knock on your door in an hour," Branch said.

"And midnight is your curfew," Frankie said.

Tessa stopped. "I haven't had a curfew since I went to college."

Frankie dumped the remainder of a box of fried rice on her plate. "This tastes really good tonight. And darlin', I don't care if you stay out until daybreak or what you do. But Mollybedamned has a curfew and it's midnight. She has to have her rest if she's to get us a couple of hundred miles on down the road tomorrow morning. And the wagon train leaves at ten, so y'all best be awake and sober by then."

"Mollybedamned will be sitting in her special parking spot before midnight," Branch said.

"Get a move on it, Tessa. I'm dying for a cigarette," Ivy yelled from ten feet down the hallway.

Tessa hurried to catch up and took Blister's leash from Ivy. "Why do you smoke when you have bad lungs?"

"They're already bad. Might as well die happy as crazy."

"Crazy?" Tessa asked.

The front doors slid open and the hot evening air slapped them right in the face. "That's where I'd be without my nicotine. I'd be yanking my hair out, slobbering and begging for a cigarette. This way I'm happy.

"Funny, it don't seem that hot when we're driving down the road with the wind blowing in our face, does it?" Ivy fanned her face with the back of her veined hand. "And I meant to tell you, girl, you are getting some color on your skin, but you need to wear something other than T-shirts because you are getting a farmer's tan. Don't imagine that Branch would mind, seein' as how he's more rancher than lawyer, but then maybe it ain't Branch that you want to impress." Ivy found a place on a bench across the street.

"What do I do?" Tessa asked.

"You wear a tank top thing so your arms will be the same color and won't look like half of them are brown and the other half dipped in buttermilk," Ivy said.

"No, not that! I know what a farmer's tan is. What do I do about Blister?" Tessa asked.

"You turn that knob right there until it's on the off place, take him over there across the road, and park him under that shade tree. He doesn't need to get overheated. And then you come back here and sit with me while I smoke my after-dinner cigarette," Ivy said.

Tessa did exactly what Ivy said but still hoped that they were far enough away from the tank if a spark hit it. Then she trotted back across the street and sat down beside Ivy, grateful that the wind was blowing the smoke away from her. She wouldn't have time to wash it out of her hair if the wind shifted.

It's not a date, her conscience yelled loudly.

I know, but Branch doesn't want to smell secondhand smoke all evening, she argued.

Ivy took a long draw from the cigarette and coughed when the smoke hit her lungs. "You are frowning. Do you not want to spend the evening with Branch? I'd be willin' to bet my last cigarette that he would be a lot of fun."

"No, ma'am. I'm arguing with myself," Tessa answered.

Ivy held the cigarette between her fingers. "I've always loved to smoke. From the first time I tried it. Changing the subject here, though. I'm worried about Frankie. She never gives up a cigarette after supper." She took a short puff and didn't cough that time. "We need to take it slower. That casino night was so much fun but it'll take both of us a week to get over it. So I want you kids to start planning fun things after we check into the hotel at night. Us old cats are content to talk to each other about the good old days and watch television."

Tessa moved closer, ignoring the smoke, and put her arm around Ivy's shoulders. "But you could do that at home."

"Yes, but we get to have family and friends in and out of our room and eating with us and arguing with us during the day when we're ridin' in Mollybedamned. It's a wonderful thing to have folks around you when you're old and bitchy," she said.

She smoked one cigarette and lit the next one from the fire of the first. "I'll pay for having two like this, but it reminds me of when me and Frankie were young and we were real bad chain-smokers then. Sweet tea or coffee and cigarettes. Sometimes it was beer and cigarettes, and on occasion it was a shot of moonshine in our coffee and cigarettes. But we always had our nails all pretty and our cigarettes right handy."

Ivy closed her eyes and enjoyed the hit of nicotine from the second cigarette. "A year ago the doctor said it was emphysema, but three months ago he said it was lung cancer and I slowed down to a pack a day then. Now a pack lasts me two days and if it wasn't for Blister, I'd probably done be dead. I've got three more months at the most, maybe less. When we get home, I've got plans made for some changes, but this is vacation and I've got Blister."

"Oh, Ivy, does Frankie know?" Tears welled up in Tessa's eyes.

Ivy patted Tessa on the knee with her spare hand. "It's okay, darlin'."

Tessa wiped at a single tear that streamed down her cheek.

Ivy squeezed her leg gently. "Don't cry. I can't stand to see folks cry alone, and if you sling snot, then I'll have to do it with you and it makes me cough. Besides, I went down to the funeral home and paid for my funeral, told 'em that I want a pack buried with me. Just tuck them under my pillow and I'll find them on my way to the big white light. But I've made other plans concerning my living arrangements. This is my last hoo-rah, but I intend to go out with my boots on and holding Frankie's hand. And when I slide up to the pearly gates, it's not going to be with a single regret."

Tears escaped through a forced smile. "Does Lola know?"

"Honey, Lola don't need that burden on her heart right now. She needs this trip to get to know her mama better," Ivy said. "Me and Frankie and Lola, we're all independent, good businesswomen, but every one of us is broken in some way and we want you to grow up to be better than any of us, but you need to know us before it's too late."

Ivy took a short draw, exhaled the smoke, and then coughed so hard that Tessa grabbed for her phone to call 911.

"Put that thing away." Ivy panted. "It's not my time yet. Go get Blister."

Tessa jogged across the street, tucked the tank under her arm like a football, and hurried back to Ivy's side. She helped her wrap the tubes around her ears and get the nose pieces in place and then turned the knob.

Ivy inhaled several times and held up her hand. "You can wipe that expression off your face now, honey. I'm going to live to smoke a few more, but that's the last time I'll try two at a time. Good boy, Blister." She patted the tank lovingly. "Now, where were we?"

"Something about going out with your boots on?" Tessa said.

"Oh, yeah. That's right. Me and Frankie have been closer than sisters even though we ain't a bit kin when it comes to blood and bone. I can't imagine life without her, don't want to, and we've already made a pact. If we don't die together, then whoever goes first will drag up a lawn chair outside the pearly gates and wait for the other one." Ivy's breathing stabilized more with every bit of pure oxygen she sucked in.

"Why ain't you married?" Ivy asked bluntly.

"Why aren't you?" Tessa fired back.

Ivy's giggle was still raspy. "Why settle down with one man when a woman could have all the men she wanted if she was discreet? Frankie had a little more of the old puritanical nonsense pumped into her brain as a child than I did, and besides, she and Lester fell smack-dab in love. Wasn't no two people in the world loved each other more than they did. No, sir! It might not have been so good for Lola, but she survived."

Tessa raised one brow. "Oh?"

Ivy's cigarette package had been lying on her lap. She picked it up and slid it into her shirt pocket. "It's like this. When a couple has children, they have to give a lot of themselves to that child, and Frankie and Lester had a love that was all consuming. They couldn't give any of it away. It wasn't possible, so Lola suffered for it. She had everything she wanted or needed, but they couldn't tear themselves away from each other long enough to be parents. It's hard to explain."

The south wind whipped across Tessa's face, flinging her long blonde hair into her eyes. She pushed it back behind her ears and asked, "Couldn't they love each other and her, too?"

"They loved her, Tessa. They really did, but they loved each other more. It's complicated, as you kids say these days." Ivy bit her lip. "You need to understand that to know Lola better. You can't give away what you ain't got to give."

Tessa hugged Ivy closer. "I believe that. You ready to go back inside?"

Ivy shook her head. "Just another minute out here with the sun on my face. Indian summer, that's what this is. It's the last dregs of summer trying to hang out and not let fall come out to play." Ivy tilted her face up to catch the sun's rays. "Kind of like us old women. We're hanging on one more month to our dream of taking a long road trip together before the cold sets in." She turned around and stared right into Tessa's eyes. "Take some advice from an old woman and don't let life pass you by while you are waiting for something wonderful to happen. Make it happen today and enjoy it when it does. Now, you'd best help me and Blister back to our room, and don't you be tattling on me for smokin' two cigarettes. I don't want Frankie to be worryin'. This is her dream trip."

"I won't. I promise," Tessa said.

Chapter Fourteen

Tessa peeled off her shorts and knit shirt on her way to the bathroom, tossing them in the general direction of the sofa on the way to the shower. She dropped the soap three times, got shampoo in her eyes twice, but was happy her hair was dry and she didn't smell like cigarettes when Branch rapped on the door.

"You look beautiful, Miz Tess. But are you plannin' on wearing shoes?" he asked.

"I was patting myself on the back for getting ready so quick and I forgot to put my sandals on," she admitted.

"I think you are adorable in your bare feet. I could carry you to the car, but if you had to get out for the ladies' room, you might get stickers since it's an outdoor movie," he said.

She sat down on the sofa and buckled her sandals. "Unless you carried me there, too."

He leaned against the doorjamb and smiled down at her. "I could do it if you want."

The scent of his shaving lotion wafted across the room when the air conditioner kicked on and stirred the air. Creased jeans, polished cowboy boots, and a plaid shirt that showed signs of an iron said he'd gone the extra mile to get ready that night. She stood up and waited a second before she took a step. With an empty bed that close and her roommate out for the evening, it would not be a good time to trip and fall into his arms.

"Are you sure you are a lawyer? I'd swear you were a sexy cowboy," she asked.

He offered her his arm. "Thank you. I can clean up good when I have a reason."

She slipped hers through it. "And this is a reason?"

"Of course it is. You are a beautiful woman and we're going out to a drive-in movie in Mollybedamned. I feel like I'm taking a step back in time to the sixties," he answered.

"And we're sixteen again and this is . . ." She stopped.

"Our first date?" he finished for her.

She picked up her purse. "But it's not a date. It's two people going out to a movie."

"Hey, I don't offer my arm to my buddies when we go out for drinks or to the movies." He chuckled.

"Then this is a date?" she asked.

"I think it might be." He led her out into the parking lot. "Top up or down?"

"Up, at least until we get there."

He opened the door for her and waited until she pulled the skirt of her sundress in before he closed it. Suddenly, she felt cramped and slightly claustrophobic. The old Caddy was big enough to haul eight people in a pinch and she'd ridden right up next to Branch for several days, so why did she have the jitters when there was at least three feet of space between them?

He started the engine and adjusted the air-conditioning. "I bet this hasn't been used half a dozen times in all the years Mollybedamned has been going places. Does this feel strange to be just us in the car, or is it because the top is up?" he asked.

"A little, and I'm not sure which it is," she admitted.

"I thought it was because I was alone in the car with you and your beauty filled the whole car," he drawled.

Tessa wiggled down into the seat and wished that she was sitting right up next to Branch like always, but that would be presumptuous on a first date. "That, Branch Thomas, is a pickup line. Does it ever work?"

He found a radio station that played current music by Blake Shelton, Miranda Lambert, Florida Georgia Line, and several of her other favorite artists. "It is a pickup line, and it does work in a bar."

They'd gone through two little towns when she looked up and saw a sign that said they weren't far from Turkey, Texas, and the town after that was Quitaque, Texas.

"I wonder how that town is pronounced," she said.

"Tur . . . keee." He drew out the syllables.

She air slapped his arm. "Not that one, the other one. Are we going to Tur . . . keee or that weird name? Is it Quit-a-eeek?"

"No, we're not going to Turkey. We're going to the other one, and it's pronounced Kit-a-key," he answered. "I looked it up on the Internet before we left. Had to get directions. It's a little place, kind of like Boomtown. Lots of teenagers frequent these places. We'll be the old people there."

Tessa liked the comfortable aura in the car. She'd been afraid things would be awkward between them but they weren't. She enjoyed his company whether they were riding in silence or talking about anything and everything.

"I don't mind, do you?"

He kept time to a Miranda Lambert tune with his thumbs on the steering wheel. "Not if once we are parked, you slide across this seat and let me put my arm around you. What have you been thinking about so hard since we left Childress?"

"Did you know that Ivy only has about three months to live?"

He took his foot off the gas pedal and tapped the brakes before he whipped his head around toward her. "Are you serious?"

"She told me today just before we left. It breaks my heart."

He pulled her close to him with his right arm and drove with his left one. "So that's what this trip is really all about. I had no idea she was that bad. What will Frankie do without her?"

"I don't know. They are so close. It's a farewell party for Ivy and she doesn't want Lola to know."

His arm around her proved that old saying her grandmother had about a good friend cutting sorrows in half and doubling the joys in life. Suddenly that big black cloud looming out there three months in the future wasn't nearly as formidable.

"I hate to hear this. I really like that old girl," Branch said softly. "Draws us up short and makes us think about the brevity of life, doesn't it?"

"I've been thinking about how it can be possible that people I barely knew only a few days ago are now important to me," she said.

Branch gently squeezed her shoulder. "Are you saying I'm important to you?"

If he didn't stop looking at her with those dreamy eyes, she was going to tell him to forget the movie and stop at the next motel.

"You are all important to me, and it is absolutely beyond words unexplainable. I've known people in New Iberia my whole life and it wouldn't make me this sad to know they only had a few months to live," she said.

He turned his head enough to gaze into her eyes a couple of seconds. "Think about it, Tessa. You've been with these people basically twenty-four hours a day for four days. If you only saw someone, say, for an hour at church on Sunday, it would take two years for you to get as close to them as you have to Frankie and the rest of us. Time is fickle anyway. It's nothing but hands moving around a clock face.

Life is reality. Living and getting to know folks' hearts, that's what matters."

"He's not only handsome and sexy, but a philosopher, too."

"So you think I'm sexy?" He checked his reflection in the rear-view mirror.

"Don't be all shy, Branch. I bet women flock around you like flies on a fresh cow patty."

Branch sighed. "Now you're talkin' about my brothers, not me. One of them got the brains and the other one got the looks."

"Poor baby. Dumb and ugly both," she teased.

"It's a burden, but I do my best to bear it without complaining." His eyes sparkled.

"Like my clumsiness? I bear it most of the time without bitchin' about it," she answered.

"You've got to put that card away," he said.

"Why?"

"Because it's only when you are agitated or nervous that it happens. Have you ever noticed that? And you have nothing to be stressed out about. Not with me."

And just like that, he'd pulled her away from the dark cloud hovering above her and brought her out into the bright sunlight.

Branch drove up to the ticket window and handed the girl inside the little building a bill. She made change and gave him a free drink voucher. "It's Friday, freebie night," she said.

"Well, thank you. Does that include a beer?"

"If you are twenty-one, but I doubt if y'all will get carded," she said.

"Ouch!" Tessa grinned.

"Well, y'all are thirty or more, ain't you?" the girl asked.

"Thank you, honey, for that compliment. We're both actually lookin' sixty right in the eye," Branch said seriously, and then drove on to let the car behind them pull up.

"Speak for yourself, cowboy. I'm almost seventy," she teased.

"I've always been drawn to older women." He found a place to park, hit the button to put the top down, and rolled the window down to within six inches of the bottom. Then he detached the speaker from the pole and hung it on the glass.

Tessa watched every movement. "Looks like you've done this before."

"Few times. There used to be one of these theaters in the town where my grandparents lived, but it closed down years ago. I'll go to the concession stand before the show starts so we don't miss anything. Popcorn, beer, soft pretzel with or without melted cheese and jalapeños, or a pickle or soft drink? Name your favorites and I'll go get them."

"Cold beer and a soft pretzel with no cheese," she said.

"Because you don't like cheese or because you're afraid you'll make a mess?" he asked.

"The latter," she answered honestly.

"Then I will get it with cheese and feed you," he said.

Watching him swagger from the car to the concession stand sent her desire button spiraling to the top of the scale. But then she noticed people pointing at the car and at the sexy cowboy and her pulse jacked on up. She was sitting in a vintage car and Branch was handsome enough to make any holy woman's granny panties sneak down around her ankles, and both were all hers that night.

Then her phone rang.

She unfastened the seat belt and fished around in the dark until she found the thing. "Hello, Mama."

"Where are you? It sounds like you are outside," Sophie said.

"I'm at a drive-in theater in Quitaque, Texas, on a pseudodate with Branch Thomas," she said. "He's gone to the concession stand so talk fast."

"Date? What are you talking about? Date?" Sophie's voice was high-pitched and shrill.

"Don't worry, I'm not going to run away with him tonight, but I did shave my legs," she said.

"My God!" Sophie gasped.

"I hope so," Tessa said.

"Don't you sass me! You know very well your father and I want you to go out with our youth director as soon as you get home. You can't date a man you've only known what? Four days?"

Tessa wasn't about to tell her mother that when she was in college she'd dated men she'd met only one time in the college bar down the street from her dorm. "It's okay, Mama. Didn't you hear me say *pseudo*? Lola and Melody went to a play at an old refurbished theater and we didn't want to go. So we drove about forty-five minutes down here in the Caddy to watch a movie. I'd never been to a drive-in, and it looks like fun," she said softly. "And Branch will be back soon, so I can't talk right now."

No way was she going to start a big fight with her mama about the youth director at this time. But something in her heart said that ship had done sailed. Strange as it was, right then her mama seemed a million miles away and this night, in an old Caddy waiting for an outdoor movie to start, was more important.

"You will call me tomorrow, promise?" Sophie said.

"I will and we'll talk in the morning right after breakfast. I usually have about half an hour before we leave. Don't worry, Mama, Branch is a good person. Someday you might meet him and see for yourself," she said.

"That's what I'm afraid of," Sophie groaned.

ᘓ

Branch bought two pretzels, two Dr Peppers, two candy bars, and a big box of popcorn. Then he added two bottles of beer to the order and asked the lady if she could put it all in a bag.

"Yes, sir," she said without asking him for identification.

"You don't card your customers?" he asked.

"You are teasing. Old guys do that to me all the time and I never catch it." She giggled.

Previews of upcoming movies had started when he made it back to the car. He slid into his seat and set the bag between them.

"Will you marry me?" he asked.

"What did you say?" Tessa whipped around to glare at him.

"It looks like I've got one foot in the grave and one on a banana peel, and I'm worried that I'll leave no one behind to mourn me. So say you will marry me and we'll drive Mollybedamned to the airport and fly to Vegas, get married, and be home by daybreak," he said.

Her laughter echoed through the night air. "Are you insane, Branch?"

He shook his head and removed her pretzel from the bag sitting between them on the seat, broke off a small piece, dipped it in cheese, and put it in her mouth. "No, darlin', I'm old but I'm not crazy yet."

"What happened? Did the smart-ass teenager behind the concession stand window tell you that she didn't need to see your ID?" she asked when she'd swallowed and sipped the beer he'd handed her while she was chewing.

"Yes, and my ego is wounded."

She turned up the cold beer and swallowed twice. "You are old and my mama called and she thinks I'm still fifteen, so I'm way too young to be out with you tonight."

"Just my luck," he said.

ᔕ

Branch parked Mollybedamned and walked Tessa to her hotel door, penned her against the wall by putting a hand on either side of her shoulders, and looked deeply into her eyes. God, she could have dived right into those green eyes and stayed the rest of the night, but Lola was in the room and she wasn't about to suggest they go to his room.

"I had an absolutely wonderful time tonight," he said.

"So did I," she said softly. "But it's because it was a pseudodate. Neither of us was nervous or antsy."

His eyes went all dreamy and fluttered shut. "Does a fellow get a good-night kiss after a fake date?"

She moistened her lips with the tip of her tongue and got ready to feel the heat, but he bypassed her lips and kissed her on the soft spot where her shoulder and neck connected. The next kiss landed on her forehead and she felt cheated. Sure, that was nice and the kisses on her neck were scrumptious, but she really wanted a real kiss to end the night.

She rolled up on her toes and wrapped her arms around his neck, closing the space between them. She met him in a steamy kiss that made her knees go weak and her whole body ache for more.

He polished off the best kiss in the universe with a buss on the tip of her nose and a husky, "Good night, Tessa. See you at ten if I don't catch you at breakfast."

And he was gone.

She managed to get inside her room before her knees gave out and she slid down the back of the door. Sweet Jesus in heaven! What had she set loose? She could not let this happen again. She had to ride right next to him for the next three weeks. She had to sit beside him at dinner and share supper in the close quarters of Frankie's room with him every night.

How in the hell was she going to do that? Not one time in all her almost thirty years had a man affected her like Branch. And for sure no one had ever made her swoon with a kiss before.

Tessa grabbed her journal and a pen from the nightstand and tiptoed to the bathroom. She eased the door shut before she turned on the light and sat in the floor, back to the tub as she wrote about that evening.

Big news first. Branch kissed me and my insides turned to mush and my brain lost its ability to think. I've never in all my life lost control of my thoughts, my heart, or my knees like that. It has to be what they talk about in castle romances when the heroine swoons. Mama wants me to write about my feelings, but I'm not sure words can begin to describe what it feels like when he touches me. There, I wrote it down. It's been like this from the first time he walked into the agency and my heart did a flip in my chest. No man has ever affected me like that before.

So with that said, I'll go on to what Lola told me in the mall about having no mother instincts. That scares the bejesus out of me. Branch kisses me and turns my hormones up to high speed, and yet if it were to ever go further than a few stolen kisses, what would happen if I inherited the lack of mothering instincts?

Now on to the pain I felt when Ivy told me she doesn't have long to live. I've gotten over the guilt of liking her and Frankie, and knowing that I don't have much more time with Ivy makes me very sad. I'm filled with a new determination to make this trip wonderful for her since it will be her last one. Frankie will be devastated when she finds out, and I hope that I can be there to help her through the time when Ivy leaves this world.

Tears flowed down Tessa's cheeks as she wrote fast and furious. Landing on the page of the journal, they smeared the ink in places. She grabbed a tissue from the hole in the vanity and dabbed at them, making a bigger mess.

"Even my tears are disastrous. I don't need to be able to read all the words though. I will never forget this pain." She blew on the paper to dry it before she shut the journal for the evening.

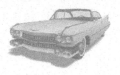

Chapter Fifteen

Ivy and Frankie giggled like little girls with a secret, whispering behind their hands, their old eyes twinkling as they got situated in the backseat of the Caddy the next morning.

Lola fastened her seat belt and glanced over her shoulder. "You two seem bright eyed and bushy tailed this morning. You want to share some of that happy?"

"Happy, happy, happy," Ivy said and then burst out laughing.

"Hush, you old fart. You'll be coughing so hard that Blister won't be able to pump enough oxygen in your worthless lungs," Frankie said.

"They must've watched reruns of *Duck Dynasty* while we were gone," Branch said.

"Watched what?" Melody asked.

Ivy nodded and then readjusted her nose tubes. "Frankie brought all the seasons of it in her suitcase and we got the hotel clerk to bring us a DVD player and this morning we are happy, happy, happy. Next time we get into a Walmart store, I'm going to buy me one of those shirts with that on the front. I may buy an extra one so I can be buried in it."

"What is *Duck Dynasty*?" Melody asked with a shiver. "And don't talk about death like that, Aunt Ivy. Besides, Mama would never let you be buried in a T-shirt."

"Modern-day *Waltons*," Lola answered.

"What is *Waltons*?" Melody asked.

"A show about family life on a farm back in the nineteen thirties and forties. It ran on television for several years back when Lola was a little girl," Ivy answered. "It's before your time, and *Duck Dynasty* is out of your league."

"You all thought that *Steel Magnolias* was, too, and now Shelby is, like, my role model, so I want to see *Duck Dynasty* for myself. Can I, like, watch it with you tonight in the hotel room?" Melody asked.

"Of course you can, honey. You might have a new role model and want to start cookin' like Miz Kay," Ivy said.

"Or grow a beard like Phil." Frankie broke out in another round of giggles.

"Or start wearing camo and ask for a rifle for Christmas," Lola chimed in.

"Hey, I'm barely getting into my new skin. Don't be trying to, like, talk me out of my blush and bashful pink this quick. But camo does sound interesting. It might show Natalie that I'm, like, out for war." Melody picked up her phone and her thumbs flew over the tiny keys.

"They do make pink camo," Tessa said. "I bet you'd look real cute in pink camo yoga pants and a tight little knit top with maybe a headband around your forehead."

"Really! This I've got to, like, see. I want the whole getup before we get home. I've got to tell Jill about it. We'll, like, check it out on the Net tonight." Melody's thumbs went back to work.

Tessa had wondered if there would be awkward moments that morning, but Branch was in every bit as good a mood as the two happy ladies in the backseat. They kept coming off with lines from the shows they'd watched and then remembering times in their lives when similar things had happened, and he laughed at their stories.

"We are going to Pampa this morning," Ivy piped up an hour into the trip. "My doctor has called in a refill for Blister's mama at the hospital there."

"Is that the tank thing that you plug Blister up to, like, when you are taking a shower at night?" Melody asked.

"It is. Blister has to suck on her tit until he's full and ready for the next day and now she's gone bone-dry and it's time to refill his mama. I call my doctor when it's time for a refill and he gets hold of the nearest hospital or medical center and they refill it for me."

"Does Blister's mama have a name, too?" Tessa asked.

Ivy patted the oxygen tank at her feet. "No, bless his heart, his mama don't have a name," Ivy answered. "Frankie, I wonder if they'd put some of that nitrous stuff in a little side tank. We could get really happy, happy, happy if we could breathe in a little of that along the journey."

"Wouldn't hurt to ask," Frankie said. "All they can say is no."

Lola picked up her knitting and started to hum. "They're wound up this morning," she whispered.

"Want to go to another movie tonight?" Branch asked Tessa. "Or how about beer, popcorn, and a movie in my room?"

"Let's plan on it in my room," she said. "After all, you paid for last night. It's my turn."

He nudged her shoulder. "Afraid to be alone with me?"

She pushed back. "After that kiss? Yes, I am."

"Oh, that little old thing. That was to cure your clumsiness, although I did think it was right cute. Mythology has it that if a handsome cowboy gives an awkward girl a kiss and he's the right cowboy for her, then she is cured forever," he said.

"I've studied mythology and I never heard that," she argued.

He touched her knee with his. "Did you study ancient redneck cowboy mythology?"

She crossed one leg over the other to get away from the heat of his bare skin touching hers. "No, that wasn't offered where I went to college."

"Too bad. You would have known about it sooner and kissed another cowboy before me. Of course it wouldn't have worked, because he wouldn't have been the right cowboy."

"Kind of like Sleeping Beauty, only this is Clumsy Lady?"

"No more, now it is Lovely Lady. I'm telling you, the kiss cured you," he said.

"Just one, or does it wear off?" she asked.

"Mythology says it's good for twenty-four hours at the very least. In a pinch it can last forty-eight hours, but the last ten of that would be kind of iffy," he teased.

"I figured there was a catch," she said, sighing.

He shifted his position so that his hip was right against hers. "It's not that bad. I don't mind helping you."

"Now, those are some pretty good pickup lines." She laughed.

"What are y'all talking about? I thought I heard something about cowboy mythology," Frankie piped up from the backseat.

Branch looked up in the rearview mirror and asked, "Did you ever hear of it?"

"Of course. My daddy knew all of the sayin's from that. Like 'Never squat with your spurs on.' Remember them, Ivy?"

Ivy raised her voice over the ever-blowing wind in that part of the state. "Oh, yeah, and 'Never drink downstream from the cattle herd.'"

"Did he hear that a kiss from the right cowboy would cure clumsiness?" Tessa asked.

Lola put away her knitting and stopped humming. "If I'd known that, I would have chapped my lips trying to find the right cowboy."

"Never heard of it, but that's not to say it ain't true," Frankie said. "Do we need to be hitting some rodeos on the way? Maybe you and Tessa could put up a kissin' booth."

"I'd sure be tempted," Lola said.

Tessa changed the subject before they started asking questions about how many cowboys she'd kissed. "Any of y'all want to move to this part of the state where there ain't nothing but dirt and sky? Not many trees and no hills, and I bet you could see a tornado coming for a hundred miles."

"Hell, no! I like the green grass in my part of the world just fine," Ivy answered.

"Not me. I want to go home, go back to school and, like, talk to Jill every day," Melody said.

"What about you, Tessa? You happy in New Iberia?" Branch asked.

"Never known any other place except when I went to college. It's home, but being a travel agent, I've often wondered about living, not visiting, other places. Clint has a rule that seems to be true. If you go somewhere and can't wait to get back home, then it wasn't meant for you to live in that place. If you go and hate to go home, then maybe you'd better study your situation a little bit."

"Where all have you been?" Melody asked.

"England twice and Scotland a couple of times, but I was always ready to come home, so I don't think I'd want to live there. Where would you like to go, Melody?"

She laid her phone in her lap and unplugged her ears from the music. "I want to see Italy someday. Maybe that's where I'll go on my honeymoon when I get married, but that's not going to be, like, until I'm old, like maybe thirty."

That set Ivy and Frankie off on a discussion about how in their day thirty was considered to be an old maid. Lola picked up her knitting again. Branch turned on the radio to a classic country station.

Tessa leaned toward him. "Maybe old cowboy kisses don't work on curing clumsiness after all. It could have to be a young, sexy cowboy who gets carded at the drive-in movie concession stand."

"Old cowboys are like vintage wine. Their kisses are more potent. That's why they can last forty-eight hours in a pinch. Those young ones don't have the finesse or the sense to know how to kiss a lovely lady right."

She sat up straight. "When I drop food in my lap at noon or spill sweet tea on you, we'll see if you change your tune."

Pampa, Texas, was big enough that they had a choice of several places for lunch, but Ivy and Frankie declared they wanted to eat at the Texas Rose Steakhouse. They dropped off Blister's mama for an oxygen refill and then headed straight for the restaurant.

"We could have gotten closer to the border since this whole road trip is about circling the great state of Texas." Branch looked over the menu.

"We're still in the zone," Ivy told him. "I'm having the biggest sirloin in the house, and those potatoes right there." She pointed at the picture on the menu. "And macaroni and cheese."

"Eating light today, are you?" Lola teased.

"I'm going to spend the rest of my natural life eating exactly what I want," Ivy said. "And smoking a cigarette after I have dessert."

"Well, go get 'em, Aunt Ivy." Melody laughed. "I'm having the same thing."

"I'm having ribs," Branch said and then moved his knee over to bump Tessa's under the table. "You might as well test out my theory about my kiss curing clumsiness tonight," he said so softly that only Tessa could hear him.

"I'm testing it right now, but are you sure you want to sit this close? Ribs might slip out of my hands and land right on your pretty white shirt," she said.

"I'm confident that I have the cure," he answered softly.

"Aunt Ivy"—Melody's eyes twinkled—"Tessa and Branch are whispering and I can't hear what they're, like, sayin' and that's not polite, is it?"

"It is not. You two save your pillow talk for when you are alone," Ivy teased.

"Yes, ma'am," Branch said seriously.

Tessa blushed scarlet.

"And I'm changing the subject before I forget because sometimes us old people do that," Frankie said. "After we run by the hospital, we're going to go to the Walmart store and get the stuff we need for supper. I'm thinking fried chicken and potato salad. We need some more plates and plastic forks, too. So Lola, make a list."

Their waitress came and took their drink orders, then brought the drinks right out and asked if they'd like appetizers. "We've got some awesome fried mozzarella cheese sticks and fried zucchini."

"Two orders of each," Frankie said. "And we are all ready to order now."

Tessa wasn't a believer, not yet, but she did finish eating messy ribs, beans, and coleslaw without dropping a single bean or dribbling on her shirt. If he kissed her a few more times and she wasn't clumsy anymore, she might patent his kisses and make a million dollars selling them to awkward women. Just thinking of other women kissing him shot a green blast of jealousy through her that she'd never felt before, not with Matt or any other man she'd ever dated.

An hour later they were on their way out of the restaurant and Lola looped her arm through Frankie's. "So fried chicken, plates and forks, and potato salad, right, Mama? Remember we're limited in the trunk, so be careful in the Walmart store."

"Yes, Mama Lola!" Ivy and Frankie singsonged together.

"I'm not your mama, so stop that," Lola fussed at them.

"But," Ivy declared as she crawled into the backseat and situated Blister, "I do want a box of those maple iced doughnuts, and I'll carry them in my lap if I have to."

"How can you think of food?" Melody groaned. "I may not eat a bite until, like, tomorrow night."

"Tell me that when we're watching *Duck Dynasty* tonight and you start bitchin' about nothing to eat in the hotel room," Frankie said.

Branch pulled the Caddy up to the Walmart store, which was only a couple of blocks from the restaurant, and all five ladies unloaded.

"I'll stay right here and wait, and yes, Miz Frankie, I will clock out." He grinned.

"Good, because I was about to tell you to get out the logbook," she said.

When they were inside, Tessa put Blister in a shopping cart's infant seat for Ivy. "You can push," she said. "I'm definitely going to start taking advantage of the fitness room in the hotel, starting tonight. Thirty minutes on the treadmill or on the stationary bike."

"You know what a shopping cart is? It's an old woman's walker but it lets her keep her dignity." Ivy moved to one side. "Here, Frankie, you can push with me."

Frankie put her hands on the handle. "I don't have to have a damned old tube up my nose."

Ivy slung her hip against Frankie's. "Not yet."

"Okay, children, stop fighting or else I'll make you both sit in the car next time," Lola said.

Ivy stuck out her tongue at Frankie, who retaliated by sticking her thumbs in her ears and wiggling her fingers.

Lola ignored their antics. "And don't go overboard on food."

"We need some decent paper napkins," Frankie said. "Last night we had to use tissues from the bathroom and they fall apart in greasy hands."

"How are we going to keep the chicken and potato salad from going bad?" Tessa asked.

"Mama's cooler is empty but there's enough ice in the bottom to keep everything chilled, and besides, we're not but about an hour and a half from the hotel," Lola explained.

Ivy picked up a bag of miniature chocolate doughnuts and a box of real doughnuts with maple icing. "We're working out a good system here. We eat in the hotel in the morning and get left by ten, drive a couple of hours and have our noon meal, then we get to our next hotel about three in the afternoon and order out or take our supper in with us. I could live like this forever, Frankie."

Frankie tossed in a bag of chocolate chip cookies. "Me, too, Ivy. I'm glad we're doin' this. We should've done it years ago and then we would have had the energy to circle the whole United States, not just Texas."

"Ain't it the truth." Ivy sighed.

ɞ

Lola squealed and pointed at a sign stuck to a fence post. "Look, it's another garage sale. And it's only two o'clock and we're only ten miles from Perryton, so we've got time because we can't check in until three."

Tessa had been dozing and almost shot straight up out of the car.

"Where do I turn?" Branch laid a hand on her knee. "Settle down. Everything is fine."

Lola pointed. "Next left, it said on the sign."

Sure enough, there was another cardboard sign with an arrow and a note that said five miles back down that dirt road was a yard sale. Branch slowed down to a crawl when gravel started to fly up into the Caddy.

"Well, lordy Lord, would you look at that?" Ivy glanced toward the southwest. "We was headed away from that so we wasn't watchin' it."

Tessa looked to her left and there was a bank of black clouds rolling toward them at a fast pace. Suddenly, lightning zipped through the sky and thunder rolled. Branch braked and pushed the button to put the top up on the convertible, turned on the air-conditioning, and told everyone to roll up the windows.

The first big drops hit the car before he could change his foot from brake to gas, and Lola sighed loudly. "You might as well turn around at the next place you can. They'll have to cover all their stuff or take it in anyway."

"I figure we're about two miles from it. Maybe it's in a garage," Branch said.

Lola shook her head. "This road is going to get really bad if the rain keeps pouring like this and we might not get back to the paved highway, so we'd better turn back."

"Oh, no! No! No! No!" Melody moaned.

"You wanted to go to the garage sale that bad?" Ivy asked. "I thought you hated them."

"No! I don't care about those silly things. My phone says no service and Jill gets out of classes in half an hour and I wanted to see what she thought of the pictures I sent her and now I can't text or call or nothin'," Melody whined.

"It's only a few minutes to the hotel and maybe you can get reception there," Tessa said. "Let me try mine. If it is working, you can use it. Nope, no service here, either. Must be the storm."

Melody put her face in her hands. "Why does this happen to me? I've been good for days."

"God is testing you to see if you can be good when things aren't perfect in your little world," Ivy answered.

The rain got harder and harder and Branch slowed down a little more. Then a loud noise that sounded like thunder caused them to swerve to the left. Ivy rolled over against Melody, who slid into Frankie's side.

"What happened?" Frankie yelled.

"I think we had a blowout, but I see a barn not too far down this lane. We'll try to make it there and hole up until it stops raining, because we'll have to take everything from the trunk to get at the spare," Branch said.

"An adventure." Ivy clapped her hands.

"I told you to stick with me and we'd have good times." Frankie laughed.

"Drive right on into the barn. The doors are open and I don't see a tractor, so I bet we can get Mollybedamned in out of this weather. If it starts to hail, she might get beat all to hell," Frankie said.

"Yes, ma'am, I'll do my best but that looks like it's pretty narrow." Branch eased the car up to the doors and held on to the steering wheel so tight that Tessa noticed his knuckles were white.

"She's veering off to the side," he explained.

Every nerve ending in Tessa's body stiffened and she could scarcely breathe. What in the hell were they going to do in a strange part of the state with no phone service and trespassing in a barn?

Frankie's tone was frantic. "I can feel it. Don't suppose there'll be anything to save of the tire."

Branch sounded as if he were in a tunnel. "We're running on the rim right now and it's slipping in the mud."

"I could get out and guide you into the barn," Tessa offered. Anything to get them out of the storm and into a dry place. Thank God they'd gotten Ivy's oxygen tank filled.

Branch shook his head. "Not in this mess. We're going to get through by the skin of our teeth, but I think we'll make it."

Tessa exhaled long and loudly when he finally parked the car in the dry. The rain sounded like gunfire peppering down on the sheet-iron roof when he bailed out and rounded the backside of the car to unload the suitcases from the trunk. In half an hour they'd be back out on the road and in fifteen minutes more, they'd be safe inside a hotel room.

Frankie wiped her brow. "I thought she'd lose her mirrors for sure."

"I'm sorry, Mollybedamned," Melody sobbed dramatically.

"For what?" Frankie asked.

Melody wiped at the tears flooding her cheeks. "I bad-mouthed her that first day and she's punishing me for it. Branch said she could if I didn't apologize. Remember?"

"Teach you to not be mean to her, won't it?" Ivy crawled out and stretched, then picked up Blister and set him down on the dirt floor. "Now you might have to sleep in a barn."

Melody's quick intakes of breath made them all turn toward her. "I can't, Aunt Ivy. I'm, like, afraid of spiders and mice and bugs and what if there's bats in there and they bite me? I could, like, turn into a vampire."

"You've been reading too much of that shit that is on the market now," Ivy said. "Frankie, that tire is ruined. But at least we're in the dry and Branch can get the spare out and—"

"Sorry, ladies, the spare has gone flat," he said from the back of the car. "Looks like we're here until this rain slacks up enough I can walk down to that garage sale place and ask for help or the use of their landline phone."

Frankie opened the back door of the car and slid into the seat where she always sat. "Hey, we've got food and me and Ivy can sleep in the car if we have to stay here. I see some horse blankets over there on the stall that y'all can spread out for beds and we'll be fine."

"What if they have fleas in them?" Melody screeched.

"Hush, child. We'll make do with what we've got. You can always sleep in the trunk. We'll even leave the lid up for you," Frankie said.

Melody wrapped her arms around Frankie. "Thank you. I might not die if I can at least have, like, that much."

"Looks to me like a farmer keeps hay in here, so hopefully, he'll come to feed sometime soon," Lola said.

"We have no technology, no tire, and we're stuck in a barn. Isn't this grand?" Ivy said. "Start the car and put the top down, Branch. When it's all the way down, you can turn off the engine. I'm calling the front seat as my bed for the night."

Frankie pursed her mouth into a thin line. "I knew you'd do that and I forgot to say it first. But then you have to deal with the steering wheel and I get the whole backseat to myself."

"Don't put a thing back in the trunk and, like, leave the lid up. That is mine." Melody opened her suitcase and took out two books. "I'm going to read as long as there is light."

"Are those vampire books?" Ivy stretched out on her back on the front seat, feet toward the steering wheel. "I need a pillow, Branch. Can you rustle up one for me?"

"Just use that ratty old bathrobe in your suitcase. You can roll it up and make a pillow out of it," Melody said. "I'm using my denim jacket."

"Smart kid when she's not being a smart-ass," Frankie said. "Branch, darlin', get out my robe, too."

"Am I on the clock?" he asked.

"Until you get our fake pillows out, you can be on the clock." Frankie nodded.

Branch took stock of the barn after Ivy and Frankie stretched out for a nap and Melody was safely curled up in the trunk with a book in her hands. Half a dozen horse blankets hung on the stall. The barn was full of small bales of hay, which meant the farmer might not come around for a couple of days if he was feeding big round bales. This could easily be his winter supply and he wouldn't have a reason to check on things.

He left the stalls and wandered toward the other side of the barn, found a tack room with more blankets on a shelf, along with a bulb hanging from the ceiling. When he pulled the cord, it lit up the room.

"That should make Melody happy. She can read all night if she wants to and she can sleep on the table if she is too cramped in the trunk," he muttered.

"Hey, what did you find?" Tessa said from the doorway.

"The tack room, with light and a big table."

She motioned toward two plastic shower curtains hanging on a wire. "What is behind that?"

He jerked one aside to reveal a toilet and a small wall-hung sink. "Guess it's a bathroom with running water and a flushable toilet. We've got a five-star hotel here, Tessa."

Lola rushed into the room. "Someone loves me for sure. You two get out of here. I need that thing right there. Is there toilet paper?"

"Don't look like it, but there's those napkins in the car. Want me to get them for you?" Tessa asked.

"No, bring the box of tissues in my knitting bag. They'll work better. And thank you. Now go!" Lola pushed them out the door and closed it behind them.

"Let's go explore the loft, Branch." Tessa said after she'd taken the tissues to Lola.

He followed her up the ladder and into the loft, where she plopped down on the hay-covered floor and propped her back against a bale. "Doesn't that smell fresh? Nothing like it in the world."

"The way that sky looks, this could last all night. We're lucky to have found a barn," Tessa said.

He sat down beside her and leaned back on the same bale. He covered her hand with his and laced his fingers with hers. The silence between them didn't need to be filled with chatter as they watched the rain falling so hard that was all they could see. Then suddenly her head bobbled and he gently tipped it over until it rested on his shoulder. With his cheek against her hair, he, too, fell asleep.

Chapter Sixteen

Water dripping on her outstretched hand woke Tessa the next morning. She didn't move a muscle, only her eyes darting around to take in the strange surroundings. Far up above her was a gray corrugated metal roof. A ray of sunshine slipped through a crack in the boards behind her head, sending a sliver of yellow across a gate at her feet.

A tingle in her left hand said someone was touching her. Her eyes shifted slowly in that direction to see exactly whose hand she held. This had to be a dream. She'd wake up any second and find herself at home in her bed with the smell of coffee floating through the apartment as her preset pot gurgled away.

"Takes a minute," a deep drawl said.

She turned her head and Branch's mossy-green eyes locked with hers. The whole storm and day flashed through her mind in a series of black-and-white pictures. "It's not a dream, is it?"

"I'm afraid not."

"I'd kill for a cup of coffee."

"I'd help you bury the body." He grinned.

"How come water is dripping through the roof if the sun is shining?"

"Wouldn't know, but it's time for me to get going to find some help so we can get out of this five-star hotel," he said.

"Don't go just yet. No one else is awake and it's so peaceful here."

He brought her hand to his lips and kissed the knuckles one by one. "Maybe that will keep your clumsiness at bay until we can find toothbrushes and coffee. Wouldn't want you to go too long without kisses of some kind."

An aura filled the stall where they were sleeping unlike anything she'd ever experienced. It was warm like summer rain, yet sparkling like the glitter of the raindrops falling from the rusty old tin roof.

She turned so that they were lying face-to-face. "I'm so glad I came along on this trip."

"Me, too." Branch's soft drawl was even sexier than normal. "I like waking up in a horse stall with a beautiful blonde."

"I like waking up next to the sexiest cowboy on earth." Her gaze met his.

"Do you always speak your mind?" He kissed her on the tip of the nose.

"Not until this adventure started, but something strange happened when I made up my mind to go. It must be some of Frankie's DNA coming through." She smiled.

He kissed the corner of her mouth. "I like it. Don't change when we get home."

The gate swung open and both of them looked up, expecting to see either Frankie or Ivy, but instead it was a gray-haired man wearing bibbed overalls and scuffed-up work boots. He removed his cap and scratched his head.

"Good morning," Tessa said.

"Who in the hell are you and what are you doing in my barn and who's them dead people in that car out there?"

Branch sat up with a start. "What do you mean dead?"

"Got two in the trunk and one in the front seat and one in the back. I didn't stop long enough to see if they was still breathing, but they looked pretty dead to me. Wasn't moving a muscle and then I heard y'all talkin' back here. Did you kill them poor people for that car?"

Tessa jumped to her feet and pushed past him. "They aren't dead. They're asleep. We had a flat."

"We had a blowout about the time that rainstorm hit and we took refuge here, sir." Branch went from a sitting position to standing. "We'll be glad to pay you for the use of it. And I'd appreciate it if I could use your phone and call for help. We lost reception on our cell phones."

The farmer tucked his hands in the bibbed section of his overalls and rocked back and forth on his heels. "Ain't got no reception for them gall-durn things out here, and me and Mama ain't got no use for a telephone. Folks want to talk to us, they know where we live."

"I'm Branch Thomas and we're on a road trip. How would I get some help with that tire? My spare is flat, too," he asked.

He scratched two days' worth of scraggly gray beard. "I reckon I can pump up a flat tire enough to get you on in to Perryton, but you ain't going to get nothing fixed today. It's Sunday and God-fearin' folks don't do business on the Lord's day. You'll have to wait until tomorrow mornin' to get a new tire. Right now I got to feed my cattle and then get ready for church, but I reckon I could take time to pump up that spare for you," he said.

"I'll gladly pay for your time," Branch said.

He finally grinned, showing teeth yellowed from tobacco. "God don't take to people workin' on Sunday, but feedin' cows and doin' a favor for a travelin' man ain't work. It's doin' what we been taught, to be kind to angels and all that, so you don't owe me nothin'," he said.

Branch extended a hand. "Thank you."

"But I reckon if you was to offer to help me with the chores this mornin', then I could accept that as a kind deed done toward me as well. And my name is Oscar Williams."

"Yes, sir, I would be glad to help you."

Oscar nodded toward the Caddy. "Your car, and it's a real beauty, is blockin' my way into the barn, so we need to load up about forty bales on my pickup truck."

"Give me a minute to make a trip to the bathroom and I'll load them for you," Branch said. "We don't have coffee to offer you but I believe there are some doughnuts left."

"Done had my breakfast, thank you. You found the bathroom, did you? It's not much but it serves the purpose for Mama." Oscar's head bobbed up and down several times. "She made me put that in when we built the barn. She helps me with the farmin' and she don't like to squat outdoors, not since she got that dose of poison ivy in places where womenfolks, well, you know." He blushed.

"Yes, sir, I do know. Look, Tessa has wakened the rest of our crew and none of them are dead."

Oscar flipped his cap back on his head. "I woulda swore that one with the tubes in her nose was a goner. Might as well throw that spare up under the hay and when we get done we'll go on down to the house and put some air in it. Probably be back here in an hour if you want to tell your people so they can get around."

"You don't think that man will take Branch off somewhere and, like, kill him, then come back here and, like, shoot all of us, do you?" Melody whispered as the two men carried bales of hay out of the barn.

Tessa had the same fears, but she wasn't going to say them out loud. "Melody, look at Branch and then look at Oscar. I believe Branch could take him down with a hand tied behind his back."

Melody stuck her chin up a notch. "Not if that old man has, like, a shotgun."

"I've got a pistol in the glove compartment and I know how to use it." Frankie yawned.

"You have what?" Melody asked.

"A .38 Saturday night special pistol in my purse and a Smith and Wesson .40 caliber in the glove compartment. And I have a license to carry a concealed weapon. Lester made me learn to shoot and sent me to the class to get my permit to carry it years ago. I ain't shot the damn thing in thirty years but I reckon I could take care of us pretty good, so stop your worryin', kid," Frankie said. "I'm going to have a warm Dr Pepper and some doughnuts so I don't starve before we get to the hotel."

"Wow!" Melody followed her to the tack room. "That really does, like, make me feel better."

Lola fell in behind Melody. "I'm going to finish off the fried chicken and potato salad. I hope they're still serving breakfast when we find a hotel. If they aren't, we're sending Branch for takeout. I want pancakes or waffles and a shower and a real bed and a long nap. How did you sleep, kiddo?"

Tessa brought up the rear. "Slept fine in one of the stalls. Didn't know that I wasn't in a five-star hotel after I went to sleep."

After an hour Tessa began to check the time every thirty seconds. They'd been insane to let Branch go off with that man. Who in the devil didn't have a telephone these days? And what if his name wasn't Oscar but he'd escaped from a mental institution? What if there were no cows to feed and he'd said that to get Branch away from the women? She didn't have a license to carry a gun, but she could shoot. Clint and her Cajun cousins had taught her years ago. Was it time to get out the guns and take up hiding spots?

The next fifteen minutes lasted three days past eternity. Ivy and Frankie argued about what food to toss and what to take with them. Lola hummed as she sat in the middle of the table in the tack room and knitted another pink baby cap. Melody paced the floor with wild eyes and her phone clutched in her hand as if the dead thing could save her life.

Finally, a rusted-out old pickup turned off the road and Tessa could see Branch sitting in the passenger's seat. Only then did she let herself believe that they were really going to get out of this mess alive.

"Mighty fine-lookin' car," Oscar said from the sidelines while Branch put the spare tire on the car and then loaded their things back in the trunk. "It's a good thing to keep cars and stuff around until it wears completely out. Folks these days think newer is better but that ain't always the case."

"Thank you," Frankie said. "My husband bought me this car and it was my first brand-new vehicle. I decided that day I was going to keep it the rest of my life."

"You done good," Oscar said. "Now, y'all have a safe trip."

"Thank you for the use of your barn." Frankie extended her hand toward him. "And for the help."

Oscar wiped his hand on his overalls before he shook with her. "You are welcome. The Good Book says for us to help strangers and pilgrims."

Frankie smiled sweet at him. "Yes, sir, it does. And if a stranger leaves a little something behind on the table in the tack room, then it's not payment but a gift."

"I reckon it would be." Oscar nodded. "And I do like doughnuts."

"I thought you might," Frankie said. "You have a nice Sunday now, Oscar."

They were on the highway headed north toward Perryton when Ivy poked Frankie on the arm. "You reckon he'll be happy with that Benjamin Franklin you left him?"

"It was worth that and more to get Mollybedamned out of the hail," Frankie said. "Look, there's a sign that says there is a hotel seven miles up the road."

"Still no reception." Melody sighed. "And it's Sunday morning and Jill isn't in school and we could be talking or texting."

Ten minutes later Branch pulled into the crowded parking lot of the hotel and Tessa almost cried. There was no way that there would be rooms at this time of the morning, not when every parking space except three at the back was already filled.

"What do we do if there are no rooms?" Ivy asked.

"We sit in the lobby and wait until there are rooms, because that hissing noise you hear is the spare going flat again," Branch answered.

"We barely made it but here we are and I'm going to wish real hard for three rooms in that place. I don't care how much they cost or what floor they are on," Frankie said.

Lola was out of the car first. "It's only ten and they usually don't stop serving breakfast until ten thirty, so we can eat while we wait."

The clerk had four rooms left in the hotel, all on the third floor and all high-end suites with Jacuzzi tubs and double queen beds. "You do realize that since you are checking in this early you will have to pay for two nights," he said.

"Yes, I do," Frankie said. "You get the keys, Branch, and meet us in the dining room. We're all going to have some breakfast before we take our things upstairs. And find out what kind of restaurants we've got available in this town for later on today."

"Do we need a password for the free Wi-Fi?" Tessa hung back with Branch.

"Your Wi-Fi ID will be Laveau, since all the rooms are listed under that name. And the password is your room number. Enjoy your stay and please call if you need anything. Here's a sheet with all the places to eat in Perryton." He peeled off a piece of paper from a thick pad and handed it to her. "The fitness room and the pool are now open and will close at ten tonight. We do have vending machines and ice machines on each floor and a small assortment of things in the little hotel store available through the door right around the corner. I can charge whatever you get to your room or you can pay for it at the time of purchase."

"Thank you." Tessa turned to Branch. "You ready for coffee and breakfast?"

"Yes, I am," he said.

She took one step, tripped over an ottoman, and fell against Branch's side. His arms went around her and held her tightly.

His lips grazed her forehead. "Guess that kiss on your knuckles is wearing off. Here, this will hold you until we can take care of it proper."

She pushed away from him. "You rat! I smell coffee on your breath!"

Branch chuckled. "Couldn't refuse a cup from Oscar's wife when he took me inside their home to introduce me, could I?"

"And that's why you were fifteen minutes later than you'd said you'd be. I was worried about you. *What ifs* kept playing through my mind and I thought that old man might kill you and come back to take us all out to get Mollybedamned."

"Frankie has guns and she would have protected you." He chuckled. "But thank you for caring about me, Miz Tess. Now let's talk about when you need another kiss to keep you from stumbling around like a drunk. I think I can work you in for an appointment this evening after supper. Maybe we can go skinny-dippin' in my Jacuzzi pool?"

She started toward the smell of hot breakfast food. "In your dreams, cowboy. Right now I'm going to eat and take a long shower, wash my hair and talk to my mother, who is going to have a hissy because I didn't call her last night."

"Do I need to tell her that we slept together but we didn't have sex? That I held your hand all night so you wouldn't have nightmares? I could tell her that I'm in the process of curing your clumsiness, too," Branch said.

She stopped and flipped around so fast that it surprised her that she didn't tumble through the archway into the dining room. Damn! She might be a believer in his kisses, after all.

"I'm not telling my mother that we slept together or that we didn't have sex or that your kisses are . . ." She paused.

His green eyes sparkled. "That my kisses are what? Wonderful? Amazing? Breathtaking?" he asked in a lazy drawl. "You are going to smile. I can see it in your beautiful blue eyes."

"Hey, you two, stop arguing and come get some breakfast," Ivy called out from a few feet away.

Tessa turned her head slightly. "He had coffee with Oscar."

"Tattletale," he said.

"And you didn't bring me a drop? You rat," Lola said.

"See?" Tessa faced him again.

Branch slung an arm around Tessa's shoulders and started walking. "I really wanted to bring all of you coffee, but I didn't want to be rude and ask."

"You are forgiven. Now pass out the room keys and go get food before they quit serving," Frankie said. "Did you get a list of restaurants?"

"Here it is in alphabetical order. Looks like you've got your choice of about three dozen places if you count the burger joints," Tessa said.

"I count them all," Frankie said. "Look, Ivy, we've hit the mother lode. Two steak houses and a couple of rib joints and a Mexican food joint, too. We've got a broad choice for dinner and supper."

Tessa left them with the list and went to the buffet table, loaded her plate with omelets, bacon, sausage gravy over biscuits, and a bowl of fresh fruit while Branch came right behind her doing the same thing.

"Looks like you might be hungry," Branch said.

"I like food and I am starving. I was too nervous to eat this morning," she said.

"I like it that you worried about me. It means you care."

"How do you know that? It might mean that I don't know how to change a flat tire."

"Those blue eyes can't tell a lie worth a damn. You care, Tessa! Your eyes say that you do."

Frankie had said something about the eyes when she told her the story of Lester coming home from the war. Was it true that when a person truly cared about another one that it showed in their eyes?

Branch stopped in the middle of the floor. "Admit it, darlin'."

"Of course I care about you. I care about stray kittens, so that doesn't mean anything." She smiled sweetly.

"Well, I care a lot about you, Miz Tess. Even more than stray kittens or puppy dogs that get thrown out on the road," he said, seductively soft.

"Then tell me who set off the sparks in your world. You said it wasn't Avery. Who was it?" she asked.

He gazed down into her eyes for several seconds. She should have gone on toward the table, but she couldn't. For the first time she was drawn to the depths of those gorgeous green eyes, and she couldn't force herself to blink or move away from him. He was baring his very soul to her. It was powerful yet humbling to have a man like Branch open up like that to her. She'd never felt such a rush, not with Matt, not with anyone.

"You," he whispered just before he blinked and the moment was gone. "You set off sparks and someday we'll talk about it."

Chapter Seventeen

Thank you, Tessa, for helping Branch bring all this stuff up here. Ivy is taking a shower. That"—Frankie pointed toward the deep tub—"is for Melody, but first she has to take pictures of the room to send to Jill. Set the luggage between the sofa and the wall and we'll sort it all out later. Tessa, can you meet me in the lobby in half an hour? Oh, and what was that thing between you and Branch in the dining room?"

"Wasn't much to it since there was a luggage cart," Tessa said. "Yes, ma'am, I can meet you in the lobby in thirty minutes. That will give me time to get a shower and wash my hair. I feel pretty grimy right now. And Frankie, I'm still trying to sort out that moment myself. It started off as a joke and then it got serious and I don't know if it ended on a joke or a serious note."

"If I know anything at all, darlin' girl, that was not a joke at the end." Frankie combed back her gray hair with her fingertips. "My hair feels like an oil pit. Me and Ivy would like to get in that tub but we're afraid we couldn't get out if we did and besides the hot water would jack our blood pressure up to stroke level." Frankie lowered her voice. "She's worn plumb out and Blister was almost empty by the time we got here. I worried about that damn tank going dry all night. Soon as she gets out of the shower, she's going to take a long nap. I wish we'd never started smoking, but when we were teenagers cigarettes didn't cause all these problems and it was cool. Even the doctors smoked."

"You sure you don't want to take a nap, too?" Tessa asked.

"I will after Melody gets bored with that tub. I figure half an hour will do it and then she'll have to get out and tell Jill all about it. I can't sleep with the noise the damned thing makes," she said. "But Ivy could sleep through a tornado so she won't have a problem."

"Then I'll see you in the lobby as soon as I can," Tessa said.

She and Branch guided the much lighter luggage cart to the next room, and she fished her room key from the pocket of her denim shorts. She slung open the door and used her suitcase to prop it open while Branch removed everything but his luggage from the cart.

The big tub over there in the corner called to her and she was planning a time to get into it when Branch turned her around and wrapped her up in his big, strong arms. She barely had time to moisten her lips before his lips found hers in a scorching-hot kiss.

Her body was pressed tightly against his when the kiss ended and she leaned in closer for more.

"That should do you for a little while longer, but if you start dropping things or get all clumsy again, knock on my door and I'll be glad to fix you right up," he said hoarsely.

"It's totally medicine, right?" She smiled. "This has nothing to do with an attraction from either of us, right?"

"Of course, darlin'. Just call me Dr. Branch."

She put her hands on his chest and took a step back. "Well, Doc, I do appreciate your snake oil, but I'm still not a believer that it works."

"You will be by the time this trip is over, Miz Tess," he drawled. "If you change your mind about that skinny-dippin' in my big old Jacuzzi, holler and I'll start the water."

"You are one wild cowboy." She smiled.

His eyes locked with hers. "Maybe I am, but you like it. See you later."

The door closed behind him and she melted onto the sofa.

"Yay, luggage and clean clothing." Lola stepped out of the bathroom with one towel around her body and one wrapped up like a turban around her head. "I'm going to do laundry sometime this afternoon. Got anything you want to add to the pile?"

"I did mine on Friday, so I'm good," Tessa said. "I figured you'd use the tub."

"I will later. Right now I need to make a couple of phone calls. What about you? Going to take advantage of the tub?" Lola asked.

"Yes, I surely am before this night is done. Right now I'm going to take a shower and meet Frankie in the lobby. She's pretty worried about Ivy, so I figure she wants to talk about her," Tessa answered.

Lola nodded. "Those two are like twins. I'm kind of glad I wasn't there when Daddy died. Ivy said Mama was so deep in grief until I came home that she feared she would die from it. But if Ivy dies first, Mama might not get over it."

Tessa removed the ponytail holder from her hair, pulling out straw and hay with it. "You ever had a friend like that?"

Lola bent at the waist and rubbed her hair dry with the towel, then tossed it over the back of the desk chair. "Sophie was probably the best friend I ever had, but it wasn't anything like Mama and Ivy. What about you?"

"Clint, my cousin and partner, has been my best friend since we were toddlers but it's not like the bond between Ivy and Frankie," she answered. "What they have is something like magic. I bet they know what each other is thinking."

"I'm not sure there is another bond like that. Sometimes I think it's deeper than the one that Mama had with Daddy and believe me, that one was bottomless," Lola said. "You'd better get a fast shower if you're going to the lobby, kiddo."

"Guess so." Tessa stripped out of her shirt and tossed it on the floor.

Frankie looked up and Tessa could feel the sadness in her eyes. *She must've found out about Ivy and she needed to talk to someone about it.*

"I got us each a cup of coffee and I went outside and had a cigarette while I waited. I'm glad we're going to sit in here. That damn barn was hot last night. I'm ready for air-conditioned comfort." Frankie motioned toward the other end of the sofa where she sat.

Tessa picked up the cup and sipped hot black coffee. It had absolutely no taste, none, nada, zilch. And yet the bitter aftertaste it left in her mouth said that it was strong enough to melt the enamel right off her teeth.

"I think Branch likes you, but Ivy says I can't interfere because I made a mess of Lola's life. If I'd let her alone about that boy she would have never run off with him and it would have died in its sleep. But then if she hadn't run away I wouldn't have you at a time in my life when I need you the most and so does Lola, so who can question fate, right?" Frankie said sadly. "Did you and Branch have time to talk?"

Tessa shook her head and took another sip of her coffee—still no flavor. The lump in her throat was as big as a baseball, and no matter how many times she swallowed it would not go down. She didn't know what to say to make Frankie feel better, but something came to mind and she spit it out. "My grandmother, that would be my daddy's mama, says that things happen for a reason. Maybe we don't understand why but they do, and if we get on down the road a ways, we can look back and see things clearer."

"I hope that's right. And I won't say anything more after this but I've known Branch his whole life and he's never looked at another girl the way he does you. There's something in his eyes and smile that tells the whole story," Frankie said.

Tessa began to relax. The next sip of coffee tasted almost like the real deal. "Is that what you wanted to talk to me about?"

Frankie's brows knit together in a solid line. "No, that's a side trip to avoid what I really have to say. Ivy hasn't got long to live."

"You know?" Tessa almost dropped the cup but got a handle on it at the last minute. *Thank goodness for the kiss,* she thought.

Frankie's face registered surprise. "Of course I know. Did she tell you?"

Tessa's head bobbed once, and she set the half-empty cup on the table between them. "But she didn't want me to tell you."

Frankie smiled, but it was still tired and sad. "We promised we wouldn't tell anyone that this is our last big hoo-rah. The blowout before we *really* retire."

Tessa scooted down the long sofa to sit closer to Frankie and laced her fingers with hers. "I'm so sorry, Frankie. You will miss her, but you'll have the memories of your whole lives and this trip. It's been fun, even when we had to spend the night in a barn."

"It has, but I didn't call you down here to talk about Ivy exclusively. It's something else." Frankie laid her other hand over their clasped hands and went on. "It's about me . . . and the future."

"Okay." The word came out as four long, extended syllables rather than two.

"The specialist says my problem wasn't caused by smoking, but I know better. In twenty years, they'll figure out that nicotine caused a hell of a lot more than what Ivy has and that it was my downfall as well," Frankie said in a monotone.

Icy-cold chills danced down Tessa's backbone. She prayed earnestly that she wouldn't hear Frankie say the words. If she didn't say them, then it wouldn't be true.

Frankie took two sips of her coffee before she went on. "We could quit smoking but we'd be miserable and it wouldn't lengthen our days at this point, so what's the use. First question I want to ask you is this. If we cut this trip short for any reason, will you go on and take the whole month off and stay with Lola?"

An acute pain hit Tessa in the temples, but she kept her hands away from her head. Maybe if she ignored it, Frankie wouldn't say those words. "Why would you ask that?"

"I need to know, because she's going to need you real bad and I want you to be near to me for the whole month," Frankie said.

"Yes, I will if it's important to you." Tessa nodded, the lump in her throat bigger now.

Frankie inhaled and let it out slowly. "That's a big relief, because me and Ivy have done lasted longer than we figured we would without wearin' plumb out. We want to make it at least one more week because it'll take that long for the plans to get worked out all the way." She paused and stared at the ceiling a few seconds before going on. "Guess I've put off sayin' the words long enough. Ivy's got less than three months to live and I've got less than that. It's brain cancer and it's one of them that got too big and badass to take out. I'm okay for today and Doc says I'll be fine for another week or two after this, but then I'll sleep more and more and one day I won't wake up." Frankie nodded slowly. "There, now it's easier since I said it out loud. So me and Ivy have got things fixed to go to a very private care facility where they'll know how to make us comfortable in our last days. We're hopin' we go together, but either way, we won't be very long apart and then we'll be together for all eternity."

Like a river during flood season, the tears rushed down Tessa's cheeks and dripped onto the collar of her sleeveless shirt. "But there's got to be something they could do."

Frankie pulled her over to hug her. With Tessa's head on her shoulder, she patted her back. "Shhh. Don't cry now, honey. I'm not in pain and probably won't be. One day I'll go to sleep and then I'll wake up on the other side. There's worse ways to go, and until then me and Ivy can talk about this trip and how much it meant to have you go with us."

"But I wanted to get to know you better," Tessa sobbed.

"There ain't no better than this right here on this journey. If we had another twenty years together, it couldn't best what we have right now."

Tessa stiffened. "Lola? Does she know?"

Frankie shook her head. "Doesn't know a damn thing and isn't going to until the day we go back to Boomtown. Only me and Ivy are goin' to our new home. Neither one of us can bear to have a day of sadness when we leave our houses, so we'll be stopping off in Beaumont at our new place. This trip is getting us some space between all that material stuff we're leaving behind and the new little stopover until we finish this life and go on. The new place needs another week to get things all arranged for us."

"Oh, Frankie, this is so hard to hear." Tessa tried to get control of the tears, but they kept flowing.

Frankie wiped her own tears away. "I never could let someone cry or smoke alone. I know this is tough, but Lola is going to need you like I needed her when Lester died. I wouldn't have survived if she hadn't come home and given me a reason to live. She was all broken and she needed me. For the first time in my life things were right between us. God sent you to me and gave you to her for this time in all our lives. She needs you to hold on to."

"She'll know something is wrong when she sees my face. I can't hide anything," Tessa said.

"And that's when you're going to tell her that Ivy is dying." Frankie gently pushed Tessa to a sitting position and stared right into her eyes. "She don't need to hear about us both at the same time. She needs to get it one at a time and let that process, but I cannot do it, Tessa. Please do this for me. I don't want the last good days I spend with Lola on this trip to be sad."

"Okay." Tessa pulled a tissue from a box on the coffee table and blew her nose. "I will do it, but it won't be easy."

"Thank you." Frankie kissed her on the forehead. "Now that's said and done, there's something else we need to discuss. I've talked to Branch's daddy, who is my lawyer. I signed a new will before we left. My oil estate is worth millions and of course Lola will inherit a chunk of it. I left a nice little donation to mine and Ivy's church and a scholarship fund to the school but not to a football player or a cheerleader. It has to go to a student who shows promise in geology and the sciences."

Tessa felt Frankie's tears on her forehead and reached for another handful of tissues.

Frankie dabbed at her eyes. "There is a sizable inheritance for you. But if you would be willing to move to Boomtown or Beaumont so you'd be closer to Lola, it will double in value. Like I said, she's going to need you, and the way I see it, you could have a travel agency anywhere."

"But Frankie," she started.

Frankie laid a finger over Tessa's lips. "I've put a lot on you today. I'm grateful that you are willing to use up the rest of your vacation for Lola and me. The rest you can ponder over. It's already in the will, so you've got time to let it all sink in. Wouldn't want you to make a decision like this today on the spur of the moment." Frankie used her tissue to wipe Tessa's cheeks. "Like I said, I'm so glad you are here for us. I couldn't love you more if I'd known you since you were born. It must be a genetic thing, because having you completes the circle for me and I'm okay with this thing that I can't do anything about."

"I can't bear this." A fresh batch of tears left more long black lines of mascara on Tessa's cheeks.

Frankie held her by the shoulders and narrowed her eyes. "We won't talk about this again unless you have something to say to me, because I want so bad for this journey to last at least one more week and maybe two. But when I see Ivy failing, we will head east and we'll get there as fast as we can, even if we have to get on an airplane and let you kids bring Mollybedamned home by yourselves." She pulled Tessa into a fierce embrace. "And I left the car to you. It doesn't have good memories for Lola, but I hope that it does for you. Enough of sadness. I want to hear about you now. The time is getting away from us even today. I figure we might have half an hour left before Melody starts bellyachin' that she's hungry. And we need to talk about something else so this won't be the last thing on our minds when we go back to the rest of the family."

Tessa gladly changed the subject. "You already know most of it," she said.

"Boyfriends?" Frankie smiled.

"Not right now. I thought I was marrying the right man and we were planning a wedding and then he broke up with me on Christmas Eve last year. His mama wasn't happy with the engagement because I'm adopted and they didn't know what kind of people I came from. His reason was that I wasn't passionate enough. He said that he needed someone with more fire and spunk than I have," she said.

"Darlin', nobody could ever say a Laveau wasn't blessed with passion. We love our menfolks, sometimes too much, but we do love them. And I was a Beauchamp before I married and honey, they don't make women any hotter than that."

"You and Ivy both have Cajun names. You'd think you'd be living in Louisiana instead of me," Tessa said.

They talked much longer than thirty minutes. Long enough for Frankie's coffee to grow cold, but she finished it anyway. "My daddy come from across the border in New Orleans to Beaumont to work in the oil fields. He met my mama when he went to dinner at his boss's house one evening, and they eloped six weeks later. Same thing with Ivy's daddy. He was from over in a little town called Jeanerette and he come over here to work on a cattle ranch and met his wife there. So we've got some Cajun in us and I don't have to tell you how passionate that blood is." Frankie patted her on the knee. "So don't you let no man be makin' you feel like that. Look at that clock up there on the wall. I can't believe we've talked this long or that I've gone so long without a cigarette." She laughed.

The elevator doors slid open and Melody stepped out with her eyes on her phone and her thumbs doing double time. "Aunt Ivy told me to come ask when we're ordering something to, like, eat or if we're going out for whatever this meal is. Two o'clock is late to call it lunch or dinner and, like, too early for supper."

"I'll go with you and we'll decide what we all want and send Branch out to get it," Frankie said. "We'll make a list for some snack food from whatever grocery store he can find for later this evening."

"I could go with him and help get whatever you want," Tessa offered.

"That would be nice. Give you some space before you have to face Lola," Frankie said softly. "But don't tell Branch anything other than the part about Ivy and only then if you have to." Frankie motioned toward the elevator. "You run along, Melody, and tell

Ivy what I said so she can be lookin' at that sheet of places to order from. I need to tell Tessa one more thing." Frankie stood up slowly. "Branch's daddy—his name is Andrew, by the way and you'll get to know him well—has an old faded velvet box that he will give you when he comes to explain things to you and Lola. It's got my grandmama's pearls in it that she wore on her wedding day. She gave them to my mama on her wedding day and my mama gave them to me when I married Lester. Lola won't ever get married, so I'd be right honored if you'd wear them on your wedding day."

"Frankie, those should be Lola's even if she doesn't get married." The lump in Tessa's throat refused to budge no matter how many times she swallowed.

"You are my future. You are the one who is going to do things right and have children that are part Laveaus and me and Lester will live on through them. And the pearls, well, I hope you will wear them."

"Thank you. I promise I will." Tessa wanted to throw a hissy right there in the hotel. Life wasn't a damn bit fair.

Frankie hugged her tightly. "That makes me happy. You let Lola put them on you that day and be sure to wear something of Sophie's, too. You are the perfect mix of us all."

ꕥ

Branch stopped right in the middle of the produce aisle beside the apples and ran his forefinger down Tessa's jawbone. "Your shoulders look like you are bearing the weight of the world, and your eyes are so sad they make me want to cry. And grown men aren't supposed to be sissies. What's wrong, Tessa?"

"Frankie told me that Ivy isn't going to live very long," she blurted out.

He sighed deeply, removed his hat and placed it over his heart. "So she knows, then?" He draped an arm around her shoulders. "Does she know about the time frame?"

Tessa picked up a small bag of apples. "Yes, she does, and it breaks my heart to see her sad."

Branch put four oranges in a plastic bag and added them to the cart.

She picked up a box of doughnuts and tears started rolling down her cheeks again. He drew her close to his chest, both arms around her right there in the produce aisle of the Walmart store. "This is even harder on you than when Ivy told you, isn't it?"

She managed a nod in among the sobs and he rubbed her back with the palms of his hands. Several people walked past them but no one mattered.

"Ivy does like doughnuts, but then so does Frankie. They should have all they want," he said hoarsely as he pulled a snowy-white hankie from his pocket and dried her tears. "Don't cry, darlin'. Frankie will manage. She has Lola and now you. You really make her happy."

She blinked back more tears. "I just met them and started liking them. Hell, not liking them. I've fallen in love with the whole bunch of them and now they're being taken away."

She handed the hankie back to him and he wiped his own eyes before putting it away. "And I'm sorry about Ivy, but if I know her at all, she wouldn't want anyone fussing or worrying. So we'll make this a wonderful journey for her and for Frankie because she'll need all the memories to hang on to when her friend is gone. I can't imagine . . ."

She pushed away from him and looked into his eyes and there it was again, that opening of the soul as well as the heart. "Me, either," she said, wondering if he was thinking about losing her as much as she was him.

It was after three when they returned to the hotel. The car provided by the hotel pulled up under the awning. The driver hopped out and grabbed a luggage cart, loaded all their purchases on it, and asked Branch which room he wanted it taken to.

"I'll push it up there, and thanks for taking us to so many places." Branch slipped a tip into his hand. "Thank you. We sure couldn't drive our car with that flat tire."

"I can make arrangements to have it fixed for you by checkout time in the morning," he said.

"Great! And tell them that we'll need two new tires, one put on the car and one to be used as a spare. Just call my room when they get here and I'll come right down with the car keys," Branch said.

"Will do, and thanks for the tip." He smiled.

Tessa helped guide the cart into the elevator. "I'm wondering where they're going to put all this stuff and how in the world we're going to get what we don't eat in the trunk tomorrow."

"We'll figure out a way. I'm hoping we don't have to sleep in any more barns, although I wouldn't be averse to sleeping with you in a big bed," he said.

"Hush," she said.

Branch tipped her chin up with his fist. "You smiled and it reached your eyes."

She tiptoed, meeting him halfway and needing the kiss more than he ever could. It didn't have time to be fire hot, but it satisfied the longing in her heart and soul before the elevator doors opened and an elderly couple stepped to one side to let them out with the cart.

"Something in there smells good. Where did you go?" the man asked.

"A Mexican place, an Italian place, a rib joint, and a burger shop," Branch said.

"And the grocery store," Tessa chimed in.

"It's the newlywed munchies, Hazel." The man kissed his gray-haired wife on the cheek. "Remember when we were on our honeymoon and couldn't get enough food?"

"Back in them days we couldn't get enough of anything." She giggled.

Branch stopped the cart in the middle of the hallway, not ten feet from Frankie's door, and grinned. "You are cute when you blush."

"So are you," she said.

He touched his cheek with the palm of his hand. "I'm not blushing."

"Yes, you are, and it's sexy. I didn't know menfolks did that, but it says you have a sensitive side and all us women like a man who's got a soft heart, especially for children and old folks. By the way, you could have told them we're not on our honeymoon."

"I didn't want to burst their happy bubble," he said.

"I know exactly what you mean. Now let's get this food into the room before those other four crew members wither up and die of starvation," she said.

Branch knocked on the door and yelled, "Room service."

Melody quickly threw it open and stood to one side.

"It's about time," Frankie yelled over the television. "My stomach thinks my throat has been cut."

Ivy threw a hand over her heart. "And I was lookin' up the phone number for the nearest undertaker. Figured I only had about thirty more minutes if you didn't get here with those ribs. What took you so damned long?"

"We didn't have Mollybedamned to drive." Branch was already busy delivering the various restaurant sacks to the folks who ordered them.

"And I believe that grocery store checker had two speeds—slow and stop," Tessa said. "But the food is here now. Everything is going to be perfect!"

"Yes, it is." Frankie blew her a kiss.

Tessa reached up and grabbed it in her hand and stuffed it in her pocket.

"Frankie used to do that when Lester blew her kisses," Ivy said.

The sun was barely a sliver of orange on the distant horizon that evening when Branch and Tessa left Frankie's room after supper. His big hand closed over hers as he walked with her down the hallway. "I get a kick out of the way Frankie and Ivy banter back and forth with each other. My grandparents are about that age, but they don't do that."

"Neither do mine," Tessa said.

Branch motioned toward a couple of wing-back chairs in front of the elevators. "Sit with me a little while and tell me about your family."

She wiggled her hand free from his and sat down in the nearest chair. "Mama is a tall, thin blonde and Daddy is tall with light-brown hair that's got plenty of gray in the temples. He wears thick glasses and is a banker at a place that takes care of the casino money for the state of Louisiana. It's not a bank like what you think of when you hear that word—only a few people work there, and their only client is the casinos. Mama teaches dance to students from age four through high school." She wished the chairs were closer together so that he could hold her hand again. "And your daddy is a lawyer. What does your mama do?"

Branch moved the chair close to hers before he sat down and picked up her hand again, holding it on his lap. "She was a lawyer, but she retired last year. Now she does whatever she wants but most of the time she enjoys her grandkids."

"How many grandkids?" There were sparks but better than that, her hand in his felt right.

"Four. My two older brothers each have two kids. Darrin has a boy and girl and Justin has two girls. This is nice, just talking like this."

The elevator doors opened to their left, and a tall, willowy woman pulled a designer suitcase behind her. Dark hair floated to her shoulders and big brown eyes zeroed in on Branch.

Tessa suddenly felt a jolt of tension, and he squeezed her hand tighter.

The woman stiffened her back, snarled her nose, and narrowed her eyes, going from stunningly beautiful to downright evil in the blink of an eye. "So is this why you haven't answered my calls or messages in days? Good God, Branch. Where did you get her? A bar? She's not pretty enough for a whorehouse."

Branch stood up, pulling Tessa with him. He slung an arm around her shoulders and glared at the woman. "Darlin', I would like you to meet Avery. Avery, this is Tessa Wilson, and don't judge her by your own half bushel. What are you doing in Perryton, Texas, anyway?" His words were beyond freezing cold.

She held up her left hand and there was a diamond the size of a dime flashing in the fluorescent lighting. "We need to talk in person and work this thing out. Did this cowboy tell you that we are engaged?"

Chapter Eighteen

The woman looked at Tessa as if she were something that she'd stepped in out in the cow pasture. Tessa should do or say something, but not a single smart-ass remark came to her mind and Frankie's gun was in the glove compartment of the Caddy.

A slow, menacing growl came from Branch's throat. "You told me you lost that ring when you broke it off."

"Well, sweetheart, I found it again and figured it was an omen. Give me five minutes to get unpacked and I'll be ready to talk." She snarled down at Tessa as if she were something dirty as she headed down the hall. "And Teresa, you can run along to whatever slum you crawled out from. He's always been mine from the first time he laid eyes on me."

"You're a brazen bitch, aren't you?" Tessa shook free of Branch's arm and bowed up to the woman. "What makes you think I'll sit back and let you move in on my territory?"

Avery's brown eyes were stone cold. "Yes, I am, and I always get what I want. It's a tiring drive up here from the Amarillo airport, so I need a shower and to get into something more comfortable. I'll call when I'm ready for you, Branch." She turned her back and disappeared down the hallway.

"Thank you," Branch whispered when Avery was gone. "Will you please stay in my room tonight and pretend to be my real girlfriend? I'll sleep on the sofa and you can have that king-size bed all to yourself."

Tessa nodded. "Of course I will. I'll have to get my things and tell Lola, but that won't take long. I haven't unpacked yet. Frankie and Ivy are going to love this drama. It'll be another story for them to talk about when they"—she paused before she spit out anything about the specialty care facility they were going to—"get home."

Branch hugged her close to his chest. "You were thinking about Ivy not having long, weren't you?"

"Yes, I was," she said honestly and took a step back. "I reckon we'd best get my things and get into your room before the hussy calls, and I will be more than glad to answer the phone when she does." She slipped the key card into the slot and pushed the door open. "Why is Avery doing this? Doesn't she have a lick of dignity or pride?"

"She's a barracuda and she wants to win this game. That's what it is to her: only a game, and she's a poor loser. The guy she left me for broke up with her and she's probably feeling the pinch. She needs to win something to get her dignity back."

"Well, since you can't drown a damn barracuda then I might have to borrow one of Frankie's guns and just shoot the bitch," Tessa declared.

Branch pulled her suitcase out into the hall and into his room. "If she thinks there's no chance, she'll go home, lick her wounds, and leave me alone."

"Poor thing must have a miserable life," Tessa said. "But she's still a bitch and I really don't like her. She has no right to look at me like I'm trash, so I'm glad to be your pseudogirlfriend for the night. And if she doesn't take the hint, I'll buy two shovels tomorrow morning and we'll bury her somewhere out here in a mesquite thicket."

Branch chuckled. "You are a force."

She reached up and grazed his chin with her knuckles. "I'll protect the big old cowboy. After all, he's trying very hard to cure me of my awkwardness. I do owe him."

❧

"You're not going to believe this," Lola said when she got off the phone with Tessa. "Mama, you are going to love it."

After the story was told, Melody said, "I've, like, got to see this woman. Do grown-ups really act like that? I thought only kids like me did stupid stuff like that."

"Kids don't hold a monopoly on stupid," Ivy said. "She's two doors down from Branch? Is that right?"

Frankie reached for the phone but Ivy beat her to it. "You old fart. I wanted to make that call."

"What call?" Melody asked.

Lola giggled. "Just be real quiet and watch two old pros at work."

Ivy punched in the room number. "You can make the next one." She held up a finger. "Hello, is this Avery? This is the front desk and we've had a bit of a mix-up. The room we gave you has been reserved and there was a computer glitch. If you will come back down to the lobby, we will reissue you a key to a different room. We do apologize and we will make this right on your bill."

Ivy handed the phone to Frankie when she ended the call. "Well, she's not a bit happy and she's using some words that me and you don't let sneak out of our mouths. It's your turn."

Frankie took a deep breath and called the front desk. "Yes, ma'am, you can definitely help me. I have a relative named Avery up here on the third floor and she's a little"—she paused and sighed loudly before she went on—"deranged. She's coming down to the lobby right now with some cock-and-bull story about you all having put her in the wrong room. If you will give her anything available on the first floor, I'll pick up the tab for the room. Tell her it's a freebie because you made a mistake and maybe she'll settle down. I'm terribly sorry. We weren't expecting her to show up here since she's only been out of the institution two days. Yes, that's right. Avery is her name, and she should be there any minute."

"And I thought teenagers were bad. This sounds a lot like you've done it before," Melody said.

"This ain't our first rodeo, Melody." Frankie nodded.

"And it probably won't be our last," Ivy said.

Lola pointed toward the door. "Let's go sit in those chairs by the elevator, Melody. She should be on her way any minute now and I want to see her. I can't believe Tessa didn't deck her."

Melody was on her feet instantly. "And I thought this trip was, like, going to be boring."

They darted out the door in their bare feet and sat down in the two wing-back chairs. Melody picked up a brochure from a pretty little round table separating the chairs and pretended to read it.

They heard the mumbling a few seconds before Avery turned the corner, suitcase behind her. She poked the down button half a dozen times, tapped her foot, and flipped her brown hair over her shoulder, completely ignoring the two ladies not three feet from her.

"What gorgeous luggage. Is that *AP* your initials, or does that mean AP is some fancy brand?" Melody asked in wide-eyed innocence.

"It's my initials. Why is this damned elevator taking so long?" Avery snapped.

"I bet they stand for Annie Phillips. I'm a psychic and I know these things. And I bet you are engaged, too," Melody said.

"You're a poor excuse for a medium. My ring says I'm engaged and my name is Avery Prescott," Avery said tersely.

"I don't wear a size medium. I'm not that fat. I'm a small. What do you wear, an extra large?" Melody asked. "And you are lyin'. Your name is Annie Phillips. Don't lie to a psychic. It's bad luck."

"This is ridiculous. I'm taking the stairs." Avery stomped to the door marked *Stairs* and disappeared, muttering the whole time.

"Well, you have a good night, Miz Annie," Melody called out loudly and then turned to Lola. "Please tell me I can tell Jill all about this. I'm about to explode and I've, like, got to tell her."

"Yes, tell Jill, but tell first Mama and Ivy. They need to know what happened. I've got a couple of things I need to do out here before I come back inside." Lola fetched her cell phone from her hip pocket and flipped through the icons on the screen. It took less than five minutes to locate Avery's Facebook page, to figure out that she posted on it regularly and it had no privacy settings, because it was all right there in living color for the whole world to see.

Miss Avery Prescott had changed her status from *in a relationship* with Luke Arthur Black to *engaged* to Branch Thomas in the last two weeks. She liked yellow roses and her precious Luke sent them often to his *sugar dumpling*, and she had quit her job and was now looking for a job in a reputable law firm.

"Amazing what people will put right out there for the whole world to see. They might as well run naked around in an apartment with no drapes or blinds," she mumbled.

Her thumbs worked overtime, punching in the toll-free number to an Internet florist that would deliver flowers within an hour if a person was willing to pay the exorbitant fee to get it done.

"Yes, sir, I want one long-stemmed yellow rose in one of those white boxes tied with a yellow ribbon, and I want it to say, 'To the love of my life. I'm so sorry, my sugar dumpling. Please come home to me. I'll be waiting in your apartment with open arms and the rest of five dozen roses.' Deliver that to Avery Prescott at this hotel.

This is the address and there is someone at the front desk where you can leave them."

She went back to Frankie's room to find Ivy and Frankie giggling all over again as Melody told the story. The kid was good with her impression of Avery's stance and the cold look in her brown eyes.

"Damn, kid. You should be taking drama classes at school. You'd be a great actress," Lola said.

"You think so? Jill said that, too, but I've got all these freckles and red hair. Who'd want me?" Melody asked.

"Think about Nicole Kidman," Frankie said. "I reckon she's gettin' paid a fortune."

"Wow!" Melody grabbed her phone and called Jill.

"So what took you so long to get back in here?" Ivy asked Lola. "This is more fun than the barn was last night."

Lola crawled up in the bed between them so they could see the screen on her phone and brought up the pictures she'd seen as she told them about the rose she'd had sent. "Tessa don't need this right now, so I'm doing my part to get rid of that bitchy woman." She lowered her voice. "I think Branch kissed Tessa already."

"Well, duh!" Ivy said, "We done figured that out, but what you did was genius. Pure damn genius. I'll pay the bill for the flower. Hey, Melody, in one hour if you'll go sit in the lobby to do your visitin' with Jill, I'll give you a hundred-dollar bill."

"Why?" Melody asked.

"I want to know when that bitch leaves the hotel."

Melody said something to Jill and shoved the phone back into her pocket. "Sure thing. I'll do it for free, though, if I can call her Annie one more time and say something about how I see a room full of red roses in her future."

"Lola sent yellow roses," Frankie said.

Melody giggled. "I know, but that way she'll, like, have another one of those fits and, like, leave all in a huff. I think she's a hoot, all hoity-toity actin' like that."

"You can do whatever you like," Ivy said.

"Including tripping her?"

Frankie held up a hand. "Hell, and I do mean hell, no! If you trip her she might break something and not leave. If anything you can help her to her car and wave until she's out of sight."

"Hey, kid, you want to stay in my room tonight and have a big bed all to yourself?" Lola asked.

"Hell . . . I mean heck, no! These two might do something wild and I want to know about it. This is way more fun than smoking pot in the bathroom at school," she said.

Lola started toward the door. "I'm going to take advantage of that tub in my room. Are we going to tell Tessa that she can come back to her own room?"

"You do and I'll kick your ass," Ivy said. "This could be the start of something wonderful, right, Frankie?"

"Yes, ma'am. We'll hope it is for sure," Frankie said.

Tessa plopped down on one end of the sofa. Feet propped on the coffee table, she asked the question that had been on her mind since Avery first stepped out of the elevator.

"What made you fall in love with that woman?"

Branch sat down beside her and covered her small fist with his big one. The rough calluses gave testimony that he didn't spend all his time behind a desk. "My mind shut down my heart," he answered.

"And what does that mean?"

"That my heart said she wasn't the right woman because it didn't feel anything, but my mind said that we were both lawyers and that made us compatible. She was charming when she got her way, and I wanted to be married."

"You wanted to be married?"

"My brothers were happy. My parents are still in love after nearly forty years of marriage. I wanted what they had."

"And now?"

"Still pretty much the same, but I've learned to listen to my heart. And you? What happened with your engagement?"

Tessa splayed open her fingers and wiggled them until his were laced with hers. "It was my fault, according to Matt. He said I wasn't passionate enough, that he needed a woman with fire and sass and that our relationship had lost its pizzazz."

"Bullshit!" Branch whipped his head around to lock gazes with her.

"That's exactly what my mama said, and pretty close to what Frankie said," Tessa whispered. His eyes were the color of the emerald waters just off the beach in the panhandle of Florida. She could always hear the calming sound of the ocean as she let herself go deeper and deeper into them.

"They're right. Anyone who loves like you do has fire and sass. I've seen it. I've felt it. Matt was crazy as an outhouse rat," Branch drawled.

"Thank you!"

His hand moved to tip her chin up. Thick dark lashes rested on his cheeks and his lips found hers in a long, lingering kiss that turned every bone in her body to jelly. She lost herself in the kiss, forgetting everything, everyone, and where she was. None of that mattered and when it ended, she leaned in for more.

He kissed her on the forehead and pulled her into his lap. "Anyone who says you lack passion, darlin', really does have rocks for brains."

"Maybe it's the person I'm with that brings out the passion."

"I hope so," he said. "Now, my darlin', as bad as I hate to say it, we have to break up this party and go to bed."

"Alone?" she asked, not knowing for sure if she was teasing or serious.

"For tonight." He cupped her cheeks in his hands and kissed her on the tip of the nose.

"I know." She untangled her arms from around his neck. "We have to face the rest of the family tomorrow morning, and they'd know if we'd shared a bed."

"By the grins on our faces. Hell, Miz Tess, not even suckin' on a lemon could erase it."

She giggled and hopped up off his lap. "You can have first shower. I'll take a lot longer than you will. Don't use up all the cold water."

Fifteen minutes later he came out of the bathroom wearing nothing but a pair of pajama pants the same color as his eyes. He paused long enough to kiss her on the top of her head as she headed into the bathroom with her arms full of her own nightshirt and toiletries.

"I left you some cold water," he said.

"Thank you." She rolled up on her toes and touched her nose with his. Later she'd give him a proper good-night kiss, after she'd cooled down enough to trust her hormones.

But when she came out of the bathroom, he'd already pulled out the sofa bed and was sleeping. She drank in the sight of him lying there on his side and envied the pillow he'd hugged up to. It would be so easy to fall in love with Branch. But . . . God, she hated buts . . . he wanted children and a family, and what if she wasn't mother material? And maybe this was just a passing fancy for them. Proximity. Not dating since their relationships failed. Too many *buts* that had to be worked out before she could commit, but he did bring out passion she'd never known she had.

Unable to sleep, Tessa curled up in the middle of the big bed with her journal. What day was it? They'd begun to run together, and she hadn't had the privacy or the time to write when they were in the barn.

Day something: This has been one weird weekend. Each feeling listed under the subtitle of emotions, I do believe I have experienced it in the past few days. First there was that angst at having the tire blowout in the pouring-down rain and then the relief at finding a barn where Branch could change it.

Excitement came when we found a bathroom in the tack room in the barn. I couldn't even worry about spiders and/or mice in the barn because of the joy at finding the bathroom with running water.

Frankie and Ivy's attitude toward the catastrophe turned the whole evening into an adventure. If anyone could take lemons and make chocolate cake out of them, those two could do it. I truly want to grow old with the same spirit that they both have.

Safety was the next emotion that I remember feeling and that came when I slept in the loft and later in the stall with Branch. I wasn't afraid of him or the surroundings or the future either time.

Then devastation. I wanted to crawl into the bed, cover my head with a pillow, and go back home when Frankie told me that she was dying. I still have to put it out of my mind or else I'll cry and everyone will wonder why. I gave my word I wouldn't say anything, but it's a burden to carry around and it's sad beyond what words can describe. In the short while I've been with them, I've fallen in love with Frankie, and to know that her time is so short is almost more than I can bear.

The dam let loose in Tessa's soul as she wrote. She scooted her journal up to her knees so that it wouldn't have even more water marks on it and sobbed quietly so she wouldn't wake Branch. Finally, she started writing again.

I want to scream at life. I want to tell it that it cannot take my newly found grandmother who is so full of spit and sass. I want to find a doctor who can make her well or a brand-new medicine that will take the tumor from her brain. I don't want her to go to sleep and never wake up. Life is unfair to give her to me and then take her away so quickly.

Comfort, even though it was small, came when Branch realized something was wrong and simply touched me on the cheek in the produce aisle. I can't tell him or anyone else about Frankie because I'm sworn to secrecy but it's so hard to keep it inside. I feel as if my heart is going to shatter into a thousand pieces.

Then there was anger. Maybe fate sent anger in the form of Avery to me as the last emotion today so that it could override the devastation and the hurt of knowing Frankie's secret. I have never been so mad that I couldn't smart off to a person but I was tonight. Hell, I wasn't that mad at Matt when he told me that I didn't have enough passion in my life for him and he'd fallen out of love with me.

Frankie is a prophet. She said the Laveaus and the Beauchamps had passion. Maybe I only had to rub elbows with the bloodline to get my dose of it, but tonight as I write about my feelings, I realize that not a one of them was lukewarm. My heart has been broken and I can't stop this flood of tears. I've known excitement, comfort, fear . . .

Oh, I forgot to talk about fear. When Branch left with that farmer, my chest tightened up and I couldn't breathe for fear that he'd never come back alive. I've never known such a fear, not in my whole twenty-nine-plus years, or such relief when he did come back with a tire so we could get away from that barn.

So now it's time to go to bed, time to smother my sobs and hope that tomorrow morning Lola doesn't notice my eyes are swollen. I've fallen in love with all of these eccentric people. In one week, I have found family, friends, and Branch. And in a short time I may have to say good-bye to them. I won't think about that. I'll focus on Melody's excitement and the comfort in Branch's touch, the thrill of his kisses, and make the best of the rest of the time I have with these wonderful people.

Chapter Nineteen

Tessa awoke with a start when the alarm went off and slapped the top of the clock, hoping that she hit the snooze button. When it buzzed again immediately, she opened her eyes and realized it was the hotel phone, not the alarm. The numbers on the clock changed as she grabbed for the receiver, dropped it, and had to lean off the bed so far that she almost fell. Her heart stopped and then raced as she brought it to her ear. It had to be Ivy or Frankie, and it was bad news if they were calling Branch's room at three a.m.

She said hello but it came out so raspy that she didn't recognize it as her voice. "Frankie?" she said.

"This is not Frankie and I don't know which one of you I'm talking to, the home-wrecking bitch or you, Branch Thomas, but either one will do. I don't know how in the hell you pulled this off but I'd bet it had something to do with that red-haired kid. She probably hacked into my computer and then pretended to have psychic powers. I could strangle her with my bare hands." The voice on the other end was shrill and angry.

"Who in the hell is this? You must have the wrong number. Oh!" Tessa gasped when she realized it was Avery. She'd expected the call right after they'd gotten to Branch's room, but the phone hadn't rung. And now at three a.m. the hussy woke her up? Those shovels were looking better by the minute.

"I'm talking about the fact that I'm in Houston in my apartment, and I might have lost this battle but the war is still on. You tell Branch Thomas that he knows I'm a poor loser and I have not lost the ability to dish out paybacks. Tell him, too, that the engagement is over so don't come crawling back to me, but I'm hitting his family like a wrecking ball and he's going to regret the day he did this."

Tessa waited for a click or something to say the call had ended, but there was nothing but silence. Branch raised his head and opened one eye. "Is everything all right with Frankie and Ivy?"

"It was Avery. She decided to go home, but she did say for you to remember that she's a poor loser." Tessa laid the receiver back into the cradle.

Branch covered his head with a pillow. "How long until we have to get up?"

"Five hours, max," she answered.

"Good," he said and in less than a minute he was snoring again.

When the real alarm went off at eight, she sat straight up in bed to the aroma of a fresh cup of coffee sitting on the nightstand beside her and the scent of Branch's shaving lotion coming from the bathroom. But there was no Branch anywhere in the room.

He had written a short message on the hotel notepad that said he had gone to help the guy put the tire on the Caddy and he would see her in the dining room for breakfast.

Tessa loaded her plate with two big cinnamon rolls and carried a cup of coffee to the table where the other four ladies were sitting. Branch was nowhere in sight, so he must still be outside with the tire people.

"How'd you sleep? Did that witch give you any grief?" Ivy asked.

"Evidently she decided to go home, because she called at three this morning. Scared the devil out of me. I thought either you or Frankie had"—she paused before she gave away too much—"gotten sick after that night in the barn. I was afraid all that dust and hay had made your lungs worse. Anyway, she was ranting about pulling something off and then she said she was a poor loser and she was really mad about a red-haired kid who was a psychic. Y'all know anything about that?"

Branch waved from across the dining room as he wove through the chairs to the table where they sat. "New tire is on the car and there's a brand-new one in the trunk for a spare. Maybe we won't have to sleep in a barn again. Y'all all rested and ready for the next leg of the journey?"

"We are ready," Lola answered. "Mama says that we'll be stopping in Dalhart at noon and then I found a little town between there and Plainview that's having a festival this afternoon. It starts at two thirty after a parade and there's a carnival and all kinds of vendors with food. Then we're going on to Plainview for the night. I've got reservations already arranged. Tessa says y'all got a call about three this morning and Avery decided to go home."

Branch braced his arms on the back of Tessa's chair. "I thought I'd dreamed that about her calling. I've been watchin' the doors and the dining room, hoping our paths wouldn't cross this morning. I've already had breakfast, so I'm going up to my room and checking on things at the office before we leave. Y'all going to have your bags ready for me at ten sharp?"

Tessa looked up at him. "Mine's already packed and ready by the door."

"This part of the wagon train will have our horses hitched at ten," Frankie said. "We're rested and ready to roll. But this redhead here has to put her things in order, so we'd best haul her up to our room and get busy."

"Speaking of a red-haired psychic?" Tessa glanced over at Melody.

"Later," she mouthed.

Lola didn't budge. "I'll sit with Tessa while she eats. My things are already packed."

"So do you want to tell me about whatever it was that Melody did? I've got a feelin' it's a real good story," Tessa asked.

"That's a story for later. Right now I want to talk to you about something else," Lola answered.

"Okay?" Tessa popped a bite of cinnamon roll into her mouth.

"There's this set of heirloom pearls in our family. Part of the Beauchamp heritage. Mama's grandma inherited them from her grandma and they've come down through the ages. Each mama fastens them around their daughter's neck on her wedding day." Lola stopped and dabbed her eyes with a napkin.

Tessa's stomach tied itself into a pretzel-shaped knot. The lump in her throat refused to go down no matter how much coffee she guzzled. Lola had found out that Frankie had offered her the pearls and it had upset her and now what was Tessa to do?

"I've been so stubborn, Tessa," Lola finally went on. "I've been seeing a man, Hank is his name, and he's gotten down on one knee and proposed to me more than half a dozen times and I always turn him down. I'm not good enough for him, but he tells me that I'm his soul mate. I don't think Ivy has much more time on this earth and I don't want her to die and not know that I'm settled and happy at last even if I am staring at that big five-oh mark in a couple of years."

"So"—Tessa was afraid to breathe—"you are going to get married?"

Lola smiled and nodded. "I told Hank last night that I'd marry him but I don't want anything big or flashy. Just him and me and Inez and Mama and Ivy and you. Maybe Melody since she's kind of won my heart on this trip and Branch and the justice of the peace."

"Does he live in Boomtown?" Tessa asked.

"He's Inez's brother and he's fifteen years older than me. And I'm not sure Mama's going to like the idea, but it will mean a lot to her to put those pearls on me and see me happy. Truth is, I don't know how long she'll last after Ivy is gone, and I should've done this a long time ago."

Tessa pushed the last cinnamon roll to the middle of the table. "But you were afraid it would turn out like the first one. You had to be sure Hank wouldn't leave you, right?"

Lola pinched off a bite and put it in her mouth, chewing slowly and swallowing before she spoke again. "I don't know how I ever gave birth to a smart kid like you. It's probably more environmental than it is genetic, but thank you."

Tessa handed Lola her coffee cup. "You'll need a drink after that sticky stuff. You are going to make Frankie very happy. Now, tell me about these pearls?"

Lola took a sip and handed it back. "They're just a strand of aged pearls. Rumor had it Mama's grandma's ancestor was a Louisiana Cajun fisherman. He started saving pearls he found when he was a kid on his father's fishing boat. He kept every one of them and when his only daughter got married, he had them strung for her as a wedding gift with the instructions that she was to pass them down to her firstborn daughter on her wedding day. I want her to put them on me when Hank and I get married, and it would be sad if Ivy wasn't there."

"I think it will, but why did you feel the need to tell me?" Tessa removed her hands and went back to eating.

"Because"—Lola took a deep breath—"it would be . . . my job . . . my honor"—she stumbled over the words—"then I would have earned the right to pass them on to you when you get married. I know Sophie raised you and you might want to wear something of hers on that day, so you can refuse."

Tessa laid her fork down and reached for both of Lola's hands, holding them tightly in hers. "I would love to wear the pearls, and it would make me happy if you would put them on me on that day."

"Thank you," Lola said. "Sometime today I'm going to tell Mama. We're planning on having the wedding as soon as it can be arranged when we get home."

"And, Lola, you are right. Ivy told me she's only got a few months left, so the sooner, the better," Tessa said.

"I knew it." Lola wiped at her eyes with a paper napkin. "I could feel something wasn't right down deep in my bones."

Mollybedamned rolled out of the parking lot at exactly ten fifteen that morning. A few puffy white clouds dotted the sky and it was about ten degrees cooler than it had been the other mornings, which made for a wonderful morning.

"Where's your knitting?" Tessa asked about thirty minutes after they'd gotten out on the road.

"In the trunk."

"Did you forget it?" Ivy asked.

Lola twisted around in the seat so she could see her mother and Ivy. "No, I do believe I'm cured, or I will be when I tell y'all something."

"Spit it out," Ivy said. "If saying something will cure you of that incessant humming and them clickin' needles, then spit the damn words out."

"Mama, I want you to put the pearls on me," Lola said.

Frankie smiled but shook her head. "You know the rule. You don't get those pearls unless it's your wedding day. Have you finally accepted Hank's proposal? What is this? About the tenth one?"

Lola's expression was pure shock. "How long have you known?"

Frankie poked Ivy on the arm. "How long?"

Ivy chuckled and readjusted her nose tubes. "Don't make me laugh. We've known since the first time he proposed. He's a good man. Maybe not in your league financially, but then money ain't nothin' but dirty paper with dead presidents' pictures on it so that don't matter. I hear that since he's retired from the postal service that he wants to do some travelin'. That what you got in mind?"

"I've been scared to death to tell y'all," Lola said.

Frankie undid her seat belt and slid forward so she could hug Lola. "I've been in the same boat about tellin' you because after that first time when I interfered and made such a mess of it, I swore to God I'd never say another word about your love life. But I'll be happy to put the pearls on you for your wedding day and then you can put them on Tessa someday, right?"

Lola twisted around in the seat to kiss her mother on the cheek. "That's the only way she'll get them."

Frankie winked at Tessa. "You okay with that?"

"Yes, ma'am, I sure am."

"Okay, then, when is the wedding?" Ivy asked.

"Soon as we get home. We don't want anything big or fancy. Just a few people and a justice of the peace."

Frankie cut her off. "And a preacher, not a justice of the peace. I don't care if you wear a big white dress or blue jeans but I want it done by a real preacher so that it will be recorded up in heaven."

"Mama, it will be recorded at the courthouse," Lola argued.

"A preacher or no pearls," Frankie said.

"Then a preacher it is." Lola smiled.

"Halle-damn-lujah!" Ivy said. "This really has been the best trip ever."

"What?" Melody jerked the earbuds from her ears. "What did I miss? Why is everyone smiling so big? Did something more happen with that Avery witch?"

"Lola is getting married," Frankie yelled and waved her arms in the air.

Ivy followed suit and hollered. "We're having a wedding soon as we get home. Halle-damn-lujah a second time around!"

Melody stuck hers up and joined the old ladies. "And I'm invited, right, Lola?"

"Of course," Lola answered. "And you're coming, too, Branch."

"On or off the clock, Frankie?" Branch teased.

"If she wants you there, you can bill me for that hour, but not another minute more," Frankie said.

"Thank God that's over!" Tessa said softly. "I was afraid Frankie might stroke out."

"Why?"

"With happiness," Tessa replied.

"She and Ivy are pretty wily old gals. Maybe they planned this journey to get Lola away from Hank so she'd realize that she was in love with him," Branch said.

"I can't believe they knew this whole time. I've agonized over telling them," Lola said.

"And now they have a wedding to plan. It might be the very thing to help Ivy hang on longer," Tessa said.

ᔓ

The festival was in a town that had a post office, two churches, a convenience store with one gas pump, and maybe half a dozen houses. The banner stretched across the street welcomed everyone to the annual cotton festival.

Two men in yellow vests were directing traffic to an open lot back behind the convenience store for parking or else around town if they were passing through. Branch held up traffic long enough to let the ladies out of the car before he drove to the back of the lot and parked Mollybedamned in a less congested area.

"I'll keep a close eye on that beauty for you. My name is Cletus. Who are you?" one of the yellow-vested elderly men said. "Too bad y'all didn't pull into town an hour ago. We'd have loved to have had it in our parade."

"Thank you. I'm Branch Thomas, and we're only passing through. The ladies thought they'd like to enjoy the festival," Branch said. "So evidently y'all do a little cotton farmin' in this part of the state?"

"Used to. In the past five years it ain't done too good for us, not with irrigation, but we still like to have our festival. It's kind of like old home week when all the folks that was raised up around here come on back and visit. We got a chili cook-off at the Baptist church and a baked goods sale goin' on across the street at the Church of Christ." The old guy brought out a package of cigarettes and offered Branch one.

Branch waved it away. "Thanks, but I never got started on that habit."

"Smart man." Cletus lit up an unfiltered Camel. "Y'all done missed the oldest person in town, Oma Ray Smith, goin' out in the cotton field and pickin' the first boll. She's ninety-nine this week and she remembers pickin' cotton when she was a kid. Looks like I got another customer here, but don't you worry none, I'll park him far enough away from your Caddy that no doors will be scratchin' up that pretty red paint."

"Appreciate it," Branch said. "We probably won't be here but a couple of hours."

"Go on and have fun. Me, I'm going to stand here and drink in her beauty while I enjoy this smoke," Cletus said.

Branch found Ivy and Frankie sitting on a bench in the shade of the post office. Two elderly ladies had pulled up lawn chairs beside them and they were talking about cotton growing and how they'd all grown up knowing how to pull bolls and pick cotton both.

Frankie grabbed his wrist. "We was waitin' on you. The other three went on to the carnival over there across the street. Me and Ivy don't care nothin' about that wild-lookin' swing thing, but we do want some cotton candy and a snow cone."

Ivy made introductions. "This here is our driver, Branch Thomas, and this is our new friends, Maybelle and Earnestine, Branch."

Branch tipped his cowboy hat and drawled, "Pleasure to meet you lovely ladies."

"Oh, Maybelle, he is charmin', ain't he?" Earnestine fanned her face with the back of her hand.

"If only we was forty years younger," Maybelle said.

He grinned and took Blister's leash from Ivy. "Here, let me take care of the pup. You concentrate on breathing."

"They're jealous," Ivy told him they made their way through the crowd.

"They should be. I'm with the two best-lookin' women here," Branch teased.

Frankie slapped him playfully on the arm. "We're talkin' about the ladies over there, not the old men givin' us the eye. And don't you be butterin' us up so you can bill me for the couple of hours we're stopping here. This is off the books for you."

Branch dropped a kiss on the top of Frankie's head. "I signed out when I parked Mollybedamned. If you'll tell me what y'all did last night to make Avery leave I might stay off the books until tomorrow morning."

Ivy shrugged and changed the subject. "Look, Frankie, there's that pistol-shootin' thing. I bet you could win one of them big polar bears."

"What would we do with the thing if we did win it?" Frankie asked.

"We could let Branch give it to Maybelle and Earnestine. It would make their day and it would show that cocky little feller hawkin' about his booth that we might be old but we can still shoot the eyes out of a rattlesnake at twenty yards."

Branch chuckled. "Those things are always rigged with bad sights on the guns."

"We know that!" Ivy and Frankie said in unison.

Ten minutes later he carried two big polar bears across the street to give to the ladies sitting in the lawn chairs. He got hugs from both of them and didn't have the heart to tell them that he hadn't won the damn things.

He'd barely made it to the cotton candy booth when Melody came running up from the other side of the lot. "Aunt Ivy, I want to get a henna tattoo. Can I please? Please? Please?"

"What in the hell is a henna tattoo?" Ivy had a ten-dollar bill in her hand, waving it in the air so that Frankie couldn't pay for the cotton candy.

Melody talked so fast that Branch could barely understand her. "It's one that only lasts a month, and there are no needles involved. And I want a butterfly on my shoulder and it costs twenty dollars and please, please, please."

"You pull Blister for me while I eat my warm cotton candy and we'll go look at them. Frankie, you think me and you should get us a tattoo?" Ivy handed off the first cone to her friend and paid the lady for both of them.

Frankie bit off a chunk of the spun sugar. "Well, hell, yeah, if there ain't no needles goin' to stick me. I'm scared to death of needles or pain but if it's painted on, why the hell not."

"Oh. My. God. Y'all aren't serious, are you?" Melody dropped Blister's leash.

"Hell, yes, we're serious. If you can get one, then by damn I'm gettin' one and so is Branch." Ivy stopped until Melody picked up the leash. "It's still nice and warm like when we were teenagers. Not all bunched up in a sack and cold as clabber."

"I'm not getting a tattoo of any kind," Branch declared.

"If you don't, Melody can't have her butterfly," Frankie said.

"You are shittin' me," Branch said.

"Nope, not one bit." Frankie grinned.

Melody danced around him. "Please, Branch. I so want to go back to school with a tat."

"It'll be worn off in three weeks," he said.

"I'll be careful and cover it up when I shower and I'll take a selfie with it tonight so Jill can show everyone how rad I am and you've got to get one so I can have my butterfly." She put her hands up in a prayerful begging gesture. "And I'll tattle on both of these old gals about what happened with Avery last night if you'll get one."

"Hey, now," Ivy protested.

"I did not promise not to tell," Melody said loudly. "Please, Branch!"

"What did I ever do to make you hate me, Frankie Laveau?" he groaned. "I've taken care of Mollybedamned and I haven't billed you for a single hour that I haven't worked."

Frankie raised a shoulder. "It's your turn to deal with a teenager. Me and Ivy are getting a tattoo. You and Tessa could get matching ones. Matter of fact, you and Tessa both have to get them and they have to match."

"Frankie!" Ivy shook her finger.

"Okay, then." Frankie's eyes twinkled. "I'll rephrase it. You and Tessa have to get one or this child can't have one. And I still want a snow cone and maybe an Indian taco before I leave this place, so you got until me and Ivy get finished with our tats and the rest of our food to decide. Until then, Melody, you don't leave his side."

"You are wicked," Branch said.

Frankie's finger shot up to an inch from his nose. "And don't you never forget it."

Melody grabbed his arm and pulled him toward the tattoo booth with hundreds of designs plastered all around the outside of the small kiosk. Lola was sitting in the chair and the artist was working on a set of interlocked wedding rings on her left shoulder.

"What do you think, Mama?" she asked. "Think I should buy a little ivory halter dress to show them off at the wedding?"

"Sounds like a plan to me. I'm having your name put on one shoulder and Tessa's on the other," Frankie said. "And I want them connected with a scrolling line. I'll wear strapless to the wedding so everyone can see it."

"Good God! Are you serious?" Ivy huffed. "We've got too much baggy cellulite on our arms to wear anything strapless. Put the damn thing on your ankle. You still got good ankles."

"That sounds like a wonderful idea, and I might go barefoot to the wedding so everyone will see my new tattoo." Frankie held out her foot. "I'm next in line and Ivy is right behind me. What are you gettin', Ivy?"

"A bunny on my left ankle and a rose on the other," she said without hesitation.

"I like it." Frankie nodded.

"Branch?" Melody looked up at him and batted her eyelashes.

He shook his head and she went to Tessa, laid her head on her shoulder, and asked, "Do you want to know the whole story about last night? If you talk Branch into getting matching tats with you, then I'll tell you, but if you don't, you will never know."

"That's blackmail," Branch said.

Melody stepped back and stomped her foot. "I'm not telling and neither is anyone else if y'all don't, like, get a tat so I can have one. And believe me, it's a real good story that y'all would love, but if you, like, don't care, then keep your bodies all pure and, like, tat-free forever. But if you do want to hear it, then you're, like, going to have to step up to the plate."

"Why do we have to get one?" Tessa asked.

"If y'all don't get one, then Aunt Ivy and Frankie won't let me have that butterfly right there on my shoulder or on my wrist, either one." Melody pointed. "And I want it so bad."

"Well, why didn't you say so? Lola, let me see your ankle. I want that happiness sign put on the top of my foot. Branch?"

"Oh, all right. I'll get the same one put on my foot. At least I can cover it up with my cowboy boots," he said.

"Yes! Yes!" Melody pumped her fist in the air and did a happy dance all around the booth. "This is so exciting. I love this trip. Love it, love it."

"What about when we get out in the boonies again and you have no reception?" Branch asked.

"I'll still have the pictures of me with, like, a rad tat and it's going to be, like, so cool because, like, not a one of those cheerleaders will have one," Melody squealed.

"If you take the word *like* out of her vocabulary and cut off her thumbs, she'd go insane," Ivy said.

"Maybe but I'd still, like, have, like, the coolest tattoo in the mental institution," Melody said. "Can I be next?"

"Nope, not until Branch and Tessa get theirs done so they won't back out," Frankie said.

From the cotton festival to the hotel in Plainview, Melody stayed true to her word and told them the story of Avery and what had happened the night before. The teenager's version was told with lots of drama, complete with voices mimicking Frankie, Ivy, and Avery.

Tessa laughed until her face hurt and when the story ended with the part about the single rose, she said, "This tat was so worth it, wasn't it, Branch? You are all wicked and I love the whole lot of you."

Branch's expression changed from happy to sad in a split second. "Y'all don't know that woman. She will get even, and it won't be nice."

"She might try, but there's five of us," Frankie said. "And believe me, old age and enough money trumps youth and a pretty face any day of the week. She'd best be careful with her threats or she might find herself working pro bono in a third world country."

"Frankie Laveau!" Ivy scolded.

"I swear to God with one hand on the Good Book and the other raised to heaven that she'd better back off or I'll take care of her sorry ass. I don't mind spending the rest of my life in prison." Frankie caught Tessa's eye in the rearview mirror and gave her another wink. "Now let's talk about our tats. I love mine and I want you to take a picture of it with your phone, Lola, and send it to Inez."

"I've got, like, the coolest aunts in the whole world," Melody said. "Jill agrees with me. I took a picture of all y'all's tats already and sent them to her."

Tessa held her foot up and looked at the tat. "My mama is going to freak out."

A wide grin erased the sadness in Branch's eyes. "I'm not tellin' my family. I intend to keep it covered up until it's gone."

Lola undid her seat belt and whipped around so she could see her mother when she talked to her. "Hank says he loves it and he'll go get a real one like it with our names engraved inside the wedding bands when we're on our honeymoon. Mama, he says we're taking a travel trailer and we won't come back for three or four months. You going to be okay with that?"

Frankie nodded and patted her on the shoulder. "Of course, honey. I'll be fine with it. Y'all can leave anytime after the middle of October. By then I'll be more than okay with it. And think how pretty the trees will be up in Vermont and those places by then. Oh, and the antiques abound in that part of the country, so you can ship stuff home to Inez every day."

Frankie's voice probably sounded perfectly normal to everyone else, but Tessa heard the hauntingly sad undertones. She quickly wiped away a tear. "Damn bug got in my eye."

"Ignorant things ain't got a lick of sense. One of them dog-assed gnats flew into mine, too," Frankie said. "Old as I am, the dumb thing ought to know that I'm all dried up and there ain't no drinkin' water in there for him."

Branch followed Lola's directions when they reached the Plainview city limits sign and pulled Mollybedamned into the hotel parking lot without a single problem.

He whistled all the way back to the trunk. "Hey, Lola, I'm glad you made reservations. I bet lots of those folks at the cotton festival stay in Plainview. It's the nearest place for hotels."

"That's what I figured, too, and I damn sure don't want to sleep in a barn the night I get formally engaged," Lola said.

"Me, either. All that hay might, like, mess up my tat," Melody said.

Frankie and Ivy were slow getting out of the car, so Tessa bailed out and helped with Blister, then held on to Ivy's arm on the way inside the big double doors that slid apart when they stepped up to them.

"Fancy things like doors that know when to open and keys that look like credit cards. I love all of it," Ivy huffed. "I think I overdid it a little at the carnival. I'm glad we brought all those Indian tacos home for supper and I didn't try to eat one of them, too. But I think maybe me and Frankie both need a nap before we eat. Reckon you could take Melody with you? Her chatterin' drives me up the walls when I'm tired, and she's so wound up about that tattoo and the wedding. I swear she and Jill have talked it to death, but she'll be all up in it again soon as we get to our room."

"Of course," Tessa said.

"I'll be okay in the morning but between me and you, I don't reckon I'll make it the whole month. Frankie is failing, too. Don't worry. She told me that you know," Ivy said softly. "If we can make it until Friday, our room will be ready and we can go on to Beaumont."

"We can slow down," Tessa said.

"Hell, no! We'll go full speed ahead until they tell us everything is in order. We'll have plenty of time to rest then and we can spend our last days talkin' about how much fun we've had our whole lives, but this trip, oh, this is the icing on the cake, Tessa."

"Thank you." Tessa's eyes welled up again.

"No, darlin', thank *you*. Lola is doing so much better with you around and Frankie, well, there ain't enough words."

ꟹ

Tessa picked up her journal that evening and thought back over what had happened since she last wrote in it. Entries were getting easier and she found that she made mental notes through the day to write about that evening. Someday when she was as old as Frankie, she'd drag out her journal and the things she'd written on her laptop and remember the way that one month in the fall just before she was thirty changed her whole outlook on life.

Day happiness: The days are going by fast and suddenly the calendar isn't as important as the hours in the day or even the minutes. So today I'm dubbing happiness for many reasons. We found the cotton festival in a little town and we went to a carnival where Frankie won two huge stuffed bears. There was no way we could bring them with us in Mollybedamned, so she gave them to a couple of little elderly ladies and they thought Branch won them special for them. It was a glorious day.

We ate cotton candy and got tattoos. Not real tats but henna ones that will fade or be washed away in a few weeks but I felt a little surge of rebellion and craziness at having even that on my body. Branch and I got symbols for happiness and there's a bit of rebellion in my heart when I look at it. That silly Melody has already taken pictures of them and sent them to her friend.

Lola and Hank are getting married and she says she's cured from knitting. Melody is ecstatic with her tat. Frankie and Ivy think it's a lark. Branch and I have matching ones and that seems to draw us closer together. And Lola got one across her shoulders that announces her love for Hank. If happiness could be contained in a car, Mollybedamned would be overflowing today.

I felt a little apprehensive and strange that the wedding pearls would skip a generation, so there's another thing to be glad about. Lola will wear them like she should and then someday they will be passed on down to me. Who would have thought I'd wind up with my wedding pearls from this trip? Or that I'd be willing to let my tattoo mama put them on me on the day of my wedding? Lord, I hope

Mama will be okay with that. Or worse yet, Maw-Maw! My Cajun grandmother can be a handful. I suppose I should call her and tell her about this whole trip.

But I won't think about that now, because I don't want any negative thoughts to ruin my happiness today.

Chapter Twenty

"Thought this old fart was never going to wake up," Ivy said the next morning when they were having breakfast in the hotel dining room. "I've got Blister and we don't need to refill his mama until the weekend, so I can always loan her a little oxygen if she needs it to wake up."

Tessa's heart stopped and her breath caught in her chest. What would happen if Frankie didn't wake up on the trip and she had to tell Lola? She couldn't begin to think about the horror of such a thing.

"Oh, hush." Frankie waggled a finger at Ivy. "All I needed was a good strong cup of coffee. Sit down here and get out your phone, Lola. I've looked at my map and we're staying in Abilene tonight. So book us a room. Looks like rain, so we'll have to keep the top up today."

Branch pointed at Lola. "And do not take any back roads to check out garage sales?"

"Never again," Lola answered. "But Mama, it's only a little more than a hundred miles to Abilene. If we leave at ten, we'll be there at noon and we can't check in until two."

A tired smile was all Frankie could muster that morning. "We've decided since it's raining to stay here until noon. That's the check-out time anyway, and then we're going to find a restaurant right here in town for dinner. We're thinking a pizza buffet would be fun today. And then we'll head toward Abilene."

"Okay, you are navigatin' this boat. I'll make some arrangements. Care to tell me where we might stop tomorrow night, and I'll go on and get the reservations made there while I'm at it," Lola said.

"Fort Worth. We want to go to the stockyards and to a bar with loud music and dancing," Frankie said.

Clapping her hands and wiggling her butt in the chair dislocated Ivy's nose tubes and she had to fix them. "That's why we've decided to go easy today and tomorrow. We want to be ready to do some serious partying."

"I thought we were going to circle the whole state of Texas," Lola said.

"So did we, but our old bones are telling us that they're getting tired so we're going to start slowly heading for home. We've got a few more things we want to do on the way but we're probably looking at getting back to our stomping grounds toward the end of the week," Frankie said.

Melody laid the back of her hand on her forehead, rolled her eyes, and groaned. "No, no, no! This cannot be so. Please let me stay at your house, Aunt Ivy. I'll do whatever you say if I don't have to go to detention for, like, two whole weeks."

One corner of Ivy's mouth turned up in half a smile as she slung an arm around the girl. "I've talked to the judge and we've made a new plan. He's going to let you go back to your regular school classes, but there is a condition. You have to go to this retirement home in Beaumont for eight hours on Saturdays and from two to five on Sunday afternoons to do your community service.

Your mother will drive you there and pick you up since you won't be allowed to drive until you are off your probation. You're going to read mail to little old ladies or do whatever you can to make them feel special."

The hand came down and Melody's eyes fixed on Ivy as if she was afraid to blink. "Are you joking? You mean I get to go to school with Jill, like, next Monday morning?"

"I, like, mean, like, you, like, get to go to, like, school with, like, Jill, like, next, like, Monday morning," Ivy said. "And if she wants to do volunteer work at the retirement place, she can come with you on weekends."

Melody giggled. "You don't do the *like* business right, Aunt Ivy. I'm going out in the lobby so I can call Jill and tell her all about this new plan, and then I'm going to do homework for the rest of this week." She started out of the dining room. "My tat will definitely still look good next Monday. Life is good."

"Yes, it is." Frankie sighed. "A nap does sound good. We need to rest up if we're going to put on our boots and go line dancin' on Wednesday night."

"Yep." Ivy eased out of the chair and pulled Blister behind her as the two of them put their heads together and giggled all the way to the elevator doors.

Lola hugged Tessa. It was quick but spontaneous, and Tessa hugged Lola back.

"Tessa, did you see Mama's eyes when I asked her if she'd put the pearls on me for my wedding? I thought she was going to cry," Lola said.

"It means a lot to her. She really does want you to be happy," Tessa answered.

"See y'all later." Lola picked up her patchwork hobo purse and hurried to catch the elevator before the doors closed.

"I thought the old gals were getting pretty tired last night. Looked to me like they were dragging when we went to their room for supper," Branch said.

Tessa stole the last bite of cinnamon roll from his plate. "You may have to line dance with Blister in your arms so that Ivy can do some boot scootin'."

"Hey, that was mine," he protested.

"There are lots more on the bar."

"Are you telling me that you want another one, too, but you are too lazy to get up and go get it?" he asked.

"I'm telling you that it's been a long time since I had an antiawkward kiss, and if I go get us each one then I'd probably trip and fall and they'd land in that woman's cleavage sitting closest to the bar." She flirted and enjoyed it. "She's so much bigger than me that she'd probably jump up out of that chair and whip my scrawny ass."

"In that case, I'll go get another plateful. But darlin', your ass is not a bit scrawny."

"And don't look at the lady's cleavage," she said.

"Jealous?" Branch turned and asked over his shoulder.

Tessa nodded. "Damn straight, and I sure don't want her to get my antiawkward kiss. I dropped my laptop this morning. Thank goodness it landed on the bed. Then I fell over nothing but air and landed facedown on the sofa in our suite."

"Wow! You really are running low on preventative, aren't you?" He grinned.

"Yes, I am." She smiled up at him.

His butt filled out those tight-fitting jeans just right that morning. The swagger in his step as he made his way across the dining area proved that Branch was one of those men that women's eyes gravitate toward when they walk into a room. No wonder Avery wanted a second chance.

A vision came from nowhere of Frankie all dressed up with her diamonds on her fingers and her gray hair styled just-so, and she was lying in a gorgeous, shiny red coffin. And in the same room, there was Ivy in a matching casket, all laid out in a red outfit with enough bling on it to rival all the stars in the sky.

She wiped away a tear. Two weeks ago she hadn't even known these people, and now they had wrapped tendrils around her heart that would never break. She shook the picture from her head and tried to focus on Branch as he brought four big cinnamon rolls and two cups of fresh coffee on a tray toward their table.

"What happened? I was only gone a minute and you have tears in your eyes." He set the tray down and moved his chair close to hers and kissed her on the forehead. "You didn't get a phone call with bad news, did you?"

"No, I got a picture in my head of Ivy and Frankie's funeral. How can I care so much after only a couple of weeks?" She captured his hand with hers and held it to her cheek.

"They're family," he said.

"Not Ivy or Melody or you."

"Sometimes family doesn't share a bloodline. Think about your mama and daddy. And I hope I'm not family, because if I am I've been committing incest in my dreams." He kissed her softly. "Maybe that will hold you until we can get into the elevator . . . alone."

"You dream about me?" She was utterly flabbergasted.

He slipped an empty plate in front of her and shifted a cinnamon roll over to it. "Every night since I first walked into your travel agency."

"Are you teasing me?"

He picked up a plastic fork, cut off a piece of the sweet roll, and fed it to her. "I'm not teasing, Tessa. We knew Ivy wasn't well when we started out, but for you to dream about Frankie, too. I wonder what that means. Do you know something I don't?"

"Grandmother–granddaughter confidentiality is as binding as lawyer–client, I do believe." She took the fork from him and talked between bites.

"Is it her lungs? She smokes as much as or more than Ivy."

She changed the subject abruptly. "Isn't that painting up there on the wall pretty?"

He frowned. "What if I stop giving you your anticlumsy kisses?"

"I've been a klutz all my life. I reckon I could continue to live with my ailment."

The frown deepened, drawing his dark brows together. "If she's sick, then my dad will know and I'll ask him."

"That's between you and him and Frankie and I have nothing to do with that business, and besides, I might be yanking your chain." She smiled.

"Only you aren't. I can read your eyes, Tessa."

"What are you going to do with two weeks' vacation? Go back to work or take a real trip somewhere?" She tried changing the subject again.

Branch leaned over and nuzzled her neck. "Tell me what's going on."

"Answer my question. What are you going to do?" she asked.

"I'm going to ranch for two weeks and enjoy every minute of it. What about you?" He kissed her earlobe.

"I'm staying in Boomtown and using every day of it to be near Frankie and Lola," she said.

"Want to take a day and tour my ranch?"

"I'd love to. I love ranchin'," she said.

"But you live in town. How do you know you love ranchin'?"

"My grandmother on Daddy's side still has a little spread up between Jeanerette and New Iberia." If she didn't get some distance between them, she was going to lead him up to his bedroom and fall into bed with him. "She has chickens and a couple of hogs and maybe ten head of cattle. They used to have more, but when Paw-Paw died she sized it down to what she could manage." She inched away and picked up her coffee. "She's a salty old girl, a lot like Ivy, but she smokes a pipe rather than cigarettes and she likes wine instead of liquor. Makes all kinds of wine herself. Blackberry, wild cherry, and dandelion wine."

He ate the first bite of his cinnamon roll. "I can't believe a city girl like you likes country life. What's your favorite part?"

She didn't need to think about the answer one bit. "Baby lambs. Maw-Maw is old-school Cajun, and she has a couple of old ewes that produce little lambs every spring. I love watching them romp and play in the pasture."

"I'd love to meet your maw-maw someday. She sounds like a pretty awesome lady," Branch said.

"I'll take you to see her if you are brave enough."

Branch finished his second cinnamon roll. "How many of your previous boyfriends were brave enough?"

She shook her head. "Not a single one. Maw-Maw is a hell of a lot more than a force. She's more like a tornado and a hurricane combined and she will grill you for hours about your intentions because the only reason a girl takes her feller to see a Cajun grandmother is because she is entertaining ideas of bringing him into the family. So it's up to you to call the shots about when you want to meet her."

"Is that a proposal?" Branch laughed.

Tessa bit her lip. She'd sure gotten his mind off the Frankie issue in a hurry. "No, sir! Maw-Maw would have my hide for a stunt like that. In her world the man takes on that job, not the woman. What are you going to do with your free morning?"

"I need to call my dad and see if he knows anything about Frankie's health," he said. "Gotcha! I knew you were steering me away from that but I want to know."

"You don't play fair," she protested as she pushed her chair back. "I'm going to put on my runnin' shoes and do laps around this hotel."

"You don't play fair, either, and soon as I talk to my dad, I'll catch up with you. I feel sluggish from lack of exercise." He rose and with one hand on her back guided her to the elevator.

"Lucky us," he drawled as soon as the doors closed. "We don't have to share."

She reached over and pushed the button to stop the elevator, wrapped her arms around his neck and tiptoed, her eyes locked with his. He bent slightly at the knees and his lips met hers, tongues doing a mating dance that sent her hormones into overdrive.

"Wow! That should cure you for a week," he said hoarsely when she took a step back and hit the button to put the elevator back in motion.

"I hope not." She smiled.

Chapter Twenty-One

After a buffet pizza lunch and a two-hour ride in drizzling rain, they stopped at yet another hotel. They'd all begun to look alike to Tessa: walk through the doors into the lobby to a smiling person who was all too glad to take that piece of platinum-colored plastic from Branch's hands. Elevators either around the corner or straight ahead. Dining room usually to the left, and not a nickel's worth of difference in the rooms. Swimming pool and exercise room somewhere on the first floor. Brass luggage carts in a little foyer between the outside door and the one that opened into the hotel lobby.

That Tuesday afternoon, she noticed that Frankie was already yawning when the clerk handed them the room keys. Melody had confided that both the old gals had gone back to bed after breakfast and slept until after eleven o'clock. It was getting serious when a sixteen-year-old kid interested in texting and selfies was worried about her roommates.

After Branch unloaded Tessa's and Lola's suitcases in the room right next to Frankie and Ivy's, Lola fell backward on the bed and sighed. "I'm ready to be home. I talked to Hank and we're going to get married next week. That'll give Ivy and Mama time to rest up a bit. I'm afraid Ivy is going to go downhill fast, and she needs to be there the day Mama puts the pearls on me for the wedding. I'd feel horrible if she wasn't, and Hank has been ready for this for years."

"Sounds like a plan to me," Tessa said.

"Would you stand up with me and be my maid of honor? You can say no and I can ask Inez, but I'd sure like it if you'd do that for me. I'm too old for a bachelorette party so you wouldn't have to do anything but be there with me," Lola asked.

Tessa fell back on the bed beside Lola and laced her fingers in her birth mother's. "I'd be honored. So when exactly is the day?"

"A week from Saturday. I told Mama this morning after breakfast and she was really happy with it. She told me that you'd agreed to stay on until your vacation is up, so maybe we could go shopping next week, get our nails done and our hair and all that girly stuff. I need to find a dress and I'd appreciate your help. Nothing long and flowing or I'll fall over my own feet." She smiled.

Tessa squeezed her hand. "I see flowing but midcalf length and maybe some baby rosebuds wound into a circlet for your hair."

"You see me as a flower child, don't you?" Lola squeezed her hand.

"Yes, I do, and I love the picture in my head. Free and unburdened of all the conventional cares of the world." Tessa turned her head to face her.

Lola looked right into Tessa's eyes. "I never thought I'd be here like this with you, but I'm so glad that it's happened."

"I never thought I'd meet you at all."

"Did it bother you, being adopted?"

Tessa turned back to stare at the ceiling. "Being clumsy bothered me but being adopted, that wasn't any big thing. Clint was adopted, too. We figured we were special."

"So your best friend and cousin is also adopted?"

It was a strange feeling, but Tessa was totally comfortable talking about this now with Lola. "Yes, his mother and mine are sisters and we're the only two grandchildren on that side. But my daddy has six siblings, so there are lots of cousins on that side. Most of them have been brought up in the country and are a lot more Cajun than I am."

"I'm glad you grew up in a big family and that you weren't the only adopted kid," Lola said. "But I'm happy, too, that you've come into my life at this time."

"Me, too," Tessa said.

When the phone rang beside the bed, Tessa let go of Lola's hand and picked up the receiver. "Hello," she said.

"Meet me in the exercise room in ten minutes? Wear your swimsuit and we'll go from there to the hot tub," Branch said.

Lola flicked her wrist in a go-on gesture. "If that is Branch, get on out of here. I'm going to discuss wedding plans with Hank and Inez."

Tessa wanted to tell Lola that her plans would change drastically and it would probably be in a glorified, exclusive nursing home, not in the living room of the lovely home in Boomtown. But she'd been sworn to secrecy and besides, she could not burst Lola's happy bubble. She loved her too much to do that—not as a mother, but as a good friend.

"I bet I can beat you there," Tessa told Branch.

"Last one on a bike owes the other one a coke out of the vending machine."

"I'd rather have a beer when we go out to get supper stuff," she said.

"Then you'd best hurry or you'll be buying me a beer."

She slammed down the phone and raced to her suitcase, threw things out on the sofa, and stripped down to her bare skin right there in front of Lola. In less than two minutes she was wearing her swimsuit with an oversize T-shirt over the top, had tucked her key card into her shoe, and was on her way out.

"I never thought I'd see the day that you'd leave things in a mess." Lola laughed.

"I've got a bet with Branch and I like cold beer."

"Then fly like a butterfly." Lola laughed.

Tessa ran barefoot to the elevator. The doors were closing when a big hand slipped between them and pushed. And there was Branch, carrying his running shoes like she did and wearing nothing but baggy swim trunks riding low on his hips and a dazzling smile.

She couldn't keep her eyes off the perfect amount of soft black hair traveling from his chest to his ripped abs to his belly button and down into his trunks. She was glad she had a shoe in each hand or she might have lost all her willpower and run her fingers through it to see if it was as soft as it looked.

He pushed a strand of hair back behind her ear. "You are so damn cute in that T-shirt, but darlin', it's wrong side out."

She whipped around and kissed him on the tip of his nose. Two could play the flirting game. She might be rusty, but she wasn't dead. "Maybe I'm wearing it like this on purpose so you'll notice me."

"Oh, honey." His shoes hit the elevator floor with a thud. "I notice everything about you every day."

"Oh, yeah? What was I wearing earlier?"

"A gorgeous smile," he said.

"And?"

He raised a finger. "And jean shorts with an orange tank top and a black bra with one strap that peeked through all day to entice me." And a second finger as he counted off what she wore that day. "Perfume that sent my senses reeling, something tropical smelling in your hair." A third finger shot up. "And cute little brown sandals that showed off your new happiness tattoo on the top of your foot and coral lipstick." The elevator doors slid open and he picked up his shoes. "Anything else you want to know?"

"I think that about covers it," she answered with a sly grin.

The fitness room was right around the corner and had a sign on the door reminding people that they were not to use the equipment without proper footwear—no flip-flops or backless sandals of any kind—and they were to use it at their own risk because the hotel was not responsible for accidents.

"Do you think we need to sign an affidavit in blood?" He held the door for her.

"Aha! I beat you in here, so you owe me a beer." She sat down on the weight bench and put her shoes on, tucking the key card in the bra top of her bikini.

"That's what I get for being a gentleman. Hey, I talked to my dad earlier."

"What did he tell you?" She hoped that Mr. Thomas had let the cat out of the bag so she and Branch could discuss the whole thing. She needed to tell someone so badly.

"Not a damn thing. He said it was covered by client privilege and that if she wanted me to know about her health, she would tell me. That it was my job to make her happy so she didn't move her money and affairs to another firm," he said. "You sure you don't know something that you're willing to share?"

Tessa sat down at a stationary bike. "I can share that Frankie is a hoot and that Ivy seems to be sucking down more oxygen every day and that Frankie is worried about her. And that Lola is getting married a week from Saturday, so save the date. And that Melody is working her little ass off to get every bit of her homework done so that she can be caught up when she gets back in school on Monday."

Branch dropped to his knees and drew Tessa close to his bare chest. The soft hair tickled her cheek and dammit all to hell, she wanted more than a few stolen elevator kisses.

"You sure you can't tell me more?" His voice was deep, seductive.

She placed one of her small hands on each side of his face and gently nipped at his lower lip. "Yes, I am very sure."

"Okay then." He rolled up on his feet and stood up.

Her eyes were level with the blue dolphins on his swim trunks right below his belly button and she could not force them away from that little white string. If she pulled it, would it reveal proof that he was as turned on as she was?

And that's when Melody poked her head in the fitness room. "Hey, y'all goin' to the pool when you get done in here?"

Branch took two steps back and started a treadmill at a fast pace. "Yes, we are."

"Why don't you forget about this and come cool off with me? I've got all my homework done and I'm bored. Aunt Ivy and Frankie are sleeping again. I've never seen two old girls sleep as much as they have this past couple of days," she said.

"Give me time to at least run a mile," Branch said.

Tessa needed to cool off more than a bike ride or a jog on the treadmill. She wouldn't mind a few ice cubes floating in the pool. What she definitely did not need was a workout and then a hot tub, not when her blood was fast rising to the boiling stage.

She should not have looked back at him. No, sir, because he'd already worked up a sweat and all that masculinity, with wet sweat on his abdomen, only added gasoline to the fire going out of control in her gut. And then he winked, slow and deliberate, and it was so damned sexy that it flat-out took her breath.

If Melody hadn't grabbed her wrist, she might have stood right there and melted into a pile of nothing but boiling hormones. But some higher power understood, and a minute later she'd shed her shirt and her shoes. She climbed to the tallest diving board and then she was flying through the air, slicing into cool water that did little to bring her hot insides down from the boiling point.

"Wow, that was a beautiful dive." Melody clapped from the shallow end of the pool, where she was getting wet an inch at a time. "Did you take swimming lessons?"

Tessa swam over to the steps leading down into the pool and sat down on the bottom one with only her shoulders and head out of the water. "From the time I was four. Mama found out that unlike dancing, I could swim, but forget golf, tennis, or ping-pong."

Melody took another step into the cold water. "Well, you are sure good at it. I took lessons and I could save myself from drowning but I'm not good at it. Why hadn't you done that before? We've been in lots of pools on this trip."

"I needed to cool off fast," Tessa admitted honestly.

Melody took a deep breath and ducked all the way underwater. She dog-paddled to the side and leaned back, using her elbows as props on the side of the pool. "Hey, do you think I need to be, like, worried about Aunt Ivy and Frankie? They don't seem as feisty as they were, like, when we left on this trip. Remember how they were yelling and carryin' on. Embarrassed the hell out of me, but I, like, understand them better now."

"You just worry about stayin' straight when we get back to school," Tessa said.

"I'm not gay," Melody protested.

"I know that. I meant straight when it comes to smokin' pot or maybe getting into fights with those hussy ex-friends of yours when they pester you about getting caught," Tessa said.

"Oh, I can whip their asses with, like, one hand tied behind my back."

"But you're not going to, because that will get you expelled or put into detention for a very long time. You are going to learn to fight with words."

Melody looked at her like she'd grown an extra eye or maybe a set of horns were sprouting out from her wet blonde hair.

Tessa splashed water toward her. "Okay, here's a scenario that you might think about. Natalie struts up to you and says that you are an idiot and to never look at her man, Creek or River or whatever the hell his name is, again. What do you do?"

"Slap the shit out of her," Melody said. "Even though I don't want the slimeball, she ain't goin' to talk to me like that."

Tessa shook her head. "No, ma'am, because that gets you in trouble for starting a fight. You grab your stomach, roll up in a ball, and throw yourself down on the floor, rolling around and screaming until a teacher comes. Believe me, she'll be standing there in shock."

"And then?" Melody was hanging on every word.

"And then you tell the teacher that Natalie is threatening you because you heard that she and her boyfriend are selling pot on the school property. You haven't hit her and it looks like she's hit you, but you didn't say that she did or that you know she's selling drugs. The teacher will have to tell the principal, who will talk to both of you."

"And what do I say?" Melody asked.

"That you are so sorry and you don't want to get anyone in trouble because you realize from your own problems how hard it is and then refuse to tattle."

Melody laughed. "That's pretty good."

"For an ancient thirty-year-old?" Tessa asked.

"I bet Aunt Ivy and Frankie can help me out, too. I'm cooled off now, so I'm going to see if they're awake. This has been, like, an awesome trip, Tessa. I love all of you." Melody stood, marched up the steps and out of the water, and was all but running when Branch appeared on the other side of the doors.

"What's she off in search of so fast?" Branch slid into the water and sat down beside Tessa.

"Instant gratification," Tessa said.

"Sounds good to me." He grinned.

"Me, too, but not on this trip," she said honestly.

"Why?"

"I wouldn't be responsible for what I might say," she answered.

"Aha! You tell secrets when you are indulging in instant gratification, do you?" he asked.

"Maybe, but then maybe I just make up stories. You won't know on this trip, though."

His wet lips kissed her on the cheek. "I'm a patient man. I can wait until we get home."

Lola had several magazines scattered around her on the bed when Tessa picked up her journal that evening. She looked up and asked, "Are you keeping track of what all we're doing on this trip in that thing? Seems like you write in it every night."

"No, I'm doing that on my laptop. This is for my emotions and my feelings about what happens on this trip. Mama gave it to me. Where'd you get all those magazines?" Tessa answered.

"In that last convenience store we stopped at for a potty break." Lola tossed one over to Tessa.

"Brides' magazines." Tessa grinned.

"Yes, ma'am. I want this to be small but perfect for Mama. Tell me about that journal thing and writing down your feelings. It's, like, therapy in a book, right?"

Tessa nodded. "I guess it is."

"Sophie always was smart. Maybe I would've been better if I'd stayed with her and your dad a little longer. But she'd often say that sometimes we have to get messed up before we can step up. I guess it takes some of us longer to realize what a chaos we've made so that we can take our place behind home plate and pick up the bat," Lola said softly.

"You know something, Lola, until right now I never thought of my journals as therapy, but I think they are," Tessa said.

"Oh, it's therapy. Sophie knew you would need something to keep you in touch with the reality of your feelings. This can't be easy for you, Tessa. Meeting us just that once and then going with us on a trip."

"It's been good for me," Tessa said.

"Well, then get your therapy lesson and I'll finish reading my magazines." Lola smiled.

Like always, Tessa picked up the pen from the end table and started to write:

Day of kisses: Branch kissed me again tonight. It's my antiawkwardness kisses and insane as it is, they work. When he kisses me then I'm not clumsy for at least twenty-four hours. I bet if Mama put me on the stage I could dance like a professional right after he kisses me.

And yet today was also laced with sadness because Frankie and Ivy made the announcement that we are slowly starting to head toward home, and I know what that means. So in spite of the aura that surrounds kisses from Branch, there is a bittersweet end coming to our journey. I've promised to stay in Boomtown for the final two weeks of my vacation and I'm glad that I did, because I can't think of being anywhere else. Lola has barely gotten her feet under her and she will need me.

It's good to be needed. Love is wonderful, but to be needed, that's a whole new emotion. One that carries responsibility. I hope I'm up to the task.

Branch still doesn't know and I feel bad that I can't tell him. But Frankie trusted me with her secret and I simply can't break that trust. She will tell the rest of the family when she wants. Until then it's our secret.

Melody is overjoyed to be going back to her school. She will have to work off the rest of her punishment by doing community service on the weekends at some posh nursing facility. I'm pretty sure that it'll be the very place that Frankie and Ivy will be living, but that, too, is Frankie's business. I can only hope that it is, because I've grown quite attached to that child. She's the little sister I never had but always wanted and in my world, adoption is part of life. So I can adopt all these people as family if I want to.

Today I talked wedding stuff with Lola and it was amazing. Totally wonderful to be included in the plans. She'll be lovely when she and Hank stand up together before the preacher in that fancy place Frankie will be living. And it's going to bring tears to my eyes when Frankie puts those pearls on her.

So on the day of kissing, I've experienced elation with Melody, wedding jitters and joy with Lola, and pain with Frankie and Ivy.

My heart is no longer empty, but it's full of feelings. I never knew that a heart could hold so much. Matt was right. I wasn't passionate with him. I didn't feel like this. His kisses didn't make my knees go weak like Branch's do, and his touch on my cheek didn't create flutters in my stomach. My heart was like a closed door in that relationship and today I'm glad that it didn't work out because if it had, I would have never known what I feel right now. Even the pain tells me that I'm alive, that I'm needed and wanted, and the joys are surreal.

Chapter Twenty-Two

"Can't I stay in my room and, like, talk to Jill about school next week and our weekend job at that old folks' place instead of going to a stockyard?" Melody groaned from the backseat of the Caddy.

"No, you cannot. It will be good for you to see the cattle drive down the street," Frankie said.

Melody did her famous eye roll and sighed. "Bull crap and long horns! I can see that any day of the week by driving from my house out to Jill's."

"You two are awful," Lola said from the front seat.

"We're teaching her a lesson about not judging a book by its cover," Frankie said.

"What are you talking about?" Melody laid her phone down. "What is the stockyards really all about?"

"It's an adult party place, but there's shopping and those old-time pictures that you can buy and lots of fun things, plus we're staying at Miss Molly's, which is a real haunted bed-and-breakfast place that used to be a bordello, so I don't think you want to stay there alone," Lola said.

Melody was now wide-eyed and the whining had stopped. "Wow! For real? Who are the ghosts?"

"I'm not sure, but since Miss Molly's was a bordello seventy years ago, maybe it's some of the folks who visited the place back then and had such a good time that they never wanted to leave," Ivy answered.

"A bordello. You mean like a whorehouse?" Melody asked.

"That's right," Frankie said. "The child who is being punished for smoking pot in the bathroom gets to stay in a haunted whorehouse tonight."

"That is, like, awesome to the max. I've got to tell Jill and I'm staying awake all night so if I see a ghost I can take a picture of it. This is the best time of my life. I'm glad I got caught smoking pot because if I hadn't, I wouldn't have ever got to go with y'all. Can I go on every vacation with you, Aunt Ivy?"

Tessa turned enough to catch the haunting smile that Ivy flashed toward Melody. "My next vacation is going to last too long for you to go, but every year August ends, you remember the summer you were sixteen and smile at all the fun we've had."

"How long is it going to last?" Melody asked.

Ivy patted her on the bare knee. "You just remember our trip."

Tessa's eyes burned, but she kept the tears at bay. She'd recorded everything that had happened since the day they'd had a parade out of town, and after what Ivy had said, she fully intended to keep writing about the days until the last one had passed. Then every year she would remember the whole trip when she got out her journal and read through it.

When she glanced over her shoulder again, Frankie was staring out her side of the car at the cows and cotton fields speeding by at nearly eighty miles an hour. Ivy was intently studying the same view from her side of the car and Melody was busy sending a message on her phone.

How would the child remember all this when she was thirty years old? How would Branch remember it? Would it be a minor blip in his mind or would it be the time that changed his whole life?

She visualized herself sitting in a rocking chair on a wide porch in the fall of the year with a journal in her lap and a glass of sweet tea on the table beside her. Would she read from the journal to the little blonde-haired girl sitting in the rocker next to hers and tell her stories from a summer fifty years before?

Lola nudged her with a shoulder. "Where were you? You looked like you got a glimpse into the past or something. Were you visiting with one of the ghosts from Miss Molly's place?"

"No, I got a glimpse of a lovely fall day someday in the distant future," Tessa answered.

"Tell me how you do that. I'd love to see where I am going to be in the future," Lola said.

"I don't know how. It happens sometimes and until it comes to pass, I don't put much stock in it," Tessa answered seriously.

Lola would find out tomorrow or the next day at the latest that she really hadn't wanted to know what the future held, because her plans were about to be turned upside down. And worse than that, her heart was going to be broken. Tessa only hoped that she and Hank would be enough to put all the pieces back together for her.

They reached the stockyards at two o'clock and Frankie already had their itinerary planned out. The first stop was at Uncle Charlie's Old Time Studio, where Lola had made arrangements for them to have a full hour of pictures taken. Frankie and Ivy went first, all dressed up in the big dresses of the day and big hats with feathers and pistols by their sides.

Melody whipped through the costumes and held up a short red dress. "I want to be a barmaid and you two should wear these and I'll lie up on the bar and y'all can cock a leg up on a bar stool and we'll all have pistols pointed at the camera."

Lola took the dress from her and nodded. "I love it. But I want to also have one made in the bride's dress for Hank."

"Pick one out, Branch, because when we get all done with individual pictures I want one with all six of us to frame," Frankie said. "If Tessa is a barmaid I think you should be a southern gambler with an ace up your sleeve."

"And an ace in Tessa's garter, too," Lola called out from behind the curtain where they were getting dressed.

Branch raised a dark eyebrow at Frankie.

"You are on the clock for this hour, so you will do what I tell you. If you mess with me I'll make you dress up like a groom and Tessa like a bride and have one of those pictures taken where she's standing behind you and you're sitting down," Frankie said.

"Gambler it is." Branch smiled.

"This is so much fun," Melody said. "I wish I had this dress for the fall formal at our high school. And this hat thing. It's, like, out-of-this-world cute. Here we come. Y'all get ready to be wowed!"

Lola threw back the curtain and three hot bar chicks stepped out. Tessa gasped when she saw Branch standing beside the fireplace mantel having his individual picture done. He had been transformed into a gambler with garters on his sleeves and a gun belt slung low around his hips. The curve of his lips made her want to take a running leap and wrap her legs around his waist and her arms around his neck. Wouldn't it be awesome if she really was a loose-legged bar maid and he was a gambler looking for a good-time woman?

"Now, that is eye candy. If he wasn't, like, a hundred years older than me, I'd take him to the dance next month," Melody said.

"That stung," Branch said.

"Don't worry, darlin'," Frankie said. "She's young and ignorant. We'll hope that the stupidity fades with the youth. Now be still so me and Ivy can have our picture made with you before she has to hook her nose back up to the tubes."

After the photographer took several shots of the three of them in different poses, Ivy put her tubes back around her ears and crawled up on a bar stool. "Y'all go and get the rest of what you want done and then I'll take them out for the ones of the whole bunch of us."

"Okay, you three hussies get in position at the other end of the bar," Frankie said. "And Branch, you're going to get in behind it and be the bartender."

"I thought I was a gambler."

"You are, but right now you're going to pour whiskey for these hardworking barflies." She laughed.

"Real whiskey. I get to drink?" Melody asked.

"Not on my watch," Frankie said.

"A little more leg to show off that garter, Tessa. A little more attitude from you, Lola, and a hell of a lot less from you, Melody," Frankie said.

The photographer kept snapping and Frankie continued her bossing, telling Branch to sit at the poker table and Tessa to act like she was about to eat him up with her eyes and to flash plenty of cleavage when she leaned over his shoulder to peek at his cards.

"I could learn to like this business," Branch said.

"That's great," the photographer said. "Y'all are naturals. How long have you been a couple?"

"They're not," Melody answered for them. "But they might be someday."

Tessa blushed. "You never know what the future holds."

"Thank God," Melody said. "I thought this whole trip was going to be awful, and it's turned out to be, like, amazing."

From Uncle Charlie's they drove to Miss Molly's and unloaded all their baggage; then Branch found a safe parking place for Mollybedamned. The lady of the place showed them to their rooms and Melody squealed and did a dance right there in the doorway when she realized she had her own private room and bath for the night.

"Y'all deserve one night of privacy. Melody gets the Miss Josie room," Frankie said.

The lady handed Melody the key and smiled at the way the teenager was trying to take in everything from the purple walls to the fabric-draped ceiling to the gorgeous claw-footed tub. "Kind of makes you wish you'd lived in a different time, don't it?"

"This is way too cool. It's like I'm really the person in the pictures we took. Thank you, Frankie. This is, like, beyond grand." Melody wrapped her arms around Frankie and hugged her tightly.

Frankie patted the girl on the head. "Now on to our rooms. Me and Ivy are staying in the cowboy room because it's got two beds and we don't want separate rooms so tonight it's going to be the cowgirl room."

"I'll stay right here. I've got to take dozens of pictures of everything to send to Mama and to Jill. This is, like, the coolest room I've ever seen. Y'all call me when you're ready to do the next thing," Melody said.

Frankie hugged her tightly. "I'm so glad you like this room, and yes, you can. Branch, darlin', push that cart on to wherever this sweet lady leads."

After he got their things unloaded, the woman took them on to Lola's room and then to Tessa's and finally she put Branch in the gunslinger's room. "Y'all have about taken up my whole place. I've only got two rooms left. Oh, and please be aware that we don't serve breakfast on weekdays. But there are lots of fine places to eat within a short distance."

Branch tipped his hat and nodded. "Thank you. I imagine I will go out and get some pastries and coffee and bring it in to the ladies. As you could see, one of our crew is on oxygen and mornings are tough on her."

"That's sweet of you." The lady handed him a key and quickly answered the ringing cell phone that she pulled from her pocket.

"A cell phone sure looks out of place in a hotel like this. I guess it's the old and the new combining," he muttered.

Ivy could barely get Melody out of her room to go down to the street and watch the cattle drive at four o'clock. But once she was there she was more excited about the whole thing than any of them. Tessa loved seeing everything through the eyes of both a sixteen-year-old kid who had a full life ahead of her and two old gals who were approaching the end of their time on earth. As the rangy longhorn cattle, herded by cowboys on horseback, made their way down the street, she was already forming the story that she'd write that night about that particular Wednesday in September.

The smell of cattle, horses, leather, and dust filled the air as the cattle passed so close that she could have reached out and touched their extralong horns. Branch leaned on a post right beside her and looked like he belonged there. Melody couldn't snap pictures with her phone fast enough.

"You aren't taking pictures?" Branch asked Tessa.

"I don't need them," she said. "This day, this whole journey, is branded on my mind and in my heart so deeply that all I have to do is close my eyes and it's all right there."

"Me, too." He took her hand in his. "Would you ever want to go back to a time when this was real, like in the cattle run days a hundred years ago?"

"I don't know. I don't expect those rooms we have would have been air-conditioned in those days or had indoor plumbing," she said. "What about you?"

Branch nodded. "I would have loved it."

"Why are you a lawyer, Branch?"

"It's a means of making a living so I can ranch and do what I want. Someday I hope to be able to quit that side of my life and only run my ranch for a living," he said.

Tessa nodded. "I understand."

"Why are you a travel agent?"

"I love helping people put together a dream vacation, but probably the biggest reason is that Clint and I get to be our own bosses. With my lack of grace, I wouldn't last three days working for someone else. Maybe we should move to this part of the state and put in a bordello," she teased.

"You aren't old enough to be a madam, and I couldn't stand it if you were one of the girls," he said.

She stepped closer to him and leaned her head on his shoulder. "Oh? I thought I'd make a good barmaid."

His arm went protectively around her shoulders. "No, ma'am. The bordello is out. But I could be one of those cowboys who herd the cattle down the street twice a day and you could take pictures in the old-time place down the street."

"Okay, now it's time for supper," Lola said. "Let's herd the six of us up to the Lonesome Dove for a steak."

Branch kept Tessa's hand in his. "You don't have to twist my arm for that."

Tessa tried to ignore Ivy and Frankie's wide grins, but something told her that they had planned this from the beginning.

"I'm having buffalo," Ivy said.

"Yuck!" Melody's pert little nose snarled. "They do have something else on the menu, don't they?"

"Sure thing. They've got grilled quail quesadillas," Frankie told her.

"Good. I like quail. I just don't like the taste of buffalo," Melody said.

Lola giggled. "Guess that backfired, didn't it?"

"Guess so," Ivy said. "But we're not home yet, so I can still have some fun with her."

Melody took over pulling Blister along on his wheels. "Don't forget I can still have fun with you, too."

The hostess seated them, took their drink and appetizer orders, and then left them to look at the menus. Melody decided on the quail quesadillas and Ivy wanted the buffalo steak. The rest of their crew stuck with rib eyes, baked potatoes, and salads.

Lola laid the menu down. "Okay, now the rest of the night is lining up like this. After supper, the kid here and I are going back to Miss Molly's to see if we can catch a ghost on film, and you four are going to spend some time at Pearl's. Mama and Ivy really do want to belly up to a bar and order a beer and dance."

"You sure, Frankie?" Tessa asked.

"Never been surer of anything. Me and Ivy are going out with our boots on. See?" Frankie held up a leg for them all to see that in addition to the bling on her fancy shirt, she was wearing bright-red cowboy boots.

"And mine." Ivy did the same, only her boots were black with hot-pink stitching.

"How come I didn't notice those?" Melody asked. "And why don't we get to go dancing, Lola?"

"Because you are sixteen and you can't go into Pearl's, and if you could, you would text it and the judge would revoke Aunt Ivy's care of you. And I don't care to dance if I can't be in Hank's arms so I'm your babysitter tonight and you are mine. We might need each other if the ghosts come out to play," Lola answered.

Frankie and Ivy both seemed pumped up, almost as much as they'd been at the carnival but not like the day they left Boomtown. Tessa leaned over and whispered in Frankie's ear, "You sure about all this? It's not written in stone. It can be changed."

Frankie patted her on the shoulder. "Do you realize that you hardly ever have an accident anymore, and that since Lola owned up to loving Hank that she's not been clumsy one time? I'm beginning to think maybe it has something to do with love, which makes me wonder if Lester really loved me because if that's what it took to cure someone, he wouldn't have stained every tie I ever bought him."

"I'll be damned," Lola exclaimed. "You are right, Mama. I should have said I'd marry Hank years ago, and I'd have saved a ton of bruises and stains."

"I didn't say I'd marry anyone," Tessa said.

"Then Lola broke the cycle when she did and now you don't have to be clumsy anymore, either," Ivy said.

And that's when Tessa began to worry. She couldn't dance. She had two left feet and she'd always, always avoided places where she'd be required to do a simple two-step or waltz. She'd been a wallflower at her high school proms because she didn't want to make a fool of herself on the dance floor. Now, what in the hell was she going to do at Pearl's? What if Branch asked her to dance and she stepped on his toes or worse?

"We have our own rooms," Branch said softly when everyone else was talking about the ghosts.

"I can't dance," she blurted out.

"Don't worry, I can teach you," he promised.

"In one night?"

"There might be a price for lessons."

"Not as thin as those walls are. I swear I could hear Melody talking to her mother as I was brushing my teeth," Tessa said.

"You heard what?" Ivy asked.

"Probably everything we said. Those hotel walls are not soundproof, so we'll have to be careful what we say," Frankie said.

Lola hummed the music from the old *Twilight Zone*. "It's so we can hear the ghosts when they walk down the hallway."

"You are beginning to freak me out," Melody said.

ᔓ

Dancing in Branch's arms was like floating on air. Her feet didn't feel like lead as he swept her around the floor in a country waltz while Ivy and Frankie sat up to the bar with an empty bottle of beer in each of their hands and two empties in front of each of them.

"Blister is liable to go up in a blaze of fire if she drinks much more and gets the hiccups," Tessa said.

"Right now, I've got better things to think about than Blister." Branch buried his face in her hair and held her so tight against his chest that she could not only hear but feel every beat of his heart.

"What are we doing, Branch?" she asked. "And what kind of name is Branch, anyway?"

"It's my mother's maiden name and since I'm the third son and they'd used up all the important names, it's all she had left. I was supposed to be a girl and my name was going to be Sally. Now, to answer your other question, what do you want us to be doing?"

"I can't think about us right now with Ivy on her last leg. I have to think about Lola and Frankie," she said.

He spun her around and then gathered her back into his arms. "But you are, whether you want to or not, aren't you?"

She was amazed that she'd been graceful. "I do not believe in love at first sight."

He kissed the top of her hair. "Me, either."

"I have to know someone, really know them before I fall for them."

He squeezed her hand gently. "Me, too."

"Stop agreeing with me."

He looked deeply into her eyes. "Yes, ma'am. We will have spent almost two weeks, twenty-four hours a day in each other's company or in close proximity by the time this trip is over. If I had asked you out on a date the first day I walked into your travel agency and each date lasted four hours, two dates a week . . . let's see, fourteen days for the two weeks, twenty-four hours for each day is . . ."

"Over three hundred," she said.

"Now divide by four and you get about seventy and divide that by two for twice a week and we would have been dating over six months. And we've only shared a few really amazing kisses. Don't you think we should take this to the next level and see where it might lead?"

"I think you are a damn fine lawyer." She laughed.

"Does that mean you'll think about going out with me on a real date when we get back to Boomtown with those two drunks up there on the stools?"

"It does," she said.

"Good. Now it's time for you to sit on a stool and for me to dance with each of them so we can go to our hotel," he said.

She didn't want to know the answer, but she had to ask. "Am I that bad of a dancer?"

"No, darlin', but you've got me hotter than a two-dollar pistol and I need a cold beer and a cold shower in that order," he answered.

Branch walked with his hand on her lower back to the bar and waited until she was on a stool beside Frankie before he held out his hand to Ivy. "May I have this dance, please, ma'am?"

Ivy jerked the tubes from her nose and left them hanging on the stool as she slid off. "Thank God. I thought I was going to have to ask some old man myself. Now I'll be the envy of every young girl in the joint. One thing for damn sure, I wasn't going home without a dance at Pearl's."

"Beer, please," Tessa told the bartender.

Frankie sipped at her beer. "It's almost over and it's kind of bittersweet. We've about used up the last of our energy, but it's been worth every bit of it."

"You could go home and be comfortable in your own house and in your own room. We could hire a full-time nurse," Tessa said.

"No, darlin'. I can't do that because I don't want that kind of memories in the house for Lola. I should go into that final sleep in a place that she never has to see or visit again. Tomorrow night, we'll stay in Huntsville, and Friday at noon when we stop for lunch, I will tell her. I'm waiting until the last minute because it's going to make her so sad. I'm so glad you'll be there to help her."

Tessa took a long draw from the beer. "But Frankie, she'll have Hank and Inez."

"She loves Inez like a sister and she loves Hank. But neither of them are blood, and it's only that kind of relationship that understands this kind of loss. Don't tell me that you've changed your mind. I couldn't bear it," she said.

Tessa shook her head. "No, I'm staying for sure, and if I need to, I can extend my vacation."

Frankie slipped an arm around her shoulders. "I love you, Tessa. When you think about this time we've had to get to know each other, you remember that I said that and that I mean it with my whole heart."

"I love you, too," Tessa said and she meant it.

Like Branch said, if she'd spent four hours twice a week visiting with Frankie and Lola, they'd be six months down the road, but since Frankie didn't have six months—or Ivy, either—she was glad that she got a crash course in getting to know them. Her mama had been right when she advised her to use her vacation time to go on vacation with these amazing people . . . her family.

Ivy didn't waste any time getting herself wired back up when the song ended. "Whew! That takes it out of a woman." She panted until the oxygen began to take hold.

"And I've saved the best until last, Miz Frankie." Branch held out his hand. "Please dance with me."

She put her hand in his and let him lead her out to the floor. "I was about to go into a pout and refuse to let you bill me for a whole day but you are forgiven since you came up with that pickup line."

When she stopped wheezing, Ivy took a long draw from her fourth beer. "She's getting real weary. After this dance, I'm going to say I need to go back to the room. You and Branch can stick around and dance long as you want."

"We'll go with you," Tessa said.

"It's been fun, but I'm glad it's almost done. Person sees things different when they see that finish line up ahead and I'm gettin' tired of this. It's not living, Tessa. It's barely surviving. I'm ready to lie down on a bed and talk to Frankie when she's awake and remember all the good times and cuss the bad times. I hope that God sees fit to take us at the same time and if he can't do that, then to make the one left behind not be lucid so we won't ever be alone."

That damned lump in her throat was back. "I can't stand to hear those words."

"It's okay." Ivy downed the rest of her beer. "It's a good thing to know the EDT. That's estimated departure time. I feel so sorry for those poor people who drop dead in their bathrooms from a blood clot or retire one day and die in their rocking chair the next day. They never got to plan a final farewell party like this one. They never got to spend every hour of every day with their loved ones, to enjoy three meals a day with them and be silly at a picture place like we did today. This is a gift from God, so don't be sad."

"I can't help it." Tessa's voice broke.

"Then we won't talk about it anymore. Will you come see us every day in the place where we are headed?"

Tessa couldn't make a single word come out of her mouth, so she merely nodded.

"Then it's all good. Now finish your beer and put a smile on your face. There's still more of this trip and we've got stories to tell and things to do."

Branch brought Frankie back and held her arm while she got settled on the bar stool. "You two ladies about wore me out. I'm going to need a cold beer. Thank goodness there's a stool left down here beside Tessa or I'd fall on the floor."

"God don't like liars," Frankie chided, but her old eyes were twinkling.

"Then he should love me, because I'm not lyin'," Branch said smoothly.

"Looks like this bunch of party animals is about ready to head to the hotel. Y'all with me?" Tessa asked.

"I am." Branch nodded. "I'll take my beer with me."

"You?" Tessa asked Frankie.

"You two kids can stay and party. Us old party animals know the way to the hotel and we can lean on each other," Frankie answered.

Tessa leaned over and kissed her on the cheek. "No, ma'am. I've been watchin' those two old guys over there at that far table trying to catch your eye and there ain't no way I'm letting you walk down the street without chaperones. Lola would have my hide if those two sweet-talked their way into your bedroom tonight."

"Honey, them old men wouldn't know what to do with two hot women like us." Frankie smiled.

"I'm not taking any chances," Tessa said. "So finish your beers and we'll go to see if Lola and Melody have had any luck with the ghosts."

Branch had just gotten out of the shower. He'd pulled on a pair of pajama pants and a tank top, but his hair was still wet and he hadn't had time to brush his teeth when he heard the gentle rap on his door.

Hoping to hell it wasn't Avery, he opened it a crack before he slung it wide open and pulled Tessa into the room. Tears flowed down her cheeks. Her hair was wet and she was dressed in faded blue pajama pants and an oversize nightshirt with a picture of Betty Boop on the front.

"What is it?" He shut the door with his bare foot and wrapped his arms around her.

"I have to talk about it or I'm going to explode. I can't bear this burden alone another day and I need some support or I won't be able to handle Lola and my heart is breaking, Branch," she sobbed.

"Ivy?" he asked.

She shook her head and the weeping got worse. "It's Frankie."

His blood ran cold as ice water. "What about Frankie?"

"I'm not supposed to tell and I have to and I'm already feeling guilty and . . ."

He picked her up like a bride and carried her to the bed, laid her down gently, and then stretched out beside her. With one arm under her and the other rubbing her back as warm tears landed on his chest, he waited.

"She's got a brain tumor and she's only got a few weeks left and she's already sleeping more and more and that's the sign that it's coming to an end and I haven't had enough time with her and I shouldn't be telling you this," she said between hiccups.

"I'm so sorry." His drawl had a definite catch in it.

"And she and Ivy aren't going home. They're going to tell Lola and you and Melody on Friday and you are going to drive them to the fancy assisted care place where Melody is going to work on weekends for community service." She paused to catch her breath. "And my heart is breaking and I can't sleep alone tonight but we can't . . ."

"We don't need to do anything." He kissed her salty lips. "I'll hold you and you can talk and I'll listen."

"Thank you," she said. "Oh, no! Frankie paid so much money for my room and I'm not using it."

"Shhh." Branch put a finger over her lips. "You took a shower or a bath in your room and your things are there and besides, money doesn't matter right now to her. I'm not surprised to hear that Frankie and Ivy are both in their last days. I'm sad because I like both of the old hussies, but I'd be worried about either of them not having the other one. It's like they need each other." Tears welled up in his eyes with a couple finding their way down his cheeks.

"Everyone needs someone." Tessa laid her cheek next to his, blending his tears with hers.

"Yes, they do, darlin'," he said softly.

"And tonight I need you, Branch. Not for sex but to hold me," she whispered.

"Is this your first time to lose someone really close to you?"

She nodded.

"I lost my grandpa when I was sixteen. He was the one who introduced me to ranching and losing him broke my heart. Trust me when I say you'll get through it because you are a strong woman, but don't believe that shit about time making it better. After a while you can remember them and the happy memories, but it's bittersweet because you'll also remember the pain. The memories, for the most part, take first place, though."

"Tell me about your grandpa. Mine died when I was too young to remember," she said.

Branch massaged the tense muscles in her back. "He was my mother's father and a ranching man, but it was a side job like mine. He told me he was happiest when he was on the ranch and not in the big oil business office in town. I remember him saying that if you gave a rancher a million dollars he'd ranch it all up in a few years but he'd be happy doing it."

"What does that mean?" she asked.

"That making a living at ranchin' isn't easy and ranchers are a stubborn lot. They'll use up their last dollar and last bit of common sense to stay on the place they love."

"I understand that."

Seconds ticked off the clock in a long, comfortable silence as his hands continued to work on her back.

"I like the way I feel in your arms, Branch," she murmured.

"Me, too. Let's get some sleep, darlin'. Things always look better in the daylight."

"I sure hope you are right, because right now the next couple of days aren't lookin' too promising."

ꟹ

The next morning, Tessa shot the journal a dirty look and walked right past it. She took a long shower, hoping that when she came out the need to write about the previous night would be gone. It wasn't, and she had thirty minutes before it was time to check out and find a place that served breakfast. Finally she picked it up and scrawled in a tight little script that later she wouldn't recognize as her handwriting.

Angry night: I don't want to write this because when I do it makes it real and I could pretend until now. I know that I wrote about it before, but now it's the last day and tomorrow Frankie and Ivy will be in that glorified nursing home and I'm angry. God, I wish I could hit something. I've never known such anger.

How could fate give them to me and then take them away? I feel like I'm already going through the steps of grief. Denial and now anger. I don't know that I can ever accept this so I'm mad and that's okay because it's my right to feel like this.

Yesterday was a fun day with the pictures and the whole business here at the haunted whorehouse. Most of all I liked the cattle drive and seeing it through Melody and Frankie and Ivy's eyes at the same time. It was old meeting new. Old fading out to give way to the new. Frankie and Ivy's last day on this trip. Melody's future on Monday at school with a new perspective.

Then there was the dancing with Branch. I felt like I was floating on air. Do all dancers feel such freedom? If so, no wonder they love it so much. And I do believe that Frankie is right. Neither Lola nor I have been as clumsy since she told us that she's in love and since I have my antiawkward kisses. So love, whether long lasting or physical, must have something to do with it. Or maybe it's all psychological and we want to believe Frankie.

I told Frankie that I love her today and I meant it. The very grandmother that I didn't want to get to know has stolen my heart and I do love her. That old saying comes to mind: it's better to have loved and lost than to have never loved at all. Loving this new family puts a whole dimension into my life, indescribable with mere words, but it's there all the same.

And I have to write about my feelings when I broke down and told Branch about Frankie. It was as if a weight lifted from my shoulders. I realize I broke a sacred secret but not by many hours, because she's going to tell us all tomorrow and I will need his support to get me through the announcement. If I don't have his support, then there's no way I can give Lola my shoulder to lean on when she hears the news.

It's so much easier to record the sequence of events than to put into words the emotions and feelings that those events create inside. Mama was wise to give me this journal for the personal side of this trip. I'll never forget this trip . . . not ever.

Chapter Twenty-Three

Tessa had almost forgotten that it was their last night on the trip, the last hotel, the last supper they'd eat from paper plates or takeout containers in Frankie's room. She'd almost forgotten that it was the final time all six of them would share meals and watch reruns of old sitcoms on television.

Almost didn't count except in horseshoes and hand grenades, though.

And the heavy feeling in her heart felt a hell of a lot more like a hand grenade was about to explode than a lucky horseshoe was touching it. She hung back when Lola and Branch called it a night and waited until Melody was in the shower to say her piece.

Talking past the lump in her throat wasn't easy, but she had to try one last time, for Lola's sake as well as her own. She swallowed three times before Frankie laid a hand on her shoulder.

"We know what you are going to say and the answer is no," she said softly. "We made up our minds before we ever left Boomtown, and we're not reversing our decision."

Ivy's expression was purely impish as she shook her head. "Come on now, Tessa. It can be a party or it can be a funeral. We've decided to make it a party. Life has been good to us so we're going out with a bang the way we want to, not all sad and melancholy. You and Lola will come and see us every day and bring us doughnuts and pizza and whatever the hell else we want that day. You'll keep my flask full and not tell a damn soul about it and make sure there's Dr Pepper in my little dorm-size fridge."

"They're going to tell you that drinkin' and smokin' will kill you." Frankie laughed until she got the hiccups.

Ivy slapped her on the shoulder. "Be damned if it won't, but since I'm dyin' anyway, I'm not givin' up either one. I bet they tell you that it's the liquor we've put away in our lifetime that's put that booger in your brain."

Frankie wiped her eyes with the edge of the comforter. "Hell, no, it was the sex. They tell young boys that pleasurin' themselves will make them go blind. Well, on girls it puts big old slimy boogers in the brain when they have too much sex and then stop dead for thirty years. I should've bought me one of them sex toys when Lester died."

They both fell back on the bed and clasped each other's hands as they laughed even harder.

Tessa clapped her hands. "This is not funny."

"Hell, yes, it's funny," Frankie said. "Living has been a blast and we're not going to let the finish line drag us down."

"Amen, Sister Frances." Ivy giggled.

Frankie shook her finger under Ivy's nose. "You call me that again and you'll be going before I do because I'll put a crimp in that hose that shoots oxygen in your shitty lungs."

"I could still whip your ass with a hand tied behind my back and a blindfold on my eyes, so don't threaten me, you old broad," Ivy said.

"Could not!"

"Could, too!"

Tessa couldn't keep the smile at bay. "You are both crazy as outhouse rats."

"That's pretty damn crazy," Ivy said.

"Not as crazy as a Missouri mule," Frankie chimed in.

"Get your stuff straight. That brain booger is wiping out your thinkin' ability," Ivy said. "Outhouse rats are crazy. Missouri mules are stubborn."

"Well, you two are both. Good night." Tessa eased off the foot of the bed. "I'll see y'all at breakfast in the morning. What time are we leaving out of here?"

"Ten o'clock on the button. We're having dinner at our new place and you are all staying to have our first meal with us," Ivy said.

"Hey," Frankie said. "Just one more thing before you go, Tessa. I wouldn't mind hearin' about your engagement to Branch before I do a swan dive off the diving board and wind up on the other side of eternity."

"Frances Beauchamp Laveau!" Ivy exclaimed. "I told you—"

"Hush. I'm going to say what I think from this minute forth. I've got a perfect excuse. My brain is getting eat up. You have to be nice because all you got is lousy lungs."

"I've only known Branch three weeks." Tessa blushed.

"Time ain't nothing but the hands of the clock moving around in endless circles," Ivy said.

"Or numbers on a calendar. Listen to your heart, not your mind," Frankie said. "Now get on out of here and let us get some rest."

Tessa heard the elevator door ding as it opened and rushed to catch it. Lola had left ten minutes ago to meet everyone in the dining room, but Tessa couldn't imagine swallowing anything, not even coffee. It had taken every second of those ten minutes to stare at her reflection in the mirror and give herself a severe lecture.

Branch held the door back with his hand until she was inside. "Last day."

"Don't remind me. I'm not sure I can face them this morning. I tried to talk them out of it last night, but they were laughing and joking and acting like it was a big party," she said.

He took her hand in his and squeezed gently. "I hope when I'm eighty years old and get the kind of news they have that I can approach it the exact same way. Be glad that you've got that kind of DNA in your system, Tessa. It's a great legacy."

"You're right. Thank you for that," she said.

Ivy waved at them when they reached the dining room. "Well, look what the cats drug up and the dogs wouldn't have. Y'all sure are slow this morning. They've got some really good danish and strawberry cream cheese to put on bagels this morning."

"I'm going home today," Melody singsonged.

"So are we," Ivy and Frankie pitched in right behind her.

"I see Hank today." Lola came in third.

They all looked up at Branch and Tessa.

She couldn't think of a single thing to say and could have kissed Branch right smack on the lips when he said, "We need coffee today."

"Well, get it poured and grab some breakfast. We're having a CEO meeting in my room soon as everyone can get there, and blastoff this morning is at ten sharp," Frankie said.

"CEO?" Lola asked.

"Yep, or is it CTJ? Frankie never can get those damn letters all straight. It's a wonder she didn't say FBI or CIA meeting. But it is an important meeting and since y'all are all members of the Molly-bedamned committee, you have to attend," Ivy said.

"CTJ?" Melody frowned.

"Come to Jesus," Ivy said.

Frankie slapped her thigh. "Well, you're on the ball today. You get the whoopee button for the whole day for that one, Ivy Dupree!"

"I'd bow, but if I did I'd put a kink in Blister's tubing and besides, the way I got it figured there's enough juice in his canister to get us to where we're going, so y'all don't waste too much time gettin' your coffee. This wagon train leaves at ten sharp," Ivy said.

"They're going to tell Lola the news. I'm glad you're going to be there." Tessa filled two cups with coffee.

"Just take deep breaths and hold my hand," he said. "Bagels for two and danish for four. We'll have to take it up to their room but I'm hungry, so if you don't want to eat half the danish, I'll polish off all of them."

No wonder people brought food to funerals and wakes. It gave folks something to talk about other than doom and gloom. It fed their bodies and in doing so kept them from going insane with grief.

"If you want four sweet rolls, you'd best add two more, because I'm not sharing mine," she said stoically.

He carefully stacked two with cherry filling on the side of the already bulging paper plate. "We need sideboards. You okay with that coffee, or do you need a little pick-me-up kiss before we go to the CTJ meeting?"

"I think I've still got a little antiawkward juice left in my system, but after this meeting I might need two kisses," she answered.

"I've got them ready and you can choose whether you want cherry- or pineapple-flavored AAJ kisses."

She cocked her head to one side and frowned. "What?"

"Antiawkward juice kisses," he said.

"You are trying to take my mind off the coming announcement and I appreciate it, but all that alphabet soup stuff confuses me. You do realize that I am a very natural blonde, don't you?"

"You don't get to play that blondie card with me, darlin'. I already know how smart you are."

Frankie and Ivy were sitting on the sofa with Melody on the floor in front of them and Lola rocking back and forth in the desk chair when Branch and Tessa reached the room.

"Melody, darlin', scoot over there by Lola and let these two have the coffee table for their breakfast. It's already nine thirty and we don't want them to ride two hours on an empty stomach."

"I'll sit on the end of the bed," Melody said.

Tessa set the coffee down and eased down to the floor, crossed her legs Indian style, and laid a paper napkin in her lap. The sundress was her last clean piece of clothing, and she sure didn't want to make a bad impression on the people at Frankie and Ivy's new home by showing up with jelly and coffee stains on her skirt tail.

"Okay, here's the deal," Frankie said. "And I'm going to spit it out because I don't know how to say it all gentle like. I've got a brain tumor that can't be operated on and it can't be shrunk with radiation or killed with chemo. It's growing every day and sometime in the near future I'm going to go to sleep and not wake up."

"And," Ivy started, "my lungs are getting worse every day and the doctor said before we left that I'd be stretching it if I lived three months."

"That said, we've decided we're not going home. We are going to a fancy-shmancy place in Beaumont. Our room is ready and we'll be there until this life is over. We'll have no tears or begging, Lola. It's our decision and we didn't tell you because we wanted this to be a fun time."

"No!" Melody threw herself on the bed and sobbed with both hands over her eyes. "I won't let y'all die. I won't."

"Darlin' girl, you don't get a vote in that part of the business, but you will be working in the place on weekends, so we'll get to see you," Ivy said.

"Mama, please don't do this." Silent tears streamed down Lola's cheeks.

Tessa crossed the room and gathered Lola in her arms, their tears mingling together as they wept on each other's shoulders. Frankie crossed the room and joined them. "You both know I can't let anyone cry alone, especially my girls. So let's get it out and be done with it, then be happy with every bit of time we've got left."

"I have to cry because y'all are crying, but this is going to be the last time." Ivy pulled the tubes from her nose and wrapped all three of them into her arms. "So let's sling snot and cry like babies just like Frankie said. And Lola, it's already done. Tessa has agreed to stay on the rest of her vacation. But you will have to postpone your honeymoon a few weeks, because your mama and I don't want to miss a minute that we can have with you and Tessa."

"But"—Frankie picked up a box of hotel tissues and ripped handfuls from the box to pass out to everyone—"we do want you to get married a week from tomorrow like you said, because I want to put the necklace on you. And we're going to get all dressed up in our bling and the wedding can be in our room."

"But Mama, we can get second, third, and fortieth opinions. We can fly you anywhere in the world. Someone can cure this." Lola grabbed Frankie's hands and refused to let go.

"I've gotten four opinions. More won't matter, my child." Frankie kissed Lola on the cheek. "Be happy for us. We have been given the greatest gift of all. We know about when our time is done, and we've used it to have fun with the people we love. We'll polish off the rest by having a good time every day when y'all come to visit. So no tears and no regrets."

"You old hussies. You meant it when you said this was a come to Jesus committee meeting," Lola said between sobs as she clung to her mother.

"We did, and when we leave this room, there will be no more tears or sadness, only happy times." Ivy replaced the tubes and sat down on the sofa.

Melody bailed off the bed, knelt beside Ivy, and buried her head in her great-aunt's lap. "I will never forget this trip."

"That's right, baby girl. Every year, you set aside an hour to sit on the porch or go to the park or lie down in the backyard and look up at the clouds and remember our fabulous trip."

Chapter Twenty-Four

The ride from the hotel to Beaumont was surreal. The rolling hills, the tall pines, the humidity said they were nearing home. And yet home would never be the same again. Two weeks in an old Cadillac with five complete strangers had changed Tessa's life forever. Those two old gals snoring in the background had engraved their names upon her heart as family. The teenager with the red eyes between them, using her thumbs to write messages to her friend, had become her little sister.

Lola wasn't her mother, but there was something there that went beyond friendship. And Branch? How could she feel like this about a man she'd known two weeks?

At the county line, Lola's strength played out. She grabbed a paper napkin from the glove compartment and buried her face in it, giving way to the pent-up tears she'd been holding back. "I . . . can't . . . do . . . this," she said between sobs.

Tessa leaned her head over on Lola's shoulder. "None of us can face it alone. It's going to take all of us pulling together to get through it."

Leaning her cheek against Tessa's, Lola tucked the soaked napkin into her purse and got out a clean one. "Thank God you are here. I feel so empty. I can't imagine how I'd get through it without you."

They reached for each other's hand at the same time, and comfort flowed from one to the other until Branch pulled up in front of a posh-looking place on the outskirts of Beaumont.

"We're here, but I have to admit I didn't think it would look like this." Branch stared at the meticulously kept grounds and the sparkling-clean windows.

"You mean this is where I'll be working on weekends? It looks like something out of Hollywood," Melody said in awe.

Frankie stretched and yawned. "Wake up, Ivy, we're here. I'm hungry, so I hope they have dinner all laid out for us and that the chocolate cream pie has a foot of meringue on the top."

"Okay, okay!" Ivy grumbled. "Well, would you look at that? Blister's light is sayin' that I've only got about twenty minutes to get inside. I understand they've got lots of little Blisters lined up ready to take care of me, but I think I'll unplug him and have a cigarette before I enter the pearly gates."

"Good God!" Lola screeched.

Ivy laughed out loud. "He will be good if he don't strike me graveyard dead before I get to see the inside of this fancy place, but I do intend to have one last smoke before I go in there."

"Well, shit, Ivy," Frankie fussed. "They do have a smoking lounge for us old smokers. You don't have to smoke out here in the heat. And it's got a fancy ventilation system so our clothes will never smell like smoke again."

"Well, shit, Frankie," Ivy repeated. "I love going to sleep at night with the aroma of eau de smoke all up in my hair and clothes. Frankie came over here and booked the whole thing before she told me and convinced me it was the way to go, so it'll be my first time through those pearly gates," she told the others.

Lola looped her arm in Frankie's. "I will never like this, Mama. Let's get in the car and go on home to Boomtown. I'll make the call and tell these people you've changed your mind."

Frankie kissed Lola on the cheek. "I didn't ask you to like it, darlin'. I asked you to accept it. Now crawl out of the car and come and see my new elaborate digs. Branch, you get mine and Ivy's suitcases out of the trunk. And Melody, you can pull Blister inside." Twisting away from her daughter, Frankie patted Mollybedamned on the hood. "You've been a good and faithful friend, old girl. Now I'm handing you off to Tessa and I expect you to treat her as good as you have treated me. Take her on lots of trips and journeys and help her make all kinds of beautiful memories."

Branch slipped an arm around Tessa. "Don't cry. This has to be hard on her. She loves this car."

"I do, too, but I love her more," Tessa whimpered.

Frankie stiffened her back. "Ivy, for God's sake, finish that damn cigarette so we can get out of this heat. Hell, I remember when you only got three drags off a smoke and now it takes you half an hour to finish one."

A man dressed in neon-green scrubs rushed down the stairs and took the suitcases from Branch. "We've been watchin' for you, ma'am. Y'all come right on in. Dinner has been laid out and a table set for six. The food will be brought in as soon as you are ready. I'm Mason, and I'm one of the many people who will be seeing to Frankie and Ivy's every need or whim."

Tessa didn't give a tiny rat's ass if there was an army taking care of Frankie and Ivy. They should be at home in Boomtown and the people taking care of them should be family.

"The doctors wear purple and the nurses wear blue," Frankie explained as she led the parade inside the glass doors. "We'll be having roast beef and hot rolls today with chocolate pie for dessert. Side dishes include potatoes and fresh green beans cooked with lots of bacon. Ivy got to choose the menu but I chose the dessert." Frankie talked the whole way across the cobblestone walkway and the wide shady veranda with gorgeous morning glory vines growing up the pillars and into the enormous lobby. "And if you will let us know what day you will be visiting, we will plan whatever you want. We have a chef and our doctors will be visiting us here so we don't have to go sit in those damned boring waiting rooms."

Mason opened the door into a gorgeous room and stood to one side. "And here we are. We strive to give only the best to our lovely guests."

An archway separated the sitting room–dining room combination from a lovely bedroom. A glass-topped coffee table between two facing sofas and a pair of those fancy lift chairs was situated next to floor-to-ceiling glass panels looking out over a beautiful garden with a fountain in the middle. Nearer to the door, the dining room sported a table with six chairs, all set up for them with china, crystal, and silver.

A vision of paper plates and barbecue, soup in disposable bowls, and takeout Chinese food flashed through Tessa's mind. If only she could take a step back, she'd do it gladly.

Beyond the archway there were two queen-size beds with a nightstand between them. Not so very different from the hotels where they'd stayed the past two weeks except in luxury. Again Tessa wished she could spend one more week in those places, back before she knew about Frankie's and Ivy's illnesses.

Frankie went straight to her bed and picked up a remote control device. "This one calls the nurse. This one calls the doctor. This one calls the chef. And this one is magic. Watch." She smiled as she pushed it. A big-screen television flipped over and descended from the ceiling. "What do you think of that, Ivy?"

"You're showing off," Ivy said.

"Am not!"

Ivy hip-butted her. "Are too."

"When you are ready for the food to be served, push the button, and if you need anything, I'm here until eight this evening and then Loretta will be your evening concierge," Mason said.

Frankie pushed the button before he had time to get out of the room and told the chef they were ready for lunch.

"In here we don't have dinner and supper." She laughed.

"We have lunch and dinner and snacks anytime we want." Ivy smiled. "Now, bossy butt, tell us where we are supposed to sit. And we ain't playin' musical chairs, so wherever she says today is where it'll be all the time."

Frankie assigned seats so that Lola was on one side of her and Tessa on the other. "See, it's going to be a lark living here with Ivy. We'll be together and we can have whatever we want, whenever we want it. And when you come to visit we'll have fun. You do not need to have bad memories in the house where you grew up or where we've made good memories since you came home to me almost thirty years ago. Trust me, Lola, I know what I'm doing."

"Will you be brave enough to admit it if you have second thoughts?" Lola asked.

"I will, but I won't. Ivy and I are going to finish up this business in style and we're going to look forward to seeing Melody on weekends and you other three anytime you can get here on weekdays. Here comes our dinner, so we'll see if the chef is any good. If he isn't, I'll fire his ass and hire a new one," Frankie said.

Leaving Frankie and Ivy alone, even in the lap of luxury, was the hardest thing Tessa had ever done. Melody sat in the middle of the backseat and cried all the way to her house. She threw herself into her mother's arms at the door, and Tessa wished that her mother was there so she could do the same.

Neither Lola nor Tessa made a move. They'd started this trip in the front seat and they'd finish it the same way. With fingers intertwined, she held Lola's hand on her thigh the whole way to the house in Boomtown.

"I can't get out. I can't go in there and face that house without Mama. She's always been here." Lola held on to Tessa's hand in a death grip.

"What would you give your mama right now?" Tessa asked.

"Anything in my power," Lola answered.

"Then get out of this car and let's go inside the house, because this is all she's wanting from us. She wants the time we spend with her to be fun and quality, not worrying with pills or food or sickness," Tessa said.

Lola let go of her hand and with a long sigh got out of the car. "I hate this."

Tessa slid out behind her. "That which does not kill us—"

Lola finished it for her. "—makes us stronger. By the time this is over I'll be able to bench-press Mollybedamned."

They walked together into the house with Branch bringing their luggage inside behind them. Cool air greeted them, but the house lacked the sparkle, the pizzazz that Frankie and Ivy brought to it.

"Want me to take it upstairs for you?" Branch parked the suitcases and the other baggage at the foot of the staircase.

Lola shook her head. "Most of it needs to be sorted and washed. We'll take care of it."

Tessa heard tires crunching on gravel, then someone running across the wooden porch. But she still jumped back when the door flew open and a tall, lanky man wearing jeans and a pearl-snap shirt went straight for Lola and gathered her into his arms. "I'm so sorry, darlin'. What can I do to help?"

She clung to him. "Just be here. Don't leave me."

The moment was awkward with four of them standing there, not knowing what to do next, so Tessa spoke up first. "I'm Tessa and this is Branch Thomas."

"I'm Hank." He nodded.

"I'll put Mollybedamned in the garage and . . ." Branch said hoarsely.

Tessa grabbed his hand and held on tightly. "I'll go with you."

They made it to the car before his shoulders slumped and he put his hand over his eyes. "Dammit! A grown man controls his emotions. He stays strong for the ladies and he doesn't cry, for God's sake. And you've already seen me go all sensitive once and that's enough."

Tessa wrapped her arms around him. "You have done all those things, darlin'. But the heart can only take so much. It's okay if you are angry or emotional. It's been a hell of a day."

"What do you intend to do with this?"

"You mean this whole situation or Mollybedamned?" Tessa asked.

"The Caddy." He opened the driver's door and she slid into the middle spot. He'd regained his composure by the time he started the engine, but Tessa could still feel the pain in his heart.

She swallowed hard and put on a brave face. "I intend to take her out every year on the first day of September. Some years it might be for a weeklong drive down the coast; sometimes it might be for a day trip to Galveston for an ice cream cone or a hamburger. But I'm going to put the top down and let the wind whip through my hair and remember Frankie and Ivy and Melody and you, Branch. And she's never leaving Texas, not even to go across the border to New Iberia to visit my folks."

He used the remote to raise the garage door and parked the Caddy back in her original spot. "Visit? You mean you're leaving her here?"

"That's right. Lola won't mind, I'm sure. Frankie didn't let Molly-bedamned leave the great state of Texas and neither will I. She's a Texas girl, full of sass, and this is where she belongs."

He hit a button on the remote to close that door and open another where his pickup truck had been parked. "Are you going to be all right? This is a big burden."

"Frankie said it was a gift, knowing approximately when a person's time is up." She smiled and then giggled and then burst out into laughter. "It's like the ending of *Steel Magnolias.* Only this isn't the end of our journey. It's more like the middle. Still, if those two were sitting on a bench like Clairee and Ouiser, they'd be arguing and fighting, and it's not funny but it is and I'm so tired of crying. And you'll think I've lost my mind. I've got to shut up. I talk too much when I'm nervous." She stopped to catch her breath.

Branch tipped her chin up and kissed her before she could say another word. "I understood every word of what you said."

It was one of those *you had to be there* moments. No one could have gotten a single sane thought from what she'd said, but Branch had lived through every moment of it, so he understood, and for that, Tessa loved him. "Who would have thought something so serious could be funny? Or that they'd make such a big joke of dying."

"Only Frankie Laveau and Ivy Dupree could pull that off." He picked her up and set her on the fender. He traced her lips with his forefinger. "You are so damned beautiful that it takes my breath away, Tessa. I love the way you fit into my arms and I love your heart."

She raised an eyebrow. "My heart?"

"Yes, your heart. It's kind and good and honest. You care for people and about them and there's not a fake bone in your body. I love that about you," he said.

"That may be the most romantic thing anyone has ever said to me." She blushed.

"Then you must have been dating idiots all your life. I'll pick you up at two at Frankie's on Sunday and take you for a tour of the ranch? If you ride with Lola, then I can have you all to myself and I'll bring you home when you get tired of the ranch."

She nodded. *How could I get tired of any place on earth if Branch Thomas was there?*

ꕥ

Maw-Maw said that you can tell the worth of a person by their eyes, and when Tessa went back into the house that afternoon, she measured Hank by that yardstick and he passed the test. He held up a glass of sweet tea and smiled.

"Hello, Tessa. I made tea. Would you like a glass?" His voice wasn't as deep as Branch's. His brown eyes were soft and kind. His hair, graying in the temples, and his tall, lanky body were absolutely nothing like what Tessa had pictured when Lola talked about him.

The strangest thing was that talking to him was not awkward and hearing him call Lola her mother wasn't uncomfortable. By definition when Hank and Lola married, he would be her stepfather, and that wasn't even weird.

She went to the kitchen and stuck a glass under the ice dispenser in the refrigerator door. "Yes, thank you, but I can get it myself. I understand we have a wedding to plan this week."

So you've got a tutu mama and a tattoo mama. Lucky you to have a proper one and a wild one, both. One of them will understand your every mood.

"I'm sure Frankie and my sister, Inez, will put their heads together and make it a bigger affair than going to the courthouse." He pushed wire-rimmed glasses up on his nose and glanced worriedly toward the bathroom door.

"Frankie is sure looking forward to putting a certain strand of pearls around Lola's neck." Tessa carried her tea from the kitchen to the den and sat down in a rocking chair. "Do you think Lola is going to be all right?"

He shook his head. "No, but she'll live with our help. You mean a lot to her and the fact that you are staying here means more to me than words can even say. I'd move in, but Frankie would have a fit if I did before we're legally married, and we're going to do everything we can to make her happy."

Lola wasn't crying when she came out of the bathroom, but her eyes were still swollen. It was the bane of a blonde to have splotchy red streaks after a weeping jag, and it would take a few hours for those to disappear. She went straight for the antique sideboard, opened a lower door, and brought out a bottle of Jack Daniel's Black Label and poured a double shot.

"I need more than tea," she said.

Tessa set her glass on the table. "Pour two of those and I'll join you. It might not be five o'clock, but it's been a hell of a day."

Hank patted the place beside him. "I saved this spot special for you."

Lola put Tessa's whiskey on the coffee table and sat down in Hank's lap, wrapping her free arm around his neck.

"I should go unpack. Which room am I staying in?" Tessa stood up, but Lola shook her head. "You come sit right here beside us so I can touch you with my foot. Don't go. I need you both."

Tessa moved from the chair to the sofa and shifted both of Lola's feet over into her lap. Like she had done so many times in the past when her mama came home from a hard day of dance classes, she massaged Lola's feet.

"Did you never expect anything or did she cover all this up really well?" Tessa asked.

A sip of the whiskey gave her visible strength. "She's taken longer naps lately and she's gotten more forgetful, but I thought that it was part of getting older. But a brain tumor? Hank, are you sure you want to marry me with that in my background?"

"I'm very sure," Hank said.

"I'm numb with shock. I need to ask her if she's got her will up-to-date, especially since you've come into our lives, Tessa," Lola said. "But how do I ask that without admitting that all this is reality and not a nightmare?"

Tessa stopped massaging and picked up the glass. "She asked me if I'd stay on the rest of my vacation, and that's when she told me that she'd fixed things. I suppose it's with Branch's firm."

"I'm sure it is and that's a relief, knowing I don't have to talk about that part of things. Did she tell you anything about the—" Lola stopped.

Tessa shook her head. "No, but I'll bet it's all laid out to the letter for her and Ivy both, and the lawyer has the papers. Changing the subject here, is that Frankie and Lester in that picture on the mantel?"

"On their wedding day. See the pearls?"

"Where is that dress? Does it still exist?"

"In her closet. It's yellowed with age but every bead was hand sewn onto the lace by my grandmother. Why?"

"Why don't you wear it? She looks to be about the same size as we are in that picture and you wouldn't have to shop for a dress and . . ."

"I will if you will." Lola smiled.

"If I will what?"

"I'll wear that dress if when you get married, you'll wear it, too," Lola said.

"Deal." Tessa raised her glass and Lola clinked hers with it.

Picking up the journal that night wasn't easy, but there would be no sleep if she didn't write things down. So she propped the pillows behind her in the big four-poster bed and started writing.

Come to Jesus day: it is written in stone. They are in the fancy care facility and Lola and I are in this house together. She's right across the hall but it seems like she's fifty miles away right now. I miss having her in the next bed from me. I miss hearing her move around in the morning and the rattle of the keys on her laptop as she typed messages to Inez and Hank.

Melody, in her sixteen-year-old innocence, did what we all wanted to do when she threw herself in Ivy's lap and sobbed like a baby. Frankie says that we must have no sadness and no regrets, but I can't. I simply cannot stop the tears or the regrets that I never knew her before. She's been only two hours away from me my whole life, and I only had to ask Mama and she would have found Lola and Frankie. I have no doubt of that, because she's the one that encouraged me to go on the trip.

My heart is broken, and that is all I can write on this come-to-Jesus day.

Chapter Twenty-Five

Poor old darlin's," Melody said softly.

"Don't you *poor darlin'* us," Ivy said from her bed that Sunday morning. "We ain't sleepin'. We're only restin' our eyes while y'all talk about wedding stuff."

"Speak for yourself. I was sleepin'." Frankie slung her legs over the side of the bed and sat up.

"Now that you are both awake, I've got a favor to ask, Mama," Lola said.

"The answer is yes," Frankie said.

"But you haven't heard it yet."

"Whatever you want, if I've got the money or the energy, then the answer is yes," Frankie said.

"I want to wear your wedding dress when I get married, and Hank and I want to have the ceremony in our church in Boomtown. Branch could pick you two up in Mollybedamned and bring you to the church. The reception will be in the fellowship hall, and when you get tired, he could bring you back here." Lola talked fast.

Tessa held her breath.

Melody's chin quivered. "But I won't get to go because I have to work here on weekends."

Lola sat down beside Frankie and held her hand. "We'll have it at seven on Saturday night so Melody can be there. Besides, she's going to sit at the guest book and Tessa is going to stand up with me."

Ivy pumped her fist in the air. "One more last hoo-rah, Frankie! I'll tell the folks here to be sure Blister is loaded up for the day. We'll rest for two days before the wedding so we'll be all fresh and bushy tailed."

"Humph," Frankie snorted. "Our bushy-tailed days are over. Lola, I'll do this, but you have to promise me that you won't do something sneaky. I don't want to go to the house or drive past it. We'll get us a limo to take us to the church and I'll put the pearls on you and then we'll come back here when it's all over. Understood?"

"Yes, ma'am. And will you and Ivy walk me down the aisle and give me to Hank, Mama?" Lola asked.

Tessa's eyes misted.

"Of course, we will. And honey, I can't imagine why you'd want to wear my dress, but it makes me happy that you do. But I see you with a ringlet of roses in your hair, not my veil. Besides, it's got a little chocolate stain on the corner that the cleaners never could get out, and I don't want one thing to taint your wedding," Frankie said.

"Hello," someone said right after a light rap on the frame of the open door.

Tessa thought it was the voices in her head when she heard her mother's voice. It still didn't register that it was real until she saw Sophie standing in the doorway of Ivy and Frankie's suite, and even then she thought she was seeing a ghost.

"Mama?" Tessa gasped.

"Sophie!" Lola's eyes lit up.

Sophie opened her arms, but when Tessa pushed back her chair, she noticed that her mother's eyes were set on Lola, not her.

"I've missed you so much." Lola walked into her arms, and the two of them hugged each other like long-lost sisters.

"It was all for the best." Sophie pushed back and studied Lola's face. "She's old enough now to understand. Now come here, Tessa Ruth, and hug us both. We all need it right now."

"Mama, what are you doing here?" Tessa wasted no time crossing the room for a group hug.

"After we talked last night, I packed my bags, put a note on the dance studio saying that I'd be gone this week, and came for a visit. I've missed you these weeks. It's the longest I've ever been away from you and I didn't like it. Even when you went to college you came home every weekend. Where's a good hotel?" Sophie asked.

"You'll stay at the house with me and Tessa." Lola shook her head at the suggestion of a hotel. "I'm so glad you are here. You can help me plan my wedding. I'm wearing Mama's dress, but there's so much more we've got to get done in a single week. And Tessa is standing up with me, but you have to be my matron of honor," Lola said. "Come and meet my mama, Frankie, and our best friend, Ivy. And this is Melody, Ivy's niece, who went on the trip with us. I'm sure Tessa told you all about us all."

Frankie sat up on the edge of the bed and stuck out her hand. "Pleased to meet you, Sophie. Look at this, Ivy. The three of them could be sisters with all that blonde hair. The only thing that is different is their height and eye color."

Sophie shook hands with Frankie and smiled. "This is a lovely place, and Tessa has fallen in love with the whole bunch of you."

"Well," Melody piped up, "we love her right back."

"Hello, ladies." Branch knocked on the door frame. Dressed in creased jeans and a pearl-snap shirt the same dark green as his eyes, he was freshly shaven and holding a black cowboy hat in his hands.

Tessa's eyes traveled from his smile to the big silver belt buckle with what looked like a brand engraved on it, down the tight-fittin' jeans to his shiny eel boots. A cowboy from head to toe—maybe the sexiest cowboy on the whole planet, and both of her mothers were staring at him.

"Come on in here, Branch, darlin'," Ivy said. "Tessa's mama, Sophie, surprised us by coming for a visit."

"I didn't know." Tessa mouthed the words silently.

He crossed the room in a few long strides, slung his left arm around Tessa's shoulders, and stuck out his right hand. "I'm right pleased to meet you, ma'am. Tessa has talked so much about you that I feel like I already know you. We have a date to go to my ranch this afternoon for supper. Would you like to join us?"

Sophie put her small hand in his. "Not today. Maybe next time. Today, I understand my old friend here and I have some wedding plans to go over. Y'all have a good time."

"We're having supper here and then going back to the house," Lola said.

Tessa caught the meaning loud and clear. *Be home before too late, because I don't know how to handle this alone.*

Branch hugged Tessa closer to his side. "I know the three of you have lots to talk about, and with the wedding coming up so fast, you'll need to work on that, so I'll have her home by nine."

"Thank you," Lola said. "Now, tell me, Sophie, are you hungry? I can call down to the kitchen and have the chef send down a tray of finger foods."

"That would be wonderful. I was too nervous to eat and too afraid to tell Tessa I was on the way for fear she'd tell me not to come, but I had to see her and I wanted to see you again," Sophie answered.

"You look gorgeous, like a gypsy in that skirt and shirt, and I love the cowboy boots with it. And you do look enough like Sophie to be her biological daughter and yet you look like Lola, too," Branch said when they were in the pickup.

Tessa let out a long sigh. "I'm in shock. And thank you for the compliment, but both of them in the same house for a whole week—I'm going to need Ivy's flask, or at the very least a new bottle of Jack."

Branch drove with one hand and held her close with the other one. "I'll make sure there's enough moonshine to keep the flask filled and get you a case of Jack if you need it. But really, once the shock of seeing each other again after almost thirty years wears off, they'll be so busy catching up and talking wedding, I bet you'll feel left out. That's where I come in, darlin'." He gently squeezed her shoulder. "We can go for ice cream or a dinner date or whatever you want. If the going gets too tough, pack a bag and come stay at the ranch."

"Thank you, Branch. It doesn't have to be a date. Just rescue me every day for a little while, even if it's only to sit on the porch and talk." She brought his hand to her cheek. "Being adopted never bothered me, but that was an awkward moment back there."

"Why?"

"Because I could feel the friendship between them and I can't explain it," she said.

"It was like it took both of them to be your mama in that moment, wasn't it?"

"I guess so, but I want to talk about something else." Tessa didn't want to analyze, talk the situation to death, or think about it right then. She was going to Branch's ranch and that should take top priority. "How far is it to your ranch?"

"Ten minutes. I'm grilling hamburgers and hot dogs and I bought a chocolate cake and a can of cherry pie filling, so we're having black forest cake for dessert, but before that we're going to tour the ranch."

"I should've brought other clothes," she said.

"You are fine." He smiled.

A few minutes later he turned off the road into a lane, across a cattle guard and through an arch with a sign swinging in the wind. "Welcome to The Ranch" had been burned into the old piece of rough wood, with the *TR* brand at both ends.

"So you meant it when you said The Ranch," she said.

"It was named that when I bought the place, and I've never changed it."

"I like it," she said.

The lane led right up to a yard fence circling a long, low-slung ranch house made of natural stone. Roses of every color bloomed in the flower bed in front of the wide porch that swept across the entire front.

"Do you have a green thumb?" she asked.

"Not me, but my foreman's wife, Gracie, does, and she loves the roses. They live in the bunkhouse with their three kids, but since I'm here on weekends, they get those days off. They're visiting relatives in Conroe today. If you come back through the week, you can meet them, and believe me, when Gracie cooks you'll get more than hamburgers and store-bought cake. My culinary skills don't reach very far," he said.

He parked the truck right outside the yard fence and helped her out, stopping long enough to pin her against the truck for a series of kisses that sent her pulse into overdrive and her heart to thumping.

"I thought you might need a little dose of medicine since I didn't see you at all yesterday," he said.

"I was getting low." She cupped his cheeks in her hands and kissed him. "I like this place. It's peaceful. The house looks old and like it could tell us some stories if it could talk."

"It was built about seventy years ago and has had a few remodels. It probably needs another one, but I'm not good at that kind of thing and those interior decorators charge a lot of money." He slung the gate to one side and let her enter first, shut it behind him, and grabbed her hand. "Tour of the house first and then the ranch and maybe a cold beer?"

When he reached for the doorknob, the door flew open, and for the second time in less than thirty minutes, Tessa thought surely she was seeing ghosts.

Avery Prescott stood not three feet from her.

Wearing tight jeans and a cute little black lace apron with ruffles over a pristine white shirt, Avery was barefoot and free of all makeup. A sassy little ponytail swung playfully from side to side and with that smudge of flour on the tip of her nose, she looked like she belonged in the house.

"I had no idea you'd be bringing company home. I parked my car around back so I could surprise you, darlin'. Come right on in, Teresa. I'm glad to see you again. Tell me again, are you a client of Branch's?"

"It's Tessa and I'm not a client, I'm his girlfriend," Tessa said.

"Don't be silly. An engaged man doesn't have a girlfriend. I'm making your favorite for supper, darlin'. There is a pecan pie in the oven and we're having fried chicken. It's not quite time to start that, so I'll pour us a glass of wine and we can talk," she said.

Branch planted his feet and refused to move an inch into his own house. "What are you doing here? Didn't I make myself clear enough, Avery?"

"It's like this. I hate losing and you love your brothers, so you are going to marry me. Tomorrow, six months down the road—I don't care about the date, but I'm moving in here as of tomorrow morning. The van is bringing my furniture and taking this shabby crap out of here," she said. "We'll discuss that after we eat. You can stay or go, Teresa, it's up to you, but this is not going to bode well for you."

"We'll talk right here, and then you are leaving," Branch said.

Avery pushed the screen door open and held it with her bare foot. "I'm pregnant, and you will marry me or else I'm going to pick one of your married brothers and claim it belongs to him. By the time the baby is born in six months, whichever brother I decide on will have his reputation ruined, probably his marriage in shambles, and he'll be lucky to get a job as a pro bono lawyer in some remote boondock town in the backwoods of Kentucky. You've got until the pecan pie is done to make up your mind which way it goes."

"You don't want children," Branch said.

Avery's smile was so sarcastic that it looked downright evil. "And that has not changed, but you do, so you can raise this baby."

Branch took a step backward. "It's not mine. Get out," he said coldly.

"Okay, have it your way, but know that you could have stopped what is about to happen." She pulled off her apron and tossed it on the floor, picked up her purse from the sofa, and slipped her feet into bright-red high heels.

The only thing that went through Tessa's mind right then was that she'd never wear red heels again.

It probably took less than two minutes for Avery to stomp off the porch, circle the house, and get into her cute little sports car, but it felt like an eternity plus three days.

"I'm so sorry about this, but plans have changed," Branch said.

"I can call Mama and Lola to come and get me. You do what you have to do," Tessa said. Could this day get any stranger? If so, she intended to be in her new bedroom with the door locked and the shades pulled until after midnight.

"Nothing doing. I met your mother, so you can come on into Beaumont with me and meet my family," he said. "But first we've got to take a pie out of the oven and trash it. I may never eat pecan pie again."

She shuddered. "Me, either. What is the matter with that woman?"

"I told you before. She hates to lose."

"I think she has a screw loose."

"Probably more than one," Branch said.

Chapter Twenty-Six

Branch's law firm was located on the penthouse floor of a twelve-story building that required a key card for the elevator to go up there. When he removed it from his pocket and stuck it in the slot, the fight-or-flight mode struck Tessa—with strong emphasis on the flight business. She expected the elevator to open into a lobby area but oh, no, to add icing to the nerve-racking cake of the day, the doors slid open silently, and there was Branch's family.

Three women and three men stared right at her.

The oldest woman had a hip propped on a long conference table, and she quickly pushed away from it. She wore high heels and a cute little fitted red suit, and her gray hair was styled in big fluffy waves. She crossed the room and hugged Branch.

"We're glad you're home. And you must be Tessa." She stuck out her hand. "We've heard a lot about you these past couple of weeks. I am Branch's mother, Martha. Let me introduce you to the rest of the family. This is Branch's father, Andrew, and his brothers, Justin and his wife, Lacy, and Darrin and his wife, Vicky."

Her handshake was firm and her smile genuine, but her eyes said that she didn't take shit from anyone, especially when it came to her family. She dropped Tessa's hand and motioned for her and

Branch to sit in the two empty chairs. Thank goodness, they were side by side or Tessa might have really turned tail and run.

"We are glad to meet you, Tessa, but Branch has never, ever called an executive meeting of the family, so forgive us if we are worried," Andrew said.

"It's my pleasure to meet y'all." Tessa melted into a chair and was very glad that Branch took her hand in his when he sat down beside her.

Darrin nodded toward his brother. "Okay, little brother, speak your mind. You dragged me away from a backyard football game with my son and his friends."

"And me from a Sunday afternoon nap and your mother from her garden club party. What's going on?" Andrew said.

Branch sat down and told them the story of how Avery had shown up on the trip and again that morning. He left nothing out, not even the part that Frankie and Ivy had had in getting rid of her, or what she'd threatened an hour before.

"My God!" Vicky's high-pitched voice echoed off the walls. "Even if it's not true, it could ruin your reputation, Darrin."

"And the firm would suffer." Andrew pulled off his glasses and pinched the bridge of his nose. "Do you think she'll really stir up that kind of stink?"

"I wouldn't have called you if I didn't," Branch answered.

"Well, then let's nip this in the bud. No need in taking it to court when it can be solved beforehand." Martha set a big black purse on the table and dug around in it until she found her cell phone. She flicked the screen several times before she hit an icon and then put the phone to her ear.

"Hello, Ramona, this is Martha Thomas," she said, and there was a long pause.

"Ramona is Avery's mama. She works at the library where Martha donates a lot of money and time," Andrew told Tessa.

Martha held the phone out and pushed another icon, then laid it down on the table. "Ramona, I have put my phone on speaker and I want you to know that I have Andrew and all three of my sons right here with me. Also Branch's girlfriend, Tessa, is here and my daughters-in-law, Lacy and Vicky."

"Girlfriend? Branch's girlfriend? Avery told me that she and Branch had worked things out and they were getting married within the month. Why would Branch have a girlfriend there?" Ramona asked.

Martha nodded toward Branch. "Tell her."

"Ramona, this is Branch. Are you sitting down?"

"Of course I am. Is Avery all right? Has there been an accident?" Ramona's voice sounded frantic.

Branch leaned in closer to the phone. "As far as I know she is fine."

"I see her parking out in the front of the house right now. That scared me when you asked if I was sitting down."

"I will talk fast." Branch gave her a condensed version of the story he'd told his family, leaving out the part Frankie and Ivy had played in getting rid of Avery at the hotel.

"Mama, where are you? I've got wonderful news." Avery's voice filled the room the moment Branch finished telling the story.

"If you don't mind putting your phone on speaker mode, I have something to say to Avery," Martha said.

"What is going on, Mama?" Avery asked.

"Yes, Martha, I will put it on speaker, and I'm sorry for this. Believe me, it will be taken care of," Ramona said.

"Who are you talking to?" Avery asked.

"She is talking to me," Martha said. "And in case you don't recognize my voice, this is Martha Thomas, Branch's mama. And here's the way things are about to play out. You are going to send that engagement ring on your finger to this office tomorrow. Don't bring it. Send it by registered mail. You will not spread any rumors or we will not only sue you for defamation but see to it that you never find another job in any other firm in this state. And I will personally go before the state bar to press charges to have your license revoked. In short, Avery, you are going to leave us alone. Is that understood?"

"I'm pregnant and it belongs to one of your sons. I've been with all three," Avery said bluntly.

Ramona's voice raised an octave or two. "Avery Prescott, that baby belongs to your last boss and you know it. You cried about it and said he wouldn't leave his wife and marry you but you intended to have the child. You told me that Branch loved you enough to overlook it," Ramona said. "Martha, I assure you, this is over right now. The ring will come home tomorrow and you won't hear from us again. Don't you leave this house, Avery! We are going to have a talk right now."

"Thank you, Ramona. Y'all have a nice day," Martha said and ended the call.

Everyone at the table stared at her, slack jawed.

"What?" She shrugged. "If they'd let mothers run the government, we'd have far less wars and lots more peace. Now I'm going to my garden club party. If I drive fast, I can get there before that rotten Jules Smith eats up all the cheesecake. Come to dinner next Sunday, Tessa. We have a family dinner at our place once a month, and next Sunday is the day."

"Thank you," Tessa said.

"Nice meeting you," Andrew said. "If I hurry I can catch a nap before Martha gets home from the party and wants to talk my ears off about the thing."

"This place is intimidating," Tessa said when they'd all left the room.

"Not as much as visiting your mama's dance studio will be to me," Branch said.

"I can't believe your mama took care of that, just like that." She snapped her fingers in the air.

Branch picked her up and set her in his lap. "You remind me of her."

"You'd put your mama in your lap and kiss her neck?"

He chuckled. "Not in looks or in size, but in the fierce way you protect what you think of as yours. I wouldn't be surprised if Ivy and Frankie aren't still with us at Christmas, simply because you won't let them go."

"I hope you are right," Tessa said. "You think we could go back to the ranch now and have supper? Anxiety makes me hungry, and after the shocks of this afternoon, I could probably eat a couple of hot dogs and a hamburger or two. Even your fancy black forest cake sounds good."

"Right after I kiss you again and show you my office."

ᔓ

It was well after four when they got back to the ranch and nearly five by the time Branch had the burgers and hot dogs grilled.

"I thought we could eat out here on the porch since it's a beautiful fall day. I got everything ready to bring out. You can go on out to the picnic bench and have a seat."

She put a finger on his lips. "I'm not here for you to wait on me. I know how to tote things from kitchen to deck and I will help. Besides, like I told you, I'm hungry, so if I help, then we can eat quicker."

He brought out a cooler with beer and soft drinks. She carried plates and flatware in one hand and a bowl of potato salad in the other. On the second trip, he had a relish tray and she brought the ketchup, mustard, and mayo.

"See." She pulled up a chair beside the table and reached for a hamburger bun. "Now we can eat quicker. And then I bet you have some chores to do. Can I help with those?"

"Do you just naturally fit in everywhere you go?" he asked.

"I told you about my maw-maw," she said. "I'm not a delicate flower. Maybe a clumsy one, but I do know how to cook, clean, and help with farm chores. Maw-Maw made sure when I came in the summer that I could clean shrimp, scale fish, help butcher a cow, and get the fryers ready for the freezer. She said I might marry a poor man someday and I'd need to know how to work."

"Wow!" He leaned forward and propped his chin in his hand. "You keep surprising me. Is there anything you can't do?"

"Ballet, jazz, tap, and lyrical dancing to start with. And I'm not sure I could ever master that knitting business, so I hope Lola doesn't try to teach me after all. I love baby animals. Cats, dogs, calves, lambs, and ornery baby goats. I'm partial to kittens but we never could have them in the house because Daddy is allergic. I'm not sure about babies, as in the human type, because I've never been around very many, but I'm scared to death that I might have inherited Lola and Frankie's genes and I won't be a good mother. Anything else you want to know?"

"Do you take mustard or mayo?" He chuckled.

"Mustard on my burger, ketchup and relish on my hot dogs."

He passed the ketchup across the table and flipped the top off a bottle of beer. "You can forget all about that idea of not being a good mother. Anyone as protective as you are and who loves baby animals will be a wonderful mother."

Her heart did one of those fluttering things when she looked up and their eyes locked. "I hope so, because I'd like to have a whole yard full of kids someday."

Cleaning up after supper took fifteen minutes. Feeding chores took thirty minutes, but they were gone from the house an hour because there was a litter of kittens in the barn and she had to cuddle each one and name all four before Branch could sweet-talk her back to the house for dessert and coffee.

The kitchen, living room, and dining room were all one big room divided by floor type and archways: a thick brown carpet covered the floor of the living area, the kitchen was brown tile, and the dining room hardwood. A hallway off the living room had several doorways, one leading into a bathroom where Branch told her that she could wash up. She caught a quick glimpse of a bed and a dresser behind the door where he disappeared.

The bathroom was tidy, with everything in place and the towels folded neatly over the racks. Neatness appealed to her, and she hummed as she washed her hands and checked her reflection in the mirror.

"Hello," she muttered. "How do you like this place? Would you be happy here? Do you want to go back to New Iberia?"

The last question made her sad. She dropped the soap, and when she bent to get it, her foot got tangled up in the rug and she pitched forward, catching herself on the edge of the tub with both hands.

Was fate telling her that she would be happy here and not to think of going home? Was that why the clumsiness reappeared so quickly?

"Are you okay?" Branch tapped on the door. "I thought I heard a crash in there."

"You did. Guess it takes more kisses when I'm stressed out," she said. "But I'm fine."

The door opened and he scooped her up in his arms. Instead of going down the hall, he carried her to his bedroom, laid her gently on the king-size bed, pulled her boots and socks off, and stretched out beside her. "What are we going to do about us, Tessa?"

"I guess we're going to follow our hearts. That's what Frankie said to do," she whispered.

He pulled her toward him and tipped her chin up with his fist. "That's not easy for either of us, is it?"

"No, but if we practice for a while it could get easier."

Her phone rang and she checked the ID. "It's Clint. He'll call back later," she murmured as she turned it off and dropped it on the floor. "You ready for practice? What is your heart saying?"

He slid off the bed, and she held her breath. She'd put herself out there, bared her soul to him, and now had done everything but tell him that she was willing to go to the next level, and he was leaving.

"Where are you going?"

"I'm following my heart." He removed his phone from his hip pocket, turned it off, and laid it on the dresser, and then he shut the bedroom door with the heel of his boot.

"I often wondered what it would be like if we ever met again. It's like we weren't apart all these years." Lola curled up on the opposite end of the sofa from Sophie.

Settled into the corner of the sofa in the living room with a glass of sweet tea in her hand, Sophie nodded. "Me, too, but then, we shared so much that year, didn't we?" She looked at her watch. "Tessa said she'd be home at nine. Just how serious is this thing between them?"

"She looks at him like you did Derek. Do you still think he's the best thing that ever happened to you?" Lola asked.

"It's a tie between him and that precious baby girl you gave me," Sophie answered. "I heard a vehicle drive up. She's here!"

"Hellooooo . . . Where is everyone?" Tessa called out.

Lola raised her voice. "In the living room. Come on in here."

Sophie patted the sofa between her and Lola. "Sit and tell us about Branch and his ranch. Did you have a good time?"

"It's been an afternoon chock-full of surprises." Tessa went on to tell them about Avery and Martha and everything that had happened.

"Kittens, huh?" Sophie smiled. "Seems like I remember a pretty boy with blue eyes named Skip Morton who liked the kittens that hung around the barn at the commune."

"Guess she comes by it honest. I always wondered. He had the strangest blue eyes. It might have been that dark tan or his dark hair that made them stand out, but hers are the exact same color. Almost indescribable," Lola said.

"Skip? Who are y'all talking about?" Tessa asked.

"Your biological father," Lola said.

Tessa shrugged. "Oh, I guess I'd forgotten about that. Almost. Having two mothers was such a shock that I'd nearly forgotten that there was a father involved. Where is he?"

"He died when you were two years old, in a motorcycle wreck in California," Lola said.

"How did you know that?" Sophie asked. "One of those other guys had blue eyes, too, so I never could decide until right now which one might be her father."

Maybe she should feel something, anything at all, but she didn't. Not relief or sadness or anything. It was as if Lola had told her that a stranger had been killed on the West Coast.

"I kept up with the four I'd been with that month, in case there was ever a medical problem with Tessa. All of them are gone now. Skip in that accident. Joe was killed in Afghanistan. He joined the army after he left the commune. And Billy Ray drank himself to death at an early age. And Mitch died early with a brain tumor."

"And then there was Tommy," Sophie said.

Lola nodded. "He was still alive last I knew. He was the boyfriend, Tessa. His mama moved to Conroe and he still comes to see her about once a year. He called after I'd been back about five years to ask for my forgiveness. Seems he'd gone into the ministry like his mama always wanted him to do and he was making amends for his past mistakes. Last I heard he was in Africa in the missionary work."

"Life!" Sophie said. "It can sure have some twists and turns, can't it? Tessa, you got any questions about Skip, your birth father?"

"He liked kittens?" she asked.

"And every other baby animal in the compound. The lambs followed him around like he was a shepherd of some kind. I swear if he'd had a flute the rats might have traipsed along behind him," Lola said.

Only one question popped into her head. "Did he know about me?"

Lola shook her head. "No, he got on his motorcycle and left the first day I had morning sickness. Several of the folks at the commune had the flu that week, and I remember his last words were that he wasn't going to kiss me because he didn't want to catch the flu."

"Anything else?" Lola asked.

Tessa wanted to see the man who'd be the grandfather to her children if he was alive. "Do you have a picture of him?"

She shook her head. "Not a one."

Sophie laid a hand on her knee. "I've got one at home. It's the only one that got taken at the compound. It's me and Derek and Lola. It was taken the day that she arrived and Skip had brought over some moonshine for us to sample, so he's leaning on the porch post behind us."

"Can I see it sometime?" Tessa asked.

"Sure you can. But that ringing in my purse says that Clint is calling again. He is about to drive me stark raving mad—he's been calling and saying y'all haven't talked in two days and if he doesn't hear your voice by ten o'clock he's getting in his car and starting this way," Sophie said.

"Yes, ma'am. I'll sit on the porch steps so y'all can go on with your conversation." Tessa hurried outside, thankful for a few minutes to be alone.

Tessa didn't know where to begin to write that night, so she chewed on the end of the pen for a while, trying to put into words what she'd felt that day.

Strange, wonderful, passionate day: I slept with Branch. No, that's not right, we did not sleep. It was wonderful, passionate, everything that I've never experienced before. I thought afterglow was something that romance writers dreamed up to make their stories spicier. But it's not true. It happens when things are right, when the moon and the stars and the heart and the mind are all lined up together. That's what makes afterglow, and I had it today. This feeling inside me was something that I actually feared Mama and Lola could see when I walked in the door tonight.

The strange part of the day was when Mama showed up and she and Lola acted as if they'd seen each other only last week and talked every day. It was strange and yet comforting at the same time. That and finding out that my biological father is dead and not feeling anything at all about that. I mean, he created half of me, gave me my blue eyes and who knows what else. And he's been gone from this earth many years. Still the heart does not yearn for something it never knew. If I'd never met Lola and Frankie, I wouldn't yearn for them. But I have and now I can't imagine life without them.

Or Branch. I don't want to ever be away from him. All I can think about tonight is that I'd rather be in bed with him than in this big old four-poster all alone.

Chapter Twenty-Seven

The cleaners did a fine job with the dress, considering that it was well over sixty years old. Fitted to the waist, the bridal satin dress was covered in a delicate lace with hand-sewn beads scattered over it. Sleeveless, it showed both of Lola's tats on her upper arms and portions of the henna tat across her back.

Frankie and Ivy wore matching blue satin pantsuits, and all their diamonds had come out of the bank vault for the day. Tessa wore a lovely blue-lace dress with a portrait collar that matched her eyes perfectly. She'd worn it when she served as a bridesmaid at Clint's wedding. Sophie wore a darker blue satin one that she'd worn to a Christmas party the year before. Neither of them had wanted to shop for a new dress, not when they could spend the time with Lola, Frankie, and Ivy.

They were all dressed and the time was drawing close to start the ceremony when Frankie took the long, slender velvet box from her purse, snapped it open, and removed the strand of pearls. Tessa couldn't take her eyes off them. They'd been worn by generations of women in her family, and today her birth mother was getting them passed to her. And someday they would be Tessa's.

"With these pearls, I'm giving you years and years of legacy, Lola." Frankie fastened the pearls around Lola's neck. "Be happy and love life. They are now yours to pass to Tessa in the future."

"Thank you, Mama." Lola's voice was thick with emotion. "I treasure this day, not because of these pearls, but that you are here to pass them on to me."

Ivy dabbed her eyes with a tissue. "Oh, hell! Y'all stop it or you're going to make me cry, and when I weep, Blister has a hard time keeping me breathing. So let's get this party on the road and stop all this sentimental folderol. Weddings are supposed to be happy. If I'd wanted a sad day, I could have stayed home and watched *Steel Magnolias*. Besides, I've seen the fellowship hall and that wedding cake is calling my name."

"*Steel Magnolias* is not sad." Melody handed the circlet for Lola's hair to Sophie. "That's a beautiful movie that makes you laugh. It's still the best movie ever made."

"Is your signature color still pink?" Tessa asked.

"Yes, it is, and my wedding will be bashful and blush, just like Shelby's was in the movie," Melody declared.

Lola rolled her eyes.

"That is Melody's trick, not yours," Tessa said.

"Mine was knitting. You think I should get out my pink baby yarn?" Lola asked.

Tessa hugged Lola gently. "Not today."

"Are you trying to tell us something?" Sophie asked.

Tessa smiled at her tattoo mama and her tutu mama. "No, I am not. And today is not about me. It's about Lola and Hank, and I heard our cue. Me first, and then you, Mama, then Lola comes in with Ivy and Frankie. Like Ivy said, there's wedding cake waiting, so let's get this party on the road."

The toast that Hank gave at the reception was what put the idea in Tessa's head. He mentioned that Lola had stuck with him through the doubts and fears of a new relationship, through the arguments as well as the joys.

Argument was the word that stuck like it had a thick coat of superglue. Tessa and Branch had bantered back and forth, but they'd never had an argument. Was this what Matt was talking about when he said that she didn't have enough passion to argue with him? That life was too dull with her?

She'd been devastated when he left, but if she lost Branch her heart wouldn't be broken, it would be shattered so badly that she'd never get over it. She'd be a hollow person like Lola had been all those years.

As matron of honor, Sophie gave the next toast, and it was beautiful. She talked about Lola being the best friend a woman could ever have and how they shared something that went deeper than a bloodline.

Tessa heard every word and clapped at the appropriate times, but the fact that she and Branch had never had a single argument stuck in her head. Maybe their passion was in the bedroom, but Maw-Maw had told her once that bedroom stuff lasts only a little while each day and the rest of the time she'd better like the man she picked out to live with the rest of her life.

What if a year down the road, Branch looked back and realized that he'd felt alive twenty-four hours a day with Avery? What if the bedroom passion wasn't enough to hold?

"Are you okay?" Branch asked.

"I'm fine, but we need to talk," she said.

"Are you going to propose to me?" His eyes sparkled.

"I told you a long time ago that Maw-Maw would skin me alive for that."

He slipped an arm around her shoulders and squeezed gently. "Are you going to break up with me?"

"I don't know," she said honestly.

"Let's slip outside while they're having cake and punch. If you've got something to say I want to hear it now, not worry all evening about it."

A slight warm breeze whipped Tessa's hair around in her face when they sat down on the porch steps. Branch tucked a strand behind her ear and kissed her on the ear.

"You go first," she said.

"You called this powwow, darlin'. So you have to go first." Branch smoothed the legs of his black western-cut dress slacks down to stack up over the tops of shiny cowboy boots.

"We never argue. I mean, really argue, as in throwing things, crying, breaking up, makeup sex, all that," she said bluntly.

"I've had that kind of relationship and it didn't last," he said.

She picked at an imaginary piece of lint on her dress. "I haven't, and it scares me that you'll think I'm boring."

"Good Lord, Tessa! You are not boring. You are the most amazing woman I've ever known. I couldn't fall in love with a boring person." He tipped her chin up and his lips met hers in a steamy kiss.

"In love?" She heard the words, but she didn't believe her ears.

"I know. It's insane. I mean, how can I be in love with you when we've known each other only three weeks but my heart tells me it's true? I've argued with it, tried to talk my way out of it . . ."

She laid a finger on his lips. "Why would you talk yourself out of it?"

He removed her hand and kissed each fingertip. "Because it was going to hurt if you wanted to talk to me to say that you are bored because I don't fight with you over every little thing. Maybe you think *I'm* boring?"

She pulled his lips down to hers in a lingering kiss. "You are the most passionate man I've ever met."

"We will argue someday, Tessa. No one lives with another person twenty-four hours a day, seven days a week, and agrees on everything that comes up or happens. But when we do, we'll settle it right then and there."

"So I'm going to live with you someday?" she asked.

Branch's hand skimmed her bare arm. "I hope so. Want to move in tonight?"

She gasped. "Don't tease me."

"I do not tease about serious things," Branch said.

She shook her head. "Not tonight."

"I love you," he said.

She shivered in spite of the warm night air. "Still not tonight, but I do love you."

"Okay, then, let's go back inside and get some cake."

She frowned. "We said that we love each other and you are thinking about cake?"

"Those were the words. We've known it for a long time, haven't we, Tessa? My heart had no doubts from the time I walked into your travel agency, and it absolutely knew you were the one when you slid into the Caddy that first morning. It took me awhile to catch up."

She tucked her hand into his. "I like the words."

He pulled her up and drew her to his chest. "Then I'll say them again. I love you. I love you. I love you. And darlin', I know why you are worried. You have no grounds, not with this old ugly cowboy. I love the sound of your voice, the way your hair feels against my nose, the way you fit into my arms, your laughter, everything about you."

"That may be the sweetest thing anyone has every said to me, and I believe it all except for that ugly cowboy shit." She laughed. "Now we can go get some cake."

Ivy yelled across the room the moment she saw them. "Lola is getting ready to throw the bouquet and we need single ladies. Tessa, you and Melody get your butts over here."

"Did you hear that? She said *butt* instead of *ass*." Branch chuckled.

Tessa rolled up on her toes and kissed him on the cheek. "Next will be the garter toss and she'll tell you to get your fine sexy butt over there to the middle of the room."

Branch winked at her. "Are you fighting for the bouquet?"

"Are you tucking your hands in your pockets when Hank tosses the garter?"

"Come on," Frankie yelled. "You two can talk afterward."

Lola and Hank walked hand in hand to the middle of the room.

"We've decided to do this at the same time," Lola announced. "So you guys line up over there and girls over here."

Branch joined half a dozen bachelors and Tessa stood behind a couple of tall girls who could reach a lot higher than she could. Besides, she didn't need to catch the bouquet. Branch had said he loved her. Her chest tightened. Her breath came in short gasps and the room did a couple of spins before she got it under control.

Well, you said the words, too. It was Maw-Maw's voice in her head that time.

Lola and Hank turned around backward and Frankie yelled, "One, two, three, let 'em go."

They faked the throws and then turned around.

"We're doing this our way," Lola said.

She and Hank went back to the two groups and Hank stretched the garter around Branch's forearm at the same time that Lola handed her bouquet to Tessa.

"But . . ." Tessa said.

"I want you to be next. I don't want to be eighty and on my last leg when I put these pearls on you." Lola hugged Tessa. "Besides, your mama would like to see grandkids and so would I."

ఌ

Tessa sat cross-legged in the middle of her bed and opened her journal. With a long sigh, she started to write with the pen from the last hotel they'd stayed in.

Mama and Daddy are sleeping, worn out from the wedding and all the preparations to get it ready. It's strange having them in this house. Lola and Hank have gone to Galveston for a couple of days, but she says she'll be calling in several times a day to be sure that Frankie and Ivy are okay.

Branch said he loves me and I said the words back to him. I meant them, and when the heart speaks there should be no buts in the way. However, this scares the devil right out of me. What ifs plague every thought as I sit down with this journal tonight. One week and four days and I have to make a decision about going back to Louisiana. Thinking about leaving Frankie and Ivy and not being here with them until the end makes me so sad that tears come to my eyes. Leaving Clint and Mama and Daddy and moving two hours away makes me as sad as staying here. My mind says to go back to my job, my security, and my family. My heart wants to be here, and I can't do both.

Frankie and Ivy were so tired tonight that I bet they sleep most of tomorrow. Bless their hearts, they were the life of the reception, though, and stayed until the last crumb was swept from the floor and the last light was turned out.

Mama and Daddy are going home after breakfast in the morning and then I'll have the house to myself until Monday morning when Lola and Hank come home. I can't bear to be in this house alone, so I'm going to pack a bag and go to Branch's ranch as soon as the dust settles from Mama's van heading back to Louisiana.

I'm supposed to be recording my feelings but today has been like a merry-go-round with each horse painted with a different word. The horse with the pretty baby blue reins and saddle is happiness for Lola and Hank. The one with the gaudy red is joy that Frankie and Ivy felt like leaving the nursing facility and coming to the wedding. That one with lots of pearls and fancy gold lettering has to be the one with "love" written on it because Branch said he loves me.

Maybe by this time next year we'll be ready to announce our engagement and Mama can have a few months to plan a wedding. Wow! He hasn't proposed and I'm thinking about dresses and cakes. It's the moment, I'm sure. Seeing Lola in Frankie's dress and knowing the story of the pearls—it's put my mind in the happy-ever-after mode. Tomorrow I'll think clearer and more rational. Tomorrow I'll make a decision about what I will do the last day of this month. But tonight, I'm going to call this the merry-go-round day and hope that I dream of Branch when I fall asleep.

Chapter Twenty-Eight

The next week passed so quickly that Tessa looked back on Sunday afternoon and wondered where the days had gone. Her mama and daddy had gone home to Louisiana, but Sophie called at least twice a day all week. Hank and Lola came home and the routine began on Monday. The three of them had breakfast together and then Hank went to the antique shop to help Inez. Lola and Tessa went to see Frankie and Ivy, had lunch with them, played board games, watched reruns on the big-screen television, or listened to them bicker about the next day's menu or tell stories about the old days.

Sometime in the afternoon Branch always came to sweep her away to the ranch for a few hours, most of which were spent behind the closed door of his bedroom. Then suddenly it was her last Sunday of vacation time and she had only three days left to make up her mind about her business in New Iberia, about her two families, about Branch. He hadn't asked her to move in with him again, but he did tell her every day that he loved her, and there was that glorious afterglow that kept happening.

Hank, Lola, and Tessa skipped church that morning and had lunch with Frankie and Ivy. That day it was fried chicken and all the trimmings and peach cobbler for dessert.

"Can you believe it, Mama?" Lola laid her napkin on the table and wiggled her shoulders in a sitting-down dance. "I ate a whole meal and didn't drop a single bite of food on me or dump anyone's glass of tea on the table."

"It's because you are in love," Frankie said and then looked at Tessa. "Both of you!"

"Hey, what's going on in here?" Sophie rapped on the doorjamb and walked right in. "Is that cobbler I smell?"

Lola and Tessa both jumped up from their chairs, and the three women met in the middle of the room in a three-way hug.

"What a wonderful surprise. Have you had lunch? We can call down to the chef and have him make you anything you like," Frankie said.

"We've eaten but I did bring doughnuts from that fancy shop in New Iberia. They make the best beignets in the whole state, so I threw in a few of those as well as a dozen regular doughnuts," Sophie said.

Derek held up the bag, crossed the floor, and set it on the table before he pulled Tessa out of Sophie's arms and gave her a bear hug. "I missed you this week, sugar."

"I missed you, too, Daddy."

"Are you coming home Thursday?" he asked softly.

"I don't know. It's a hard decision," she said.

"I know, sugar, but whatever you decide, I will support you. It's not that far from there to here but you know I'd rather have you a mile away in your little apartment. Now go give your mama a hug. She misses you as much as I do."

She leaned against his broad chest. "Thank you, Daddy."

"Hey, hey, looks like the gang is all here," Branch said from the doorway and held up a white paper bag. "I brought along a dozen of those chocolate chip cookies from the bakery in Beaumont that Ivy and Frankie like. Reckon we could get some coffee from the kitchen?"

"Later," Frankie said. "Right now we're all full but in an hour we'll break out the beignets, doughnuts, and cookies and have us a celebration feast."

Tessa left her father, tiptoed so she could kiss Branch on the cheek, and slipped her hand in his. "I'll have to stay today," she whispered. "I can't leave when they just now got here."

"It's okay, darlin'," he said.

Branch handed Frankie the bag, and she set it on the end table beside her recliner. "You been doin' all right today, Miz Frankie?"

"She's fit as a fiddle and sassy as hell. I think she made up that brain tumor so she could stay in here with me while I'm dyin'," Ivy smarted off.

Frankie's finger shot up to point at Ivy's nose. "Don't pay no attention to her. Her brain is oxygen deprived. And besides, she's old as dirt."

"Girlfriend, I'm only a few weeks older than you are."

Frankie grinned. "Cradle to grave."

"You're damn right, but if I die first and find out when I get to them pearly gates that you were fakin', I'm going to let Lucifer have you. I'm not goin' to talk Saint Peter into letting you dust the heavenly gates for him. And put that finger down before it goes off and kills me graveyard dead," Ivy said.

"What is cradle to grave?" Sophie asked.

"We were born the same year and we've been together ever since. We're plannin' on dyin' the same year so we can be friends from cradle to grave," Ivy said.

Branch helped Ivy to her bed and fluffed her pillows so she'd have a nice place to settle down. "We don't need to talk about that grave business today."

"We, young man"—Frankie pointed at him—"will talk about what we want."

"Yes, ma'am." He grinned as he sat down beside Tessa and laced his fingers in hers.

"Is that all you got to say?" Ivy narrowed her eyes.

"Well, I did have something else to say but it's not to you two fussy old gals," Branch answered.

"Well, get on with it. I'm needing a nap," Ivy fussed.

Branch suddenly let go of Tessa's hand and dropped down on one knee in front of her. It took a full five seconds before she realized what was going on and then her heart skipped a beat before it leaped ahead on a full head of steam.

"Tessa Ruth." Branch looked into her eyes and there was no one in the room but the two of them. "I fell in love with you the first time I saw you sitting behind the desk in your travel agency. It took my mind a while to catch up with my heart, but it's there now. I wanted to do this while it was still September so that looking back in years to come we will always remember September as being our month. I love you. I can't imagine life without you and I don't care if we have a twenty-four-hour engagement or if it lasts two years. I want to know that you will marry me, so please say yes."

He popped open a royal-blue velvet box to reveal a round sapphire encircled with thirty small diamonds. "The sapphire is the color of your eyes and there are thirty diamonds surrounding it—one for each day in September. I knew it was the right one when I saw it at the jewelry store."

She sighed, squealed, and fell into his arms. "Yes, Branch. Yes, I love you. Yes, I will marry you, and yes, I will move in with you until Mama can plan our wedding. Frankie, will you stay awake until Thanksgiving? We can get married the Saturday after that in the church. If you don't think you can, we can move the date up."

"I believe we can make it that long," Ivy said. "The doctor came in today and said that we are holding our own with this new medicine."

Branch stood up and swept her into his arms like a bride. "We'll see y'all tomorrow."

The applause followed them all the way down the hall and out the door, where he put her in the passenger's seat of his truck and kissed her with so much passion that it brought tears to her eyes.

"I love you," he said simply. "I will always love you. When we have our first big argument, I will love you. When we are eighty years old and our hair has gone gray, I will love you."

"Me, too, Branch, on all of what you said. I will always love you, through the bad times, old age, and gray hair, the good times and everything."

Epilogue

One year later

Tessa sat down on the porch with a brand-new journal in her hand. This year she would again write something every day for the entire month of September. She picked up the pen and flipped the journal open to the first blank page. That's what her life had looked like a year ago before the trip started. It was a blank page that morning when she crawled into the front seat of Mollybedamned and began the journey that would change everything.

She rocked and enjoyed the lovely fall day, not so very different from the sunny day when they'd had the parade down Main Street the year before. September in the South is fickle. It can be hotter than the devil's pitchfork, or it can be the beginnings of semicool weather. It's never cold by any means, and certainly not chilly, but it can be a little cooler than the triple digits that August is capable of bringing.

The Ranch was forty miles north of the Gulf waters, but that morning, Tessa could shut her eyes and imagine a little salty taste in the breeze blowing up from the south. She picked up the pen and started to write.

It's really still twenty-one days until summer is officially over, but today the weather gods blessed us with a drop in temperature and a cool day. Mama and Daddy are here for a long weekend, and they left to go to some little seafood restaurant down near Sabine Pass.

When she and Daddy come to town, they stay with Lola and Hank, their new best friends, at the house in Boomtown. It would be awkward to most people, but I'm no stranger to that word and it works for us, so that's all that matters. I'm waiting for Branch to come in from the feeding chores. After supper, we're taking Mollybedamned out of the garage and driving to Beaumont for ice cream. I still keep a journal even though I don't write in it every single day. But sometimes when emotions fill my heart to the brim, I simply have to write about them.

The baby in the antique rocking cradle whimpered, and she touched the rocker with her foot to set it in motion. The dark-haired child snuggled down and made sucking noises.

Tessa smiled and kept writing.

The doctors were right about Ivy and Frankie. They made it long past that original diagnosis. And after Hank and Lola's wedding they went with us to church a few Sundays. They never wanted to go back to their homes, but we did talk them into coming out to the ranch two times to have Sunday dinner with us. They saved their strength for us and I'd actually begun to think maybe they'd kick the whole illness.

Branch and I were married in the church in Boomtown on the Saturday after Thanksgiving. I begged God not to take them until after my wedding. I wanted Frankie to actually see Lola put those pearls around my neck and pass them down to me. And the Almighty granted my plea. Daddy walked me up the aisle with Mama and Lola right behind me, and the three of them gave me away together. I wore Frankie's dress and the pearls and Mama's garter for something old, blue, and borrowed all in one, and Daddy put a penny in my shoe. My something new was beautiful pearl earrings from Branch.

When I started down the aisle, Branch smiled and met me halfway. The preacher wasn't expecting that and neither was I, but he told me later he couldn't wait for me to get to the front of the church. I loved it and hope someday when he walks his daughters down the aisle that their grooms love them that much.

All my Louisiana relatives came for the wedding and the church was packed. That Maw-Maw left the state of Louisiana at all was a miracle. But she fell in love with Branch and declared that she'd be coming back with Mama and Daddy real often.

Tessa laid the pen down. Maw-Maw had come back to bring the cradle in early summer, and then when the baby was born she'd clapped her hands when she saw a full head of dark hair and declared that this baby had a good healthy dose of Cajun blood. She promised she'd visit again at Christmas and bring along the rocking horse that all the great-grandchildren had played with and by then she'd take the cradle back for the next baby in the family to use. Tessa checked the sleeping child and kept writing.

It was a lovely day but it wore Frankie and Ivy out so much that I was afraid neither of them would be there the next day. But after a couple of days, they were back to their old sarcastic barbs. I didn't realize it at the time of the wedding, but two weeks afterward the doctor told me that I was six weeks pregnant. No morning sickness and I figured all the stress was what had stopped my periods. I mean, after all, the pill is only ninety-eight percent effective, right? But surprise, surprise!

Our mantel is filling with pictures these days. There's the one of all six of us in the old-time picture shop, one of the family at Hank and Lola's wedding and again at mine and Branch's wedding, our wedding shot with him sitting down and me standing behind him (Frankie got such a kick out of that one) when we were at the stockyards, and too many to count of the baby.

She was born the first day of August and her name is Frances Ivy Thomas. Branch and I argued about the name because of her initials, but I won the battle. We call her Frannie and she's having a nap right now so she'll be ready to take her first ride in Mollybedamned. She has her daddy's dark hair and my blue eyes. She's not the little blonde-haired girl I dreamed about that night so I know there will be more children and one of them will definitely be my little Martha Elizabeth, named after my amazing mother-in-law and my maw-maw.

She looked out over the roses, still blooming profusely, and nodded. Branch had been right about her motherly instincts. Maybe she really had gotten the parental part of her DNA from her birth father.

"Wherever I got it, I'm almighty grateful to have it," she mumbled and kept writing.

Just before our wedding we had our Thanksgiving together out here at the ranch. Maw-Maw brought fresh shrimp and Mama made Southern-style cornbread dressing and it was a big feast. Frankie and Ivy and Maw-Maw got along from the first and watching them in the kitchen was an experience. They tried to teach me how to make pecan pie but I swear all I could see was Avery's face so I made Mama make it. Maw-Maw and I made a lovely gumbo but they wouldn't let me eat as much as I wanted because I was getting married in two days and Maw-Maw said it would bloat me up like a roadkill possum. Try taking that picture to the wedding with you!

We had a quiet Christmas with Frankie and Ivy and Lola and Hank. And two days later they called us to come in a hurry. We got there and they were both sleeping peacefully, but the doctors said it wouldn't be long. I crawled up in bed with Frankie and she put her arm around me. Lola got on the other side and when Frankie roused up enough to open her eyes, Branch took a picture of us all piled up together in her fancy bed. Her last words were, "Four generations of Laveau women right here together." We didn't know the sex of the baby at that time but I believed her and wasn't a bit surprised when they told me that I was having a daughter.

Frannie whimpered again and Tessa rubbed her chubby little cheek. The baby settled right back down to sleep. "That's a good girl. If you can wait for your supper until Daddy gets home, you'll enjoy your first trip in Mollybedamned so much more than if you are hungry and gnawing on your fists."

Tessa read the last paragraph she had written and started writing again.

Melody was lying beside Ivy and when we tried to wake Ivy to tell her that Frankie was gone, she'd slipped into a coma. She passed a few minutes after midnight with all of us on the bed with her, holding her hand and kissing her on the forehead. It wasn't sad but a sweet release. Still, when I look at the pictures on the mantel of us with each of them, tears flow down my cheeks and I have no control over them. Cradle to grave. Only it went beyond the grave for Frankie and Ivy. They made it to the pearly gates within minutes of each other.

Even after Ivy and Frankie were gone, Melody and Jill stayed on as weekend help. They tell us that they've never seen two young girls so good with the elderly ladies and that everyone loves them. Who would have thought it the way she whined that first day about having to go on the trip? She called me early this morning and her voice cracked as she said, "Remember this day a year ago?"

Lola stopped by with a gorgeous antique cream pitcher to remember this day. It looks beautiful on the mantel with the two that I bought on the trip. She says she'll add one a year on the first day of September and someday Frannie can inherit the whole lot of them along with my journals. I may have to buy a curio cabinet in a few years just to hold them all. The fancy little bowl I bought on the trip is in the nursery and holds Frannie's tiny little hair bows.

So in a few minutes, Branch will come home from the barn and I'll nurse Miss Frannie, then we'll get Mollybedamned out of the garage and take Frannie out for her first ride in the car. I'm thinking maybe we'll go to the ice cream store and then drive through the cemetery to put fresh fall flowers on the two graves.

September. It was a time for new beginnings, for fate to play out a hand, for me to find my birth family, and to fall in love with Branch. Right now I'm thinking of the song that was playing when I walked into the church. It was an old song by Anne Murray called "Can I Have This Dance." When the lady from the church sang it I had her change up the first few lyrics that said she would always remember the song that was playing and slip in the words that she would always remember a day in September.

Tessa laid her pen down, closed the journal, and went out to the gate to meet Branch. He slung an arm around her and kissed her on the forehead. His eyes were still dreamy and soft when they looked at her, even after a year, and although they'd had their arguments, they'd followed Maw-Maw's advice when she told them to never take an argument to bed with them.

"How are my girls doing this first day of September?" he asked.

"Frannie is getting fussy. She has your appetite and I've started my new journal. Someday there will be fifty or more lined up in the bookcase."

"Yes, there will, and we'll take them down often and read them so we don't forget," he said. "But right now I believe we have a baby to feed and a ride to take. How about a hamburger at your favorite café to start off this September?"

She slipped her hand in his. "That sounds absolutely wonderful."

Author's Note

Dear readers,

From the time the characters in *The Wedding Pearls* entered my world, I loved them. They shared their hearts and, more importantly, their souls with me. They told me their innermost fears and joys and allowed me to put their stories on paper. When I finished *The Wedding Pearls*, I felt as if I'd been on the trip around the perimeter of Texas with these strong characters, and my heart was heavy as I told them all good-bye. But it was necessary for me to say good-bye to them, even if it was with tears, so that you could meet them and tell them hello.

I hope you enjoyed taking this trip with Tessa, Branch, and the rest of the family, including, of course, Mollybedamned and Blister. They became so real to me that I expected to see Mollybedamned parked beside our local drugstore and to find Tessa, Branch, Melody, Frankie, Ivy, and Lola inside having a pimento cheese sandwich and a fountain drink for lunch one day on their journey. I could sit on the bench outside the drugstore and imagine Mollybedamned right there in front of me. I could hear Frankie's laughter inside the store as she and Ivy bantered back and forth. And I swear I caught a glimpse of

Branch in his tight-fitting jeans and cowboy boots ushering the ladies back to the Caddy.

It's summertime here in southern Oklahoma as I finish this story, but you'll be reading it in December. Merry Christmas to all of you—my family, my fans, my friends, all of you amazing people who support me by buying my books and sharing them with your neighbors and friends.

Cuddle up under that brand-new fluffy throw that your great-aunt gave you for Christmas, get a glass of wine or maybe a whole bottle, and relax as you crawl into Mollybedamned, the '59 Caddy that takes them on the journey, and set out on the road trip of a lifetime.

I'd like to thank my editor, Kelli Martin, for her absolutely amazing help with this book. From helping find the perfect title to all her suggestions to make this a stronger story, she's been there for me. I'm so privileged to have her in my corner! Thanks also go to the whole Montlake crew, from the publicity team to the folks who made the fabulous cover and to all those folks who work so hard behind the scenes—you are all appreciated more than words could ever express. And thank you to my agent, Erin Niumata, who took me under her wing when I was barely getting a start in this writing business and who has stuck with me through thick and thin. Once again, big hugs to my husband, Mr. B, who continues to support me even when he has to eat takeout five days in a row so I can write "just one more chapter."

And thank you to all my readers who buy my books, read them, talk about them, share them, write reviews, and send notes to me. I'm grateful for each and every one of you.

Until next time,
Carolyn Brown

About the Author

Photo © 2015 Charles Brown

Carolyn Brown is a *New York Times* and *USA Today* bestselling author and a RITA finalist. Her books include contemporary romance and cowboy romance, with a penchant for country music, and historical romance. She and her husband have three grown children and enough grandchildren to keep them young. When she's not writing, she likes to sit in her gorgeous backyard with her cats and watch them protect their territory from crickets, locusts, and spiders. She resides in Davis, Oklahoma.